THE DARKEST WINTER

SAVAGE NORTH CHRONICLES, BOOK ONE

LINDSEY POGUE

AN ENDING WORLD NOVEL

The Darkest Winter

Savage North Chronicles Book One
By Lindsey Pogue

Editing by Lauren McNerney
Proofreading by Sarah Willmarth
Cover Design by We Got You Covered Book Design

Written and Published by Lindsey Pogue
101 W. American Canyon Road, Ste. 508-262
American Canyon, CA 94503
Printed in the USA

978-1-63848-875-0

ALSO BY LINDSEY POGUE

THE ENDING WORLD

<u>Savage North Chronicles</u>

The Darkest Winter

The Longest Night

Midnight Sun

Fading Shadows

Untamed

Unbroken

Day Zero: Beginnings

<u>The Ending Series</u>

After The Ending

Into The Fire

Out Of The Ashes

Before The Dawn

Beginnings: Origin Stories

The Ending Series: World Before

<u>The Ending Legacy</u>

World After

OTHER SERIES INCLUDE:

<u>Forgotten Lands</u>

Borne of Sand and Scorn Prequel

Dust and Shadow

Earth and Ember

Tide and Tempest

Saratoga Falls Love Stories

Whatever It Takes

Nothing But Trouble

Told You So

For more information visit: www.lindseypogue.com

To all The Ending Series fans, near and far.
Thank you for making my dreams come true.
I wrote this for you.

PROLOGUE
ELLE

I struggled to open my eyes and discern where I was. Crammed. Head throbbing. I could barely make out the windshield as I blinked to focus.

"If I've said it once, I've said it a hundred times. *It's all a conspiracy.*" The male voice sounded far away, frenzied yet familiar. "You thought this was a democracy—that we had a say in what happened in this country? Who were you working your fingers to the bone for, before the shit hit the fan? You're delusional if you think it was for yourself."

My mind spun and cold air nipped at my skin.

The voice was laughing . . . An echo I'd heard many times before, grating and almost hysterical.

The radio crackled. "Here you all thought *I* was the delusional one."

Thud—thud.

Blood pulsed through my head and ears, gravity pulling on me as I hung upside down.

Thud—thud.

"You think everyone going mad was accidental? The joke's on you, my friend. The joke is on *you.*"

The clawing fear dulled as I tried to remember what happened. *I was driving . . .*

My arms hung heavy as a biting pain shot up my tendons, sending me back to the cusp of unconsciousness.

"Wake up, world! Or whatever's left of us. You are *not* in control. You never were. It was all a smokescreen, and they played you like my uncle Earl's fiddle."

The radio crackled again, and his voice faded in and out as I blinked, registering the shuffling sound beside me.

"Sophie?" I rasped.

One boot. Two boots. Upside down. They were covered in blood.

It was not Sophie.

I needed to scream—to get out of the vehicle and find the kids —but all I could think about was endless sleep.

"If you survived the pandemic, it was for a reason." The radio voice looped through my head as blackness consumed me. "Welcome to the goddamn Apocalypse."

PART I

DECEMBER 7
FOUR MONTHS EARLIER

1

ELLE

I couldn't stop my foot from bouncing as Dr. Rothman and I sat in silence. The pipes in the wall clanked as the heat kicked on and off, trying to keep up with the arctic temperatures seeping into the building. The soft gray hue of the setting sun filled the room, washing over the mahogany bookshelves and mauve carpet.

"Elle," Dr. Rothman prompted from her chair across from me. "Do you want to say more about your dreams?"

I leaned back into the couch and picked at the loose thread in the cushion. The thread had been there since my first visit nearly a year ago, and I wanted to cut it for her every visit since, but it didn't seem appropriate.

"I'm not sure what else there is to say," I told her. "It's like I hear things in my room, see a dark form standing at the end of my bed, and I can't move or speak."

"It's an ominous presence," she clarified. "Not like a guardian watching over you, but something dark—monstrous, perhaps?"

Monstrous was a word for him, but I shrugged. "It's just a man."

"Is it *him*?"

I peeled my eyes away from the maddening cushion string and

7

looked at my therapist. Her straight, black bob brushed against her shoulders as she lowered her brow, awaiting my reply. She was the most patient, immaculately put together person I knew. But then, I didn't know very many people. I told myself I liked it that way.

"Elle?"

I stared at her. Was it possible to dislike someone and feel gratitude at the same time? I wondered it every time I was in her office. I hated the expectant expression that always creased her brow, both stern and soft, and the way she made me feel beholden to her. I'd made a point to never feel beholden to anyone ever again. But she was different.

"You requested this meeting today," she reminded me.

"Yes," I said, clearing my throat. "It's him. It's always him. I can feel his presence even if I can't always see him in the darkness."

"Does he ever move?"

My hair stood on end, imagining he stood beside me now. I knew how it would feel—a cold sweat, frozen in place, and unable to breathe. "Yes. He moves."

"But he doesn't touch you?"

"Not in my dreams. He . . . watches." I stared at my fingernails, the nude paint chipped from picking at it the minute I got off the ship. I could remember the last time I let him touch me, like it was yesterday. It was as if his skin was still beneath my fingernails and I wanted to scrub it away. "It's like he's haunting me."

Dr. Rothman shifted in her chair, the leather protesting as she swung her right leg over her left. "You think it's brought on by his recent death," she guessed, drumming up an image of my stepfather, good ol' Dr. John, all over again.

I was more compelled to explain than to agree. "Sometimes I blink and he's still there."

Dr. Rothman lifted her chin. "Elle, have you ever heard of sleep paralysis? When a person's caught between sleep and wakefulness?"

"Yes," I said. "I've heard of it." I tucked my dark hair behind my ear, uncertain I liked where she was going with this.

"Then you might know it's common, especially in people with poor sleeping habits or who struggle to get a good rest."

"You think that's why Dr. John keeps visiting me in my sleep?" It didn't seem likely, but then I didn't have a doctorate in psychology like she did.

"Well, you said yourself you feel awake, and it feels like he's there—real and inside your room." She pursed her lips, which meant she was in analysis mode. "In sleep paralysis, the inability to speak and move generates fear, naturally, which feeds panic. It's common to hallucinate apparitions, sometimes even hear them."

"Well, I definitely don't see ghosts or aliens," I said wryly. But I had heard him whisper my name in my sleep. The hair on my arms stood on end again, and I rubbed the back of my neck.

"No, you see something much worse, don't you?"

I cleared my throat. She got me there. I'd take the boogeyman over Dr. John standing next to my bed any day.

The heater kicked on again, and I stared at the vent in the floor, listening to its soothing hum as my mind drifted. "I panic," I admitted. "I blink, like it will make him disappear, but he's still there, like he's really in my room." My heartbeat thumped harder and louder in my ears, remembering.

"But you've had episodes like this before, with other dark figures that were not your stepfather."

"Not for a while."

Dr. Rothman's mouth quirked in the corner, pleased. "So, you're enjoying the shooting range then?" Of course she was pleased, the shooting range had been her idea, to give me *a sense of control* in my life, my safety in particular.

I could practically feel the weight of a pistol in my hand, the strain of my forearms as I pulled the trigger. It was power and control. It was sanity when my thoughts were dark and desperate. "Yes, the shooting range has been helping." Until now.

"Good. What about relationships? Have you explored any since Ben?"

I snorted. "No. I don't think I'm ready for that." The early stages of a relationship were easy—they were mostly physical, and you could be whoever you wanted in the beginning. It was being *real* with someone I wasn't ready for again. The crumpled brow. The pitying gaze. The unspoken judgement. The self-loathing that followed.

"Self-discipline is hard for you, Elle. Six months ago you might've rushed into another relationship, but you haven't. Restraint is a big step." Dr. Rothman smiled this time, big and wide the way a proud mother might. Maybe she was the closest thing I had to a mother, even if she was probably thirty-five, only ten years older than me. To a stranger, we might've resembled each other with our slender frames and brunette hair, though she was more like six feet to my five-foot-seven.

"What about your letters to your mother? Are you still writing them?" Dr. Rothman blinked, waiting.

Though I hated to disappoint her, I shook my head. "I'm not sure I see the point. She'll never get them. I haven't heard from her since the day she left, I don't even know if she's alive." My mother took off when I was six and never looked back, leaving me and Jenny with the worst kind of devil—one that everyone else adored. My visit wasn't about my mother though.

"I got a call from his estate," I blurted, remembering the older woman's voice on the other end of the line. *This is Sandy Fields calling for a Miss Eleanor St. James.* I'd been playing her words over and over for the past four days, uncertain what to do. "Dr. John left me everything."

"Did he?" Dr. Rothman lifted an eyebrow. It was nice to know my stepfather could still surprise her too.

"His executor wants me to go to Eagle River to deal with his affairs." I met her blue gaze. Anywhere near Anchorage was the last place I wanted to be. "So, it's not just the dreams that have been bothering me," I admitted.

She was pensive a moment, turning her pen over in her hand before she leaned forward, resting her elbows on her lap. "While I didn't expect, nor would I wish, for your past to show up at the foot of your bed, I think it's good these things are moving closer to the surface, instead of weighing you down in a past you can't control, lingering in a childhood you didn't choose. It's your adulthood that matters, right? The *now*. The monsters from your childhood can only haunt you if you let them, and this is the closing of a huge part of your life."

"What are you saying?"

She clasped her hands in her lap. "I think the more you try to understand the monsters you've created in your mind, the more you can expel their power over you and move on."

"Monsters I've *created*?" I repeated flatly.

"Your stepfather is in the past, and yet he still follows you around. He is one man—a dead man as of last week—who has set the stage for all others. You'll never see him again, and yet he's in your life incessantly, in all that you do. He's in every man you meet and refuse to trust. He's in your dreams at night. While it's natural to internalize the past, it's not healthy, and it doesn't have to be that way, not forever. John is just a man, a horrible man, but he's *only* a man and only has the power you give him."

While Dr. Rothman's words made sense, it was far from easy to flip a switch and make him disappear, no matter how badly I wished he would.

"Let me ask you this," she said and straightened her shoulders. "If you saw him standing in front of you on a busy street, what do you think you would do?"

I imagined him wearing a gray trench coat with his clean-shaven face and hollow brown eyes. His salt and pepper hair would be slicked back without a strand out of place. He would smile the same false smirk that always gave his mood away.

My stomach turned.

"You're having a visceral reaction about a dead man."

My eyes narrowed on her of their own accord.

"Good, then you see my point. Feelings tend to govern us, not the mind. Find a way to move on from feeling the way you do because your brain already knows he can't hurt you anymore."

Feelings were everything, a warped heap inside me—fear every night as a child, knowing he was outside my window in the shadows, or dread when I could hear him breathing beside my bed and the air shifted as he reached for me. I let out an uneven breath, exhaling the tightness in my chest.

"Are you going to Anchorage?" Dr. Rothman finally asked.

I definitely didn't want to, and I wasn't sure I should care what happened to his things. I met her gaze. "I'm undecided."

"Maybe it's time to end this for good, Elle."

Even if crawling into an obscure, dank hole of horrific unknown was preferable, I knew she was right. "You think I should go."

She blinked at me.

"I figured you'd say that."

"It's why you came."

Reluctant, I nodded.

"Who knows, maybe you'll find your monsters are old and shriveled now," she said, smiling.

"Ha." A strand of hair fell in my face as I sat forward on the couch. "That's an amusing image." I tucked it behind my ear again.

Dr. Rothman looked at her watch, and though she said nothing, I knew my session was up.

"Well, that was fun." I stood up with a stretch and grabbed my bag from the cushion beside me. It was old and covered in patches collected from the ports the cruise ship I'd worked on had stopped at over the past four years. *All the places I had gone, searching for a life far away.* And yet I always came back. Something unexplainable seemed to tether me to this cold, dark place.

Dr. Rothman stood. "Go to Eagle River, Elle." Her blue eyes rested on mine with a subtle command in them. She wasn't saying it as my therapist, but as my friend.

I nodded, non-committal, as the phone on her desk buzzed. She picked up the receiver, and I opened the door to leave.

"Oh, Elle?"

I glanced behind me.

"Happy Birthday." A full, knowing grin engulfed her face, and she winked at me.

I hated birthdays.

"Thanks," I muttered, and with a wave, I shut the door behind me. The hall was long, and I passed a few more offices on my way to the exit, before I stepped outside.

I folded the collar of my down parka up around my neck. The cold, crisp winter air stung my face and the inside of my nose. Snow lined the sidewalks and the rooftops of downtown Seward, but the harbor glowed with muted lights of blue and orange. Like the bay as the clouds set in, my mind felt foggy. Why did life have to be so exhausting?

Begrudgingly, I dialed my sister's number and put the phone to my ear. How long had it been since I'd spoken to her? Months? Nearly a year? I pursed my lips as the phone rang and rang before it went to voicemail.

"It's JJ. Leave me a message." *JJ?* I hadn't heard that nickname in a while. But that was Jenny, short and to the point. Typical.

"It's me," I said, uncertain why I'd called her to begin with. Jenny wasn't the type of sister to console or commiserate with. She ran away the day we turned fifteen and led a life I knew almost nothing about. I didn't blame her for leaving—I would have gone too, if she'd told me she was running away—but I did blame her for never looking back.

I cleared my throat. "I'm not sure if you've heard, but Dr. John's dead. He left me the house, and—well, I'm thinking about going back for a few days." I glanced down the sidewalk, knowing deep down she wouldn't call me back. Regretting my call altogether, I hung up. Leave it to my identical twin to make me feel perpetually alone.

The screen darkened, and I gripped the phone tighter in my gloved hand. The ginormous cruise ship at port sounded its horn, and I peered at it longingly for the first time. I could leave with the ship tomorrow, spending the next week calling guests into the studio to take overpriced, choreographed photos that would end up forgotten in a drawer a month down the line, or I could be well on my way to Anchorage by then, headed to the one place I swore I would never return.

Despite the appeal of drifting out to sea, I knew what I had to do.

2

JACKSON
DECEMBER 7

"Come on, babe," I called down the hallway as I swooped the lasagna off the kitchen counter. I nearly tripped on Hannah's favorite polka-dot slippers. Luckily, she'd made my favorite dinner, which more than made up for it. It was still warm, and Grandma Ross's recipe made my mouth water just thinking about it, especially coming off twelve hours of patrol with little sleep. The scent had my stomach barking at me.

"Babe—"

"I'm coming," Hannah sang. Since the end of the first trimester, she had a permanent lilt in her voice, a happiness. Pregnancy, I'd come to realize, suited her, and I couldn't help smiling as I swung the side door open.

I kicked it back with my foot as the cold air breezed through. The stack of firewood against the garage was low. Great. The neighbors had their Christmas lights up and I hadn't even started mine yet. I added that to my ever-growing honey-do list, along with finishing up the crib and *starting* my Christmas shopping. I glanced at the calendar hanging on the fridge. I still had a solid two weeks left. I'd be fine.

"Coming, coming," Hannah sang again. Her boots dragged

against the carpet as she hurried toward the door. At eight months pregnant it was more of a toddle than a run, but it made me uneasy nonetheless.

"Babe, be careful," I told her, nodding to her coat on the rack. "And make sure you're bundled up. It feels like it's below zero out here."

"Jackson, honey," she said softly. "I'm pregnant, not nine."

With a slight head tilt, I glared at her, eliciting a wink in return. "Warm the truck for me?" she simpered. "I'll lock up the house."

"I'm on it." Clicking the fob in my pocket, I remotely started the truck. It grumbled to life in the garage as I stepped out onto the breezeway. The front yard was covered in white. It wasn't surprising given it was dead winter, but the streets looked unplowed, just as neglected as they'd been at dawn when I got home. The last thing I needed to worry about was Hannah driving to work every morning on dangerous, unplowed roads, risking an accident and turning our unexpected bliss into another devastating loss.

I cleared my throat and stepped into the garage, elbowing the garage opener on the wall. The door groaned and protested open.

"It smells like a carburetor in here," Hannah grumbled as I opened the back door of the truck and slid the lasagna inside.

"It's called grease because this is a garage—*my* garage," I warned her.

"I have an infuser—"

I turned to her with breakneck speed. "No more lavender," I told her. The garage was the only place left in the house that didn't tickle my nose every time I walked into it.

Hannah lifted her chin with feigned offense. "Suit yourself." She walked around the front of the truck to the passenger side. "Do you think Kyle and Kelsey will have kids?" she asked as I opened the door for her.

"Um . . . I have no idea." I took her hand and helped her into the cab. "Why? You willing to ignore the fact you don't like Kelsey if she'll give you nieces and nephews?"

"Maybe," she said and settled in with a sigh. Her cheeks were already red with exertion and the cold, and her golden eyes gleamed. She was small, even with a belly double the size of her beer guzzling uncle, Sal. "Kyle would be a good dad," she mused. "He's so much like our father."

Yes, her brother *would* be a good dad, but not just because he was like his father. Kyle Ross didn't wear his heart on his sleeve like I did, and he didn't hold grudges either, he thought life was too short for that. But he had a perspective many others didn't, his six years in the infantry had seen to that. He'd seen more of the world than he'd bargained for, and if he had kids, it would be difficult for him. He above any of us knew how precious life was; he'd watched it slip through his fingers more than once, something he only talked about when he'd had too many beers and his heart felt too full. For now, he had a revived relationship with an old flame to navigate, and them moving in together was enough of a hurdle for the time being.

Thinking about Ross as a dad and knowing my own faults, I wondered if I would be a good father. Would I be too tough? Too rough around the edges, like Hannah often teased me? Would I baby her to the point of suffocation since she isn't supposed to exist as it is? I wanted to think I'd be a good father, even if it scared me shitless.

"Where'd you go?" Hannah asked, watching me.

I chuckled and shook my head. "I was just thinking about the impending chaos. This time next year we'll have a little girl to pack around with us."

Hannah's meditative smile curved into a grin. I knew that look. She had a secret, something I would either love or hate.

I crossed my arms over my chest and waited. "What is it, Han? Spill."

With a trill of a laugh, she dug into her purse and pulled out an ultrasound image. "I got it at the doctor's yesterday—"

I took the image of our daughter with greedy fingers. "How could I have forgotten—and you're only just showing me?" I turned the image around in my hand.

"You were exhausted when you got home. I didn't want to wake you."

"You should have," I admonished, admiring little shadowed ears and her little nose. "Holy shit," I breathed.

Hannah stared at me, expectant.

"This is really happening."

"Yes, it is," she said with a laugh. "You said that last time."

"I know, because sometimes I can't believe it." I would be a father. It wasn't a hope or a wish anymore and felt more real than ever.

"And . . . I've decided on a name," she whispered.

I met her smiling eyes. We'd considered plenty of names in the past, but after three miscarriages it became harder to discuss, to hope. This time, I wanted it to be up to her.

"Molly, after your mom."

My heart squeezed so tight my eyes burned. "But—" I cleared my throat. Adaline Ross had made her wishes known the day she found out she was getting a granddaughter. "What about your mom—"

"I like Molly," she said simply. "My mom will get over it." She brushed the back of her mitten-covered fingers over my cheek. "I want our daughter to know about your mother and learn about your culture. I want her to be a part of that world, too."

I leaned in and pressed a kiss to Hannah's lips, inhaling her— burnt amber, and of course, a hint of lavender. My wife was the light I'd found in self-pitying darkness, the one who'd saved me from myself and the bottles of bourbon I'd used to drown myself in every night. She was the woman I most admired, and even in the seven years I'd known her, she never ceased to amaze me.

Resting my forehead against hers, I stared down at Molly's image in my hand.

Unfortunately, it will never happen.

The chances are low. I wouldn't count on it . . .

We'd heard it all, and had our hearts torn to shreds three times in the process, but eventually we'd proven them wrong. Six weeks turned into the first trimester, which turned into a month from Hannah's January due date, and we were finally allowing ourselves to not only hope, but to expect—a baby . . . A family.

"Molly Adaline Mitchell," I said softly. There was no reason Molly couldn't have both of her grandmothers in spirit. "It's perfect."

"Yes," she said. "It is." Hannah tucked a loose hair behind my ear. "And you're looking a bit unkempt, Officer Mitchell. I'm surprised your superior hasn't written you up yet."

"He wouldn't dare," I chuckled and handed her the sonogram for safekeeping. "But we will be late, and he might give me lip for that."

Hannah clasped the seatbelt with a sigh. "Oh, all right. If we have to go."

"Don't sound too excited," I muttered, and closed her into the truck. I hurried around to the driver side, my boots clomping against the cement, and then climbed inside and shut the door, locking us into the draftless cab. "You got me all distracted and now the truck isn't warm."

"I'll survive," she said, pulling the visor down. She ran her fingers through her long, blonde hair as she eyed herself in the mirror. "I feel fat but not gross fat," she mused. "*Healthy* fat."

Chuckling, I backed down the driveway, pulling carefully onto the road. "Healthy fat is a good thing, right?"

Flipping the visor up, Hannah sat back in her seat, settling in for our fifteen-minute drive toward Ross's new condo on the other side of town.

"Yep. Though, I have to admit the sleeping part of pregnancy is getting more difficult."

"Only a few more weeks, then you'll really feel sleep deprived."

"No," she said. "*You* will." She grinned, but she was right. Between twelve-hour patrol shifts and a newborn, our lives were about to take crazy to another level.

I turned out of our neighborhood and headed toward the highway. A car passed me, going the speed limit, but on unplowed roads it made me nervous.

"You should call him," Hannah said, her voice low and contemplative.

It was a tone I knew well, and I glanced in the rearview mirror to scour the road behind me.

"Jackson—"

"I will," I told her.

"I'm serious. I want your dad to know his granddaughter and be a part of her life if he wants to."

"I know, I'll call him. I promise. I've been preoccupied with the extra shifts and all the bureaucratic bullshit going on right now. They've been giving us the runaround about all the extra caution—crime throughout the country is on the rise, you know?"

"Yes, so you told me the last time I brought this up," she reminded me.

My dad and I had three obligatory calls a year: Christmas, his birthday, and mine. Other than that, I didn't think about him all that much. I never forgave him for forcing me to leave my Yup'ik family and heritage behind after my mom died, because he couldn't cope.

"I'll call him tomorrow on my lunch," I promised, and squeezed her hand reassuringly.

She squeezed back. "Good."

In three weeks, I would be the odd man out—me against two girls. I needed to get used to picking my battles, and losing them.

DECEMBER 8

3

ELLE
DECEMBER 8

D riving to Eagle River was the longest two and half hours of my life. Olive, my clunky, green CRV made the trip without too much protest, though the ride was anything but smooth. The rattling in the dash bothered me more than usual, but I suspected that had something to do with my anxiety about going home more than poor Olive herself. Traffic in Anchorage proper didn't help either, and if I was honest, Jenny blowing off my call hurt, even if I should've expected it.

I turned onto the frontage road. The Not A Through Street sign wasn't the only landmark anymore. The other was a giant husky head with the big black font around it: Frontier Dog Tours. It was a weather-ravaged sign, but I'd never seen it before, so it couldn't have been more than seven or so years old at most.

Inwardly, I chuckled. Dr. John must've been elated to learn he was getting neighbors, a bunch of loud, four-legged ones that would no doubt disturb his morning coffee on the back deck of his secluded, modern ranch house.

I didn't think much more about it as I neared the estate. It wasn't a mansion, but it was large and sprawling, just like the land he and my mother built it on.

The driveway opened on the left side of the road, and I slammed on the brakes. There was an old Ford pickup in the driveway, the same spot Dr. John's Mercedes used to sit during the summer.

It took a split-second to remember he was dead, and another second to recall he would never own a truck so old and rusty. Either the sweet-sounding executor, Sandy, was more badass than I thought and had arrived early for our meeting, or I had a different visitor. I wasn't quite ready for either one.

Pulling in beside the truck, I shifted Olive into park and peered through the windshield at a sight I thought I'd never see again. The house was just as I'd remembered it, with tall, floor to ceiling windows, and an arched roof. Despite the snow, I could even imagine the yard in the summer, perfectly manicured by Bruce, our gardener.

I hadn't thought about him in years. He was a nice, retired Navy man who loved to talk about the good old days when life was equal parts work and play, and people tended to their garden for the satisfaction of creating something with their hands, instead of paying someone else to do it. He let me take pictures of him so I could practice using the digital camera Dr. John had given me on my sixteenth birthday. That was a bittersweet day, and I shook my sudden chills away.

I opened the car door, bracing myself for the blistering cold. The sky was graying as the clouds rolled in, so I hurried to collect my things from the back and made my way to the front door.

Weeks of snow covered the yard, but I knew there were lily beds underneath, one of Bruce's most prized accomplishments. He'd shown me how to garden in a place hardened by permafrost most of the year, and how wood ash mixed with soil added more nutrients, encouraging life in unexpected places. *Life is beauty*, he'd told me. I scoffed at it then, but it was Bruce who told me you could see beauty in everything through a camera lens—you could focus on exactly what you wanted and capture it for an eternity. He told me to use photos as proof of what life could really be like.

As I stepped onto the porch, I eyed a set of fresh, large footprints in the snow that followed a covered path around the house. "Hello?" I called.

A gust of wind raked over me, coldness seeping into my spine.

"Hello there," a man called out and stepped around the side of the house. He was over six feet tall, with broad shoulders, a gray goatee, and short hair that stuck out beneath his ski hat. "Can I help you, Ma'am?" He looked me over, eyes shifting from my face to my luggage and back.

"Actually," I said as he took a few steps closer. "I'm wondering if I can help *you*. I'm Elle St. James. This is my house." The words were clunky and forced even if they were true.

The man stopped a couple yards away—close enough for me to notice he had mud on his clothes, and what looked like dog hair, too. There was nothing overtly sinister about him, but something was off—something that made the hair on the back of my neck and arms stand on end.

His dark, close-set eyes narrowed on me. I was about to ask him to leave when he smiled. "You're Dr. John's daughter, aren't you?"

"One of his *step*daughters," I corrected, as politely as possible.

The man offered me his hand. "Thomas Mitchell. I run a dog kennel down the road. There have been several break-ins in the area lately, those end-of-the-worlders with any excuse to steal what isn't theirs." He glanced at the house. "I've been checking in on the place from time to time since John went to the hospital."

I was glad to hear John hadn't died in the house even if I knew it was a morbid thought. I wasn't sure I could handle being in the house at all let alone knowing he'd died there.

Thomas shoved his hands in his pockets. "I was sorry to hear what happened to him."

"Yes, well, thank you, Thomas, for looking in on the place."

"You can call me Tom, Miss."

I nodded. "I'll be here for a few days, so you're off duty."

He pursed his lips and lowered his chin in understanding. "Very well."

I turned for the front door.

"Will you sell?"

I looked back at him. "The house? Yes," I said, the answer rolling easily off my tongue. "I hope to have it on the market within the next couple days."

"You don't waste time," Tom said with a grin. "I admire that."

I smiled as politely as I could, but I didn't want to prolong my visit any more than I had to. "Yeah, well, I have a cruise ship leaving this weekend in Port of Seward, and I need to be on it." I switched my luggage from one hand to the other, and glanced up at the dark clouds. "I better get inside and get the place warmed up. It looks like a storm's coming in."

"It's supposed to be nasty, Miss. Like I said, I'm right down the road if you need anything."

I waved a thank you, and Tom finally turned to head for his truck. As soon as he was inside and backing down the drive, I reached into the pot of frostbitten plants and grabbed the hide-a-key rock Sandy had left for me.

With steadier hands than I'd expected, I put the key in the lock. I hadn't been home since I'd bolted on my seventeenth birthday, eight years ago. Glancing through the windows, into the dark house, I expected to see Dr. John standing in the hallway, watching, but the vast surrounding forest was all that reflected back at me.

After a few jiggles of the knob, the latch turned, and I pushed the door open. A waft of cold, stale air hit me, and I lumbered inside with my things. I shut the door, closing myself in the musty house, and let out a deep, even breath as I turned around. *It's just a house.* The unwanted memories were like photographs I could lock in a box and shove under my bed to forget about. I could do that.

Unwrapping my scarf, I switched the entry light on and abandoned my things by the door. First things first—the thermostat. After three steps and a shimmy into the frigid room, I clicked the heat on and the unit kicked to a roar in the attic. It was noisier than I remembered, but it worked.

Dr. John always had the best of everything, which meant it was state-of-the-art in its day. Money afforded a lot of luxuries, and elaborate charades, like trips to Sea World, cruises to the Caribbean—perfect family outings that were all for show. But it also meant everything was weather-proofed, so I could bank on working water pipes too, even if the house had been uninhabited and left to the elements for a few weeks.

Heat hissed from the vents in the ceiling, and I rubbed my jacket-clad arms in anticipation of warmth. I was uncertain how to proceed as I peered around the living room.

The interior was just as I'd remembered it, stark and masculine, but precariously clean. The remote was in the black tray in the center of the coffee table, the metal coasters stacked in their holder beside it. The same gray suede couch sat in front of the fireplace with the large flat screen mounted above it. The only noticeable changes were a pair of worn, wool-lined slippers that sat next to the recliner, and a set of bifocals resting on a Holy Bible on the side table. I hadn't been expecting that.

To anyone else they would be normal items—an old man's glasses left behind. Dr. John hadn't worn glasses when I'd known him, though, and he definitely wasn't reading the Bible back then either. Even the slippers seemed strange too, like they were too comfortable, too casual for him. Dr. John Tomlin was a man of control and precision. He didn't have time to relax or read a book. He was severe and calculated and always knew your weaknesses. *You want a new camera? Here's what I want in return . . .*

Dr. John was an older man to begin with, wealthy and suave all his life, which is probably how he caught my mother in his net, not that I knew much about her other than her taste in men had been amiss. But I imagined his back stooping more and more as he turned into a lonely, regretful old man alone in his big, fancy house.

Taking a deep breath, I unclenched my teeth and stared at the Bible on the side table. At which point had he decided to leave me everything, knowing how much I hated him? Knowing I'd been willing to blackmail him to never have to see him again? *Pictures never lie.* Bruce had told me that.

Then it dawned on me. Bruce had known.

A cold, heavy mass pressed against my chest as I took in a shallow breath. *Bruce knew.* I let the unexpected truth settle in. For the first time, I realized why he asked me so many questions about Dr. John, and why they'd been fighting in the driveway the day Bruce left and never came back. Part of me was heartbroken, but elated when Dr. John kept his distance for nearly a year. It was all part of a plan—a deal brokered between them I knew nothing about.

My mind swirled with understanding, and I shivered as the house creaked in the howling wind. No more shadows, I thought and switched on the table lamp to brighten the somber afternoon. The watermark on the coffee table caught the light, and I thought of Jenny. She'd purposely left a sweaty glass of ice tea on it one summer.

Defiance had been her armor. I hadn't realized it for the longest time. She was a smart-mouth, unruly girl that Dr. John learned quickly wasn't worth the risk. She spoke her mind, was loud when he wanted quiet, talked back when he demanded submission.

Meanwhile, I was too afraid of what would happen if I challenged him. I never considered the ramifications of silence would be worse. I was the one who was punished for her disobedience, and deep down I think she knew that. But then Jenny had never thought much about anyone other than herself. She'd been convinced our mother would never leave us because moms don't do that, and when I told her to grow up, I think she'd written me off for good.

The hardwood floors, brittle from the cold, creaked as I walked through the rest of the house. The kitchen was smaller than I remembered but much the same; six chairs nestled around the long, oak dining table with only a single place setting for one.

I crossed the living room toward the hallway and hesitated outside the first room on the left. My room. As much as I wanted to keep the door closed, my hand reached for the doorknob and opened it.

Somehow, I'd convinced myself that Dr. John would've turned it into a gym or a guest room after I left, but it was exactly as I'd left it, save for the open drawers and discarded clothes I'd left in my wake. There were no incriminating photos though, nor a nasty note telling him there were more where that came from. He'd straightened it and kept it clean, his need for control ensured that.

The lotions and body sprays that littered my dresser were the same ones I'd left behind. The quilt my mom made for me when I was born, the one that matched Jenny's, was still folded at the foot of my bed.

Fleetingly, I wondered if Jenny was right—that there was more to our mom's abandonment than Dr. John had told us. She had always been meek and submissive, so I hadn't been surprised the day she finally broke and disappeared into the night, like an ailing cat slinking away to die alone in peace.

I clenched my hands at my sides, my fingers sweltering in my mittens.

Suddenly too warm to breathe, I pulled off my beanie and rushed out the bedroom door, slamming it shut behind me. I walked over to my purse and grabbed my phone to dial Sandy. I was closing a chapter, not opening an old, gaping wound. I couldn't afford to spiral right now, and I was finished allowing them to have any more power over me. Screw them all—John, my mom, even Jenny. Soon it would all be a distant memory.

4

ELLE

S andy cancelled our meeting about the house because of a sudden cold. To distract myself from a wasted day in my own personal hell, I had a taxi driver drop me off at Taps, a local hangout with cheap drinks and a decent bartender, so said the driver. He was an older man who smelled of cloves and wore a leather biker jacket, which gave him some street cred in my book, even if it was illogical, but his recommendation didn't disappoint.

Walking through the creaking door of Taps was like stepping into the past, complete with Formica tabletops, pleather swivel-seat bar chairs, and herringbone wood paneling along the back of the bar. The only thing I didn't see was Patrick Swayze with his flowing brown locks and his arms crossed over his chest, looking pensive and ready to rumble.

The jukebox played low in the background, a song with a melodic country twang, but the place was warm and wasn't a dark memory box like Dr. John's, so I stayed. The scent of stale beer and musty wood was the least of my worries.

I shrugged out of my coat and hung it on the worn, wooden coatrack by the door. My North Face jacket was pretentious beside the beat-up leather one from the 90s and the trench coat draped beside it. The two men sitting at the bar stared at me, probably thinking the same thing. They nodded at me as I walked in, a bottle of beer in each of their hands.

With a quick nod in return, I pulled out an empty seat at the opposite end of the bar, smiling warmly at the bartender. He was an older gentleman with a balding, shiny spot on his head, over-grown beard, and a large beer gut.

He smiled back, his face open and bright, like Santa himself. "You a tourist?" he asked, studying my attire. Other than a long-sleeve shirt that covered my curves differently than his, we didn't look all that dissimilar in our jeans and snow boots.

I shook my head and pointed to the Jameson two shelves up. "Here on business. A whiskey, please."

He flipped a highball glass over and poured two fingers full. "A whiskey it is," he said with a slight whistle. He placed the glass on a small napkin square and slid it to me.

I slid him my debit card in return. "You can start a tab."

"You got it." He turned to the cash register.

"Thank you." I lifted the glass to my mouth and pretended not to notice the lipstick stain on the rim. Though drinking was never really a vice of mine, I felt almost desperate for it, and with a quick swish of the glass, I swallowed the spicy liquid down in one gulp. I reveled in the trail it blazed from my throat into my stomach and licked my lips.

"You're a whiskey girl, huh?" The bartender's brow crinkled. If I wasn't mistaken, there was admiration in his non-question.

I shrugged. "By default. It's the only thing my stepdad wouldn't drink."

"Ah. I see." Amusement curved his lips.

Did he? His eyes fixed on me, measuring me up as I pulled out my phone to check the severity of the impending storm. Maybe the bartender had an inkling, since I assumed he was good at gauging people. It *was* part of his job, assessing if a patron would cause trouble and determining when one more drink was one too many.

In a state with freezing temperatures most of the year where the natural beauty could be equally cruel and terrifying, I assumed he'd seen a lot of desperation in people's eyes in his lifetime. I was probably no different.

As I was about to put my phone back in my purse, I noticed twelve unread emergency alert texts. I clicked the first message open. Below the image of a man, it read: Anchorage manhunt for assault and battery charges. I tapped it closed before I could read the rest. I'd been getting more and more notifications lately, and I didn't need to hear about all that shit right now. I was on a mission to forget my problems, not get sucked into the desperate state of the world and humanity—both of which were completely out of my control.

There was a reason it took a certain type of person to thrive in Alaska. The arctic nights could stretch long, and dark thoughts ran rampant; a never setting sun in the summertime could create just as much disquiet. We lived in a place so far removed from one town to the next, it was easy to get lost in the restlessness. Traveling with the cruise lines helped, even if it was to have subpar conversations and get outside of my head for a week or two at a time.

"I'll have another, please," I said, running my fingers through my hair. The strands fell down around my shoulders, still not as long as they used to be—but getting there. I'd cut my hair after I'd left Dr. John's house. He preferred Jenny and I with long hair, and illogically, I'd kept it short for years after, as though it might help keep him away—until I started seeing Dr. Rothman.

The bartender filled my glass again and slid it back to me. I turned it around and around, contemplating what I might do with the money I made from selling the house. Buy a new one? Move away from this place? I actually liked living in Seward. Being here, so far from the ocean, was strange. Moisture wasn't heavy in the air like it was in Seward. Eagle River was further removed and cold in a way that made my bones ache at their core, and my body stiff. The whiskey though . . . I tossed it back, breathing out an invisible fire. Oh yeah, one more of these would do the trick.

"Looks like they have another update for us," the bartender muttered.

The outbreak in the lower forty-eight had been making the headlines for the past week, a possible chicken flu outbreak from an unsanitary factory, which seemed to happen more and more frequently. With the increasing FDA regulations, I wasn't sure I bought it, even if people around here were starting to get a tad nervous. We imported most of our food, so what was to keep the outbreak from spreading all the way out here?

Tugging the elastic band from my wrist, I pulled my hair up into a ponytail and turned to the flickering light of the television. I wasn't sure if the heater was cranked up to a hundred degrees or if the whiskey was finally making its way through my veins, but I was growing uncomfortably warm.

The bartender turned up the volume on the flat screen.

"—Influenza hospitalization is at an all-time high. Joseph Hillman is in Georgia now—outside of the Centers for Disease Control and Prevention—awaiting an announcement from the Director-General of the World Health Organization, Kenneth Donaldson. Joseph, have you heard anything new since this morning?"

The screen flashed from the brunette news anchor to who I assumed was Joseph Hillman, standing outside the CDC. He was wearing a measly scarf and windbreaker, and a surgical mask hung around his neck. "No, Veronica, there's been nothing new officially reported. The Virginia and Georgia departments of health still request everyone stay indoors as much as possible while they continue to investigate the multi-state outbreak of what's said to be an avian flu. Now, the U.S. Department of Agriculture is said to be helping them with this, but there's been nothing official reported. We already know they think the outbreak might've started at a chicken plant in western

32

Colorado, but, again, there has been nothing officially announced."

"Any idea why the East Coast would be so affected by an outbreak in Colorado? Have they claimed they are the same virus, or why they've had such difficulty containing it?"

Joseph shook his head. "No, they haven't stated whether they're connected, though there's plenty of speculation circulating. We know there was an outbreak reported last week at two different plants owned by the King Corporation. Forty-two people were initially infected, and only six of them survived and remain in critical condition. Without knowing much more, you can imagine the panic here on the East Coast with so much uncertainty."

Veronica's eyes crinkled with apprehension. "With all the spreading panic, the CDC seems to be more quiet than expected."

Joseph nodded. "There's been a lot of vague talk, which makes most of us standing out here wonder if they're still working on their answers. Hopefully, we'll know more after their official statement tomorrow." A gust of wind whipped over him, causing his scarf to flail around his body.

Veronica cleared her throat. "Has the King Corporation had anything to say about all of this?" I had to wonder just how off script she was going.

"Unfortunately, they could not be reached for comment."

"The number of sick reported in Wales yesterday were staggeringly high as well. Is it possible it's the same disease?"

"Again, there's no way to know for sure." Joseph looked exhausted and a bit perturbed by her questions, perhaps because he was standing out in the cold, or perhaps it was because he didn't know the answers to very much at all.

He switched his microphone from one hand to the other. "One thing I *can* tell you," he started, a bit reluctantly. "Is that historically speaking, the CDC operates on the basic principle that disease knows no borders. Statistically, this means in today's interconnected world, diseases can be as dangerous as wildfire, spreading from an isolated village to any major city in the world in as little as thirty-six hours. This information was on their website last week, and as of today, I could no longer find it."

Despite his calm and collected demeanor, the reporter's foreboding tone gave his anxiety away, and a shiver shimmied down my spine. If the CDC wasn't providing answers during a rising panic, that probably meant everyone was screwed.

The guy at the end of the bar set his beer down with a clank. "Thank God we're way out here," he muttered, but I couldn't breathe as easily. The sticky fingers of fear crept over me. Just last week I'd met hundreds of people on a cruise, traveling from around the world, and my stomach knotted as I considered how many of them could've been sick.

"Can I getcha another?" the bartender asked, eyeing my empty glass.

"Um, yeah. Please." I tried and failed not to wonder how long before a virus like that was out of control and what that would even look like.

"The name's Terry, by the way," he said with a weak smile. Either he could see the alarm on my face, or he felt it himself.

"Elle," I said, flashing him a wavering smile back.

Terry poured me another shot, heavier this time. "It's on the house."

5

ELLE
DECEMBER 8

M y mind was spinning as Terry drove me back to the house. His old truck was loud and rattled over every bump in the road, making my stomach churn more and more as each minute passed. Although I'd had three or four shots, it wasn't until I'd stood up to leave the bar that I realized just how drunk I was.

"I'd wanted to forget the past tonight," I slurred. My tongue was heavy and thick in my mouth. I laughed. "I think I've accomplished that."

Terry chuckled. "I think you did, Miss Elle." He was a nice man, I'd decided. Among other things, I'd learned that he was very proud of his grandkids from Juneau, but wished he saw them more.

The headlights flashed on the dog kennel sign that was coming up fast. "It's right here," I directed.

Terry hit the brakes, thrashing me forward, and turned onto the frontage road. Had I ever been so drunk? I nearly lost the contents of my stomach as he drew closer to the driveway, and I wasn't sure I ever wanted to be this drunk again.

As we pulled into the driveway, I thanked Terry for the ride and fumbled to remove my seatbelt. "That was fun. We should do it again." But as the words came out, I knew I would never see him again.

"Here," he said, shifting the truck into park. He was about to climb out and help me when I held up my hand, the passenger door swinging open. "I got it. Get home to your wife," I told him. My mouth tasted sour, but I hadn't even thrown up yet. Not that I could remember, at least.

I stumbled out of the car.

"Take care of yourself, Miss Elle."

I flicked him a goodbye wave as I ran as fast and steadily as possible to the front door. The snow was cold as it clung to my face, the wind like sheets of ice against my skin, but internally, I was on fire. My insides rolled and burned, like they were smelted in a caldron, churning until I couldn't take it anymore.

I clung to the porch railing and doubled over. Everything scorched its way up my throat as I expelled it into the hibernating rose bushes. My entire body trembled, and it took everything I had left in me to hold myself upright and not fall to my knees.

This sucks.

Pulling in a deep breath, I peered out at the driveway. Olive was parked under a thin blanket of snow, Terry was gone, and everything was dark. Despite the sweat dripping down my temple, I needed to get inside where it was warm before I froze to death on the stoop.

I fumbled for my keys, using the doorframe to lean against. I couldn't focus. I could barely make my fingers work, and it felt like something rotted inside me. I didn't feel drunk anymore; I felt like I was dying.

Minutes passed, or maybe only seconds, before I was in the sweltering heat of the dark house. I slogged into the kitchen. All I could think about was drinking water, but lifting my arm to reach a glass from the cupboard was nearly impossible. I stuck my cupped hand under the faucet instead, sighing with relief as cool water rolled off my skin.

Chills immediately followed, then momentary numbness, which was a welcomed sensation. Bending over, I slurped the water overflowing from my hand as quickly as I could, but it wasn't enough. I needed more water. My stomach rumbled, my insides twisting into knots, and before I realized what I was doing, I was hauling my ass down the hall and into the bathroom.

I couldn't breathe, and tears stung my eyes. I peeled off my suffocating coat and the scarf around my neck. *What the hell's happening to me?*

I switched on the light and dropped to my knees on the tile. I needed to purge every rotten thing inside me if I would survive what felt like pure misery.

I retched into the toilet bowl over and over, until my insides were raw and cramping with pain. Nose running and eyes too heavy to keep open, I rested my burning cheek on the cold toilet seat. "God," I pleaded. "Kill me now."

DECEMBER 9

6

JACKSON

DECEMBER 9

I stared at the clock on the dash. It was barely 1:00 a.m. and I still had another three hours before I got a break. My mind was numbing over, and I wondered how many more frantic calls I would have to take before my good Samaritan side wore off completely.

The long, drawn out beep of an emergency alert broadcast blared through my speakers, peeling a layer of haze back from my mind. I ran my hand over my face, dreading what came next. I wasn't sure I could take another Amber Alert tonight.

"The following message is issued at the request of emergency management. Due to the possibility of a viral outbreak, a mandatory quarantine has been issued for all cities in Alaska with five hundred or more civilians. Alaska residents, including those in Juneau, Anchorage, and Fairbanks, are asked to stay tuned to television and radio stations for further updates."

I blinked out the window at the black morning as the recording repeated. Things had gotten crazy in the past twenty-four hours, but quarantine? I reached for my phone and dialed Ross. Even if I was certain he would've told me about this if he'd known, he was my superior and would have far more information than I did.

The phone barely rang once. "Are you hearing this?" he said in answer.

"Yeah. You didn't know?"

"No, I mean—the chief said things were worse than they were letting on, but he never said the word quarantine."

I stared at the radio, waiting for it to beep again—for another Emergency System Alert that would explain what the hell was happening, not just contribute to the spreading fear. "Should we meet up at the PD and—"

"Shit—he's calling. I'll hit you up in a sec." Then the line went dead.

Could things have worsened so much overnight? It was hard to tell out here where everything seemed normal, parked at an abandoned gas station on the side of the highway. Normal except for the paper-thin mask I was wearing as a result of an unexpected fever outbreak. *Just a precaution,* we'd been told.

Out here, the roads were white and desolate like any other winter night. In a matter of hours, I'd only passed a few cars on the stretch between Anchorage and the surrounding boroughs, but that's how the back roads were in a territory where miles of wilderness stretched between one unincorporated town and the next.

Chief Gonzalez's request, that all units remain on-call, was justifiable when we thought it was to maintain order due to the spreading hysteria as conditions in the lower forty-eight worsened. But *quarantine* meant contagions, not food poisoning and chaos as the rest of the US scrambled to make sense of everything. How had it spread so fast? Or maybe everyone was just finally catching on. The past twelve hours had been a blur of breaking up bloody-knuckled fist fights, responding to car accidents from sick people who shouldn't have been behind the wheel, and catching an arsonist in Sutton that claimed he wanted to know what it felt like since the world was ending, anyway.

If government officials had downplayed what was happening, they'd risked everyone's health and safety, and I wasn't bionic.

Troopers were just as susceptible to contagions as everyone else, and we'd been on patrol for over twenty-four hours, since we'd got the call at the dinner table. My lasagna was still on my plate when we headed to the department for bullet-proof vests and masks.

I tore the mask off my face and clenched my hand around it. The damn masks wouldn't do anything if a perp was infected, and I hit the dash with my fist. It creaked in protest and the computer screen shook, but I didn't give a shit. There was no way to know if I'd caught the virus in the span of the last twelve or twenty-four hours, and now I might pass it on to Hannah when I got home.

I scrubbed my hands over my bristly face again. "Fuck," I groaned and leaned my head back against the seat. I needed to compose myself before I called Hannah to see how she was feeling. And I needed to figure out where I was going to stay because I wasn't taking my potentially sick-ass home until I was cleared.

I took a swig of cold coffee, though I didn't need it. My body was already wound tight, my adrenaline kicking in. Staring into the darkness, I tried to control my racing thoughts. Regardless of whether or not I was sick, Hannah was in danger if the illness had already spread this far. *Molly* was in danger. Hannah wouldn't survive if anything happened to this baby, not after we'd already lost so much and come so far with this pregnancy. Losing Molly would be devastating for both of us, and dread began to burn a hole in my stomach as I imagined the possibility of it.

"All units—" I glared at the radio. "10-19 for a 10-10 in progress. Lasson Street in Eagle River. Tango 3 is on the way, requesting backup. Caller is advising that there's a 12-gauge shotgun and 2200 on the premises."

I was only ten minutes away, but for the first time in my six-year career, I hesitated to answer the call. I hadn't heard back from Ross and had to make the split decision to respond and risk getting sick or worse, or ignore it and be the cause if an innocent was injured or killed.

Loyalty. Integrity. Courage. "Shit." Despite my better judgement, my oath made it impossible to ignore the call.

As I reached for my radio, my cell phone rang, vibrating and screaming at me from the passenger seat. "Finally." I grabbed it, watching a Dodge Ram speed past me down the highway as I brought the phone to my ear. "Ross—what'd he say?"

"Mr. Mitchell? This is Nurse Crawford at the emergency clinic."

My breath caught in my throat. *Hannah.* "What is it—what's happened?"

"Your wife was admitted thirty minutes ago." The nurse's voice was raspy, like she was winded and distracted. "She's in surgery."

"She was what?" I could barely speak through my terror. "The baby . . ." Hannah still had a few weeks before she was due.

"Mr. Mitchell . . ." Nurse Crawford paused, a pause that implied impending bad news. "You better get down here." There was a crash on the other end of the line—a commotion of back and forth muttering that drew closer. "Take him to room two-seventeen, through that door," she commanded, and then the connection was lost.

"Hello?" I shouted into the phone. "What the . . ." My mind spun with a million questions as I threw the truck into drive, fishtailing on the slick road as I turned toward the city.

A Vise-Grip cinched inside my chest as my worst possible fears became reality. The roads blurred, and I wiped the tears from my eyes as I pressed the pedal down as far as it would go. Hannah would be fine. Molly would be fine. *Everything* would be fine . . . I just needed to get there.

7

JACKSON
DECEMBER 9

I barreled through the hospital doors of the emergency room, passing a sea of patients that filled the waiting room, ignoring the stench of body odor as I hurried to the glassed-in front desk. The haggard woman with long, silver hair eyed me from behind the counter, taking in my uniform. "Can I help you, Officer—"

"My wife," I rasped. "Where's my wife—Hannah Mitchell?"

The woman's dark eyes fell, and she nodded down the hall. "She's in surgery, Mr. Mitchell. She had an accident."

My knuckles whitened against the counter. "An accident?" She was supposed to be asleep, warm and at home in bed. I turned for the double doors that separated everything else from the waiting room.

"You can't see her right now—Officer!"

I rushed down the hall of the small clinic. I didn't care about the rules and they couldn't stop me.

The hinges of the electronic doors screeched as I burst through, glancing fervently between the three closed rooms to my right. Surgery meant something bad happened, and there were complications.

"Hannah!" I shouted, even if a voice told me she couldn't hear me.

"Sir!" the nurse called.

I peered through the window in the first door. An exposed, dark-skinned foot was all I could see, but it was enough to know it wasn't Hannah, and I ran to the next. I peered through the second window, at the bloodied sheets on the floor. Someone had died in there, or was dying. And when the woman in scrubs moved out of my line of sight, I saw polka-dot slippers stained with blood discarded on the floor.

Air rushed from my lungs, and my heart froze in my chest. A wave of disbelief washed over me, taking with it every willful shred of hope I'd brought in with me.

Another scrub-shrouded person moved around the table. Blood soaked the sheet covering the mound of her stomach.

"Sir—"

I startled.

"You can't be in here, sir." The nurse tugged on my arm, but I couldn't pry my eyes from Hannah. Was she still alive? Was the baby dead?

"Sir—"

"That's my wife!" I growled, glaring at her.

The nurse swallowed. "I know, and I'm sorry, Officer Mitchell, but if you want her to live, you can't distract Dr. Fines. Please," she said, gesturing toward the waiting room. "Sit." Her voice was calm and practiced. But I wasn't like all the other husbands and fathers she'd talked to before. That was *my* wife and *my* child, and I did not understand what the fuck was happening. "You said there was an accident—"

She gestured toward the waiting room again. Patients were everywhere, blurs and outlines in my panicked haze, and the scent of sickness permeated the building.

"I know this is hard, and I'll explain to you what I know."

Uncertain if I should listen to her, to take even an immeasurable step back, I glanced back inside the operating room, at the nurse peering over at me. I sucked in a breath.

Hannah needed their attention, and I was only hurting her by causing a scene.

"Right this way," the nurse murmured and rested her hand on my elbow. The severity of what was happening became a whirling tornado of uncertainty, and tears blurred my eyes as I followed her back out to wait with the others.

I listened for the creak of the operating room door and for the doctor to run out and reassure me everything would be okay, but the door never opened and the doctor never came. In my gut I knew nothing would ever be okay again.

The electric doors swung closed behind us. "There was an intruder," the nurse explained, letting go of my elbow.

I paled. "A what?"

"Someone broke into your home—"

"A looter?" Dispatch had been flooded with reports all night.

The nurse shrugged. "An older man brought her in—Mr. Hutton." Whether it was a courtesy extended because I was a trooper or because I was a distraught husband, I wasn't sure, but the nurse handed me the intake report.

Neighbor heard a scream and gunshots. Ran next door and found the victim on the kitchen floor. She was barely conscious and holding her stomach.

I'm not sure how long I stared blankly at the paper before I dropped the clipboard and it crashed onto the linoleum. I couldn't read it. I couldn't bear it. Not when it was my wife fighting for her life in my house . . . holding my daughter. I could barely catch my breath.

The nurse crouched down for the clipboard. "He called 9-1-1 when he found her, but there was so much blood he brought her in himself."

Her words were like distant horns, blaring and soft at the same time. They echoed through my head as I imagined Hannah scared and in pain, alone in our *home*.

"Officer," the nurse said tentatively. My gaze drifted to her. "The intruder shot her in the abdomen . . . She lost the baby."

I stumbled to the side table in the waiting room and lowered myself down. "No," I said, shaking my head. Molly's room was nearly ready and her clothes were already picked out for the drive home from the hospital.

The automated doors opened with a click and the doctor marched out. His face mask was resting under his chin like he could barely be bothered to come out and speak with me as he pulled one bloody glove off, then the other. His eyes were grayed, and his jaw was a few days unshaven.

"I'm sorry, there was nothing we could do," he said unceremoniously. "I did all I could, but she'd already lost too much blood." He rubbed his temple. "Her organs failed. She didn't make it." His words hadn't even sunk in before the surgeon turned on his heel and hurried back down the hall, too busy to explain anything more. "I'm sorry," I heard him mutter again, and then the automated doors shut behind him.

It was like I'd been pitted and hollowed out. I was a vacuous, abysmal void of incredulity. "I just saw her." She'd given me a kiss, told me to be safe, and waved as Ross and I had drove to the station.

I shook my head, refusing to believe any of it.

"I'm so sorry, Mr. Mitchell—" but the nurse's sympathetic voice was like air to a nascent fire. "Oh, God. No," I pleaded and let my head fall into my hands.

Hannah wasn't gone. It didn't feel real. "No . . ." I repeated, standing. I ignored the ache in my bones and instant fatigue. The doctor was wrong. He didn't try hard enough. There was still hope.

My legs gave out before I could take two steps, and I stumbled back into the wall. The nurse reached out for me, but covering my face with my hands, I slid down to the cold linoleum. I was an abyss of emotion unlike anything I'd ever felt. Gaping. Raw. Empty pain. And yet so full and brimming, I couldn't catch my breath.

"I'm so sorry," she said again, but they were just words—sounds with no meaning.

Molly, our little miracle, was gone. She was supposed to be spoiled rotten and perfect.

A woman coughed somewhere in the room and I looked over. An indistinct horde of faces stared back at me.

I glanced down at my uniform. My blue fatigues had held a meaning once, but I was no longer a state trooper. I was a man whose world had just fallen apart, and my wife and child were dead.

I peered up at the nurse. I opened my mouth, but nothing came out. Clearing my throat, I tried again. "Can I see her?"

"Of course, you—"

"Hey!"

A man pushed himself off the far wall of the room. He had tattoos on his face and neck, and looked like he'd seen better days. "I've been waiting for hours. Am I gettin' this broken arm looked at or what?"

The clinic was small, and couldn't have had more than a handful of staff. The few staff around were bustling in and out the doors and answering phones.

"I've been here longer!" A woman shouted

The man with a broken arm pointed at the nurse, eyes narrowed. "I want to talk to management or something—"

I didn't care about them and their bullshit problems. "Sit your ass down," I told him. "Wait your turn."

He took a step back, but I didn't think it was because of the uniform. He scowled, but said nothing more.

"I need to deal with these patients," the nurse said softly. "You know where to find her."

Hesitant, I stepped past her. "Mr. Mitchell?" I peered at the nurse over my shoulder. "I'll give you as much time as I can, but we'll have to wheel her out when we need the room."

I continued walking. Somehow, amidst the indescribable pain, I could also feel nothing at all. Reluctant to open the door—to see what remained of my wife and daughter—I peered in through the window slat and did my best to brace myself. I couldn't leave without saying goodbye. I wasn't sure I could leave at all, not without her.

Lowering my head, I choked out a sob and squeezed my eyes shut before I could bring myself to open the door and step inside. I walked over to the curtain with a ragged breath, and pulled it open all the way.

A blanket covered Hannah's stomach, and a small, infant-sized shape was wrapped in linen in the incubator beside her. My feet froze where I stood at the end of Hannah's bed.

Her face was gray and slackened, not like she was simply sleeping but like she'd been gone for hours already. Her lips were less rosy, her skin more ashen, and as she lay there, I feared her as much as I missed her.

"Baby . . ." The word was only air exiting my lungs as I struggled to breathe.

Stepping around the bed, I took her cold hand in mine, wincing as I sat down on the stool beside her. I couldn't see her through the tears, but I knew it was better that way as I brought her cold hand to my lips. "Han, you can't leave me. I need you baby—" I sucked in a breath.

Last time I saw her, she was smiling, threatening to give me a haircut when I got home. Now she would never touch me, never sleep beside me again.

Tears dripped down my cheeks, onto her hand and down the soft skin of her arm. Another sob burst from my chest and I rested my forehead against her shoulder. I couldn't do this—I couldn't bear a life without her playful griping and dimpled smile. There was no reason to go on living without her.

8

JACKSON
DECEMBER 9

T he phone rang. Then it rang again, forcing my mind to stir. I wiped the crusted tears from my eyes and cracked my back as I unhunched myself and straightened. I wasn't sure how long I'd sat beside Hannah or for how long I'd wept, but at some point, I'd fallen asleep. The fog in my mind hadn't cleared and the nightmare hadn't faded. Hannah was still lifeless in front of me—her fingers cool and stiff in mine—and it all came crashing back down on me.

Biting back another sob, I rose to my feet, my body yelling at me to stay with her, to never leave her side. But I couldn't stay in the operating room forever. It wouldn't be long before the nurse came in to take her from me. What would I do then? And I couldn't leave her exposed like this any longer, undressed and cold. But she couldn't feel the cold, I realized.

I stared at the pale skin of her throat, waiting for her to swallow or give me some small sign that somehow she still breathed. That was crazy, though. Her stomach was cut open beneath the sheets—I knew it was. I didn't need to look, nor did I want to.

I peered up to the clock above the doorway. Then blinked and rubbed my eyes as I leaned closer. It was 6:15 in the morning. Five hours? I'd been sleeping for *five* hours? How had no one come to get me? In the recesses of my mind, I remembered shouting and banging in the hallway that had stirred me from my sleep, though none of it made any sense.

Reluctantly, I pried my fingers from Hannah's, hating that it felt like a final goodbye, and dared to look at Molly's body, still swaddled in the incubator. I couldn't bring myself to go over, petrified what I might find. But I had to eventually. I needed to get them out of here and lay them to rest.

With a steadying breath, I leaned down and pressed my lips to Hannah's forehead. "I love you so damn much," I whispered. It was all I could do to grit back another breakdown.

The phone continued to ring down the hall, grating on my last nerve as it went unanswered, and then it dawned on me. I had two very important calls to make. Han's mother and father in Hawaii needed to know what happened, and her brother . . .

The Vise-Grip cinched around my heart again, and I could barely stand the weight of dread, pressing against my chest. How was I going to tell Ross his baby sister was dead?

I braced my palm against the wall, willing myself to stay upright. My limbs were heavy with grief and exhaustion, and my mind was a cloud of insecurity, yet when I pulled out my phone to make the two most heart-breaking calls of my life, I had to be strong. I had never been the strong one, and now I needed to be their rock.

Dragging in a ragged breath, I readied myself to make the call. I thumbed the tears away, like it might actually help, and I stepped into the hallway.

When I saw I had no cell service, I felt . . . Relief? Distress? Defeat? I looked at the metal doors, which were open this time, and dropped my hand to my side. Only four people were left in the garage-sized waiting room, but the air smelled foul, like sour gym clothes in a sauna.

A nurse with a red bun and stalky legs I hadn't seen before

attended to an older woman with blood on her forehead, while another woman vomited in the far corner of the room.

"Excuse—" I cleared my throat, voice rusty. I stepped toward her. "Excuse me, Nurse?"

"What is it?" She didn't bother looking up from the bandage she placed on the elderly woman's head.

"Where's the doctor?"

"Which one?" She rose to her feet and tossed a soiled rag into the cart beside her. "Never mind, it doesn't matter. Dr. Fines left for a family emergency, O'Donnell is passed out in the break room, sick, and I'm not sure about the others."

When she finally looked at me, I could see the sickness in her blue eyes. She looked jaundice, and it wasn't only exhaustion and overwhelm. The nurse was unwell. We all were, I could feel it in my blood, sucking out what little life was left in me.

The governor's ESA had come too late. I wasn't one for facts and figures, but I knew it only took one person to infect a colony, history had proven that much. Despite its remote outposts and frozen lands, Alaska was no exception.

I cleared my throat. "My wife is dead," I said dumbly.

"I'm sorry for your loss, Officer." She pushed her supply cart over to a little girl sleeping in the last chair and placed the back of her hand against the girl's forehead, brushing a loose curl behind her ear. The little girl inhaled deeply, her throat rattling, but she didn't wake.

"What I mean is," I continued, "she's still in the operating room with a—my daughter."

The nurse seemed to finally see me, *really* register my standing there, and she looked at me. Her name tag had a photo of her. Penelope Hernandez: Medical Assistant.

"The doctor said he'd come for her but he never did," I explained.

The nurse rose to her feet, coughing into her shoulder as she surveyed the room. "What's your name?"

"Jackson Mitchell. My wife is Hannah Mitchell, and she was in here for a gunshot wound to the stomach."

The nurse's brow furrowed with sympathy, and she shook her head. "I'm sorry about your wife," she said again, though this time she seemed to mean it. "I don't want to lie to you, Officer. We're a small clinic, our rooms are full, these people have been waiting to see the doctors for hours, and we're short staffed. I don't see it getting better anytime soon. I'm not even sure we'll be able to function as a clinic for much longer. We're running low on supplies and there's no one to run anything." Her voice pitched. "We've all got it—it's only a matter of time before. . ."

"Before what?" A new, spiraling kind of fear racked through me.

She glanced at the TV mounted on the wall. Two news anchors sat behind a desk, the camera panning between them. The segment title read: 70 million hospitalized in two days stokes fear in officials world-wide. Some are coining 'End of Days'.

"They're all dying," she choked out. "They're not getting better. They say it's the H1N1/12 sickness." Her eyes scoured my face, waiting for me to understand. But how could I? It had only been hours since I'd fallen asleep. It was happening too fast, and it made no damn sense.

"People aren't just looting anymore—they're losing their minds. We're all going to die."

"Hey," I said as firm and softly as I could. "You are not going to die." I said, pronouncing every word. If she *was* dying, there was nothing to stop me and everyone else from following behind her. And freaking out wasn't an option for me—not with Hannah and Molly to tend to.

Summoning every shred of willpower that remained, I dug deep for what was left of my calm-and-collected reserve and led her to one of the empty chairs that didn't have unidentifiable fluid on it.

"You're just exhausted—we're all exhausted," I told her and

pointed to the television. "They will figure this out. We just have to hold on a little while longer." The lies were pouring out of my mouth. "You've been at this for hours, haven't you?"

She nodded with a sniffle and blew a strand of red hair from her face. Her blue eyes were red-rimmed. "Yes."

"You just need some rest."

"I *am* exhausted," she admitted. "I could use a couple hours to sleep." She needed more than that given the gauntness of her face.

I glanced at the old woman in the chair opposite us, her eyes were closed and her mouth was open. Her chest was rising and falling with each shallow breath. I wasn't sure why she hadn't left, maybe she had no place to go, or maybe she was too sick, but the nurse wasn't helping anyone by staying. "You've done what you can for these people. You should take a break."

She nodded in pure defeat, as if she only needed someone to give her permission. "I only need a few minutes. I'll be okay after that."

The nurse rose shakily to her feet and looked down at me, still crouched beside the chair. "I can't promise your wife and child will get the attention they deserve," she explained, voice level this time. She wiped her brow with a shaking hand. She was ailing before my eyes, and I stood and took a slight step away from her, even though I knew it was already too late.

"It's not clinic policy—in fact, it's against the law—but if it were me, I would consider taking my family somewhere to be looked after properly, where their bodies will be cared for."

Horror replaced the dread and despondency that turned in my gut and inched its way up my throat. "You mean take them with me?" I imagined holding my dead wife in my arms and the weight of a tiny lifeless baby in my hands. "Take them out of this clinic, to God knows where?"

She coughed again, and this time I felt the air shift between us. The nurse was right. This was the plague and no one was coming for my family. None of us had much time left, my weakening muscles and fatigue were proof of it.

A wave of calm washed over me at the thought. If I didn't make it through the virus, I wouldn't have to go on living without Hannah and Molly.

"I'm saying," the woman started again—her voice more raspy than before. "Do what you want, no one will stop you."

She grabbed a jug of water from behind the desk and chugged it down, wiping her mouth with the back of her arm when she was finished. Then, she disappeared into a hallway in the back.

I peered around the waiting room of borderline corpses. No one was coming for any of them. No one was left to help. We were on our own now, and Hannah deserved better than this. I couldn't stay here and I wouldn't leave without her, uncertain what would happen to her body or if I'd ever see her again.

Spotting an abandoned stretcher from the hallway, I went over to it, grabbed hold, using it to brace me up in my daze, and wheeled it into the room where my wife and child lay. I pushed it up beside the operating table, forcing thoughts of insanity aside as I tried to validate what I was doing, taking a dead body from the hospital—*two* bodies. I stared down at Hannah's beautiful face, remembering the way her golden eyes smiled, even when she was trying to be serious, and the way her eyebrow lifted ever so slightly when she really meant business. I committed it all to memory, praying the day never came that the memory faded.

Then, clenching my jaw, I gathered her body into my arms and placed her on the gurney. It was impossible to ignore the blood staining the white sheets, so I grabbed a clean one from the cupboard and draped it over her, hoping it would help me forget, but it didn't.

When she was on the gurney, I pulled the sheet up higher, covering her shoulders and then her face, and strapped her body in. The significance of what was happening poked holes in the failing armor I grasped onto. I needed to do this. I needed to get out of here; I just needed to be strong a little while longer.

Rallying what remained of my fortitude, I turned to the incubator. It was essentially a shoebox housing a newborn corpse swaddled in linen, and knowing it would break the very last pieces of my heart, I reached in and gathered Molly into my arms. I drew her to my chest, holding her for the first time.

Fearing I would regret not seeing her at least once, I peeled the layers around Molly's face back, even if it was only to say goodbye. My hands shook and my lungs constricted as I peered down at her. Her eyes were closed. Her nose was tiny, and her cheeks were chubby. She was perfect—tiny—but perfect. She was my daughter, the only one I would ever have, and I never got to meet her.

Our little miracle. She was probably gone before Hannah could take her last breath.

Eyes blurred with tears, I lifted her closer and kissed her tiny forehead. "Goodbye, little one," I choked out. Then I placed her in the crook of her mother's arm, wishing I could join them.

❄

"10-33, we have a 5150 at The Gardens. Are you still in the area?"

Sitting in the truck outside my house, I listened to the dispatcher's voice over the radio. She requested one unit after the other and no one responded. It was nearly eight o'clock in the morning and the sky would be dark for another couple hours still. The snow had let up though.

I glanced around at the quiet street.

"Unit 33, come in. Over."

Hands shaking with rage, and vision blurred with tears, I pulled out my cell phone and dialed Ross. I'd never heard back from him. I didn't know if he was okay, and even if he were, he wouldn't be for very long after I gave him the news.

I squeezed my eyes shut and told myself to prepare for the worst, so I was glad when the call went straight to voicemail. I tried Hannah's parents next, my fingers pulling up their number without thinking much more about it. It needed to be done. It was that simple. The call went straight to the operator. "We're sorry, your call cannot go through. Please try your call again later."

"All units," the dispatcher's voice came through the radio again, but I tuned her out, dropped my phone on the console and forced myself to open the driver door. Hannah deserved more than this, she needed to be at peace, and I needed to be the one to make that happen.

Body stiff and my mind not nearly numb enough, I got out of the truck, welcoming the 7°F windchill that accosted me. Trudging through the snow to the other side of the truck, I braced myself to take Hannah and the baby in my arms once again. Hannah's body felt heavier than before, my legs less steady. My strength drained from me with each step toward the house.

But still, I hesitated at the stoop, staring at the door handle. The last time I carried her through this doorway we'd just bought the house and had spent our last ten dollars cash on burgers from Bud's in celebration.

I closed my eyes and took a deep breath. I could almost smell the scent of her amber perfume mingling with French fries.

I wouldn't walk into an empty house this time. There would be blood, probably signs of the struggle. *And there would be evidence and clues.* For the first time, my sadness was overshadowed with rage, and a small, minuscule part of me bloomed with optimism and retribution.

As Hannah grew heavier in my arms, I ignored the churning in my stomach at what was to come, and turned the unlocked handle and stepped inside. Fleetingly, I knew I needed to thank Mr. Hutton for doing what he could to save Hannah, and I would ask him what information he had that would help me in the process—if he was even still alive.

I bit my lip and peered around the living room. It was trashed, but the flat screen was still there, so was the computer on the desk. My cop mind inventoried everything as I walked over to the couch and laid Hannah's body down, the baby with her, and my muscles felt an instant reprieve. I unfolded Hannah's favorite blanket from the back of the couch and placed it over their bodies.

The scanner on the bookshelf against the wall went off, and amidst my numb mind, I heard another 5150 call and the victim being DOA, and that's when I made the connection.

Blinded by a frenzied understanding, I headed down the hallway, straight for the bedroom. The blue comforter was perfectly made, and nothing was out of place, save for my gun locker, which was shot open. My 12-gauge and .22 were missing. A few bullets were strewn on the ground, but the boxes of ammo were gone. Whoever broke into my house was willing to leave a pregnant woman for dead just to have them.

I kicked the locker with a roar and pounded on the wall so hard my fist went through it; the pain replaced the hurt for a single second, but it was enough. I cursed. I kicked. I wailed. The intruder was someone who knew I was a cop and would have guns. They had to have known.

I stomped back down the hall, so close to the edge I could feel myself teetering between recklessness and all-out fury. I would find the person who did this, but I wouldn't kill them. I would do something much, much worse. But when I saw the bloody skid marks in the kitchen and a lifeless male form, my feet would no longer move. My breath caught in my throat.

A tuft of red hair tumbled across the tiled floor in the wake of my footsteps, and I eyed the man's knotted, shoulder length hair and torn long-sleeve shirt. I flipped him onto his back; his brown eyes open and glazed over, his cheeks lined with dried blood and a fingernail slash. It was Charlie, a man who lived a few houses down and owned a tree service I'd inquired about a few years back. He had a bullet wound in his chest.

She'd fought back.

Hannah had told me years ago she'd never remember the code to the gun safe because she would never use it. I wanted her to be able to protect herself, so I put a revolver in the most obscure, accessible place I could imagine—the top shelf in the pantry.

I strode across the kitchen, feeling a strange sense of relief, and I opened the floor-to-ceiling cupboard. The gun was gone, the cloth it was wrapped in discarded under my boot. The revolver hadn't saved her life, but it had given her a fighting chance.

The images came fast and hard; Hannah's surprise in seeing him, her fear and inevitable pleas as she covered her belly, and her determination to protect our child until her dying breath. Alone, with no husband to protect her, she'd given him hell and took him down with her.

Insurmountable pride and regret filled every inch of me. Then came anguish.

I kicked Charlie's body, shouting and cursing him until I couldn't hold myself up anymore and fell against the side of the fridge. The guns were gone, but the door was unlocked and anyone could've taken them. Even Mr. Hutton might have, if he were smart.

Tremors shimmied up my leg and rattled the retribution loose. Hannah killed him and in doing so she took the revenge holding me together. I couldn't punish him because he was already dead. Impending recklessness and despair circled me, like vultures waiting to feast.

I'd done so well because of her, I'd become the man she saw in me the first day we met. But I hadn't been here to save her, and without her I wasn't strong enough to be the man she'd want me to be now.

I climbed to my feet, stepping through the blood as I reached for the handle of tequila in the cupboard above the fridge.

I couldn't get the cap off fast enough before I brought the bottle to my lips, heavy and full as it was. I was a drunk, and I'd always be one. I think those were my dad's words the day I swore I'd never confide in him again.

I took one swig after another, desperate to numb the pain, until I could no longer breathe and had to stop to catch my breath.

The bottle hung at my side, my heart pounding in my chest and the familiar warmth of liquid-oblivion coursing through me. A small voice somewhere told me I should call Ross again, or try to find him. But he was probably dead, or sick and would be soon.

I flicked on the porch light and stared out at the backyard, covered in snow. The only thing visible aside from the fence was the spruce where Hannah had asked me to hang a swing. "*It will be perfect in the spring and summer. I can rock her back and forth by the garden.*" I hadn't had the heart to tell her she never had a green thumb.

The scanner continued to click and buzz incessantly in the living room.

I took another slug from the bottle. Then another. I drank until my throat was raw and it felt like I'd burned the sickness stewing inside me away. Then I turned back to the couch where Hannah lay. Did I bury her in the frozen ground or sit with her until I drank myself to death? Ross wasn't around to ask; I was alone.

When the scanner went off again, I set the tequila down on the table with a clunk and pulled the radio off the bookshelf, smashing it over the back of the dining room chair to silence it permanently.

Taking another swig from the bottle, I let the fear and sorrow overwhelm me until I could no longer see through body-wracking sobs and a veil of tears. I had a long night ahead of me, followed by an excruciating forever.

DECEMBER 10

9

ELLE

DECEMBER 10

Whehen I stirred from the fathoms of dreamless sleep, my body ached and what felt like a furnace burned in my core. My veins were like tunnels, blazing with fire.

The floor creaked somewhere in the house, and my murky thoughts sharpened as my eyes flew open.

It took a heartbeat to remember anything beyond the ache in my abdomen, tender from retching; my throat was raw and sweat covered my skin. But despite all of that, my body felt renewed, alive in a way it never had before. I stretched, waking my taut muscles from hibernation.

The pale blue promise of morning crested over the treetops, breaking up the dark shadows outside my bedroom window. It must've been nine or ten, if the sun was rising—unless it was sunset. I wasn't sure how long I'd been out, but I recalled the bar and shots of whiskey. Big mistake.

I sat up with a groan, my head throbbing a little, and peered around my old bedroom. That was not how I'd seen the night playing out. I wasn't even sure what day it was. It was as if I'd been asleep for ages, and yet my body felt like it had been only a matter of hours since I'd lurched over the toilet, puking my insides out.

The floor creaked again, somewhere in the living room and louder than before.

Dr. John's face flashed to mind, but I pushed it away.

I heard the sound of a shoe scuff, loud and heavy.

Another creak.

Someone was in the house, and I braced myself for them to appear in the hallway outside my open door.

Trembling and weak, I held my breath and climbed as quietly from bed as I could. The rug was stiff beneath my bare feet, the cold air brushing over my warmed skin.

I stopped as the floorboards shifted beneath my feet, but there was no noise to follow, and no one appeared in my doorway. What were the chances it was Sandy Fields? She had a key. Or was it a random robbery, and they didn't know I was here? I thought of the faces at the bar, and the men who might've followed me home.

The kitchen door leading out to the garage creaked open, and I heard a male voice muttering. It wasn't Sandy Fields in the house.

Heartbeat skipping from a thud to a full on sprint, I scoured the morning shadows for my phone. A cold wave of dread washed over me when I saw my pants on the floor in the hallway, phone sticking out of my pocket, discarded in the craze of my fever. *Shit.* I always did that. I'd told myself it would fall out of my pocket one day into a toilet bowl and I would be sorry, but not as sorry as I was now, knowing someone was in my house and it was so far out of reach.

I stopped just shy of the doorway, shoring up my nerve to rush out and grab it before the intruder came back into the house. I could hear him rifling through the garage, looking for something. He was loud and careless, and I was thankful. I knew exactly where he was.

I peeked around the door frame. My pants were only a few feet away. If I didn't grab my phone now, I might not get another chance. Exhaling, I dropped to my knees and crawled out into the hallway, praying he would stay in the garage a few minutes longer. I reached for my phone as a tall man with broad shoulders stepped back into the dining room, the threshold creaking under his weight. He was facing my direction as he peered frantically around. I didn't dare move.

"Where is it!" he growled, and knocked an empty water pitcher off the table—the sound of shattering glass filled the house as it hit the ground.

My chin trembled, trying to see who it was in the morning shadows, uncertain why it mattered. I might've survived the fever simply to die at the will of a stranger.

As if something suddenly occurred to him, he lifted his head, facing me fully and headed right toward me. I swallowed a whimper, uncertain if he'd actually seen me. Then, he stopped mid-step, and I saw the recognition on his face.

"You!" he shouted. It was Thomas, the neighbor, only he was a menacing version whose eyes rounded, and he seethed when he spat my name. "Where did you hide it? I need it—now!"

I ran back into my room and slammed the door shut. My hands shook. My eyes blurred with fearful tears, and my mind screamed at me to do *something* as I glanced around the room.

Thomas's footsteps were heavy and quick behind me, and without a chair to bolster beneath the doorknob, and the dresser on the other side of the room, I scrambled to find a solution. I yanked the metal curtain rod off the wall just as he barreled through the door.

"Get away from me!" I shouted, ramming him in the chest with the finial on the end.

He stumbled back, but then kept coming toward me. "Give me his medical bag you little bitch," he ground out.

"It's in his bedroom!" I shouted. It was a lie. I didn't know where the hell it was or if Dr. John still had one.

"You're lying—"

I jabbed him with the finial again, but it was like he couldn't feel it, each blow only knocking him off balance for a millionth of a second before he was lunging at me again.

Desperate to hurt him enough to pass, I rammed him in the stomach and then the chest, until he tore the rod from my grip like he was unfazed and I was nothing more than an annoying wasp.

I ran for the lamp on the side table, ripping it out of the wall and threw it at him. Thomas stumbled back this time, onto my bed and I ran past him, gripping my phone in my hand and praying I could put enough distance between us to use it.

I'd only taken a few steps before something solid slammed into the back of my head, and I fell to the ground, a smarting pain shooting down my neck. Everything around me swirled, and I winced as my skull began to throb.

The vision of Thomas was a blur as he gripped hold of my shirt and rolled me onto my back. He wrapped his hands around my neck, making me gasp, and brought his nose within inches of mine. His hot breath pressed against my face as he shouted, only I couldn't make out the words. They boomed and blared, but his grip was too tight. My body began to burn so intensely I thought I might implode. I gulped for air and hit my fists against his arms and face, but it was pointless. His grip was ironclad—crunching my windpipe—and my vision began to gray.

Thomas was killing me.

The heat was alive inside of me. It blazed and flickered against my skin, trying to get out as he smashed my head on the hardwood floor.

This could not be my end. Dying at the hands of a man in a place I swore I'd never return? I hadn't gone through years of therapy to come back and die in this godforsaken house.

Resolve turned to hardened clarity, and I used every ounce of energy flickering inside me and lunged for Thomas's throat. Every muscle in my body lit like fire, coursing with an unbridled strength I'd never felt before. Every cell was alive and pulsating as I clutched his neck in my hands, unable to stop myself from squeezing. I was a forge of red-hot hatred, and tears stung my eyes. Fire burned in the tips of my fingers, and my body shook with a fury that scorched away every lingering fear.

"Screw . . . you," I choked out, half in shock as I felt the power in me surge.

Thomas let go of my neck and hit at my hands as I squeezed tighter—grew stronger. The fire inside stirred, blooming in the depths of me, and I felt it leave my body with a final squeeze. Thomas's eyes widened and bulged. His face reddened and his tongue fell from his mouth as he let out one last, silent scream.

As he gurgled his last breath, I shut my eyes. My muscles deflated as the last of the energy flowed from my fingers. Then, I curled into a ball and cried.

※

I peeled my eyes open to the brightness of day and stared up at the taupe ceiling. My head was pounding, but my body felt lighter. The heaviness was gone, so was the heat.

Jolting upright, I saw the dead man wilted beside me. Thomas's eyes were still open; his mouth was agape. There were burn marks the shape of fingers around his neck, and I clasped my hands over my mouth and scurried backward until I was flush against the wall. Shaking.

He was dead, and I had killed him.

I stared down at my trembling hands. What had I done? What could I *do*?

Tears filled my eyes as I tried to bite back the impending sobs. I'd never killed anyone before. I had ended a human life with my hands. I turned my palms over, scouring them for burn marks, fisting my fingers, searching for the fire I'd felt consume me—every fiber, every inch. It was impossible. And yet somewhere deep down, I could still feel it writhing inside me.

I looked at Thomas again; emotions clamoring through me, exacting whatever pieces of my sanity were left. Fear. Regret. Confusion. Relief. He was going to kill me and I'd killed him first. I *killed* him. My fingerprints were seared around his neck to prove it.

Staring at my hands, I tried to understand. They were just hands with fingers, like they'd always been, and they were unscathed.

I glanced from the burn marks on Thomas's neck to my hands, remembering the euphoric release as the fire, scorching within me, leached from my fingertips. Then, I turned to the side and retched.

10

JACKSON

DECEMBER 10

There was movement in the darkness—a rustling, a jolting. My mind stirred as my body shook. No, I was being shaken.

I smelled the stench of decay before I registered the blunt fingertips at my waist, and my eyes flew open.

A hulking form crouched beside me, tugging at my belt.

"What the fuck—" I jerked away, my body stiff and sore as I reached for my holstered gun, but it was too late. It was already in the man's hand.

"I can't," he muttered through chapped lips, peering down at the gun in his shaking hands.

"What?" I scrambled back as he tightened his grip on the Glock. His blonde hair was matted to the side of his head, his body covered in a sheen of sweat. "Put the gun down," I told him. "Put it down." Even in a liquor-induced coma, I could find my voice. "Sir —put it down," I said more calmly, but my insides were scream-ing. My muscles were weak and my head was throbbing. I willed myself to focus. "You can have anything you want in here—you want more guns? I'll get you more guns."

The man shook his head, tears streaming down his ruddy cheeks. He looked no older than I was.

"I can't," he cried. He aimed the barrel at me. I'd had a gun pulled on me before, but never my own. Never had I been so close I could see the yellow flecks against the blue in the eyes of my assailant. "I just can't." His eyes met mine with finality. "I can't stop it. I can't stop any of it!" He gripped the gun more firmly.

I swallowed the bile rising in my throat. He would kill me. I didn't need the virus to kill me or to drink myself to death; the lunatic sitting on my living room floor would do it for me. I'd wanted to die and now I was getting my wish.

Even so, my instinct was to flee, to talk him down and save my skin. I lifted my hands, no longer stupefied, but afraid. "You don't want to do this, man."

His gaze shifted from the gun to me—he looked through me. "I have to," he wheezed. The saliva was white and gathered in the corners of his mouth, and he was ill, unlike anything I'd ever seen. "It's the voice!" he cried, making me jump. "I have to."

"Put the gun down, man. I'm a state trooper, bad things will happen if you shoot me."

The man laughed, the sound reverberating through the house, vaguely reminding me how empty the place was, how cold. "There's nothing you can do," he said.

Before I could process anything else, he pressed the pistol beneath his chin and pulled the trigger.

I doubled over and covered my ears too late against the ear-splitting bang. "Shit," I hissed, blinking as the room spun and the sound reverberated through my body, concussive and visceral.

Heaving out a breath, I grabbed the gun from his slack hold and slid it across the room, backing away as fast as I could. I stopped only when my back slammed into the wall, and I blinked.

I stared at the dead man on my floor and ran my hand over my face and through my hair. Brains splattered the wall—brains and blood dripping onto the floor. I'd seen gunshot wounds and fatal motorcycle accidents; I'd seen what an overdose looked like—puke and needles and blood. But this was different—this was my home, this was my life —and bile rose up my throat faster than I could scramble to the door.

I was barely on the porch when I doubled over and hurled everything out over the railing. The tequila burned my nose and throat, my muscles twisted, and my eyes watered as I heaved out a steadying breath. *What the fuck just happened?* I wiped the moisture from my eyes and spit the remnants of vomit from my throat as I sat down on the porch step.

I dragged a chestful of air into my lungs, then another, and stared out at a world of white. The snow had stopped, but not before the roads were piled high and abandoned. My street was eerily quiet. The neighbor's front door creaked open and shut with the breeze. There was no residual noise from the overpass ten blocks down, no engines roaring in the distance or horns honking. There were no birds chirping. I peered up at the leafless trees that lined my street. It felt as though I was the last person left. Chills trickled down my spine as gray daylight filtered through the clouds.

I glanced at my truck in the driveway and did a double take. It was beaten to hell; the windows were smashed and the side paneling was dented, like someone had come at it with a sledgehammer.

Gritting my teeth, I rose with achy knees and retreated back into the house, prepared to shoot the man on the floor again, just for good measure. That changed the instant I stumbled and stopped beside Hannah's covered body.

Part of me needed to remove the blanket to prove she was still there, but I hesitated. Hours of oblivion had come at a price—I had no idea how much time had passed or what it had done to her.

What would she look like? *Worse* wasn't how I wanted to remember her. But the part of me desperate to discover it was all a dream couldn't resist. As I inched the blanket back, her dappled skin sent my pulse racing and my heartbeat thrashed in my ears.

I dropped the blanket again. I couldn't do it. I couldn't look at her, but I couldn't move her body either. Where would I take it? What would I do with it when I got there?

Unsteadily, I began to pace. Two break-ins. Too many deaths. The world was silent, and the news was right. It was the end. It was the fucking end, and I needed protection. I needed answers too. Where was Ross? Where were Kelsey and my dad? I couldn't be the only one left, even if the world seemed to be standing still.

I stared at the dead body on the living room floor. Even if the madness was following me everywhere I turned, I couldn't be the only one left. I looked at the body in the kitchen. If I did nothing, soon it would be impossible to stay.

Forcing my mind to forget the hangover or sickness, whichever it was, I went to the closet and pulled out a set of sheets. Not the Egyptian cotton ones that were Hannah's favorite, but the old ones I used to have in my old apartment that we never used.

I covered the man in the living room first, unable to stomach the hole in his head. Then covered the rotting man in the kitchen. In a matter of hours, our home had become a crypt, a lonely, condemned house, and I couldn't stay here anymore. I grabbed what was left of the tequila, walked to the sliding glass door, and peered out at the backyard. This is where Hannah would want to rest.

I took a long pull from the bottle, and set it down again. Uncertain where I'd left my phone, I headed to the bedroom for Hannah's on the charger on the bedside table. Seven missed calls from Ross. The tension in my neck eased slightly, and I almost laughed. The son of a bitch might still be alive.

I clicked his number to call him back, but it went straight to voicemail again. I hung up and called again. Then again before I finally left a message. "Ross . . . If you're alive, I need to talk to you. I'm at the house . . . you should come." My throat swelled with regret. "At least call me back as soon as you can." Biting back the tears, I exhaled a ragged breath. "I hope you're okay, brother," I said, then I hung up.

Hastily wiping the tears from my eyes, I called 9-1-1 to report the bodies on my living room floor, but the line only rang. I tried the police department next, the menu giving me too many extensions—none of which worked—before I ended the call and strode back out to the living room. My wife and child were dead on my couch. Two intruders were rotting on my floor. And I was running out of time and options.

Imagining Hannah and Molly in a hole in the ground shredded me, but I would do what I had to.

I would find a place to take the bodies, clean up the house, and then I would bury my family in the backyard. After that, I would drink myself into oblivion and find Ross, if I hadn't heard back from him by then.

DECEMBER 11

11

ELLE

DECEMBER 11

"*Elle, I missed your calls, I'm sorry. But—look, I know you're going to look for me, but don't. Okay? I'm . . . not well—just, don't come to Whitely, okay? It's not safe.*"

I'd missed a call from Jenny somewhere between the bar and waking up shaking and half-naked on my bedroom floor after crying myself to sleep. Every ounce of energy had been drained from me, just like Thomas's body, still crumpled beside me on the floor when I'd opened my eyes. It hadn't been a nightmare.

I stared at my closed bedroom door, chewing on the broken skin on my bottom lip.

Don't come to Whitely.

Jenny's message was eerily calm despite her being sick, perhaps on the verge of death. It made me think she might be okay. I was okay, wasn't I?

I thought of Thomas's burned neck and studied my hands for the hundredth time. I was alive anyway. I pushed the growing hysteria as deep down as it would go. There was a logical explanation for all of this.

My hands were still normal, my fingers wiggling and my skin unchanged—I could almost convince myself the night of terror was only a hallucination caused by the fever, that it hadn't actually happened. Or maybe I was just losing my mind. It wouldn't be that surprising.

Yet, when I cracked opened the door, Thomas was still there. A lifeless mound I couldn't bear to see, covered by a blanket. I shut the door again, staring at it. I could feel it inside of me still—the fire—moving around like some foreign being was crawling beneath the skin, only it was electrified, an incessant, dull hum.

Squeezing my eyes shut, I exhaled. Jenny was my focus, not what partial memories lingered from my fever-induced haze.

The sound of an explosion emanated from the television in the living room, and I abandoned my useless pacing outside the bedroom door to watch the news footage. The afternoon gray filtered in through the windows and filled the house, still in disarray from the morning.

"—video came in last night," the male voiceover explained. "Chief Gonzalez, of the Alaska State Troopers, says the lack of a police force in such a remote, expansive state has always been an obstacle, making the average response time outside of the city between fifteen and thirty minutes. But this . . ." The camera swept up and down a cluttered, downtown street, eerily devoid of traffic. Two vandals wearing black clothes and Halloween masks ran in and out of the frame, between buildings and around abandoned vehicles.

"And here is viewer footage from somewhere in the Government Hill neighborhood." The screen cut to suburbs where an abandoned car in the middle of the road was covered in an inch of snow with the shape of a body still inside. "Please be advised, this is unedited and possibly disturbing footage," the news anchor said, his voice grim. The images changed from one neighborhood to the next. "Viewer discretion is advised."

Another video flashed onto the screen, of a house across the street being filmed through the window.

"There've been gunshots inside for the last twenty minutes. I don't know if it's Jim or Barbara—they've always been nice people." The woman's voice cracked, and I leaned forward, holding my breath as I closely watched the house cast in dying sunlight, uncertain what would come next. My heart thumped once, then again, and then a gunshot and flash of light lit the screen.

I jumped where I stood and covered my mouth.

"Oh my God." The woman behind the camera whimpered. "I don't know what's going on over there." The footage shook as she broke into a coughing fit. "I called the troopers, but no one's come yet. I keep thinking it's too late—I mean, what do they keep shooting at?" She cleared her throat, her breaths asthmatic and shallow.

The lights in the room flashed on and she squealed. "Turn the lights off, Eddy!" They flicked off almost immediately and a little boy whined. "Go back into the room. Close the door—go!"

The camera whirled as she hurried around, coughing and shepherding the boy into the hallway, until she went back to the window, coughed, and refocused with another shallow breath.

"My husband took our car to work this morning, and I haven't heard from him since." She sniffled. "The troopers have to come—they have to, right?" The little boy began to cry in the background. The woman cursed, shrieking for him to be quiet before the video went black.

"Footage has been sent into KTUU from around the city. And while some Alaskan citizens are trying to flee, others are preparing to hunker down and wait it out."

A man in a hockey mask flashed on the screen. "We knew it would come to this, inevitably," he said, severe as he rested his elbows on his knees. He leaned closer to the camera, peering around at a storage room I couldn't make out. "You'll get supplies and prepare for the worst, if you want to survive. No one is coming for us. We're on our own. It's the end of the twenty-first century as we know it." Suddenly, the man's eyes widened with excitement.

"Survival of the fittest!" After a hoorah and a fist pump, the screen went black.

Finally, a cell phone recording scanned a large room in what looked like a hospital, overwhelmed with sickness. "The number of dead world-wide is unknown, but unofficial reports claim more than half of the United States is infected. The Coast Guard is blockading all ports to prohibit further spread of the deadly virus. Since the Governor's ESA on Tuesday—"

I clicked the television off. There was nothing left inside of me to throw up, and every clip was the same. Each one made the dread knot tighter inside my stomach. Each new face and disturbing story was a blaring taunt that if the fever didn't get me, someone else likely would.

I got it, we were fucked, and I had to figure out what I would do before I let it all implode and fear prevented me from getting to Jenny. She was all I had left, and she was in Whitely. My sister needed me.

Glancing at my bedroom door, I told myself that Thomas was dead; there was nothing I could do about him, not anymore, and if I continued to wait for 9-1-1 or *someone* to arrive, it could be too late for Jenny.

I walked to the French doors facing the deck and stared out at the world shrouded in white, the grim sky promising a storm. Whatever I decided to do, I had to keep going. If I stayed here much longer, I might not be able to leave.

When Dr. Rothman encouraged me to return home, I don't think she'd expected this. Was she even still alive? I hoped so. She never wore a wedding band, but I hoped she wasn't completely and utterly alone, like I was. *Except for Jenny.* Whitely was only a few hours away; I couldn't live with myself if I didn't at least try to make it to her.

Decision made, I plopped down on the couch and pulled on my boots. Her living in such a small, remote town had to have some advantages. Maybe it meant the fever would pass quickly and by tomorrow night Jenny and I would be passed out on the couch, bored out of our minds and watching black and white movies, like we used to. My heart ached with hope, even if I knew full well that wasn't likely.

It took only minutes to pack my things strewn around the living room, but I knew I'd need what few clothes I had. Donning my scarf and parka, I flung open the front door. The instant I saw old Olive covered in snow, I knew it would be impossible to get to Whitely if I didn't have a better vehicle.

I peered over my shoulder at the garage door. Dr. John used to have a Bronco—one that rumbled and grumbled like it could take on anything. Turning on my heels, I headed across the house, wheeling my small luggage behind me.

Relief eased the tension in my shoulders when I saw the old Bronco was still inside. I snatched the only keys on the hook beside the door and stepped down into the mess Thomas had left in his search for the medical bag. I had no idea what he'd wanted it for, but he was crazed enough to try to kill me in order to get it.

Stepping over the hammer, nails, and different-sized screws strewn across the ground, I clutched a corner of the car cover and flung it up and over the Bronco. It was just as mean looking as I remembered it. The black paint sparkled, even in the dingy garage light, and the mud tires looked like they could chew up anything that came their way. I almost thanked Dr. John for such a glorious, unexpected gift.

As I walked around the front of the Bronco, tugging the cover the rest of the way off, I debated calling the police again, but it was clear they weren't coming, not soon anyway. Not after what I'd seen on the news.

I opened the driver side door and paused. I might've had good intentions going to find Jenny, but after what I'd seen on TV, other people clearly didn't, and I hadn't spent the last year with Dr. Rothman working on my needlepoint. She'd helped me work through sexual abuse, abandonment, being victimized, and all the crap that fell in between. I wasn't going to forget all of that now.

Peering through the passenger side window, I stared at Dr. John's gun safe against the farthest wall. Like most Alaskans, he enjoyed his seasonal hunting trips, and how stupid would I be to go out there into the madness without a way to protect myself? I could use a gun, even if I hoped I wouldn't need to.

My feet didn't wait for me to contemplate any of it. I had no idea what I would find in the safe, but if there was anything inside, I would take it. I expected to find his old shotgun and some bullets, maybe. If I was lucky, he'd have a handgun in there too.

I spun the combination lock, assuming his tendencies hadn't changed, and I was right. One perk of having twin stepdaughters, Dr. John didn't have to choose which birthday combo he'd use.

When the door creaked open, I let out a breath of relief. His 20-gauge stood tall, shiny and clean, but it was the smaller case and the ammo box that made me smile. I set the gun case on the worktable and flipped it open to find a Glock 17. A sigh of relief escaped my throat, and I squeezed my eyes shut. I closed the gun case and walked back to the Bronco, snatching the box of ammo along the way. My day was getting better already.

12

JACKSON
DECEMBER 11

"I regret to tell you that as of midnight on the 10th of December, over 80 percent of the world's population has been reported or is assumed dead. It is estimated that the death toll will continue to climb. This news is devastating, I know, but all is not lost."

I broke the rest of my Ford's busted window out as the president yammered on, her voice more white noise against the bone-chilling wind, turning what few parts of me weren't marinated in tequila to ice. Maybe another drink would remedy that. I glanced at the bottle belted in the seat next to me, making a mental note to stop at the store at some point to grab some bourbon, my trusty old friend. Moving the bodies and cleaning the blood from the house was a haze. Good. I had bloodstained hands as proof it wasn't just a horrific dream and that was enough.

"Some of us are surviving. This is how we will fight our enemy —by not giving up, by being resilient and resourceful, by surviving. We are not a species that will go out quietly, so I task those of you who are still alive with one essential purpose: live."

"Shit." I swerved around a Nissan stopped in the middle of the road that seemed to come out of nowhere. I'd only seen two other cars in motion, and with vehicles scattered everywhere—some

80

abandoned, others mausoleums—it was easy to forget that someone else might be on the road, or that I wasn't actually the last person alive.

I blasted through a red light and turned onto Elmore Road. The American and Alaskan flags flapped half-staff in the oncoming storm as I drew closer to the police department.

I might've been drunk, but I wasn't stupid. I knew that the instant I decided to step out of my police vehicle, especially one battered to shit that looked stolen, I was probably barbecue. To anyone inside, I'd look either crazy in my blood-covered uniform, or like a threat. And it was clear the world didn't care about the rules and repercussions much anymore.

Everything was falling apart. The world had fucking lost it—*I* had fucking lost it laying Hannah and Molly to rest in their grave.

I pulled the truck to a stop out front of the building and hesitated to get out. Not because I cared what would happen once I did, but because I feared what I would find inside. An empty place with no sign of Ross or any other familiar, friendly face still breathing. I thought of the inconsolable man hovering over me when I woke. How many others were like that? Was *anyone* I knew still alive?

It didn't feel like it. Ross's townhouse had been empty with no signs of a struggle and no note. The APD was my last hope.

Unbuckling the tequila, I lifted what remained of the contents and took a gulp. I wasn't quite drunk enough to start spiraling yet. I took one pull, then another, eyeing the darkened windows for signs of life. On any other Friday I might've stopped by to harass Ross still stuck in his office, filing reports and making follow-up calls to eyewitnesses and bereft families. Today, I just prayed he was there.

I pushed the driver side door open and stepped out of the truck, my jacket catching in the wind. The afternoon was darkening to evening, and soon there would be only a whirl of white.

The longer I stood there, the more quickly my buzz diminished. Unclipping my pistol from my belt, I slowly made my way toward the front door. Footprints were visible in the snow, coming and going from the entrance, though it was hard to make heads or tails of them packed on top of one another. My gut told me someone was inside, but I would find out for sure soon enough.

Aiming my Glock, I pulled the door open and stepped inside, then swept the room to my right. An acerbic scent took me aback, followed by a growl that reverberated from down the hall behind me.

"Drop the gun, asshole!" A familiar voice warned.

With an audible breath, I smiled. "Does your mother let you talk to her with that mouth?" I turned around, ecstatic tears in my eyes.

"Jackson—Jesus." Ross barreled over and wrapped his arms around me. "You're alive, you lucky son of a bitch," he breathed. He took a step back as his shadowed blue eyes scoured my face.

"Where have you been?" I asked. "I tried calling you back."

Ross shook his head and put his hands on his hips. He was still suited up in his blues like me, and he looked haggard, also like me, but other than the dark circles under his eyes and some scruff, he looked like the same ol' Ross. He wasn't senseless, just sleep deprived, and I would've wept if I had any tears left in me.

"I'd been passed out in my office up until about an hour ago. I woke up to Drago's nose in my crotch." He glanced at the German shepherd licking my hand. "My phone's in my truck, I guess. Probably dead." He shook his head, his brow quirked with uncertainty. "I've been a little out of it the past couple days. I wasn't sure I was going to get through that fever. It's all sort of a blur."

I peered down at the dog sniffing my boots. "Where's Calvin?" I asked. Drago never left his partner's side.

"No clue. On patrol, at home—dead." He shrugged, his confusion a relief after wondering if I'd ever see him again. "I don't remember if he was here when I stopped in to puke my brains out or not." He looked squarely at me. "There are bodies in the back. Demetri, Steph, Barnes . . . I was moving them out of their offices when Drago growled at you coming in. I figured I should cover them up or—" He shook his head. "I don't know what to do with them. I don't know what *we're* supposed to do." He nodded to the break room. "Have you seen the news?"

I shook my head. I didn't need to see the news. I'd seen enough with my own eyes to know we were up shit creek. A soundless police department with blinking overhead lights and the scent of bile in the air was only a reminder.

"I turned it on to another ESA saying we're fucked and to shelter in place. What the shit is that going to do?"

I stood quietly and listened as he processed what I already had.

Ross crouched down and ran his hands over his buzzed head, scrubbing and scrubbing until I thought he might rub his scalp raw. Then, he stopped and peered up at me. "The quarantine came too late. We might be up here in our own piece of winter wonderland, but all those ships coming in every day, all those tourists—that shit has spread like wildfire."

He walked to the phone at the reception desk and pounded on the keys as he brought the receiver to his ear. "Shelter in place, my ass." He grumbled something else and shook his head again. "I've tried calling Kelsey a hundred times in the last twenty minutes. I need to go to Fairbanks and check on her, she's staying with her mom. I have to know if she's all right."

"Then you should go," I told him. It was the only thing that would give him peace, and maybe, he'd be luckier than I was.

Waiting with his ear to the phone, he peered at me through dark eyes that were rimmed with red and swollen from too much sleep. I knew his question was coming; it was only a matter of time, and I averted my gaze.

He slammed the phone down when there was no answer, weary, and stepped back around the desk. His eyes narrowed and he scratched the side of his face, slack-jawed and staring at me. Then, he leaned closer and sniffed. "Are you drunk?" His eyes landed on the blood on my sleeves, like his relief in seeing me was beginning to fade away and he was finally seeing me for the first time. He stared at my untucked lapel and scruffy face. My hair was shaggy compared to his, but then it always was. I was a rebel that way.

I don't know what else he saw, but his back straightened and his jaw clenched. "I went by your house that morning," he said, hesitant. "After we heard the report I wanted to check on Hannah, but she wasn't there—no one was, only a body." I watched with bated breath as his memories from before the fever fell back into place. "I checked Regional and Providence—she wasn't at any of the hospitals—"

I shook my head. "No, she wasn't."

"Where's Hannah, Jackson?" he croaked. "Where's my sister?"

My chin trembled as I grappled with the words. "She's gone."

13

ELLE

DECEMBER 11

T raffic was fine leaving Anchorage, until the highway took me right over downtown, where the shipyard barricades brought traffic to a complete stop. I stopped behind the biggest mass of cars I'd ever seen.

The Coast Guard had done what they'd said they would and blocked off the Port of Alaska. I could see the barges and tankers docked as I drove around stopped vehicles on the overpass. Shipping containers were suspended in midair, abandoned. And yet with all the congestion stretched out in front of me, everything was strangely still. Traffic was a gridlock. Very few officials manned the barricades below; a few flares flickered in the dying daylight.

I rested my elbow on the door, rubbed my temple, and heaved out a sigh. I was never a patient person, but this was excruciating. I was stuck in a sea of taillights and white puffs of air streaming from tailpipes. No one was moving.

I peered longingly at the other side of the highway. There was no traffic. No one was trying to get into the city; everyone was trying to get out. I was tempted to bust through whatever barrier was covered by the snow and continue south.

The Bronco's heater hissed, and the fuel gage sunk to less than half, and I still had fifty miles until Whitely, according to my phone's GPS. Honking would do no good, and waiting wasn't an option.

Leaning over the passenger seat, I strained to see down at the Corolla in the next lane. A woman in the driver seat had her head back on the seat rest, her eyes were wide, and her mouth was gaping.

I blinked. Swallowed. I sucked in a breath. Then, prying my eyes from the second dead body I'd ever seen in my life, I looked out at the sea of vehicles. This wasn't a traffic jam, it was a graveyard. I didn't know how many of the drivers were dead or just slow to catch on, like me, but I wasn't going to sit among them a second longer, regardless.

I glanced around, feeling like a rebel as I contemplated what to do next. Whether I backed up or found another way off the overpass, I would be breaking a dozen laws. But then I'd already committed worse than reckless driving today.

Shifting the Bronco into four-wheel drive, I cranked the steering wheel left and inched my way up the median. The Bronco protested in the thick, unmanned snow, but I was up and over it in seconds.

Fleetingly, I worried I would get pulled over and would have to pay a massive fine I wouldn't be able to afford, or worse, I'd be arrested and Jenny would think I'd never tried to come. But the further I drove without sirens and troopers to stop me, the faster I went until the city was lost behind me and the highway opened up with only a few cars parked on the roads. None of them moved.

I'd known things were bad, but I hadn't expected the world to be stopped all around me. Was *anyone* alive on the roads? I couldn't bear to look, so I kept my eyes forward as I hauled ass to Whitely.

The coastguardsmen at the docks might've been the only other people alive, other than me. While that didn't seem logical, nothing much did anymore, and I'd tried not to think about any of it. Between getting to Jenny and failing to ignore the deep burn in my blood, my thoughts were plenty occupied. I flexed my hands on the steering wheel.

Minutes went by. Then what felt like hours.

Finally, I turned onto the frontage road toward Whitely. I half expected them to glow red through the quilted fabric. No matter how much I tried to tell myself it was a freak accident or twisted memory, the fire was back. I could feel it stirring in my veins, bubbling up from somewhere I couldn't fathom.

My nostrils flared. I gritted my teeth. I steadied my breathing.

I'd done everything I could to push the burn away and write it off the first time. I wanted it to be part of the fever—a fluke nightmare with some rational explanation I was too incoherent to remember. I took a deep breath in, held it, then exhaled the tension coiling in my arms and shoulders. As the Whitely Tunnel came into view ahead, I realized it was all that was left between my sister and me. I glanced up at the sky and the black clouds settling in. I didn't know what I would find in Whitely, but I couldn't go back in the oncoming storm. I *wouldn't* go back.

Entering the tunnel, dimly lit by blinking lights, I followed the one lane road under the mountain. It was the only way to get to the secluded city.

To tune out my escalating panic, I clicked the radio on, hoping for more news about the lower forty-eight. I needed something else to think about. I needed news about a cure or where people were retreating to for safety, *something* to give me hope. Maybe they'd discovered it was all an elaborate hoax, like Orson Welles' radio-broadcast of "War of the Worlds," which had caused a widespread panic.

I turned the dial, wading through one static-filled station after another.

"—enemy has swept through every nation, attacking discretely, killing indiscriminately." Eyes wide, I looked from the road to the familiar female voice on the radio. "We lost thousands before we even knew we were under attack. Many have already fallen, and many more will fall. But we cannot give up the fight." I nearly forgot to breathe as I processed what she was saying.

Under attack? Was the president saying she thought it was chemical warfare? I considered Russia and Iran, but neither made sense. The outbreak was worldwide; millions of people were dying. No, billions of people were already dead.

"Over the past century, through technological achievements, we made our world smaller. We made the time it takes to communicate across oceans instantaneous, and the time it takes to travel those same routes nearly as fast. We made our world smaller, and in doing so, we sowed the seeds of our own destruction: a global pandemic."

I gripped the steering wheel more tightly, grateful for the dull light at the end of the cement tunnel. If the president was alive, that meant she had a plan. She would figure something out eventually. I just had to stay alive and find Jenny in the meantime.

I pressed my lips together. My sister *would* be on the other side of the tunnel. She had to be.

"Survive. Thrive." The president continued, urging listeners to pray for guidance. "Learn from our mistakes. Let the world remain big. And most importantly, live." The broadcast petered out and static returned.

I scrambled for the volume. "Shit." That couldn't be all. I turned the station dial maniacally, trying to find something else— more information, anything.

What were we supposed to do next? I glanced furtively between the road and the radio. "What the *hell* are we supposed to do?" I shouted at the president.

A bank of snow threatened to block the end of the tunnel, but I could see Jenny's complex a few miles in the distance, ugly, towering, and ominous, yet somehow a beacon. I plowed through the snow, shifting the old Bronco into four-wheel drive again. I wasn't taking any chances. But just as I was through the mound of snow, I ran over something, and my head crashed into the window.

"Shit!" I hissed, cupping my ear. I slammed on the brakes as my ear rang with pain, shooting into my scalp, and through the tears burning the backs of my eyes. A car was abandoned on the side of the road, but I ignored it. Growing more desperate and angry by the second, I gritted my teeth and drove faster. I needed to be out of the car and off the damn road. Jenny and I would figure out what to do after that. She was always the problem solver, even if I didn't agree with her solutions most of the time.

I followed the road around the side of the snowcapped mountain, going faster than I probably should have, and ran over another bump. This time, however, I was more prepared. I braced myself and maneuvered around the ones I could see in the growing darkness, listening to static as the radio continued to seek a clear channel. Then the static broke. When I heard the scratchy, high-pitched wail of the words highway and hell blare through the speakers, I immediately dialed past, glad to know KWHL was still playing their adequate end-of-days soundtrack for survival inspiration.

But the only other station that came in was the president's speech, her words looping the same as before. She offered no solution. There was no safe haven. I switched to AM, praying there was someone—*anyone*—else broadcasting. I scanned over Mozart's Serenade no. 13, assuming it was a schedule set, or they might've broadcasted something more pertinent to the situation we were in. I scanned and scanned, finally stopping when I heard a man's animated voice bursting through the speakers. I held my breath to listen and prayed for good news.

"—you heard it from me. It's like I've been saying. They don't want you to know what's really going on. It's all part of the plan— the end of days wasn't just some biblical story, it was part of a master design." His enthusiastic laughter made my skin crawl. "Naysayers said I was crazy, but what do you think now? I hate to say I told you so, but . . . I did. I told you so. They'll tell you there are safe places to go, but can we really trust them after all of this? I don't—" I switched off the radio. The last thing I needed to do was listen to the ranting of someone crazier than I was.

I didn't allow myself to even consider that his words might've been true as I parked the Bronco just outside the apartment building, next to an SUV covered in several days' worth of snow. I peered up at the ugly, looming high-rise in the middle of picturesque Alaska. There had to be a hundred rooms, at least, but only a dozen windows were lit up while the rest remained ominously dark.

Jenny's warning boomed back to life. *Don't come to Whitely.*

Whitely was well known in Alaska. It was a city under one roof and all that was left of the abandoned military base after a big earthquake in the 60s. It was a hamlet, happily perched on Prince William Sound. The PW Tower housed two-hundred-plus residents —doctors, elected officials, and fisherman alike. Though Whitely was a place of renowned beauty, it also bred ghost stories and strange disappearances, making it one of Alaska's most famed and intriguing oddities.

Cut off from the rest of the world by a single road that wound beneath the mountain, Whitely seemed the perfect place to hide away until the outbreak blew over, yet I wondered if I wasn't making a dire decision by going in. The longer I sat in the Bronco staring up at it, the more uncertain I became. What if there were others like Thomas?

What if there were others in there like me?

Regardless, it needed to be done. Pulling my cap down over my ears and zipping up my jacket, I opened the gun case I'd set on the floor and pulled out the pistol and a full magazine. I stared at the Glock momentarily, wondering if I was being paranoid. I didn't want to scare people by walking in there with a weapon, but after Thomas and the news reports, I couldn't take any more risks than necessary.

Inhaling a steadying breath, I told myself this was what I

needed to do and pushed open the driver side door, shoving the pistol in my waistband as I braved the cold.

Mountains surrounded the town, barely the size of an Anchorage city block, and abandoned Army barracks stood like watchmen on either side, black, gaping mouths and eyes where windows and entrances used to be.

A cruise ship was anchored at the pier, and I had a sickening suspicion being a port to the Alaska Marine Highway would not work in this town's favor.

My footsteps moved more quickly, and in a rush to get to the front steps, I tripped in the snow and fell to the ground. My knees collided with the frozen cement, my palms following.

"Ugh!" I growled, letting the sting settle a bit before I pushed myself up off the ground. The building's exterior lights barely illuminated the darkness as I climbed to my feet. There was only so much a girl could take in a twenty-four hour timeframe, and I was losing my grip. I kicked the lump in the snow, my foot colliding instantly with an unyielding mass and my ankle twisted at contact. With a silent gasp, I drew back my leg, stifling a maddening cry, then froze.

Stripes. I could see colorful, delicate stripes, and I leaned closer. I brushed the snow away and screamed. A hand—a glove-covered hand.

Stumbling back, I scanned the sporadic white mounds on the ground, understanding instantly. I darted inside, desperate to separate myself from the frozen wasteland of dead, and I slammed the door shut behind me as quickly as the hinges would allow.

I stared out at the bodies like they might suddenly move. They were frozen, and logically, I knew they would never move again, but that didn't make me feel any better. Squeezing my eyes shut, I placed my palm on my chest, desperate for it to stop racing, and turned toward the building's interior.

"Hello?" I called, glancing around at the stark, drab walls. The place was dead quiet, save for the papers taped to the walls that settled back into place in my wake. "Hello!" The building felt similar to an old office building, but there were no bustling receptionists wearing too much makeup and there was no droll elevator music playing from the overhead speakers. I wasn't sure what I smelled, something musty and yet faintly sweet, like an overripe banana. And the cold that clung to my skin turned hot with fear.

The florescent lights flickered overhead. The pipes in the walls clanked. I pulled my beanie off as the warmth of the building pressed against me like a heated blanket. The doors shuddered in a gust of wind, but I heard no one.

While I assumed I was in the lobby, there was no reception desk or directory for reference. There was nothing to denote it was the entry of the building, save for a corkboard with flyers on the left wall just before the elevator, and directional signs hanging from the ceiling. I took a step closer.

The word Stairs was painted over a door, offset to the right.

Offices were denoted to the left, Mercantile to the right, and long tunnels stretched in both directions.

A building like this had to have a managerial or administration team of some sort, and that's who I needed to speak with if I was going to find Jenny's apartment. A phone rang in one of the offices down the hall, so I followed the arrow left.

No one's alive. The thought taunted me as I broke into a run. Someone had to be alive—they were calling. I ran faster, my ankle smarting with each step.

Light poured out of an open office door into the dimly lit corridor, but the phone stopped mid-ring as I stopped in the doorway of the mayor's office. "Hello—" I hedged in the doorway. A woman with a mahogany-red ponytail slept with her hands folded under her head on her desk, her head turned away from me.

Tentative, I stepped inside. She had a loose, sleeveless blouse tucked into pressed pants, tight around her waist, and a clipboard with a list of names rested on the desktop beside her.

The heat inside me swirled, and I tried to catch my breath as my heart beat faster and faster. JJ St. James was on the top of the list. A line was struck through it.

Jennifer June St. James. Did the line mean she was dead or better? Most of the people on the list would've had a line through their name if it meant they were dead, wouldn't they? If billions of people were dying, almost all of them would be crossed out.

I stepped closer and reached for the clipboard slowly, so not to startle the woman I prayed was sleeping.

"Ma'am?" I whispered. The scent of vomit hit my nose just as I saw it pooled around her face, and I jumped back. Her eyes were open to slits, but I saw their discolor and knew what it meant. My insides twisted.

I barely caught sight of her nameplate before I ran from the room, right into a sign on the wall I hadn't noticed before. The overheads flickered, casting the paper in a light show of shadows. Big, bold red letters were scribbled on it: Q3. On a normal day I wouldn't give it a second thought, but one word screamed in the back of my mind. *Quarantine.*

Sweat was slick on my upper lip and beneath my layers of clothes. The building was suddenly sweltering. I peered down the hall, at the stairs that would lead me to Jenny. I didn't want to find out where Q1 and Q2 were, or any other quarantine that followed, so I decided to take my chances on the tenth floor. That's where she lived, even if I didn't know which apartment.

On wobbling legs, I lunged into the stairwell. I took the steps two at a time, ignoring the sting of my sore ankle. "Jenny!" I shouted, forcing myself to focus as the harrowing realization I might be the only one alive in the entire building overcame me.

She was better, just like I was better, and if Jenny was anywhere, she would be in her apartment, not down some dark hallway that housed bodies I wasn't sure I could bear seeing.

I knew she wouldn't be able to hear me ten stories up, but I called her name all the same, the sound of my voice—the sound of *something*—putting me more at ease.

"Jenny!" I yelled again. She'd complained in one of our infrequent calls about moving her things up ten floors, but having never been there, the apartment number escaped me. Her reclusiveness had always bothered me, but only now did I realize how bad it had really become.

Up and up I went, climbing each floor of the tower until I thought the stairs would never end. I finally reached the tenth floor and flung the door open, wheezing as I gasped for air.

"Jenny . . ." My voice was barely a whisper as I scanned the hallway. There was a corridor to the right and one to the left. Thighs screaming with fatigue, I veered to the right. I had to start somewhere, and I would pound on every door until I found her. "Jenny!" I shouted, inhaling the stale, hot air that permeated the floor. It didn't smell over-ripe like the floors below, which flared my hope.

I knocked on the door of the first apartment. "Hello? Is anyone there?"

When I heard no movement, I pounded on the next. "Jenny, it's Elle! Is anyone in there?" I couldn't bring myself to say alive. "I'm looking for my sister, Jenny St. James." I pounded harder. "Hello!"

I sprinted to the next apartment. The door wasn't latched and opened as my knuckles grazed it, but no one was inside. The fact there was no body made me hopeful. They could've gotten out of here before things had gotten too bad. *Jenny might've gone with them.*

As hopeful as the thought made me, tears blurred my vision as I reached the next apartment. "Hello," I rasped, voice weakened by desperation. "Jenny, it's me." If she wasn't answering, she was likely dead. If she'd left . . . how the hell would I ever find her?

I tried the knob, but like most of the others, it was locked and I moved on. I knocked on 1005 and 1006, then moved on to 1007 and 1008. "Somebody!" I yelped as the hysteria crept in.

I peeled off my jacket, my skin feeling like fire. Was I the only fucking person alive? I pounded on door 1010. "Hello?" Sweat beaded my brow, and my lungs pulled manically at whatever air they could get. I was hyperventilating, the panic swarming me like a cloud of bees blocking out the last rays of the sun. I couldn't breathe.

I leaned back against the wall and covered my face with my hands as the sobs tore out of me. Thomas's face flashed to mind, along with the scorch marks on his body. The corpses I'd seen outside, the sea of cars—all of it drowned any semblance of hope. What was I thinking coming here? I didn't care about my hands anymore, or the churning burn inside me. I couldn't do this alone.

As my legs gave out, a door creaked open down the hall. I stilled and my head popped up. I blinked and glanced around. "Hello?" I wiped the tears from my eyes and held my breath.

A girl, probably seventeen or eighteen, stuck her head through a doorway, her strawberry blonde hair pulled up in a long ponytail.

"Oh, thank God." I ran over to her, forgetting how crazed I must've looked.

Her eyes shifted to the gun tucked in at my hip and she slammed the door shut.

"No! Please—please don't shut the door. I need to find my sister. She lives on this floor—Jenny St. James. Please—you're the only person I've seen." I knocked stubbornly, desperate. "Do you know her?" She had to, right? They all lived in the same building. They were all neighbors. "She's my twin—she looks just like me . . ."

I shut my eyes, pressing my warm cheek against the cool door, praying she would open up. "Please," I whispered. "I need your help."

The door creaked open, stopping where the chain lock ended.

"Oh, thank you—thank you! Do you know where Jenny lives?"

The girl's blue eyes narrowed on me, assessing me. Then, they softened. "JJ lived there," she rasped and nodded to the last door at the end of the hall.

I rushed to the apartment, wishing for a miracle. The door was unlocked, but it wasn't until I opened the door that I registered the girl's words. Lived—it's where JJ *lived.*

Tears dripped down my cheeks as I stepped inside. "Jenny . . ." The light was on, flickering like the lights in the hallway, and there was blood on the kitchen floor. I gasped. "No . . ." I scoured the rest of the apartment, rushing to the bedroom where a sick person would sleep, but her queen-sized bed was disheveled, and empty. The oak dresser across from it had nothing on top to gather dust and the flat screen mounted on the wall was turned off. The only thing in the room was a side table, a wrought iron lamp with a black shade sitting on it.

I walked back into the living room and stared at the black suede couch and white walls with only a large, silver framed mirror to adorn them. I stepped closer to the coffee table, half-expecting to see a ring in the tan wood from where she always set her cold cups down without a coaster. But there was no ring.

Everything in the apartment was crisp and clean and sparse, which wasn't Jenny at all. She was a whirlwind and a mess, and for the first time I was grateful for it. This wasn't Jenny's house— JJ was *not* Jenny. It was all a huge mistake.

As I allowed myself to hope, I saw a loaf of gluten-free bread on the counter, blackberry jam, and an open butter dish. It was Jenny's favorite snack when we were kids—the sweet and the salty with a little crunch. And she was allergic to wheat.

All I could do was stand there, motionless and my mind adrift. Blood splattered the counter, soaked into the grout around the tile.

I'd known she was sick, but we were twins. She was supposed to be fine. But then I realized, *I* wasn't fine. Something was wrong with me, the virus was still inside me, alive, likely eating me from the inside out. Maybe this time tomorrow I would be dead, too.

My gaze caught on a single photo, hung on the fridge. I stepped closer.

It was us. Its edges were well-worn and discolored. We were young, probably ten or so based on the tie-dye t-shirt I was wearing, but I didn't remember taking it. Stepping over the blood, I pulled the photo off, the magnet clanking to the ground.

The floor creaked and the girl from next door stepped into the doorway, arms wrapped around her middle. Her legs were exposed in her boxer shorts, half covered by an oversized sweatshirt, and she looked as scared and miserable as I was.

"Do you know where she is?" I asked.

The girl blinked, her shoulders heaving as she gripped her middle tighter.

I stepped closer, desperation clawing inside. "Have you seen my sister or not?" I asked her.

She nodded, her chin trembling. "They took her away on a stretcher."

I forced myself to utter the words. "To quarantine?"

The girl lifted a petite shoulder and licked a tear from her lips. "I don't know."

"You don't know? Did she go to quarantine or not?" I bit out.

"I don't know," she barked back and wiped her nose with her sleeve. "I never saw her again. My mom told me to stay upstairs and not open the door or leave this floor—she made me swear."

I nodded because it didn't matter. I'd seen the list. Jenny was on it, her name crossed off. It was clear what it meant. And there was blood everywhere in her kitchen to prove the rest.

"Where did your mom go?" I asked, daring to hope she might still be alive.

The girl shook her head. "She was helping the people from the cruise ship on the first floor. I've been calling her, but she hasn't answered."

The unanswered call . . . "She's the mayor." It was only a half question, and my chest tightened before she could even answer.

The girl's red-rimmed eyes widened, and she stepped closer. "Have you seen her?" she asked.

Reluctantly, I nodded.

The hope in the girl's eyes blurred with tears and she choked out a sob. "She's dead? My mom's dead?"

I didn't answer her; I didn't have to.

Her mom was dead. So was Jenny.

I didn't wipe the tears away as they poured down my cheeks. My heart broke for me and for the girl. For the mother who had kept her daughter safe, even if she knew she wouldn't make it herself.

The girl doubled over, barely able to catch her breath, and I wrapped my arms around her, pulling her against me.

She grabbed at my shirt, clasping on like I was all that held her upright, and in my sister's apartment, as the world crashed down around us, we cried.

14

JACKSON
DECEMBER 11

I stood at the sliding glass door in my kitchen, staring into the night-shrouded backyard with my arms folded over my chest. The porch lights lit the snowflakes drifting through the air, falling to the cold earth, where the garden would've been in spring.

Hannah's stone covered grave was marked as my mother's had been in her village the day she was buried, a sentimental offering of peace resting between two top stones. I felt strangely closer to my mother as I stared at them.

For my mother, I'd left a fishing pole, the one she'd helped me make from a willow branch and reed grass when I was six. For Hannah, I left my wedding band wrapped in a pair of polka-dotted baby socks.

Do I look like the kind of girl who would date a drunken stranger from a liquor store?

I could picture Hannah's lifted eyebrow and tilted head perfectly; she could scold me with a single look, and the day we met was no different. Defiantly, I wanted to reach for the wine bottle on the table and guzzle it down. Maybe if she were angry enough with me for falling off the wagon, she would come back from the grave and give me a ration of shit.

Drago yawned, and I looked back at him as he stretched from his spot in my recliner. I was just happy someone was using it. Shoving my hands in my pockets, I stared at the wine bottle again until my eyes were so blurred and wet I couldn't see its silhouette anymore.

The toilet flushed in the bathroom down the hall, the door opened, and I thumbed the tears away.

Ross walked into the kitchen. His shoulders were slumped more than before, and he nodded to the wine bottle. "I figured you would've chugged it by now. I wouldn't blame you."

I glanced at the photo of Hannah and me pinned to the bulletin board. "She would," I told him. My hair was longer in the photo; it would've been down to my ears if it wasn't so wild in the wind, like hers was, blonde locks whipping around us. The sun was out and we were both smiling, as she leaned in to kiss my cheek, the wind threatening to blow us away.

I almost smiled, but it ached too much.

"I didn't figure you were a wine drinker anyway," Ross muttered.

"I'm not. Someone gave it to us a while back. I told Hannah she could have some, it would've been fine, but she never drank it. She never threw it away, either."

"I remember when she told me she'd met the guy she would marry at a liquor store, and that you were a drunk—no," he shook his head. "Her exact words were 'functioning alcoholic'." Ross looked at me with shimmery blue eyes. "I told her she was fucking crazy." He picked up the bottle and turned it over in his hands. "Why do you think she kept it?"

I stared down at my hands, trembling as the remaining liquor left my system. "To remind me how strong I am," I said, but my voice was paper-thin. "She was standing in line at the liquor store," I told him, remembering her paisley purple bandana wrapped around her head, blonde hair disheveled, and a dozen woven bracelets that looked handmade around her wrist. "She was such a hippy," I mused. "But I wanted her. Especially when she glared at the cashier who'd told her she couldn't use the bathroom unless she was a customer." I looked at Ross. "You know what she said?"

"I can imagine." He wiped a tear from his eye, unable to look at me.

"I can pee on your floor instead, if you want me to." Even in the cloudy darkness her smile shined through. I wanted her smile to be real. I needed it to be.

Ross clasped me on the shoulder and took a deep breath. "You'll get through this," he told me. "You and I both will, okay?"

With Ross standing there, the thought almost seemed possible. I peered back at him, seeing the fear in his eyes. He didn't know what awaited him in Fairbanks. Kelsey might be alive, or she might be dead. She may not want to leave her mom. Everything was still so uncertain.

He sniffed and wiped his nose with his sleeve. "Leave it to women to make us weep, right?"

Closing my eyes, I could almost feel Hannah standing next to me, her hand on my shoulder. She'd want me to take care of Ross, for us to take care of each other. I picked the bottle up off the table, opened the back door, and threw it against the back fence as hard as I could. Unexpected relief flooded me as it shattered. It was gone. I'd made a choice, for her, and now I could move on.

"If you don't hear from me right away, give me a few days to see what's what," Ross said, thoughtful. "I'll at least call you by then and we'll figure out what to do."

I understood why he had to leave, just like he understood why I had to stay in Anchorage to check on my dad. But it didn't make his leaving any more comforting.

"I better get on the road." He grabbed his jacket and lifted the satellite phone. "I'll call you." He tucked the handheld CB radio under his arm. "Or, I'll try you on Channel 07."

I nodded.

"Worst-case scenario—"

"This *is* the worst case scenario." I pointed to the sat phone clutched in his hand. "If I don't hear from you, I'll come to Kelsey's mom's in Fairbanks."

Ross shook his head sharply and glanced around the house. I could imagine him mentally ticking off all the reasons we both knew we shouldn't stay in the city longer than necessary. "No, don't come to Fairbanks. If something happens—"

I held up my hand. "I—"

"Shut the fuck up, Jackson, and listen to me," he commanded, knowing exactly what I'd say. "*If* something happens and you don't hear from me, you don't stay here either."

"I'm not staying here," I said, peering around at the tainted memories. "I can't."

"Go to my house, stay as long as you want." He pulled his keys from his pocket and handed them to me. "I know where the spare is if I need it."

His keys felt strange in my hand.

"My Tacoma is in the garage. Use it, if you need it. I'll take my work truck."

We knew nothing about the virus or what was happening to the rest of the world. We were alive, but for how long? A thousand things could go wrong from now to tomorrow, and we were only dancing around them. "I'll head northeast," I told him, staring up from his key ring. "If I don't hear from you, I'll head to the back-country, somewhere away from this place."

Ross nodded. "Leave me a note, a crumb trail—whatever the hell you have to do. I'll find you," he reiterated. "Even if I have to wait for the snow to melt."

That was months from now, but he was right, the roads were getting worse and we still had months of winter left.

I shoved his keys into my pocket. Bravado aside, we stood in silence a moment, me imagining the impending days of uncertainty. Ross was all I had left.

"Well, wish me luck." He exhaled, long and deep, then swallowed thickly. He hadn't uttered the words aloud, but he worried his wife was dead. Why else hadn't she figured out a way to get ahold of him, or answered her phone—or her mother's.

"Be safe, brother," I said, pulling him in and wrapping my arms around him.

"You too. Tell the ornery son of a bitch I'm glad he's okay, when you see him."

I nodded, because I wasn't sure what else to do, and whistled for Drago to follow us as we walked out to Ross's truck. It felt like a knife ripped at my gut with each step. I didn't have a good feeling about this.

He and Drago climbed into the patrol truck, Ross waved for good measure, then they drove away.

Shoving my hands in my pockets, I stared at my lifeless street and walked back into the house. It was time to say goodbye to this place, and to my wife—for the last time.

15

ELLE
DECEMBER 11

Hands braced on the sink, I stared into the mirror, not so much looking at myself but staring straight through. At nothing. At everything—a blur of an angry, resentful past and terrifying, uncertain futures. So much of the past had been awash in regret and bitterness, and what was it all for? I thought my problems *before* were bad, but this . . . What was the point of surviving if everyone else was dead?

Sophie wasn't dead. Why? And why wasn't I? What made us special? I stared at my white knuckles, gripping the edge of the basin. I knew what made me dangerous, but *how* I'd gotten this way was the unanswered question. I covered my face, smiling like a lunatic. "What the hell is happening to me?"

Heaving a sigh, I dropped my hands and studied the calfskin gloves I'd raided from Jenny's top drawer. I was able to touch Sophie without hurting her when I'd had my snow gloves on; I'd held her against me, too lost in my own grief to realize the danger I was putting her in. While I was determined not to allow the slip again, not until I knew what was happening to me, the gloves gave me a temporary buffer, and that was about all I could ask for.

It hurt to think about it. My head, my body . . . everything ached from crying and Thomas's attack. I'd done my best to ignore it, but under the weight of everything, it grew more difficult. I needed sleep, a lot of it, but that would have to come later, too.

Mind throbbing, I dug through my bag for the emergency ibuprofen stash in my coin purse. I laughed silently to myself. *Emergency was a word for it.* I unlatched the coin purse and fingered through a few coins clinking around, but I didn't feel the pills. "Damn it . . ."

I leaned down and closer to the light to see inside. I'd taken them already, I remembered. I'd needed them after Thomas slammed me onto the wood floor. "Shit," I hissed, borderline desperate. I was close to throwing the coin purse across the room when a beige piece of paper, inside the pocket, caught my eye. It was Jenny's riddle. I'd forgotten about it until now.

What people said about twins was true. Even if Jenny and I were never close, there was a connection between us I couldn't easily explain. I knew when something was wrong, even without her telling me, just like I knew the envelope was from her the day I received it with no return address, before I even opened it.

I unfolded the discolored corners and re-read the words that seemed familiar at one time, but they still made no sense. *The sound of silence will set you free. In the silence there I'll be.* Jenny had never been sentimental, so I knew it was a song lyric or a riddle she wanted me to figure out.

"So, the note you sent, is it a riddle I'm supposed to figure out or something?"

She laughed, but it wasn't with humor. "Yes. Have you?"

"Have I what?"

"Figured it out yet?"

"The quiet will liberate me? Is that a threat? Maybe morbid song lyrics?"

"No," she said, but her amusement faded. "Keep it until you figure it out, okay?"

"We're not nine anymore, Jenny. I don't have time for riddles—"

"Don't throw it away, Eleanor." Her sharp tone wasn't entirely surprising. She was the dramatic of the two of us; always had been. But there was a tinge of panic in her voice that I hadn't expected.

"Why not?"

"Because, Elle, just don't. Figure it out first—promise me." For all of her theatrics, I was always the gullible one, and even though I knew she was probably playing with me, there was still a pique of uncertainty I couldn't shake.

"What if I don't want to play?" I asked. It was our first year of college, me at a community college while she miraculously got into a university in Juneau. With what money I didn't know. Dr. John had cut her off the day she ran away. Waitressing tips barely paid for my books. Or, maybe it was all a lie. I'd never visited her at the university, I only remember she used it as an excuse to never visit. Just like I used school as an excuse to stay away.

"Elle, please. Just . . . keep it, okay? At least until you figure it out."

"What if I never figure it out?"

"Then keep it forever," she said.

I stared at the words, churning them over in my mind. I'd do some Googling later and play her game. "Fine," I agreed. "But if it's something stupid or some prank, I swear I'm sending you a box of dead spiders in the mail, and you'll never know when it's coming." Jenny hated spiders, she sobbed whenever there was one in her room, dead or alive.

"Okay," she said easily, which meant it must've been a good riddle if she would risk my wrath.

I'd never figured the riddle out. I'd put it in my purse that day, got too busy with flunking school, and eventually forgot about it.

The floor creaked in the adjacent room and I stilled.

"Elle?" Sophie's voice was soft and hesitant in the living room.

"Yeah?" I pulled my sleeve down and wiped my nose. I hadn't realized I was crying.

"Can you come here for a sec? There's something you should see."

I ran my fingers through my loose hair, resigned to look like hell since I was living in it. "Uh, yeah. Give me just a sec."

"Okay." I heard Sophie's retreating footsteps and let out a breath. What the hell was I going to do now? I couldn't leave Sophie, but I couldn't stay here either.

I stared at my reflection like it would somehow produce answers; really seeing myself for the first time in, well, I wasn't sure how long. Days, nights—they all blurred together—incoherent, tumultuous moments that bled from one memory to the next.

My eyes weren't just green, but looked sickly and swollen. The shadows beneath them made my cheeks hollow. When was the last time I'd eaten anything?

Clearing my throat, I grabbed a rubber band from my purse and tossed my hair up, then turned on the faucet. I didn't wait for it to get warm; I didn't *want* it to get warm. I reveled in the chills that rose on my arms and neck as I splashed cold water on my face; the jolt I needed to pull myself together for a while longer.

After my face was dry, I tugged the gloves over my deadly fingers and abandoned my things in the bathroom for the time being. Stomach rumbling with hunger, not nausea, I made a mental note to raid Jenny's cupboard sometime soon.

I didn't bother closing the door behind me as I walked to Sophie's apartment. There was no one left but us.

Or so I thought. I stopped in her open doorway and stared at three new faces. A small boy and a girl, maybe six and nine years old, sat on the couch. Their pajamas were filthy and they wore their coats zipped to the collar like they couldn't get warm. Sophie handed them both a glass of water, which they eagerly accepted. She then held out a glass to the older boy, a Latino kid with dark hair and features, crouched over a tablet in the recliner.

Sitting on the edge of the seat, his fingers frantically tapped on the screen.

They were kids, and they were alive. If there were five of us, there were likely others. The world didn't feel so unrecognizable knowing that.

"Hello," I whispered, leaning against the doorjamb. I offered a tentative wave.

Four sets of eyes shifted to me. The little girl with ratty brown hair and wet eyelashes blinked at me. Her nose was pink and her chin quivering. The little boy's eyes were red and his cheeks flushed, but he only stared at me, uncertain.

"That's Thea and Beau," the older boy said. "I'm Alex." His eyes narrowed on me, but his features eventually softened. "Have we met?"

I shook my head. "I don't live here," I told him. "But, you might've met my twin sister." I glanced between the three of them. "I'm Elle. We thought we were the only ones left."

Thea blinked at me, curiosity lifting her brow. Beau, older and less curious, continued to study me, clearly distrusting.

"Alex is in my class," Sophie explained as he continued to swipe at the tablet in his hand.

I had a dozen questions to ask them, but as the little girl sat there shaking, I knew it wasn't the right time, so I stuck with one question only. "You all know each other then?"

Thea shook her head as Sophie tucked a blanket around her. "He found us," Thea whispered, wiping her nose with the palm of her hand. I handed her a tissue from the box on the coffee table.

More questions continued to swirl. "Found you?"

Thea's head bobbed as she blew her nose. She looked around, uncertain what to do with the used tissue, and finally offered it to her brother.

"Here," I said, stepping closer. "I'll take it."

Thea handed it to me tentatively, staring at my gloves. I was about to pull my hand away when she dropped the Kleenex in my palm and then slurped down half the glass of water. She licked her lips when she finished, inhaling to catch her breath.

"Have the three of you been sick?" I asked, unable to resist. "Have you had the fever?"

"Yeah," Alex said, groaning as he lifted the tablet up and moved it around, like he was trying to get a signal.

"What about you two?" I asked. "Have you been sick?" The need to understand was gnawing at me. "I'm worried we might still be contagious—"

"We've been sick," Beau finally said. "First me, then Thea."

"Then Mommy—"

Beau elbowed her, making her grimace.

"Damn it," Alex grumbled as he set the tablet on the coffee table, scowling at it. "There has to be a way to get news."

"The Internet's been in and out all day," Sophie said. "The cable for the TV isn't even working anymore. But you can keep trying."

I peered around her apartment, noting the sweeping landscape photos that donned her walls, and the lack of family photos. Growing up in a house I wished had less family photos, I tended to notice those things. I stepped up to a cluster of frames beside the television, seeing a little Sophie with leg braces on and a miserable fake smile on her face. The mayor was pretty, if a little severe with the same blue eyes Sophie had, and red hair that was much darker. Sophie's father had the blonde hair, was tall, and definitely younger than Dr. John, even if there was still something similar about him.

My stomach grumbled and I flushed.

"We have cheese and crackers," Sophie said. She glanced from me to Alex, who shook his head, then to Thea who nodded happily.

"I like cheese and crackers," she chirped, suddenly a little less afraid.

Beau looked at his sister. It was the same look I gave Jenny when she said something out of turn. Like Beau didn't want to impose, or maybe he wasn't sure if he could trust Sophie yet.

"I like cheese and crackers too," I added with a smile and patted my tummy. "And I'm starving."

Finally, Beau looked at Sophie and nodded as well. "Yes, please."

"I'll help you," I said, following Sophie into the kitchen.

"Alex," Sophie stopped short. "There are coloring books in my desk in the bedroom, will you grab them for me? The colored pencils too?" She nodded to the kids, then into the dark room behind him.

Alex stood, hesitated before he went into her bedroom, but flicked on the light.

I saw a cutting board leaning against the wall beside the microwave and grabbed it as Sophie pulled out a block of cheddar cheese from the fridge. Like Jenny's, the galley kitchen looked out into the living room, only Sophie's was remodeled with new, expensive stainless steel appliances.

"My dad is a chef," she explained. "Was—I guess, I'm not sure if he's okay or not."

"Is he here in Whitely?"

She shook her head. "He was on a yacht in Barbados, last I heard." Her voice trembled and I wrapped my arm around her shoulder as she tried to stifle the tears back. "I'm fine," she said.

"No, you're not," I told her. "None of us are. You're allowed to be sad and worried."

She nodded, but brushed her tears away and put the brick of cheese on the cutting board.

"I hope you like flowers," Alex said, setting the books and pencils on the coffee table.

Sophie cleared her throat. "There might be games in the closet," she said loud enough so Alex could hear her. "I can't remember if my mom took them down to the classroom already."

I handed her a knife from the holder. "Thanks," she said, voice quiet. She was fair skinned and willowy, but though she looked fragile she was strong. I already knew that much. She could've been curled up on her bed still, sobbing hysterically. "Alex found them in the Heston Building," she whispered and nodded toward the kids.

I had no idea what the Heston Building was. "Is that a bad thing?"

"It's the ruined Army bunkers next door."

That structure had looked legitimately abandoned during my drive in—it didn't even have glass on its windows or functioning doors. I frowned. "What were they doing in there?"

"I have no idea." Her voice was low, but pitched. "Alex thinks they watched their mom kill herself. I'm not sure I buy it though."

"Why not?"

"Elle, their mom is Katie Gunderson. She was my teacher . . . she would *never* do something like that—ever. I've known her for years." Sophie dropped the knife and braced herself against the countertop. Her glassy eyes shifted to the living room. "Why would she take them out in a blizzard and make them watch something like that? It doesn't make any sense." I knew that look; I'd felt it many times. Sophie was beginning to spiral.

"I think," I started, uncertain what exactly I should say when none of the pieces fit together or made any sense. "I think we need to prepare for the possibility that those of us who have survived the outbreak will never be the same."

Sophie's eyes narrowed on me. "What do you mean?"

"I mean . . . Do you feel different?" I hedged.

Her brow furrowed deeper. If I wasn't careful I would scare them, hell, I was petrified. "Like how, exactly?" she asked in complete bewilderment. If Sophie's reaction was anything to go by, she definitely didn't have what felt like dragon's breath simmering under her skin, and I pushed that knowledge away to dwell on later.

Grasping for words, I shook my head. "Just tired, exhausted—

Maybe your teacher was sleep deprived and didn't realize what she was doing."

"You've seen something like this," Sophie said. She was clearly observant too.

I crossed my arms over my chest and leaned my hip against the counter. "Yeah—I guess, sort of."

"Is that how you got that bruise on your jaw?" Alex asked, stepping into the kitchen.

I straightened, my gloved hand going to the side of my face. I hadn't noticed a bruise.

"Look," Alex said, changing the subject. He set the tablet down in front of us. "There are reports about people losing their minds. They thought people were acting out of fear, but this man survived the virus and when he woke he set everyone else in the hospital ward on fire, dead or alive—kids, women, children."

"An *effect* of the fever," I realized.

He shrugged. "It's speculation."

I skimmed over the article, grateful Alex covered whatever image was beneath his hand.

"But—" Sophie shook her head. "Why would she take them out there, wearing only their pajamas and their shoes? Was she trying to freeze them to death or something?"

He shrugged. "Why would a doctor who paid gobs of money to go to school to save people's lives, suddenly decide to kill them?"

"So some of the survivors are insane?" Sophie gasped. Yes, I wanted to tell her. Thomas had proved that much.

Alex leaned in. "I think their mom tried to push them out a window."

My gaze flashed to the kids. They muttered quietly as Beau helped Thea with her coloring page.

"I saw her body and the fear in their eyes, it outweighed the sadness. Like maybe they weren't sure she was dead and that she might come back or something. Beau wouldn't say anything more."

"Those poor kids," I murmured and pulled the crackers out of their sleeve to place on the plate. It was clear that sickness was no longer the enemy; it was whatever had been left in its wake. "We have to be extra careful," I told them.

Sophie shifted from one foot to the other. "What are we going to do? Just stay here forever?"

"We can't stay here," Alex said. "There's a gym full of bodies. It's only a matter of time before—we just, we can't."

"The quarantine," I remembered.

"There's a post about this place in British Columbia." Alex tried to show us, but the Internet connection was lost again. "Shit," he muttered. Scratching his buzzed head, he sighed. "It's a gathering place in Hartley Bay."

"Hartley Bay?" I glanced between them.

"It's supposed to be safe," he explained, but I wasn't sure I believed it. That was easily a thousand miles from us, unless one of them knew how to captain a ship. I'd visited once for a photoshoot. It was very secluded and on the ocean, much like Whitely, which scared the shit out of me. The quarantine might not have been necessary if there hadn't have been a horde of people from the cruise ship to complicate things. Hartley Bay would be a place where boats from all around the world could sail into if they wanted, madmen and survivors alike, seeking a safe place to stay. Unless Hartley had extreme measures in place, there would be nothing to stop them.

The lights flickered and Thea shrieked.

"It's fine," Beau admonished, and Sophie handed me a piece of cheese, then Alex walked into the living room to deliver the plate of food.

The cheddar was like candy on my tongue and my stomach wanted more. I cut another piece off the block for Alex and then myself while Sophie lit a candle on the center of the table.

"The backup generators came on this afternoon," she

explained. "We're used to the power going out here," she looked at Alex, then at me. "But once the fuel is gone . . ."

I leaned my elbows on the counter and rested my head in my hands. The crippling question of *what now* inched its way in, settling nicely next to fear.

"There're tons of posts online about hold-outs throughout the country," Alex said, and I admired the optimism in his voice. "Around the entire *world*, but nothing close enough we can get to." Alex showed me the list. A place in the San Juan Islands in Washington, an Army base in the lower forty-eight, two places in Canada, Greenland . . . The list went on but Alaska wasn't on the map.

"Canada's the closest," Alex said. "If we can get there, we might have a chance." I wasn't sure who this kid was, exactly, but I admired his bravery and his grit. I didn't, however, know if we were ready to take a road trip to Hartley Bay, me and four kids.

"How do we know we're the last ones left in the building?" I looked at Alex. "There have to be others if we're still alive." I waited for him to say something about his parents or for melancholy to shadow his gaze.

"We looked for their dad," Alex said, peering out at the kids. "He wasn't anywhere I could find him. I'd bet there's no one else left in this building. They would've found us by now."

Deep down I knew he was probably right. I'd been calling and shouting and no one had heard me.

Sophie sniffed and put the cheese back in the fridge. Her mom was still down there. Jenny was down there somewhere too.

Sophie covered her face with her hands and stood in front of the fridge, the door hanging open.

Alex looked at me, his green eyes wide.

"Her mom," I mouthed and pointed down to the first floor.

His face fell, softened, and he cleared his throat. "We'll find a way to say goodbye," he promised and hesitantly rested his hand on her shoulder. "Before we leave, we'll figure out a way." Something occurred to him and his eyes flicked to Sophie's stomach. He leaned in. "Are you okay?" She met his eyes, and he glanced down at her stomach again, pointing.

My heartbeat thudded to a stop, and I stepped closer. "Are you pregnant?" I whispered.

Sophie's face flushed and her hands went to her stomach. Slowly, she shook her head. "No. It's—I'm not. It was a false alarm." She brushed past us and tossed the dirty knife in the sink.

I glared at Alex. "I thought you guys were just friends?"

"We are, I mean—I guess we are." His eyes widened as he registered my implication. "It wouldn't have been mine," he groused. "We met for the first time on Monday. I just moved here."

And yet somehow, he knew she thought she was pregnant. I was curious, but had more important concerns. I needed to figure out what we would do. What *I* would do with two teenagers and a couple of kids.

Alex nodded to my gloves. "You cold or something?"

I fisted them at my sides. "It's a germ thing," I lied. I told myself they wouldn't know any different; I was a stranger to them anyway. But I felt bad all the same. I might've been a stranger to Sophie six hours ago, but now, I wasn't sure what we were. Survivors? Orphans? All of us were both, and we all needed somewhere safe to go.

I smacked my fist on the counter. "The Coast Guard."

"Brilliant," Alex said, pleased. "What about them?"

I eyed him skeptically. He was strangely collected in all of this. "What were you doing outside?" I finally asked him. I eyed him closely. "Where have you been all this time?"

His features hardened and he straightened his shoulders. "I needed to get away from my uncle, Jimmy. He wasn't what you would call a standup guy." He pointed to his fat lip.

"He hit you?" Sophie's question was more of an incredulous rasp than a whisper.

"With a shoe," he grumbled, his cheeks reddening. "Look, I

don't know what happened or when." He looked at Sophie. "We got into an argument, and I took off. I needed air, and the next thing I knew, I was waking up in a warehouse. Which, trust me, was better than his shithole apartment."

Alex met my gaze, almost defiantly, like he was waiting for me to ask him more questions, but I could see he was hiding whatever confusion and fear he had beneath his stoic exterior. I knew that facade—stay busy and focused. It was the only way to keep your shit together.

I nodded, a silent forfeiture of prying questions.

"So, the Coast Guard?" he prompted.

"There's a blockade at the docks in Anchorage. We could head back there, see if they're still set up—they'll know what to do. There were a few of them when I was headed this way. They'll likely know more than we do." I nodded reassuringly, convincing myself it was a good plan. That it was a solid plan, perhaps our only plan. "They're our best option."

"All of us?" Sophie asked. Her eyes darted between me and Alex.

"I would assume . . . I guess. That's up to you guys." I glanced out at the two smaller children. I didn't know the first thing about parenting, but I knew I was all they had at this point. "We'll leave notes for their parents, in case their dad comes back, but I can't leave them here. Whether you both stay or not."

Sophie looked down at her hands, fiddling with a piece of plastic cheese wrapper.

"We could leave a note for your dad too," Alex told her.

I didn't want to push her, even if I knew it was our only real hope of finding safety and answers. Sophie needed to decide what she would do on her own, we all did.

"Yeah, I'll do that. In case he survived and comes home." She could barely speak the words. While I'd lost an estranged sister, she'd lost her entire family.

"Mull it over," I told her. "You have time." If my body odor was anything to go by, we all could've used showers and fresh clothes. "We need to get some rest."

Alex and Sophie nodded.

I stared in at Thea, curled up against the arm of the couch. "We leave tomorrow then, when there's a break in the snow." Decided and relieved there was a plan, I grabbed an over-ripened twig of grapes from the bowl on the counter and decided a shower was exactly what I needed to wash away the fog of the day. "Oh." I turned around and touched Alex's shoulder.

He jumped back, like I'd electrocuted him, and I pulled my hand away.

My heart raced. "Sorry—I . . . Are you okay?" I eyed the fabric of his long sleeve to make sure I hadn't singed him. I hadn't felt a surge or burn, not like I had before.

Alex's eyes narrowed on me, transforming his expression into something wary. "Yeah, I'm fine." But I could practically hear the gears grinding in his head.

I cleared my throat. "Bring any weapons you have," I added quietly. "Just in case."

"What makes you think I have any weapons?" I wasn't sure if I'd offended him or if he was just being cautious after whatever had just happened, but he sounded affronted.

"Because you're a guy and you live in the wild state of Alaska. I assumed you'd have a weapon—a baseball bat or hockey stick maybe?"

He lifted his chin. "I'll find something."

Sophie watched us, just as confused as I was at whatever had just happened. But I didn't want Alex to think I was a threat, so I headed for the door to give him some space.

"Where are you going?" Sophie asked. "You can stay here, if you want to."

I shook my head. "Thanks, but I'm going to shower, then raid my sister's closet. I didn't come prepared for the Apocalypse."

16

JACKSON
DECEMBER 11

I was used to dark roads and snow flurries, but tonight was more ominous than most. I couldn't shake the feeling there was more to come—more than the gut-wrenching loss and dead bodies, more than fever and the end of our reign on the food chain. The foreboding hadn't gone away when I'd found Ross at the PD, and it worsened when he drove away.

The radio stopped scanning and the static cracked. "This is a broadcast from Hartley Bay, British Columbia."

I frowned at the radio, uncertain how Eagle River was picking up a signal from so far away.

"We've established a safe haven for survivors. We have food and water, plenty of generators and fuel, at least for now. We have military equipment, including a naval ship, and plenty of soldiers who are more than capable of defending this place." It was a not-too-subtle warning to looters and lunatics. Smart.

"We welcome survivors who are willing to work hard to gain back some of what we lost—community, protection, and hope. If you have applicable skills that will help us get this place up and running as efficiently as possible, we need you. Until things get straightened out, assuming they ever will, we're all we've got. We'll broadcast daily, if possible."

Using my blinker out of habit, I turned down the frontage road that led to my father's place. A safe haven was a nice thought, even if I knew it would fail. Too many strangers, especially scared ones, would be difficult to manage, and I didn't trust anyone, not anymore.

Eagle River was a city community in the municipality of Anchorage proper, but you'd never know it out here where the spruce trees lined to the Chugach foothills. A place in the middle of nowhere would suit me much better than a salvaged city.

I clicked the radio off as I passed the only other estate nestled on the left and continued toward his property.

The instant I saw the lights on in his house, I grew hopeful, then wary. If he was alive, he might not be the man I remembered. Then something a lot like guilt snuck up on me. If my father was dead, all the arguing and distance between us over the years would become a heavy regret.

I turned Ross's Tacoma off and peered around the yard. It was the same as I remembered. His truck was in the drive, covered in what looked like a few days' worth of snow, but that wasn't surprising. He was ornery, but he wasn't stupid. If he'd watched the news at all, he'd have stayed inside.

The dog kennels were on the side of the house, butting up to the garage; his newer, craftsman-style home was nestled in a copse of trees, a hamlet far enough away from town that he felt removed and his dogs had room to roam. His huskies were everything to him. I'd always told myself I was just glad he had *something* in his life, even if he'd pushed his family away. Or was I the one who'd pushed him away first?

I shoved the driver door open and tugged the hood of my jacket over my head as I climbed out. I'm not sure when cold shoulders turned into an irreparable resentment, but I figured if anything could bring my father and me back together, it would be the end of civilization.

Shoving my hands in my pockets, I trudged through the unshoveled snow up the path to the front door. The wind had died down, but the cold had seeped in, and my sore muscles ached in protest. Even getting out of the shower before I'd left had been a chore, and while the alcohol was gone, the sickness still lingered. I could feel the pressure of it behind my eyes and in my bones. Or was that exhaustion?

The motion light flashed on, and I braced myself for a slew of barking huskies, but they never came. In fact, they were strangely quiet. I glanced from the lit window of the living room back to the shadows of the kennels. My dad loved his dogs, but seven inside the house seemed excessive, even for him. Curiosity winning out, I bypassed the porch and headed around the side of the house to the kennels.

Through the light and shadows of the motion light, I could see two of the kennel doors open and discolored snow inside. My footsteps ceased as I slowly reached for my gun. I peered around the yard. Something was definitely off, but I took a few steps closer to the gate. I noticed blood in the snow first, then I saw the dog's foot then registered the outline of it. It was covered in a layer of snow.

Heart suddenly racing, I scanned the rest of the kennels. Some of the dogs were still in their houses, but all of them were dead. I peered around the yard as chills trickled down my back. This didn't feel right. My dad wouldn't have killed them unless something had happened.

I crouched down beside the last dog, brushing off the snow. There was a bullet hole in its gray and brown head. Its body was frozen and it had been dead for some time. I picked up a spent rifle casing.

For the first time I wondered if the dogs—if all animals—were affected by the virus, just like humans, and if they'd turned, my dad would've had to kill them. I stared at the dogs. It didn't make sense, and I wasn't sure why, but I didn't think rabid, crazed animals was the reason they were dead, especially not with half of them still in their beds.

Gun in hand and dread a weighted anchor in my gut, I hurried as quietly as I could up the steps to the back door of the house. Either a crazy fucker had been here or my dad had lost his mind, and I wasn't taking any chances.

The back door was cracked open, and gripping my gun tighter, I slowly pushed it open. For the first time since I'd woken to my intruder, the fog around my mind lifted, and I stepped inside. My palms were sweating. My heart was pounding. I had no idea what I would find.

I swept the kitchen, resisting the urge to shout for my dad. The living room was messy, but it didn't look torn apart. His desk had a few files strewn on top, but they weren't rifled through. His sparse leather furniture was as it should've been, the pillow on the couch still molded to the shape of his head.

My gut churned as I registered the silence; each footstep seemed to echo as I made my way into the bedroom. The flannel bedding was balled up, but he wasn't in it. The top drawer of his dresser was open and I walked over. Socks—that's all it had. It was a hiding place, I realized as I noted the small key stuck in the lock of the gun cabinet. It was empty.

I flipped the light in his bathroom on and stilled. Everything in the medicine cabinet was strewn about the countertop. The drawers and cabinets under the sink were open, the cleaning products, towels, and toilet paper were pulled out. Comet was sprinkled on the floor. The first aid box was open and gauze and cleaning pads littered the ground. Dad had been searching for something, maybe to try to save the dogs.

I ran through the house and back into the cold. The motion light flicked on again as I ran toward the garage. There were footprints in the snow I hadn't seen before. They were smaller than mine, but not by much, and I'd know the outline of his moccasin slippers anywhere. Snow covered some of the footprints, but there were still enough to follow the trail.

Some of them came and went from the house, but those along the kennel fence line were deep and overlapping, like he'd been pacing back and forth. I followed them in circles until I noticed a few veered off toward the woods. I grabbed a flashlight from the truck and followed them.

The tracks were hot and cold, but like illegal poachers in the spring, I could sniff out a trail when I was looking for one. When I saw my dad's Winchester was half buried in the sparse shrubbery a few feet ahead, I knew I was on the right trail. He'd shot his dogs, tossed his gun, and he was headed toward the neighboring property. As the puzzle pieces began to fit together, I dreaded what they would amount to.

"What the hell were you doing out here?" I muttered, and grabbed the rifle. Even through my gloves, my fingers were cold and numb. I hadn't dressed for a trek in the snow, and my body was beginning to protest.

Pulling the rifle strap over my shoulder, I shined the flashlight in front of me, and trudged deeper into the woods. I considered turning around to grab another layer from my truck when I saw the neighbor's house through the trees.

The windows were dark and the garage door was open. Given the uncertain circumstances, making my presence known would probably get me killed more than it would save me, so I shut my flashlight off and crept closer in the cover of darkness and thin veil of falling snow.

A vehicle was parked in the driveway out front, a small SUV that looked like it hadn't moved in days, maybe longer. It was late and the unlit windows could've meant whoever lived there was sleeping or dead.

I hugged the shadows on the side of the house and peered into the garage. Without moonlight, I could barely make out the outline of a heap on the floor. I flicked the flashlight on; it was a discarded nylon car cover.

An open gun safe against the far wall caught my attention, and I stepped inside the garage. Some of the boxes from the shelves were sideways and upside down on the floor and what looked like the contents of a toolbox were scattered across the floor around the workbench. Someone had been looking for something in here too, and I had a feeling that person was my father.

My footsteps echoed as I walked over to the gun safe. A shotgun stood inside with a box of 12-gauge shells that belonged to it. Whoever it was, they hadn't been looking for a gun. I ran my fingers over the strap of the Winchester hanging against my back. *He* hadn't needed a gun or he wouldn't have discarded his own.

Or, maybe he'd been looking for a different type of gun. I crouched down to the shelves near the bottom. A box of 9mms and an empty magazine were tucked in the corner, but no pistol.

I glanced at the door to the house. Someone could have it inside, but why leave the shotgun? I stared back down at the car cover. Or, someone took it with them when they left. I wondered what reason my dad might've had to take the neighbor's car.

I clicked off the flashlight again. I would find out soon enough.

I walked to the door and tested the handle as quietly as I could. It wasn't locked. Hoping this wasn't some elaborate trap, I creaked the door open and peered into a dark dining room and connecting living space. There was no movement inside, and no sound, other than the refrigerator kicking on and off.

"Hello?" I said. Lifting my gun, I aimed it through the doorway. "I'm Officer Mitchell. I'm a state trooper. If anyone is in the house, please step out with your hands up now." I waited with bated breath. There were no creaking floorboards or mutterings I could hear. "I am armed and entering the house. Do *not* shoot." I cursed myself the instant I uttered the words. A crazy bastard wouldn't give two shits if I wanted them to shoot me or not.

I had no choice. I needed to know why my dad was still here. I stepped further in, gripping my gun tighter with every step as I swept the living room. The air was frigid inside, a good indication no one was home, or alive, at least.

Shadows played with my eyes, and the living room was ransacked. The closet was torn apart, books were pulled from their shelves. Everything looked expensive, down to the fake plant in the corner of the dining room. They were wealthy, whoever they were.

I stopped outside the first door in the hallway, the only one that was visibly closed from where I was standing. Sidling up against the wall, I reached for the knob. "Hello," I tried again with no answer. "Dad?" I twisted the handle and pushed the door open, stepping inside with my pistol held out in front of me.

A human form covered with a blanket lay at the foot of the bed. The sheets and comforter were thrown back; a lamp was broken on the floor. There was a curtain rod on the ground in front of me, and drapes in a heap against the wall. There'd definitely been a struggle.

I turned and headed down the hall to the next room. There was an office, and two other rooms, each with four-poster beds and matching furniture, that had been untouched. Other than a hair-brush with dark long hair in it resting on the vanity in the bath-room, there was nothing in there that seemed out of place either. The house was empty.

Lowering my weapon, I flicked the hall light on and stopped in the doorway of the first bedroom. The unease writhing inside told me it was my dad underneath the blanket; the trail had only led one way.

I bent over and grabbed the fleece blanket. Like a Band-Aid, I pulled it off. Thomas Mitchell lay underneath, his eyes closed and his mouth partially open. Blood covered his jeans and stained his flannel shirt. And his damn moccasin slippers were dirty from trekking through the snow. "Pop . . ."

I swallowed the swell in my throat and crouched down beside

him. The light from the hallway was all I needed to see he'd been dead for at least a day. I'd known the chances of him surviving were low given so few people had woken up from the fever, but finding him in the fetal position, abandoned in a stranger's house was heart-wrenching.

My eyes burned as I stared at the old man he'd become without my realizing it. Talking on the phone, was one thing, but I hadn't seen him in nearly three years. Like some of the others, he'd survived the virus only to lose his mind afterward. By the looks of it, he had been killed in self-defense. The room was torn apart and someone had covered his body with a blanket, a gesture of remorse and fear, not pride or malice. A part of me felt guilty for not getting here sooner, even if I knew it would've prevented nothing.

Spotting shadows on his neck, I leaned closer. They were burns. I clicked on my flashlight and studied the strange markings. As my mind turned with possible scenarios, all I could think was that they looked like handprints—the thumbs overlapping around his Adam's apple, the rest of the fingers gripped around the back of his neck. Even then, it didn't make sense, unless the person's fingers were on fire, which was impossible.

The fingermarks were smaller than a man's, thinner than most too, and I could see the bruised impression of fingernails.

I glanced around the room again, seeing it differently this time. Photography hung in frames on the walls and an array of books filled a large case next to me. There were toiletry sprays and mists on the dresser, a pink jewelry box in the corner, and a bra stuck out from under the bed. A teenage girl had done this? It didn't add up.

"Pop," I breathed, staring back down at his neck. "What happened here?"

DECEMBER 12

17

ELLE
DECEMBER 12

S nowflakes hit the windshield as we made our way down Seward Highway. The storm that had come in overnight kept us cooped up in the tower for longer than I'd hoped, but it gave me and Alex time to clean the mayor's office of bile and the scent of rot. We'd draped the mayor in a blanket so that Sophie could come in and say goodbye.

I didn't dare touch the body though. Despite the past few days, it was still difficult to be around death, and the virus was still dangerous for all we knew. It not only left bodies in its wake, but insanity and perhaps impossible, inexplicable . . . *things*, even if I was the only one who seemed to have experienced it. Who knew what it could still do to us.

I glanced at Sophie in the rearview mirror. She stared out the window into the darkness. On a normal Saturday night, she'd probably be home having dinner with her family or out watching a movie with her friends. Instead, she was grieving for her mom, and praying for her dad.

"He'll see the note," I told her. "He'll come find you if he's alive."

She didn't respond, but I didn't expect her to. There was a slim chance he was alive, an even slimmer chance he'd make it back home or find her if he did. Getting from one part of the world to another seemed impossible now.

Alex turned in the passenger seat to look back at Sophie and the kids, dozing to sleep beside her. For having been only recently introduced to Sophie, Alex was attentive, more than I would've expected. The past few days changed a lot of things, though.

Under different circumstances, had my sister's death been peaceful, I would've gone in search of her body to say goodbye and lay her to rest properly. I would have stayed to mourn instead of running away as fast as I could to find refuge. But our reality was gruesome and wicked. The smell of the quarantine areas made it nearly impossible to stomach. I knew she was dead. I didn't have to see it. Mostly, I couldn't bear to see what had become of her and have to remember her that way.

"How are you doing?" I asked. Alex put on a brave face— something I could tell he was used to doing, but the end of the world meant even the toughest would break eventually.

He rested his elbow on the windowsill and his hand on his head. "I'm fine," he said, but it wasn't convincing.

"It's okay if you're not," I told him. "This is . . ."

"Insane?" He looked at me.

"That's an adequate word."

Alex bit the side of his cheek and shook his head. "Honestly, I feel like something is wrong with me for not caring that my uncle is dead."

I'd felt the same way when I heard about Dr. John. "It doesn't sound like you were very close, or that he was all that great of a person."

"No, he definitely wasn't. He only took me in to collect as much money as he could before I turn eighteen." He glanced at me. "I'm actually surprised he didn't step up the day my mom died. At least he would've had a better couch for me to sleep on."

"I'm sorry," I said. "About your mom, I mean."

Alex readjusted in his seat, clearly uncomfortable with the conversation, so I changed the subject. "I won't ask how you know, but I'm glad you could hot-wire the Pilot." I grinned.

Alex's gaze flicked to me and he scratched the back of his neck. "Sort of comes with the territory."

"What territory is that?"

"Hanging out with the wrong crowd. When you move from family to family, you don't have time to make the good kind of friends."

Dr. John used to tell me horror stories about foster kids getting shuffled through the system, and the terrible families they had to live with. When I was younger I thought whatever my life was with him, it was better than the alternative. It wasn't until I was older that I realized half of what he'd told me was to keep me close.

"Well." I sighed. "I think it's safe to say your street smarts will come in handy now. Lucky us."

His mouth quirked in the corner. "Yeah. Maybe."

We passed a sign for the city a couple miles out.

"I've never been to Anchorage," Sophie whispered. "Not really anyway."

"No?" Alex looked back at her. "Don't worry, you're not missing much."

Sophie continued to stare out the window, though it was too dark to see anything. "We drove straight through from Fairbanks to Whitely." I thought about the photo I'd seen of her in leg braces. She was like a porcelain doll in so many ways, from her pale freckled skin to the quiet hesitance in her voice that made her seem just as fragile. But beneath her mild manner stirred something more. I saw bits of my old self in her, a willpower she just hadn't discovered yet.

Sophie unfurled a blanket and covered herself and the kids.

"Want me to turn the heat up?" I asked. I was so warm, I hadn't thought to turn it up very high.

"I'm okay." Sophie snuggled deeper into the corner of the door.

I stared out at the white road that stretched in front of us. Only a few more minutes until we had more answers and safety. We just had to get there.

"Everything okay?" I glanced at Alex. His gaze was a hot iron on the side of my face.

He stared at me a few seconds longer. "I think so," he finally muttered.

My gloved hands tightened on the steering wheel. "Were you— uh—able to get any rest along with the others?"

He nodded noncommittally. "A little." Alex leaned back in his seat, finally focusing somewhere else. "I've been thinking about what that guy said in that message from Hartley Bay." He'd heard the radio broadcast yesterday in a final attempt to glean more information after the Internet petered out completely. Being in Alaska, it was hard to say if it was because of the frequent snow-storms or the lack of manpower to maintain the stations.

"What about it?" I asked.

"They have military, food—we'd be safe there."

"Maybe," I told him. "But getting there won't be easy." I pointed to the thick snow in the roads that prevented us from going more than thirty miles an hour. "Even with four-wheel drive it would take forever to get there. I'm not saying we can't or shouldn't, but I think we should check with the Coast Guard first." The truth of it was, Hartley Bay would be our only other choice if the Coast Guard fell through, and I couldn't think about that with only an hour of sleep and four other people to take care of.

"Yeah, I hear you. Maybe there's another broadcast." Alex leaned forward and turned on the radio, to static at first, then he pressed SEEK.

"—conspiracy!" a voice thundered on the other side. "I've been saying it for years and I'll say it again: it was bound to happen. You give the government too much power and they'll abuse it, just like they've done in every war since the dawn of time."

"Not this guy again," I muttered as Alex turned the volume up.

"They use us to fight their wars because we're expendable to them. This *virus* only proves it. Why else wouldn't they have found a cure? Why else would so many of the *very few* of us who have survived be out of their goddamn minds? I'll tell you why," he continued. "It's all part of their plan—it's just another genocide, only this time it's disguised as a plague."

Sophie sat forward, gripping the back of my seat. "Do you think it's true?"

Alex shrugged. "Maybe. I mean, it could be."

"All the lunatics out there now," the radio voice continued, "if they weren't crazy before, they surely are now, and what better way to get rid of the rest of us than trial by fire—they want to see who will survive because it's survival of the fittest and that's who they want. The strong. The mighty. They're—"

I clicked off the radio.

"Hey—" Alex grumbled.

"We don't need to hear this," I told them.

"Who is that guy?" Sophie's voice was barely a whisper.

I shook my head. "I have no idea, but he's clearly cracked."

My seat trembled as Sophie clung to it tighter. "What if he's right?" She'd already been through enough for one day, I didn't need the psycho on the other end of the radio adding to her nightmares.

"What if he's not?" I asked, glancing back in the mirror. "He's just stirring the pot. We have enough to worry about right now, we don't need to add his conspiracy theories to the mix."

"The government could do something like that," Alex said, and it wasn't a question, but a legitimate concern. "I'm just saying. They could do a lot of things—they *have* done a lot of things— things we don't even know about."

"Yeah, but all governments around the world?" I asked. "They wouldn't be able to agree that the sky is blue or that the earth is round out of spite, let alone plan a mass genocide of the entire world." I leaned back in my seat and let out a heavy breath. "He's just a loon trying to scare everyone."

"It's working," Sophie muttered.

"Exactly, which is why we don't need to listen to it. It's not helping anything, and I'm not worried about the world, I'm worried about the five of us. He's a conspiracy theorist, he said it himself, and we can't get distracted with what-ifs and maybes when we're trying to figure out what the hell we'll do, here, in this moment."

Alex wanted to argue with me, but gratefully, he didn't. I was exhausted and we'd been through enough for the time being. I couldn't handle another heap of bullshit quite yet. "We just have to stay focused," I murmured, mostly to myself. "See what the Coast Guard have to say—"

"Did you see that?" Alex sat forward in his seat.

I peered through the falling snow, toward the exit as we drove closer. One light flashed. Then another. It was a roadblock at the Brayton Drive exit, and I slowed.

"It's the Coast Guard." Sophie pointed to a man in a Humvee at the roadblock. Cars were stopped along the turnoff, but the engines were off. The coastguardsman was the only person I could see. He was there, living and breathing. I wasn't sure if I wanted to cry with joy or hold my breath.

I followed the path worn in the snow toward the coned-off area where the man was parked and brought the Pilot to a stop. He climbed out of the Humvee and hurried over, looking a bit worse for wear; he was unkempt, his uniform was tattered, and he was underdressed given the weather. Then again, it had been a long night for all of us. I couldn't imagine what the Coast Guard had been dealing with.

I rolled down my window as he drew closer.

"Evening, Miss." He tried to smile welcomingly, but he blinked and shivered in the snow. "I'm Petty Officer Donahoe. It's been a while since I've seen a car. You're a welcomed sight."

His grin widened and a flake of floating snow caught in his mustache.

"So are you." I nearly laughed with relief. I couldn't contain my smile. "We were just in Whitely . . . It's not good," I said quietly.

Officer Donahoe shook his head. "No, it's not. None of it is. We're rounding everyone up at the bus depot by the trooper detachment. Just take this exit here and head to Tudor Road." He pointed down the turnoff. "You'll see the signs."

"But what's happening?" I asked. "Does anyone know? I mean, how much danger are we still in?"

He smiled and held up his hand. "I know you've got a lot of questions, Miss. But there's protocol and all that. They'll fill you in when you get to the station," he reassured us.

I nodded, but was anxious for answers and reluctant to move on until I got some. "Thank you," I muttered, even if I had a feeling they'd be tight-lipped about it. "Even in chaos they won't tell us what we need to know," I said, rolling up my window as I pulled off the highway.

"*Especially* in chaos," Alex echoed. "Did you see his hands?"

I glanced at him. "What do you mean?"

"They were practically blue. He didn't have gloves on."

"He was sitting in his truck before we pulled up," Sophie said, though it sounded like she was searching for reassurance. "He didn't need them in there."

We all stewed in silence as I headed into the city. It was huge and sprawling compared to Whitely, and yet it was eerily still, just as it had been when I was stopped on the overpass. It was difficult to imagine there were any survivors at all, but again, we were alive, so there had to be others.

Spray-painted signs and cones marked the turns to the bus depot, and I felt a strange sense of excitement the closer we drove. The officer said there were others, and seeing them would help it feel a lot less like we were the last five people on the planet.

Turning at the last sign, I pulled into the parking lot. It was filled with cars just like I'd hoped. To the right of the bus depot was a complex of industrial buildings, and I could imagine all of the offices bustling with what city officials and lawmen and women remained as they scrambled to figure out what to do with all of the survivors.

I pulled into a vacant spot at the edge of the lot and shut off the engine. We'd finally made it. I unclipped my seatbelt, but none of the others moved. I glanced back at Sophie, staring out the windshield toward the bus station. "What's wrong?"

"What will happen when we go in?" Sophie asked. "Are they going to separate us?"

Alex looked back at her, then at me. In my excitement to get answers and find a sense of community again, I hadn't thought about what would happen to us after.

I turned in my seat to face them both. "I won't let them separate us. They have no reason to." It was a true statement. I had no idea what protocol would be, but I would do everything I could to make sure we remained together, for now at least. I looked Alex in the eyes, seeing the fear I knew all too well in them. "As far as I'm concerned, I'm your only living relative, all right?"

He nodded.

There was no getting around the fact that our lives would change again once we knew what was going on and how the Coast Guard were instructed to handle all of this, but we needed to know so we could start to move forward and have some semblance of closure.

I looked at Sophie, waiting for an agreement.

"All right," she finally said.

"We stick together," I whispered. "We don't split up, not until we know what's going on." I nodded to the kids. "Let's wake them up before we freeze to death out here."

Sophie unbuckled Thea's seatbelt as I turned forward once

again to gather myself. We were here. We were safe. We would have answers and protection—the kids would have protection.

Alex climbed out of the passenger seat and opened the back to help with Beau. "We're here, bud. Time to wake up."

I got out of the car and pulled the pistol out from under the seat. The Coast Guard didn't need to know about my gun until they found it for themselves. Sophie watched me as I shoved it in my waistband and pulled my shirt and coat over it. "Just to be safe," I said, flashing the most reassuring smile I could. I grabbed my wallet from the center console, then I shut the door. Someone had already tried to kill me, and now I had four humans to protect. The way things had been going, I didn't think anyone could blame me for being prepared.

"I'm still tired," Thea whined as Sophie bent down to zip her jacket.

"I know. We'll get to sleep more soon." She took Thea's little, mittened hand in hers and we headed around to Beau and Alex on the other side.

Together, we walked toward the bus depot building. "Stick together, okay you guys?" I looked specifically to Thea and Beau. "We're a family if anyone asks." Beau's head tilted, uncertain. "That way they'll keep us together," I explained. They both nodded.

"Is this where the police are?" Beau asked. He hadn't spoken all that much since they showed up at Sophie's, but his voice was wary enough to know he was worried about something.

"I don't know," I told him. "But there will be people here who can help us."

Beau peered at the domed-like building, but said nothing else.

The five of us walked briskly through the snow, toward the entrance. The wind was biting cold, even if the snow was only falling intermittently.

The depot was large and surrounded by a parking lot, one luckily big enough for everyone to park. As we approached the large, glass double doors, I'd expected to see hordes of people standing inside. Instead, people were sleeping on cots lined up against the wall, and the main floor was practically empty.

When we walked through the doors, only a few people milled around on the other side of the building. They seemed more like passengers waiting for a late-night bus than survivors seeking refuge. The ticket counter was empty and dark, clearly unused. There were no coastguardsmen hustling around or radios crackling in and out. And it didn't smell right, either. A scent I couldn't quite put my finger on lingered in the air.

There was nothing here—no stock of food or water. There were no EMTs or even a buzz of worry, just a dozen or so people sleeping and a few others talking on the other side of the room.

"Hold up." I held up my hand, and we stood at the entrance as the door came swinging shut. Something didn't feel right. It was hard to tell if it was the fire inside me roiling or if it was fear of what I couldn't see or sense. "Stay here," I whispered.

"Elle—" Sophie reached for my arm.

"I'll be okay." I looked her in the eyes and offered her a reassuring smile. I could feel the fire in my fingers, hot and aching, and knew if anyone in here would be okay, it was probably me, even if I feared finding out either way. "Alex," I said, glancing at the car. "If anything happens, you start that thing again and you get everyone the hell out of here."

His dark eyes were wide, but he nodded with understanding.

Turning on my heels, I walked swiftly toward the two men at the other end of the room whose faces lit up when they noticed me approaching. I glanced at a frantic woman, pacing back and forth in front of someone sitting in a chair against the furthest wall. The pacing woman's clothes were wrinkled, and she looked a little worse for wear, but I felt the same way. At least she was alive, and she had someone with her. Maybe the place was a funneling station and they would tell us where to go from here.

I walked toward her, curious what she knew. The two men a

dozen yards away eyed me, but I wanted to talk to *her*; she wouldn't still be here if she didn't feel safe, and woman-to-woman, she would be straight with me.

"Excuse me," I said, stopping beside her. "Ma'am—excuse me." I raised my voice, noticing the woman with a short dark bob that sat in the chair across from her. Finally the pacing woman noticed me and looked up, hurrying toward me.

"Hi. I'm Elle," I offered, forcing a smile. I wondered if this was a situation where pleasantries were expected. "Um, where the hell is everyone?"

"Oh," the woman grinned. There was a flicker in her shimmering eyes that lit the deep lines of her face and the dark circles under her eyes. "Aren't you pretty," she said, like I was a five-year-old girl. "Just like my sister."

"Excuse me?"

"You're just like my sister, Trish." She nodded behind her with an unnerving smile, at the woman in the chair. "Hurry, come say hi." Her foul breath hit me in a wave and I had to turn my face away.

Whatever apprehension I'd been feeling flared to blaring alarm.

"Come on." She waved me closer to her sister, unmoving from where she sat like she couldn't be bothered to stand. "You'll love her. We're just sitting down for tea."

But as I drew closer, the hair rose on the back of my neck and arms, and my footsteps, along with my smile, faltered. Her sister's eyes were painted on, her legs and arms crossed and unmoving. Her sister wasn't her sister at all. She was a mannequin.

I stumbled back.

"Come," the woman said, tugging on my arm. "You'll love her."

I yanked my arm away, glancing between the crazy woman and her giant doll.

Shaking my head, I turned on my heel. "We're getting out of here," I said, loud enough the kids would hear me.

Fear darkened their faces.

"Now," I told them.

"Where are you going?" the two men behind me said, but I didn't stop to chat. I knew they were following behind me.

Sophie and Alex turned the kids toward the exit as the door opened and the officer from the Coast Guard stepped inside.

"You made it," he announced.

"No," I stopped behind the kids. "We're leaving." I grabbed Thea's hand. "Let's go."

Donahoe raised a gun and aimed it at me. "No. No. I don't think so."

I gripped Thea's hand tighter, nearly crushing it.

"I told you it's been a while since we've gotten anyone new. You can't leave so soon." He said it apologetically but I could see the delight in his eyes.

I took a step back and bumped into a hard body, then spun around. The two men were right behind me, the five of us surrounded by three men, one with a gun.

Letting go of Thea's hand, I nudged her closer to Sophie and the others behind me. "Let us go," I said with false bravado, and pulled the pistol from my waistband. "And I won't shoot your friend." I stepped as close to the wall as I could so I could see the three of them, and aimed the barrel at the tallest man who looked like he could do the most damage, especially since he was the closest to us. Like he could read my thoughts, the tall one smirked, and a wave of chills washed up my spine.

"I *will* kill you," I promised him.

The kids scooted up beside me. I could feel their warm bodies and hear their whimpers. The men must've taken me half-serious because they stopped a few feet away.

"Kill who, Ted?" Donahoe asked. "Meh, you don't want to kill him. Then Kathy there, having her little tea party, will get all worked up, and trust me, that's no good for anyone."

I glanced from Kathy creeping closer, to Ted, watching the way his eyes sparkled with excitement as Donahoe carried on beside me. All of their clothes were dirty, but Donahoe was in uniform, and even Ted wore a neon vest like he worked for the city or maybe the Coast Guard too. Regardless, they were definitely insane with zero desire to help us.

"Maybe not good for you," I seethed, my gaze shifting between the two lascivious men who were getting their jollies off watching us fidget in fear. "But one of you will be dead, and I'd be okay with that."

"Look lady, you kill one of them, then I kill one of you," Donahoe said. "Capeech?"

My gaze darted to him as Sophie gasped. His gun was aimed at her chest. Then Ted grabbed onto Thea, pulling her into him, and she screamed.

"Let her go!" I shouted. One gun was pointed at Sophie and a lunatic had Thea. "You won't hurt them," I blurted, praying it was true. They wanted us for something or they wouldn't have tricked us into coming here. They could've killed us on the road if that was their intent.

Donahoe shrugged. "Correction—we don't *want* to hurt you all, at least not yet. The meat's more tender if we don't."

I nearly dropped the gun and had to steady myself so as not to stumble back. I glanced around the room, realizing the people on the cots were either dead or they weren't real, just like Kathy's sister. I couldn't tell which with the blankets covering them. This place wasn't a funneling station, it was a corral and they'd herded us here like cattle.

"But, you know, killing you now or later, it doesn't really matter much. Either way we get what we want in the end."

"Sick motherfuckers," Alex growled, and Sophie had to grab

onto him as he took a step forward so that he didn't get himself killed.

Beau trembled against my leg, grabbing hold of me and crying for his sister.

"What are you waiting for then?" I asked, trying to keep them talking while I formulated a plan. I could kill Donahoe who had the gun, but I wasn't sure the others didn't have a weapon they weren't showing me. It would be stupid of them not to, and Ted had Thea. "What *do* you want?"

"I'll take you," Ted said leaning in as close as he dared with my gun still pointed at him.

Thea's cries turned into screams again and Kathy hurried closer, shouting nonsense in reply. It's like she wasn't even human anymore, but a starving wildling needing to feed.

"Shut the kid up," the other man growled. "Shut them up! Shut them the fuck up!" He pushed Kathy away and she fell onto the ground. He kicked at her, like she was a dog he had to teach a lesson, and she whimpered like one too.

A gunshot rang through the building, piercingly loud, and we all ducked instinctively. Donahoe fell to the ground, writhing in pain, and I aimed my Glock at Ted's chest as he stood in temporary shock, watching as his friend collapsed to the ground. I pulled the trigger.

Ted fell to his knees, then I shot him again for good measure as another shot rang through the air, taking the lunatic beside him down, dead with a single shot.

The doors on the other side of the building flew open and Kathy ran out into the winter night screaming.

A man came out from behind the ticketing area, one I hadn't seen yet. My gun shook in my hand as I aimed it at his chest, adrenaline whooshing through me.

"I will not hurt you," he said slowly, carefully. His voice was low and reassuring, but I wasn't sure I trusted it. He held up his hands so I could see them, and his gun. Had he not just shot two of the men who were threatening to eat us, I wouldn't have believed him for a single second, but I lowered my gun, registering the kids, crying in a human ball on the floor.

Frantic, I spun around. Alex and Sophie covered the two children, all of them with their hands over their ears and tears streaming down their faces.

Donahoe was crumpled in front of the door barely breathing, but he wasn't dead yet.

The man with the gun stepped closer. He was huge with broad shoulders and dark features, like most Inuit descendants. He would've been fearsome had I any time to think about it before he trained his pistol on Donahoe.

"Cover your ears," he told us. He looked at me and lifted an arched eyebrow. "And look away." He nodded at the kids.

I covered my ears but was unable to look away as he shot Donahoe in the head. The gunshot echoed through the building, and I waited contentedly as the dead man's chest fell for the final time.

18

ELLE
DECEMBER 12

E ven with a flannel blanket wrapped around me, I was still shaking. I'd shot a man—I'd gone from never hurting a living soul to killing two men in a span of forty-eight hours. I massaged the incessant pounding in my head, desperately trying to keep it together until I knew more about our mysterious new friend. His house was shabby chic with a touch of glam, which I hadn't expected. It felt normal, which was nice for a change, and the warm scent of vanilla hung faintly in the air.

Books and folded maps were stacked on the side table next to the plush leather chair across from me in the living room, and a satellite phone lay on top. Our host hadn't said much, but he was clearly capable. After the bus depot we'd followed him back here. After he'd told us to eat whatever we wanted in the kitchen and pointed to the bedrooms upstairs, he'd disappeared outside and I hadn't seen him since.

Thea moaned in her sleep, and I peered down at the pallet of blankets Alex and Sophie had made for the four of them on the floor. It turned out they hadn't wanted food or space—they were only concerned about not being separated from each other. They craved warmth and needed rest, which outweighed any apprehension they'd had about being in a stranger's house.

I watched the four of them, bodies rising with rhythmic sleep. The sound of their soft snores made my eyelids begin to droop, even if my mind was a muddied mess.

The front doorknob clicked and opened, and our generous host stepped inside. It seemed silly not to know his name, but there hadn't been a good time to exchange pleasantries. A bottle of amber alcohol sloshed in his hand as he stopped in the entry, staring down at the kids camped out on his living room floor.

"Safety in numbers," I whispered.

He glanced at me huddled in the corner of the couch. Then he looked at the flicking candle beside me.

"I left the lights off, like you said. I hope the candle is okay." I prayed it was. I hated the darkness. "I saw the matches above the fireplace and—"

"It's fine," he said and glanced around the room, like he didn't recognize it or maybe just didn't know what to do with himself now that it was inhabited. He stepped over Sophie's feet, sticking out from beneath her blanket, and he shrugged off his coat and tossed it on the stairs. His quiet reserve and fortitude made me think he might've been a trooper or military.

"I don't want to risk anyone noticing the lights through the drapes," he explained. "The candle's fine." He claimed the leather seat beside the unlit fireplace. His stubble seemed thicker in the flickering shadows, his features harder and more mysterious.

"I understand." I wanted to be invisible too. I pulled the blanket up around my neck.

"You can turn the heater up," he said, eyes shifting to the staircase. "We might as well use it while we've got it."

"It's okay," I told him. I wasn't cold—I wasn't sure I would ever be cold again at the rate my insides were burning—but the blanket brought me comfort and I gripped it tighter. "How much longer," I asked. It was one of the many questions on my mind. "Until the power goes out, I mean?"

He let out a breath and stared into the empty hearth. "A couple weeks. Maybe less. Between the storms and lack of maintenance, it won't be long."

I'd assumed as much, and even though I dreaded the day, I was too exhausted to care. "What were you doing at the depot?" I couldn't help but ask the question that had been stirring for hours.

He finally looked at me. "I was at the trooper outpost across the parking lot getting this file of maps and saw you drive in," he said, nodding to the folder he tossed on the floor by the side table when we'd first arrived. "They're going to help me plan where I'm heading next."

"I see." My voice was barely a whisper as *what now* blared like a bullhorn in my head. I had planning to do too, and I didn't even know where to start. At least we were safe for the night.

"Thank you, for everything," I said. "It's hard to trust strangers right now, but you've been very kind."

He looked at me, and just as quickly he glanced away. "You've used a gun before?"

"Oh, uh"—I sunk lower into the couch—"yes, but not like that." The weekly practice had been for self-defense. But shooting at a target down range was nothing like staring down at a human being that would never breathe again.

"It'll get easier."

"It already is," I thought aloud. The gratification I felt, knowing Thomas or Ted could never hurt or frighten someone again, made me sick to my stomach. Killing people wasn't something I wanted to be easy, yet part of me hoped it would continue to be.

He studied me a moment, the candle flickering as I let out a deep breath. "You're holding yourself together pretty well." I wasn't sure if it was a skeptical observation or a compliment.

I laughed, if a little hysterical. "I'm waiting for it all to catch up with me." I leaned my head back on the cushion and stared up at the ceiling. "I had a mini breakdown earlier, but I think I'm due for another."

"Only one so far?" he said wryly.

"In the last six hours." I smiled at him.

His amusement faded and his gaze shifted to the bottle in his hand. It was bourbon. He hadn't opened it yet, but he gripped onto it so hard his knuckles were white. "You're lucky then." He turned it around in his hand, eyeing it like he wasn't sure he really wanted any. Drinking was definitely one way to deal with the world ending; I'd done that already and woke up with glowing fingers. I figured it was best not to tell him that part though.

"What happened tonight is only the beginning of whatever comes next," I said. "It will get worse before it gets better."

"Yep," he drawled, and I watched the battle inside him end. The demons won, and he shut his eyes and took a long pull from the bottle.

"I'm Elle, by the way."

He pulled the bottle from his lips. "Jackson," he exhaled and rested the bourbon in his lap. He glanced over at the kids. "Are they all yours?"

I shook my head. "We met last night." I peered down at Alex curled up in a ball of blankets, sleeping like he hadn't in days. Beau was sprawled out beside him with his mouth open, snoring softly. "But I guess they are now, aren't they," I realized aloud. "They were the only survivors I found in Whitely." It already seemed like so long ago as my mind grew fuzzy with warmth and the promise of sleep. "My sister was gone, but they were there."

Jackson stared at me, but I didn't take it personally. It wasn't even at me, he was staring through me, at a memory that made his permanent frown deepen and his knuckles whiten again. He was disappearing to somewhere dark inside his mind before my eyes.

"This is a nice condo," I said, trying to reel him back in. I had a hard time imagining such a mountain of a man living in a place like this. "It's way nicer than my apartment in Seward."

Jackson pulled his gun and holster off and set it on the floor next to his pile of maps. "It's my buddy Ross's place." He nodded to a framed photo on the wall behind me. It was two troopers in uniform, Jackson holding a graduation certificate. A woman with wavy, long blonde hair smiled between them, her arms over their shoulders. "She's pretty. Is that his wife?"

Jackson stared at the photo so long I didn't think he would answer. Then, he looked away. "His sister, my wife."

My mouth opened, and I blinked dumbly as I tried to think of what to say. "I'm sorry," was all that escaped.

"Ross went to check on his wife."

"I see," I hated to ask, but I couldn't help myself. "Is she okay?" I assumed I knew the answer, but I still hoped that maybe she'd made it. More survivors would make it seem like there was actually a chance everything would right itself again.

Jackson shrugged and took another drink from his bottle. "He was supposed to check in today." He picked up the satellite phone. "You know as much as I do at this point."

Aside from the soft slumber of sleeping children, the room grew silent. It was clear Jackson wasn't sure he'd hear from his friend again.

"If he survived the fever, and he's a trooper, I'm sure he's fine," I tried to reassure him, but it was clear Jackson didn't want my sympathy. He preferred the bottle to conversation, and if his friend coped like he did, it might be days before Ross cared enough to check in. "I'm sure you'll hear from him soon."

Jackson's eyes cut to me. "So, you're an optimist then?" He smiled with feigned amusement.

I wanted to see a full, real smile. I could imagine it was wide and welcoming. Big guys had a way of surprising you with their big hearts, even if it seemed unlikely as Jackson brought the bottle to his mouth again.

"No," I said. "I'm not generally optimistic. I'm one of the most miserable people I know, but—" I squeezed my gloved hands into fists beneath the blanket, knowing I had to be or I would lose my mind.

"But?"

"But I have to be as positive as I can, for them." I nodded to the kids. "So here I am, trying to be optimistic."

Jackson studied me more closely than before, his brow furrowing before he leaned his head back in his chair. "So . . ." He exhaled. "From Seward to Whitely to here, huh?"

"I was taking care of my stepdad's estate—he died recently—"

"I'm sorry."

"Don't be," I told him. "I'm not. He was a monster." I ran my fingers through my hair and pushed Dr. John from my mind. There were worse things out there that could hurt me now. "I went to his estate in Eagle River, planning on selling it when all of this happened. I knew Jenny was sick, so I went to Whitely after that, hoping I would get to see her again . . ." I stared at the flickering candle flame. "She was already dead."

Jackson took another swig of his bourbon before he stared quietly up at the ceiling. "My father lived in Eagle River," he said, then was contemplative for a few deep breaths. "He had a mushing business for the tourists, up near the mountains."

Cold-hot fear lapped up the back of my neck, and the fire inside me pulsated in tandem with my heartbeat. "He was a mush-er?" I whispered.

"The son of a bitch loved his dogs more than his own kid. He lost his mind though, at least, that's what I think."

I glanced back up at the photo of Jackson in his uniform and the certificate he held in his hand. *Jackson Mitchell.*

Thomas Mitchell. Tall and broad shouldered, just like Jackson, though Thomas had lighter skin and hadn't looked like an Alaskan native. I saw Thomas looming in my doorway all over again, felt him grabbing onto my neck.

"Your mother?" I hedged, petrified to know the answer.

"She died a long time ago, with my baby sister in childbirth." His head turned to the side. "You know, it was the strangest thing. The way he died . . . I can't get it out of my head."

"Your dad? What do you mean?"

"Someone strangled him."

I could feel my fingernails digging into my palms through the gloves. "How could you tell?"

"I know what bruises around a neck look like. And you'd have to be strong to crush a man's throat with your bare hands."

Only bruises?

Jackson's hard-set eyes fixed on me. "Would you think I was crazy if I told you I think it was a woman who killed him?"

I cleared my throat this time, the heat of the room and the low burn inside practically eating through me. I wasn't sure how my cheeks weren't on fire. "I guess a woman could be that strong," I said, but the thing was, I *wasn't* that strong, there was no way I could've done that under any other circumstances. "But what makes you think it wasn't a man?"

He held up his large hands, twice the size of mine, and wiggled his fingers. "Small hands," he said. "And fingernails. But there was something weird about it."

My thoughts stilled.

"Burn marks." He shook his head. "I've been trying to figure it out."

Of course he was, because what had happened was impossible. And somehow the only decent adult I'd met since I'd woken up after puking my brains out was the son of the man I'd impossibly killed with my bare hands. "This world is unrecognizable now," I rasped, trying to breathe through the lump in my throat.

Jackson needed to know it was an accident—it was self-defense, and I had no choice. His father would've killed me.

As a trooper, Jackson might've understood, but as a son? I couldn't bring myself to tell him. I didn't want to risk him throwing out the kids; and I wasn't ready to figure this survival thing out on my own. And how did I explain the fire without scaring them all? The thought hadn't escaped me that maybe they *should* be scared, and maybe I should be alone.

Tears burned my eyes and escaped the brim of my lashes. Just as quickly, I tried to wipe them away.

Jackson cleared his throat. "Are you okay?"

I shook my head. I wasn't okay. I was probably losing my mind like the other crazy people running around the city, and it was only a matter of time before I did something to hurt one of the kids, the way I'd hurt Thomas.

I covered my face and tried to hold back the smothering despondency. *None of this is going to be okay.*

Thankfully, Jackson wasn't a man of many words, and he stood up, his boots making the floorboards beneath the carpet creak. I heard the glug-glug-glug of bourbon sloshing into a cup, then it clanked quietly against the coffee table. "In case you need it," he said, and his footsteps retreated up the stairs.

I waited until I heard his bedroom door shut before lifting my face. A mug full of bourbon sat on the coffee table in front of me.

Jackson had no idea who was sitting in his house, or who he'd saved. As the kids continued to sleep, I stared into the candle flame and I cried my eyes out as silently as I could.

DECEMBER 13

19

JACKSON

DECEMBER 13

I woke to the sound of the heater clicking on, and the scent of something savory and sweet filled the air. I peeled my eyes open and blinked up at the ceiling. My head was a spinning punching bag and I felt just as beaten.

The bed squeaked as I rolled over. I'd passed out between listening to Elle's intermittent sniffles and the ticking of the clock on the guest room wall. I glanced up at it; it was nearly noon.

Pushing myself up, I peered down at the quarter-empty bottle of bourbon beside the bed. It could've been worse; I could've downed the entire thing and been nonfunctional today. But I had a trip to start planning, one without Ross.

I heard a clang downstairs, which meant an intruder was stealing the silver, or the kids were still in the house. I half expected them to be gone when I woke up, but I knew they had nowhere else to go, especially since the Coast Guard wouldn't be any help.

Grabbing my boots from the floor, I pulled them on, ignoring the laces. I wasn't awake enough for that. I climbed to my feet, grabbed the bottle, and opened the door. Whispers filled the air, and footsteps pattered against the tile floor in the kitchen. Another pot clanked, and my stomach gurgled as I inhaled the aroma of bacon. I tried to remember the last time I'd eaten.

I raided Ross's bathroom for deodorant, washed my mouth out, and splashed cold water on my face, before I headed down the stairs. It was weird waking up in his house, and yet it felt oddly comforting too. At least I'd slept, *really* slept, for the first time in days.

The living room had been cleaned up and looked just as Kelsey had left it, save for my things around the leather chair. The pallet of blankets was gone. The fancy pillows were put back where they'd been on the couch. It was like Elle and the kids had never been there.

"He's coming!" one of them hissed, and the little girl scuttled out of the way as I turned into the kitchen. The narrow space was filled to capacity. The younger ones were putting plates on the table, their wide eyes peering up at me. The teenagers were behind the stove, the boy flipping a pancake while the girl drained bacon grease into a mug. The only one missing was Elle.

"Morning," the older girl said, setting the grease pan in the sink. She was shy or scared, and I didn't blame her for either. I hadn't looked human for a while now.

I stood dumbly in the doorway. "Morning."

"I'm Sophie and this is Alex." Then, she nodded to the kids. "That's Thea and Beau. We wanted to make you breakfast as a thank you for letting us stay here last night."

"That's . . . unnecessary," I said as my stomach rumbled again. "But thanks."

"Wow, that was a big one," Thea said with a giggle, staring at my stomach. She couldn't have been more than six or seven. "This is your seat right here." She pointed to the chair at the head of the table. It was Ross's spot during family dinners. I pulled the chair out and sat down as Alex brought over a plate of pancakes, Sophie following with the platter of bacon.

They all wore clean clothes and looked refreshed after their ordeal at the bus depot, more than I could say for myself, and they were more animated than I could ever be in the morning.

I was about to ask where Elle was, worried she might've thrown in the towel after her internal battle last night and left the kids with me, when the front door opened and she bustled inside. She was wearing a black down parka and beanie, and held up a frozen can of orange juice concentrate. "Look what I found," she said, divesting her jacket.

"Yay!" Thea clapped.

"It's her favorite," Beau grumbled in explanation. They were definitely siblings, but as for the others, I doubted it.

Elle draped her jacket on the back of a dining room chair and handed the can to Sophie who was already pulling out a pitcher.

"Where'd you find that?" I asked, wondering if she'd walked all the way to the store just for juice.

Her cheeks reddened, and she shoved her hands in the back pockets of her jeans. "I, um, raided the neighbor's freezer."

Well, that was clever, seeing how they no longer needed it.

She cleared her throat. "I made coffee. You want a cup?"

"Please."

"Black?"

"Definitely. I need all the help I can get this morning."

Thea set an empty glass next to my plate. "Is it because you drink so much?"

"Thea—" Sophie chided.

I almost smiled. "Yeah, kid. Something like that."

"My mommy drank a lot too. I think that's why—"

"Thea!" Beau shouted at her.

Thea's lips pursed and she glowered at him.

"All right," Elle said, setting a cup of coffee down in front of me. "Let's wait and argue after we've had breakfast."

Sticking her tongue out at her brother, Thea blew out a breath as she climbed into her chair.

"Thanks for the coffee," I said as Elle pulled out a chair beside Thea.

"Of course." She cooed as she took a drink from her own steaming hot mug.

Thea eyed her, clearly disgusted. "I don't drink coffee. It smells bad."

"Good," I told her. "It puts hair on your chest."

Her eyes widened. "Really?"

I shrugged and lifted the collar of my thermal shirt, pretending to peer down at my chest. "I'd say so."

"He's teasing you," Beau told her. "You're so gullible."

"Nuh-uh."

"Yeah-huh—"

"Beau, Thea . . ." Alex interrupted before they could go another round of back-and-forth. "Take a pancake and a piece of bacon, and pass them to Jackson."

I helped Thea lift the plate of pancakes as her little arms shook, and I took one before passing it along.

Everyone settled into an uncomfortable, close-proximity silence. It was the worst kind.

I took a gulp of my coffee and watched everyone's eyes darting around at one another. The only one who seemed oblivious to the awkwardness was Thea.

She picked up her glass of orange juice and slurped it down. Only when it was half gone did she come up for air. "It's really good," she gasped, and licked her lips.

"I'll bet." It wasn't until I took a bite of bacon that I thought to say the same thing. I shoved the rest of it in my mouth without ceremony.

"I like a lot of butter on mine," Beau said, and he put a small piece on Thea's pancake and helped her spread it around. I hadn't realized kids were such good buffers, and as difficult as I thought it might be to have them there, I appreciated that they were, too.

"I hope you like bacon and pancakes," Elle said. "We didn't want to wake you to ask."

"I do. But I'll eat anything," I told her. "Something my wife always appreciated."

Eyes flicked to me and the room grew quiet again, the sound of forks and knives clanking louder in the void of conversation.

Desperate for a distraction, I cut into my pancake. It was the first time in days, excluding my brief talk with Ross, that I had been around people, and even if it made me feel uncomfortable, I was strangely grateful for it too. "This is great, thank you."

"Do you want syrup?" Sophie held up the container.

I glanced up at her and shook my head. "No. Thank you." I forked a piece of buttered pancake into my mouth and decided I missed food more than I thought.

"I didn't mean to snoop," Alex said, "but I saw all the maps in your file of the backcountry. Are you leaving the city?"

"We heard about a safe place in Hartley Bay," Sophie added. "Is that where you're going?"

I shook my head. "I'm thinking about Whitehorse."

Elle took a sip of her coffee. "What's in Whitehorse?" She glanced away as she set her mug down. I could hear the hope in her voice, but it was misplaced. There was nothing there for them. Not like in Hartley Bay, if what I'd heard about it was true.

I glanced around the table at expectant faces. "A place far removed from all of this bullshit," I said, forgetting the youthful ears at the table. "A lodge I've been to before, out in the middle of nowhere."

"If you know where you're going, then why do you need the maps?" Sophie asked, taking a bite of bacon.

"Because you never know what sort of trouble you're going to run into, and those maps have dozens of locations the department has raided over the years, which might come in handy."

Beau licked his fingers. "What kind of places?"

"Squatter houses, backwater distilleries—places where I might find shelter and supplies if I really needed them. I'll be leaving in a few days," I told them. "You're welcome to stay here as long as you like. Ross won't need the place and he's not the type that would mind anyway."

"Thank you," Elle said quietly.

We ate the rest of our breakfast without much more conversation, though Thea and Beau bickered back and forth when they grew too restless. I was lost in thoughts of Whitehorse and Ross; Elle and the kids were likely dreading their uncertain future, one I'd already come to terms with.

I looked at Elle, staring into her coffee cup. She was still wearing her gloves, which was strange, but it wasn't my business, just like my quirks were none of hers. She stared so long I wondered if she would blink.

I imagined she was frantic inside, considering what she would do with four kids in a civilization that had only just begun to crumble. Conveniences would be gone. Safety would be fleeting.

While my plate was wiped clean, hers was barely touched.

"Elle?" Sophie said with a tentative smile.

Elle stirred from her fog, her eyebrows lifting. "Huh?"

"Are you okay? Do you want more of anything?"

Elle's smile was forced and she shook her head. "Nope. I'm good. My stomach must've shrunk since it's been a while since I've had an actual meal."

Everyone seemed to buy that explanation, and it was probably true to some extent, but I saw the same fear in Elle's eyes I'd seen the night before. She was on the brink of a breakdown. I couldn't imagine my life six months from now, let alone what it would look like if I was twenty-something and suddenly had four kids to care for. Traveling would be more difficult; vehicles would have to be larger, which meant more fuel would be needed for their thousand-mile trek to Hartley Bay. Elle would have to provide enough food to feed five mouths instead of one, and she would have to find safe lodging for all of them, too. It was not going to be easy and yet I knew she was going to do it, I could see it in her false smiles and forced optimism as she tried to convince them and herself that everything would be okay.

Alex got up to get more orange juice for the kids.

"I'll grab the coffee," Sophie said, and my mouth was moving before I could stop myself.

"I can't promise you'll all be safer with me," I told Elle just above a whisper. I had to get the words out before I changed my mind. "And it's not going to be an easy journey, but you can come with me as far as Whitehorse."

Elle's eyes shot to mine.

I swallowed the rest of my coffee down and set my mug on the table. Hannah would want me to help them, and watching Thea stick her finger in the syrup and grin at me with reddened cheeks because she was caught playing with her food, meant I was a sucker already. It pulled at my heartstrings, and I couldn't live with myself if I didn't do what I could to help them get to Hartley.

I cleared my throat. "You'll be on your own after that."

Elle's chin trembled and her eyes filled with tears that twisted my insides. A woman crying—the hardest thing to see. I stood up and pushed my chair from the table. "Thanks for breakfast every-one. I've got work to do."

Elle reached for my arm, her gloved hand resting on mine. "Thank you," she whispered and wiped a rogue tear from her check as quickly as it fell. "Thank you."

DECEMBER 14

20

ELLE

DECEMBER 14

The vertical blinds were cracked on the sliding glass door, allowing sunlight to filter in over the dining table during the first break in the snow. Jackson and I pored over unfolded maps and lists strewn across the table.

He was right, there were squatter shacks all over in the back-country, and while some of them were noted on some maps to have been torn down on public land, others had been identified and forgotten.

I looked down at my ever-growing list of supplies we needed to accumulate before we headed out of the city. Yukon Territory was nearly an eight hundred mile journey on good roads, not accounting for weather or unplowed road conditions. According to the maps, the towns we'd pass heading east would be few and far between, and very, very small. While the thought of running into less people was inviting, the uncertainty of being so far away from what conveniences were left was disconcerting. We needed a few days' worth of supplies at least, and I tried not to dwell on what would happen once we got to our destination.

Thea hummed behind us on the stool at the counter, oblivious to our consternation as she turned the printer paper she'd found in the office over to start a new picture. She seemed to be the most adjusted of all of us, like she'd already forgotten Whitely and the cannibals from the bus depot. Her cries still haunted me, and every time I closed my eyes, I saw the three flesh-eaters grinning at me, and could smell Kathy's stinking breath and see the mannequins strategically placed to provide survivors with a false sense of safety. I envied Thea's ability to shut it all away and draw pictures of her family, even if most of them were dead.

"I'll try the AM stations again," Sophie said from the living room. She and Alex had been searching the radio for a Hartley update all morning.

We needed a crank radio if we were going to receive updates during our journey, I realized. The last thing we needed was to miss an announcement that the sanctuary had fallen apart and a warning not to come. I added it to the second page of my list, below flashlights, extra matches, first aid kits, and candles.

"The kids should have their own packs," Jackson said, taking a drink from his coffee mug. I was glad to see he was doing a little better than the night we'd met him. No longer lost in dark thoughts that had him swimming in bourbon. "And only the necessities."

"You don't think all of these things are necessities?" I asked, looking down at my list, which included the prepared food and clothing we needed to stock up on. I didn't know much about children and teenagers other than they were always hungry and grew quickly.

Jackson shook his head. "There's a difference between stock and necessity. When we have to hide or run—which you already know may be the case—we'll have only what we can carry, the kids included."

Thea looked up from coloring, and glanced worriedly between us.

"And," he continued, "their bags better have what they'll need to survive."

I cleared my throat. "Thea, why don't you go see what Beau is doing upstairs," I said with a smile. "Make sure he's not getting into any trouble."

"He probably is," she said and rolled her eyes. With a giggle, she climbed down from the stool and skipped into the living room.

When I looked at Jackson, he was staring at me. "You can't protect her from everything," he said. "They need to understand how different life is now, and how to be prepared if they're going to survive."

His words were grim, but true, and while I appreciated them, Thea and Beau were still only children. It seemed like delicacy was needed all the same. "They already know what the world is like," I told him. "It doesn't have to be on their minds every waking hour."

"Why not? It's on yours."

My eyes narrowed. "Yes, well that's different."

"Why? What if you're not around to worry about them? They need to be just as alert and aware of what's happening as you are."

"I understand we all have a big learning curve, Jackson," I said, taking a gulp of water. Fleetingly, I remembered that soon there would be no power or running water, and that was only the start. "But it will all come in time. It's only been a few days of craziness. I don't want them to be too horrified to close their eyes, like I am."

Jackson's ever-present frown deepened, then a flash of something softened his face, and he looked back down at his maps without saying another word about it.

While I understood his reasoning, *I* needed time to process and plan so that I could keep them as safe as possible, and keep my sanity too. Having to worry about the kids freaking out more than they already were was an added stress I didn't need right now.

"I've been thinking," I said, folding my arms on the table. "We have the Pilot and you have the Tacoma, but maybe we get another vehicle for Sophie or Alex to drive. We could take more supplies that way."

Jackson didn't bother looking up from his map. "That's more fuel we'll have to find along the way." He drew a line with a

Sharpie across the page, a straight shot from Eagle River to White-horse across the border. I looked at him, praying he wasn't planning on stopping in Eagle River on our way out of Anchorage but was too afraid to ask.

"So, you think three vehicles is a bad idea?"

He took another swig from his mug and circled a town called Slana. "If we're heading northeast on the highway, these are the towns we'll be passing." He ran his index finger along the road, tapping on Nelchina, Tolsona, and Mentasta Lake. "They're unincorporated villages, most with no fueling stations or even stores, for that matter—everything is going to be few and far between. If we're going to take another vehicle, we'll need to bring as much fuel with us as we can, which means less of everything else. I'm not saying it's a bad idea, but it's something to consider."

"Is that your nice way of telling me no?" I lifted an eyebrow. He'd made it clear he wanted to bring the necessities only, and it was his show, I'd already promised him that.

Jackson glanced up at me, his hazel eyes shifting over my face. All I could think about was how much I didn't know about living off the grid or survival—whatever we were calling it. And it was all a reminder of how grateful I was to have him sitting across from me, even if he was the gruffest man I'd ever met. Not for the first time, I was curious to know more about him.

"What was it like?" I asked him, knowing I'd learn nothing if I didn't at least try.

"What was what like?"

"Being a trooper? I used to cringe when I'd see them around town, wondering if I might get pulled over. And I've never even been in trouble with the law, well, not really."

He leaned back in his chair and crossed his arms over his chest. "*Not really?*"

I shrugged. "I ran away when I was seventeen," I told him.

"A rebel," he murmured. Intrigue danced in his eyes. "I can't say I'm surprised."

"Oh? And why is that?"

"How often did you go to the shooting range?" he asked.

I answered him with a question, "What makes you think I went to the shooting range?"

"The way you hold your gun—stiff, like you've only ever used it routinely. And hunting with a handgun is illegal, so I know you don't use one for that." This time he stared at me, expectant. "Do you?"

"Well, you said it yourself, I'm a rebel."

"Let me guess, you used to go shooting with your dad—a father-daughter thing?"

"No," I blurted, shaking it off with a laugh. "Definitely not."

Jackson didn't smile though, and the silence stretched longer than I was comfortable with. I opened my mouth to speak. "Well—"

"*Because* of him?" he asked.

His words shocked me, though I wasn't sure why. Jackson was trained to read people. I glanced back down at my list. "Something like that. But, we're getting off point." I lifted my sheets of paper. "Maybe you should look over my checklist and tell me what you think the necessities are. It will save us some time, don't you think? Then I can start scrounging them up." While I said it with more sass than I'd meant to, it was probably the best idea I'd had all morning.

His dark eyebrow lifted.

"Seriously," I said. "Help me make a list you're comfortable with, and I'll go to the mall and gather what we need—"

"You're not going to the mall." Jackson leaned forward, adamant. "Every person left alive has had that same idea. And trust me, that's not something you want to worry about."

"Okay, well—"

Shouting echoed from outside, followed by rapid gunfire, and Jackson and I crouched at the table. The instant I heard the first panicked murmur from the other room, I shot through the house.

Jackson pulled his gun from his holster, and jolted after me into the living room.

"Get out of the window!" Jackson shouted. Sophie and Alex whipped around, the blinds rustling back into place. Jackson stilled them the best he could and peeked out one of the slits, eyes wide.

Beau and Thea ran down the stairs, eyebrows drawn together and fear glistening in their eyes.

"It's okay," I told them, pulling Thea into my arms.

Alex grabbed a baseball bat by the door as another spurt of rapid fire, somewhere around back, rang out outside, and I reached for Beau.

Jackson motioned all of us into the office to hide as he ran back into the kitchen toward the backyard. The rapid fire continued, my heartbeat keeping time, round for round.

"Who's doing that?" Thea whined as we ran into the office.

Sophie pulled her up into her arms. "I don't know, but we have to be quiet, okay?" Her voice was as unsteady as my legs, and I closed us quietly inside the room.

Shots went off again. It had to be a scare tactic. There weren't enough people alive to be shooting at the masses.

Beau whimpered and grabbed hold of Alex's legs, wrapping his arms around them like he thought he might leave. Alex clung to him tighter.

I peered around at the office. It was small and the five of us were cramped against the desk. The rapid fire ceased. Heavy breaths and rustling seemed to echo in the room as I listened for movement in the other room. The sliding glass door opened, slow and nearly silent, and I pulled the pistol out from the back of my pants.

I cracked the door open, looking for Jackson. He came around the corner before I heard his footsteps.

"We're going," he said. "Now."

I hurried the kids from the room as a blood-curdling scream reached my ears from outside, followed by a screeching plea. I felt the color drain from my face. I could imagine whoever was out there begging for their lives on the promenade that weaved its way through the townhomes.

We stopped at the door and I reached for the kids' jackets. "Come on," I said, tossing Alex and Sophie theirs. I helped Thea slip into hers while Alex helped Beau. I hadn't realized there was anyone in the neighborhood left besides us. Now I wondered how many there actually were.

"I'll get the bags upstairs," Sophie said.

"No—" Jackson shook his head. "There's no time. Out. Now." He glanced out the front window again, then opened the door. He peered around the carport and down the walkway before he stepped back inside. "Get them in quietly," he told us, then looked at Alex. "Get ready to start the car—don't start it until the kids are in and you see Elle coming out, I don't want the gunmen to hear you too soon. Then, you drive."

"Drive where?" Sophie asked, voice frozen in a whisper.

Jackson looked from me to Alex. "Get on Turnbull Street, and follow it to the park at the edge of the city. Don't stop or turn back for anything. Park behind the ivy-covered fence. I'll meet you there."

I took a step toward him. "Jackson—"

"I'll keep an eye out back," he said. "Get them out," he told me. "One at a time. No noise and keep your heads down. These crazy fucks don't know we're here yet, let's keep it that way."

I nodded as Jackson headed toward the backyard again to keep watch.

Heart racing a million miles a second, I peered out the front door and edged my way out to see down both sides of the walkway. There were vehicles in the carport, but no one was rushing out, like we were. There was no movement.

Thea stifled a scream and Beau wrapped his arm around her.

With a nod of understanding, Alex went out first, timid but unwavering as he made his way a few spots down to the Pilot, and he opened the driver door as quietly as he could. He slid into the front seat, and closed his eyes as he slowly pulled the door shut after him, careful not to latch it too loudly.

Rapid fire rang out again, and a cacophony of men shouting filled the afternoon air. It echoed in the world silenced by layers of snow.

Sophie took Thea in her arms, burying her face in Sophie's neck and trying not to cry aloud for the lunatics to hear. I crouched down to Beau as he took Sophie's proffered hand and looked him in his gleaming blue eyes. "We'll be right behind you," I promised. "Make sure your sister is all right when you get inside, okay? You'll be fine, I promise. We're right behind you."

I had no idea if I could or should promise such a thing because I had no idea what was going on, but getting out of the complex was clearly paramount, and I wasn't going to question Jackson. I nodded to Sophie. "Go."

Quickly and quietly, she made her way to the car, her feet crunching in the snow as she took wide steps, Beau rushing to keep up. Once they were inside and all their heads were down, hidden from sight, I glanced behind me toward the kitchen. I didn't know if I should run for the car or wait for Jackson, but before I could decide he hurried toward me.

"They're lighting the buildings on fire," he said, "smoking people out."

My eyes widened.

"Get in the car and go. I'll meet you at the park."

I didn't want to leave him, but I saw the decidedness in his eyes. I saw the fear. "Go," he mouthed, and darted up the stairs, taking them two at a time. I wasn't sure what he was doing, but I had four terrified kids waiting for me.

Peering out into the cloudy afternoon, I could smell the smoke in the air. I knew in that moment that we would never be completely safe, ever again.

❄

Twenty minutes later, we sat on the curb in the alleyway on the far side of the park, hidden by the ivy wall. Alex had navigate the snowy, desolate streets well enough, and now we waited in suspended silence, watching the sky turn gray with smoke as the complex went up in flames ten blocks down. The gunfire had ceased, but there was no sign of Jackson yet.

"Where is he?" Sophie whispered from the back seat. "Shouldn't he be here by now?"

Thea began to whimper. "Is he dead?" she squeaked.

"No, he's not dead." He *could not* be dead. But the tightness of my throat and the dread riddling my voice said otherwise. What the hell had he gone back for? What could possibly have been so important? He hadn't been the most stable person since we'd met him, but he wasn't crazy. He wouldn't go out there after them, would he?

"What was that all about anyway?" Alex asked from beside me, his voice quiet as the horror settled in.

I wasn't sure of the answer, other than more crazy assholes terrorizing innocent people.

"There he is!" Beau shouted and pointed over the console as Jackson's charcoal gray Tacoma came around the corner.

There was a collective sigh, and tears filled my eyes as he got out of the truck, glancing furtively around as he lifted a rifle from the back and hurried over.

I climbed out of the car. "What were you doing? You scared the shit out of us."

He lifted the rifle. "Grabbing this and the maps."

"Now what are we going to do?" Sophie asked, opening the back door.

Jackson looked from her to me. "We're going shopping and getting the hell out of this city." He met Alex's gaze and offered him the rifle. "Do you know how to use one of these?"

Alex nodded. "Not a rifle specifically, but I can figure it out."

"Why?" I gulped. "Are they coming this way?"

Jackson shook his head. "We're going to the mall," he said and looked at me, clearly apprehensive. He handed Alex the gun. "Time for Gun Safety 101, the brief version."

21

JACKSON
DECEMBER 14

I was only half surprised to see a vacant parking lot when we arrived at the mall, though it didn't mean no one was inside. We parked the vehicles down the street so as not to bring too much attention to ourselves and made our way around the detached tire shop in the back.

"In and out," I told everyone, as we made our way around the main building's boxy exterior. I glanced over my shoulder at Elle bringing up the rear, her pistol in hand. While she seemed hesitant using it at the bus depot, she knew how to handle one, which was comforting. And her hesitation was understandable; I might've been worried if killing people came easy to her.

The mall was one story, the oldest one in the city, and definitely not the nicest or most popular, but we didn't want flashy, we wanted forgotten. At least, I hoped. The adrenaline still surged through me, like an electrical spark in a combustion chamber, and my heart hadn't stopped pounding since the house. There were at least five shooters, and they'd been out for blood. I wasn't going to take on five of them, half with semi-auto tactical rifles and a penchant for fire. And a very small part of me hoped they *would* eradicate every last crazy fuck that still breathed, though I knew there would be no hope in convincing them I wasn't one of them. The elderly woman I saw them shoot in the back of the head was proof of that. At least we were far enough away we couldn't smell smoke anymore, even if we could faintly see it billowing from the other side of the city.

I stopped at the corner of the building and peered at a snow-covered front lot. There were two cars, one in the middle, the other at the furthest end, and both were covered in several days' worth of snow. There were no new tire marks that I could see, which meant the place wouldn't be crawling with survivors or completely ransacked.

Waving on the others behind me, I headed around to the front. In less than a week the world had been ruined, and I'd seen enough blood and havoc to know whatever this world was coming to was only going to get worse as desperation spread. That's why we needed to stick together for the time being, and we all needed our own supplies. We couldn't be caught unprepared again.

I held my hand up outside the door of Pete's Pet Shop, a store-front just shy of the mall's main entrance. I peered through the window, cupping away the glare from what little sunlight peeked through the clouds.

The outline of cages was all I could see, so I hurried past the window and continued toward the main entrance.

"We have to go in," Beau said, and as I spun around to tell them to keep moving, he jiggled the door handle.

"Beau—" I bit out.

Elle reached for him and he glared at us both. "We have to go in—we have to let them out." He locked eyes with me, single-minded and resolved.

Alex tried the door again first, trying to kick the lock open with his foot. I wasn't about to shoot it open and draw unwanted attention, so I shook my head. "Let's keep going."

"There was a side door," Beau said, and he backtracked and disappeared around the building, out of sight. Elle looked at me, torn, and followed the others after him.

"Damn it," I muttered. Quickly scanning the road and side-walks for onlookers, I jogged after the rest of them, my jaw clenched. Now was not the time to wander off.

A side door hung open behind Elle as she stepped inside. Biting my tongue, I gripped my gun and scanned the room as I followed. I was about to remind them of my only rule, to do what I say when I say it, if they were going to stay with me. The last thing I needed was one of their deaths on my conscience. But my curses fell short when I saw Beau and Thea crouched down next to two rabbit cages. Both rabbits—one black and the other gray and white—were dead.

The darkened store smelled of feces and there was little noise given the twenty-by-twenty foot space. Cages lined the walls, but given the cold temperature of the room, the power had been out in the shop—probably the entire building—for a while.

"They starved to death," Beau said. With tears in his eyes and anger pinching his features, he stood and began opening every cage on the wall, animals dead or alive. Thea stared at him from her crouched position by the bunny cage, the rest of us also watching him as he became frantic.

"We have to let them out," he cried. When one of the mouse cages wouldn't stay open for the live ones to climb out, he began to cry.

"Hey, hey, hey," Elle said softly, grabbing a bungee cord off of one of the dead rabbit cages that held the water bottle in place. She tied the mouse door open for him. "We'll make sure they get free, okay?" She rested her gloved hand on his shoulder, and her green eyes were wide with promise. Even if Elle didn't think she knew what she was doing when it came to taking care of the kids, it came naturally to her.

Beau sniffled and stuck his hand into the mouse cage, wiping the tears from his eyes with his other hand as a tan mouse ran up his arm. Its tail curved for balance and it trotted up to his shoulder. With another sniffle, Beau cupped the mouse in his hand and set it on the floor to freedom, then did the same thing with the last mouse alive in another cage.

It was more heartbreaking than I'd expected; the rabbits had no food or water in their cages, yet the aisle beside me was lined with it. The feeder crickets were dead, and so were the iguanas on the top shelf with no heat lamp. The similarities weren't lost upon me. The world was stocked with surplus goods and supplies now, but staying alive long enough to use them would be the hard part. At least we had a fighting chance, the animals locked in buildings and cages around the world did not.

Though the store seemed empty, save for us, there were a half dozen aisles to be cleared, so I left the kids and Elle to mourn for the animals. I swept one aisle and then another, finding nothing more than cat and dog toys, bags of pet food, empty aquariums, some fish that needed food, and a row of chemicals and shampoos. There was little left we could do, and the looming list of supplies and food we needed to find, including a place to stay tonight, settled back into place.

I noticed movement against the far wall and a longhaired, gray cat jumped down from the top loft of its cage behind the glass wall of the cat kennel. It meowed when it saw me, and pawed at the glass.

"Beau," I called.

The pitter-patter of feet approached me and Thea grabbed my hand as she jumped cheerfully up and down. "Kitty!"

I stared down at her, surprised by the strength in her little fingers wrapped around mine.

Beau ran over, his eyes lit up. "She's alive!" he said, opening the door to the cat room.

"How do you know it's a she?" I asked, but all the kids filed into the back room after him. Beau's smile widened as Sophie opened the cage, allowing the cat to jump out. The cat purred and rubbed its gray body against Beau's leg with another meow. He reached down, more than happy to pet her.

Alex scooped a handful of kibble from a small bin and poured it on the floor at their feet.

I watched the kids through the glass, realizing it was the first time I'd seen any of them really smile. Strangely, it gave me a slight glimmer of hope.

Elle walked up beside me, a stack of slow release fish food capsules in her hands. She watched the kids with a softness that made her look younger, more innocent. "Thank God for that cat," she whispered. "It just made the day a bit more manageable." She sighed, and I watched the way her mouth curved up in the corner.

"I hate to be the bearer of bad news," I said, "but they can't keep her." Realistically speaking, anyway. We didn't even have a place for us to sleep tonight or know where we would be tomorrow, let alone have the capacity to carry around a cat and its food. "She'll be better off on her own."

Elle watched as Thea giggled at the cat rubbing up against her, and she sighed again. "Yeah, I know."

❄

The old mall was dark and some of the stores looked looted, but not as much as I'd expected. It was either forgotten about like I'd hoped, too far out of the city proper, or there weren't enough people left to care what it had to offer. Unexpectedly at ease, we headed straight for O'Riley's Rucksacks and Sporting Goods. The chances of it having been ransacked were nearly certain, if the boutique wine store was anything to go by, but the chances of gathering what we needed looked better by the minute.

Still, we kept to the shadows against the storefronts, checking the darkened windows as we went. Elle and the kids' footsteps followed quietly behind me.

The air was stagnant and chilly, but other than the scent of stale grease that clung to the cool air from the food court across from us, there was no foul, human smell, which put me even more at ease.

The music store was untouched, so was the Sunglass Hut. The cell phone and As Seen On TV kiosks in the center of the walkway were still covered, like everyone had closed up for the night, assuming the next day would be like any other. The cigar shop looked looted, so did the hair salon; they were small shops and easier to break into. Or maybe someone had just left in a hurry.

I knew we might potentially walk into the worst situation yet. But somehow, deep down, it felt like it was going to be okay and I pushed on. My gut hadn't steered me wrong before, and it wasn't the booze talking this time. So when I saw the rolled-up gate to O'Riley's, I held up my hand, hoping the five of them would listen this time and wait outside while I went in.

It was a large store, manageable, but dark, and I clicked my flashlight on as I examined the shadows. Boots and tennis shoes lined the furthest wall; a tent was displayed in the center of the room, fishing and camping gear on racks and shelves lined up beside it; guns and hunting gear were in a large display case to my left, and as I stepped closer, I noticed the case was open and the key in the door, though the cabinet wasn't empty. In fact, it looked like nothing had been touched.

I scanned the coats and sweatshirts on racks scattered across the rest of the store—camouflage, colorful sports jerseys, and North Face alike. Some of the clothing was discarded on the floor, but the place wasn't in shambles.

I wasn't sure which terrified me more, that there weren't enough survivors to raid the surplus of supplies they would absolutely *need* to survive the winter and protect themselves, or that there weren't enough *sane* people left to think of survival in the first place.

Moving closer to the gun counter, I nearly tripped on something sticking out from under a clothing rack. When the flashlight lit up a khaki-covered leg and a boot, I stepped around the carousal of down jackets, expecting to find a body, and froze. My heart dropped into my stomach. My gun lowered instinctively.

It was a family.

A dead man lay on the floor, russet-face grayed and mouth open with days' old vomit on the ground around him. His dark hair was longer and matted in areas like he hadn't showered in a while, but even through his dark scruff and gaunt cheeks, I recognized him. Calvin Ayala—Drago's human counterpart—was dead, and beside him, his wife was slumped against the wall, hugging an infant swaddled in pink-and-white striped fleece against her chest.

Calvin's rucksack was open and only half full of supplies.

They hadn't made it. I'd figured he and Drago had gotten separated amidst the confusion, but I hadn't thought about Calvin after that. He'd been on paternity leave; the week of the virus was his first week back.

The baby and the wife died first, I guessed. Otherwise they wouldn't be entombed in this place for all time. Calvin would've stayed with them, knowing he was going to die anyway and he likely welcomed it. I would have, anyway.

"Jackson." My name was a whisper in the still air.

Calvin and his family, Hannah and Molly, my dad, Elle's sister, the kids' parents, and maybe even Ross were all dead—good people who'd met horrific ends, while so many wicked survived. It wasn't fair, and it didn't make any sense.

I stared at the baby girl, grateful I couldn't see her, but my eyes burned and my chest ached all the same. I forced myself to swallow, to blink. I stared at the woman's solitaire wedding ring and thought of Hannah's—simple and classic. I didn't want to forget those things. I couldn't. And yet somehow it felt like I already was.

"Jackson?" Elle's voice was both a beacon and a blaring horn. Being with her and the kids was a distraction I'd begun to welcome, and yet it felt disloyal to begin letting go so quickly.

"Jackson," Elle said again, her voice soft and uncertain as she stopped beside me. I wasn't sure which had come first, the tears or Elle covering their bodies with a blanket, but even as their faces disappeared, I could see Molly in my arms and Hannah in the hospital bed, and I wasn't sure how I could've forgotten the chokingly bitter taste of misery.

22

ELLE
DECEMBER 14

After distractedly sweeping the rest of the sporting goods store, Jackson had left me, Sophie, Alex, and the children to fend for ourselves. He hadn't said a single word, but I knew it was probably for the best, for his sake, at least. I worried about him, and I wanted him to be okay, but the look on his face had been a desperate sorrow, and I knew there was nothing I could do or say that could mend that. I'd never seen a man look so stoically undone.

Having warned all the kids to steer clear of the gun counter, without mentioning the bodies covered beside it, they perused the store in search of fur hats and beaver mittens—clothes that would keep them warm in the coldest situations.

I, on the other hand, couldn't stop thinking about the family still hidden behind the coats and how gut-wrenching their final moments must have been. Had Jackson known them or had the sight of them hit too close to home? I couldn't move them or lay them to rest, so I had to stay focused.

I stared down at the six backpacks lined up on the ground in front of me; one for each of us, assuming Jackson wanted one. I wasn't sure he cared much about anything at the moment, but it was the least I could do.

Whatever our journey and wherever we were going next was going to be dangerous and cold. Windstorms, snow, and the unexpected were the only three things we could bank on moving forward, and we needed to be as prepared as we possibly could.

Hangers scraped against the racks, zippers whizzed up and down, and Sophie and Thea muttered as they looked for boots that were small enough to fit Thea's feet.

I leaned back on my heels, the thinly-padded floor unyielding against my knees, and took a mental note of the kids' backpacks: safety whistles with a built-in compass, hydro packs, fleece blankets, granola bars and an MRE, utility knives, headlamps, Chapstick, and travel toiletries. All the contents were evenly divided, and that was only half of what we still needed.

I set the rope, mini stove, butane, batteries, first aid kit, four additional MREs, and the matches aside for Jackson and I to carry. We had maps and ammo we'd have to carry too. Running my fingers through my hair, I tugged slightly on the ends like it might jostle thoughts loose, and I let out a deep breath. I was forgetting a dozen things, I just needed to take a step back and think.

This morning we'd planned out the next three days, now we were scrambling and off kilter. *I* felt off-kilter. Even if staying here the rest of the day was risky, it felt necessary. We had to land somewhere and had a trip to properly stock up for.

Jackson's heavy footsteps preceded him as he returned to the store and stopped outside the entrance. Without ceremony, he plopped down. I could only see his shoulder and the bottle in his hand. He was in no shape to go anywhere either.

Sophie and Thea came around a shoe aisle, a pair of small fur-lined boots in Thea's hands. She sat them by her pack as Sophie handed me two canisters of 36-hour survival candles. "Here you go."

I smiled, stunned. "I was thinking about grabbing these," I told her.

"Hopefully they'll help you sleep better." Her eyes were intent on mine, and she smiled sympathetically, almost knowingly, then tore open a pack of women's wool socks to divide up among our bags.

"Soph—do you think these fit him?" Alex asked as Beau shuffled toward us in his untied boots.

She crouched down in front of Beau as my mind spun a little. Had I been talking in my sleep again? How did Sophie know I wanted the candles, no, that I *needed* them to sleep better? Even though Dr. John had been further from my mind than ever before, there were other monsters that still crept closer when the world was still and my mind was quiet. I thought too much of Thomas and his final breath. I thought about the men in the bus depot and how differently things could have ended.

I peered over my shoulder at Jackson. He sat in the same position, his head back against the door frame, only he'd begun to rotate a liquor bottle beside him. Once again, the bottle looked mostly untouched, like he was battling with himself over how much he should drink.

Thea stopped beside me, looking at Jackson quizzically.

"He'll be okay," I told her, but I might've been lying. I didn't know Jackson much at all. He seemed strong, but it was what I couldn't see that worried me most. First impressions could be deceiving, if I was any example, something Jackson would eventually learn. He *would* know the truth about his father one day. It just couldn't be now, not when the kids and I needed him. I hated myself for thinking it, but I had no other choice.

"Maybe he needs a nap," Thea said through a yawn. Grabbing two thinly rolled blankets from beside the packs, she shuffled down the aisle toward him. I didn't have the heart to stop her as she waddled with a bundle under each arm. Her boots were a little too big, I noted, but they would have to do.

Tentatively, Thea stopped beside Jackson, staring at him briefly before she set the blankets on the ground and precariously scooted his bottle out of the way. Jackson looked at her, his prominent features shadowed in the unlit hall.

"It's a little scary out here," I heard her say, peering around the empty building. Ignoring her fear, Thea unrolled one of the blankets and draped it over Jackson, and then she unrolled one for herself and sat on the floor, leaning her back against him. Using the crook of his shoulder as a pillow, she pulled the blanket up to her chin and shut her eyes.

I wasn't sure how long Jackson stared down at the top of her head, a few breaths at least, before he finally wrapped his arm around her. Squeezing her closer, his shoulders began to heave.

DECEMBER 18
FOUR DAYS LATER

23

JACKSON
DECEMBER 18

The wind was blistering cold; it felt like -50F and seeped through each layer with a 40mph bite. It stung my sweat-dampened skin, and each step was a struggle through the endless field of 4-foot snow as we made our way toward the shack. The storm howled and whistled as we stepped into the trees, their spindly tops complaining against it.

All of us needed shelter, and I prayed the shack was still there.

I peered behind me through frozen lashes, beyond the veil of snow toward the Tacoma and Explorer I could no longer see in the thickening storm. We'd gotten a bigger vehicle, but that was the first mistake in a slew of many. The Explorer would be no good to us if the engine continued to overheat, so we'd left it behind, for now, and continued our trek in the middle of a blizzard, to the cabin we hoped was still standing on the fringe of the wilderness.

Sophie followed my footsteps as best she could, making each of my imprints her own. Elle came behind her in our single file line, Thea wrapped in her arms. Alex brought up the rear, the snow meeting his knees with every step, and Beau clung to me, growing heavier by the second. The windchill was numbing, and the packs on our backs might as well have been made of stone, weighing us down as we trudged through the tree line.

I'd been too busy worrying about ghosts and crazy people to have considered the possibility of freezing to death. But I could imagine it now. Winter was relentless and didn't care that the week had been fraught with one hurdle after another—food scavenging, finding safe shelter, snow drift road closures, car issues—the list went on. For all we knew, the shack—our final saving grace—was buried in ten feet of snow, untended and left to the elements since the squatters' removal two years ago. Or, maybe someone else had the same idea I did, and they might not take kindly to visitors.

Either way, there was no turning back now. The storm worsened, and I closed my eyes, imagining the map tucked inside of my pack and Copper Creek that snaked beyond the patch of pine trees jutting from the surrounding snow. We just had to make it another quarter mile. A few more steps . . . a dozen more heartbeats.

Beau gripped onto me tighter and my arms strained. It had been nearly forty-eight hours since we'd set off for the Yukon, and we had only gotten as far as Copper River Valley, somewhere around Chistochina, an unincorporated village only halfway to the Canadian border. Despite what happened next, we couldn't continue like this. Modern man hiking in the savage north without the proper equipment or know-how was suicide.

My muscles burned and ached with exhaustion as we stepped over a fallen trunk. I told myself everything would be okay; it was freezing but we were insulated well enough, even if the situation wasn't ideal. No one would die, even if it felt like we already were. I told myself we were close, that we just needed to get over the crest of the hill and the cabin would be right there, abandoned and worse for wear, but it would be there, and we would be fine.

We would be fine.

Glancing back, I took in three bobbing, hooded heads, slowly coming up the hill behind me.

They would be fine.

The trees groaned from above and snow clumps fell to the ground like falling bricks. Everything creaked—the scant branch canopy above, my bones brittle with cold.

When the frozen river came into view, my looping reassurances fell short. I scanned the bank, finding only pines, spruces, and an unending white. Was the cabin gone or had my navigation been off? Was it still a quarter mile north? My heart, pounding from exertion, dropped into my stomach.

"Is that it?" Sophie asked, her voice muffled by the wind. She pointed further downriver, to a thicket of leafless trees surrounding a shack no bigger than an en suite. I could barely see the rooftop, but it was all the fuel I needed.

My feet moved with renewed purpose as I schlepped down the hill. The snow crumbled beneath each step, but I barely noticed it. The exhaustion in my bones was only a distant ache. The numbness of my face would soon wear off.

We would be fine.

The time it took to get to the cabin felt painstakingly slow, even if our pace quickened. As all the possible scenarios of what might be awaiting us played through my head, each felt possible. Not even the most dire possibilities frightened me; they were more bothersome than anything, taking up space in my mind when I needed to find solutions instead. If I had to dig, I would dig. If we had to pull whatever dangers were inside the shack out, I would— if we couldn't get in and I had to attempt a snow cave, I would do that too.

As the cabin—a patchwork of wood and scraps of metal— came back into view through the trees, I noticed a small steel pipe chimney, and searched for a door. It was faintly outlined and half buried in snow, but it was there.

I set Beau down, unzipped the folding shovel from my pack, and dropped to my knees in front of the door. Elle plopped down beside me, wisps of her dark hair whipping around her face as she used her gloved hands to rake the snow away. Sophie and Alex did the same, Alex using the boiling pot for a scoop. Beau and Thea also scooped and dug until we had finally moved enough snow for me to be able to pull the slatted wood door open. It nearly fell off its hinge in the wind, and Elle grabbed hold of it as I peeked my head in.

I held up one hand to caution everyone, leaving the other on my gun as I stepped inside to be sure it was safe. The interior was dark, save for the fleeting dull light leaking in from the doorway and inconsistencies in the poorly constructed walls. It was a drafty, oversized shoebox, but it was empty, and the wooden chair and broken table would suffice as firewood for now.

I waved the others inside.

Heaves and sighs followed a bustling of footsteps and nylon arms and legs rubbing against each other as everyone crammed inside. "Come on—shut the door," Elle said breathily. The air was so still and suddenly quiet, it echoed every breath.

Sheet metal siding blocked most of the wind, and I opened the rusted wood-burning stove to find it was full of ash.

"I need matches," I said, forcing my fingers and legs to work in tandem as I broke the wooden legs off of the rickety old chair. "Thea—your coloring book." I nodded to her pack.

Sophie helped her wiggle out of it, and within seconds the pages were crumpled beneath the broken chair legs, and a burgeoning fire lit the room.

Crouched in front of it, I blew more life to the flame, urging the fire to catch faster and the smoke to clear. I silently pleaded the rusted chimney pipe would hold out as long as the storm, and I took my gloves off and held my hands up to the flames. I allowed the heat to seep into my bones as the fire grew. It was warm against my windburned skin, and my nose and fingertips began to thaw.

Sophie and Alex pulled their hoods back and took a deep breath for the first time, like they were coming up for air.

"Can everyone feel their fingers and toes?" Elle asked, and

when the four kids said no, I almost smiled. "Let me rephrase that," she said, still catching her breath as she peeled off her coat. "Does anyone have frostbite?"

The kids pulled off their gloves as they shivered in place; white puffs of air filled the room.

"No," Alex said, checking his hands and then the rest of them.

"Good, now put your gloves back on until this place warms up a little," she said, brushing the snow off Thea's hood and shoulders. Sophie did the same with Beau.

I blew more life to the fire as Elle glanced around the shack. "Thank God for this place," she muttered. "You were right."

Barely, I thought.

When the fire was roaring, I stood aside, waving them over to gather around it. "We'll stay here until the blizzard lets up," I told them. "Stay close to each other, though, and keep warm." I nodded to their blankets rolled up beneath their packs. Soon they'd be dripping with melting snow. "The fire will take the chill out of the air, but"—I stomped on the plywood floor—"it's not going to be a sauna or anything. Dry your blankets first, then we'll dry any wet clothes."

Shoulder to shoulder, the kids knelt around the stove with their hands so close to the cast iron I worried they might burn. Thea removed her gloves first, a smile tugging at her lips as she basked in the warmth.

"It's going to be like this all winter, isn't it?" Elle asked quietly as she stood beside me. She stared into the flame. It was as if she'd been telling herself once we got out of the city we'd be okay, and finally realized it wasn't that easy. "This really is our lives now."

I looked at her, seeing that silent fear in her green eyes I'd come to recognize.

"Yes," I told her. "For now. But soon you'll be in Hartley, and none of you will have to worry about this." It was a reminder to myself of the solitude that awaited me, and the structure and community these kids would have if they were ever going to feel normal again. "But you'll have to wait for spring."

Elle blinked from her haze and looked at me, incredulous. "Spring?"

"Unless we want this to be our reality for the next month, we need to find somewhere to hunker down and wait out the winter." I crouched down and fumbled with puffy, gloved fingers before pulling the map from my bag. "This is where we are," I told her as I unfolded it, rising to my feet. "Somewhere here, off Glenn Highway—still nearly five hundred miles from Whitehorse."

I looked into her eyes, waiting as the implications of continuing our journey to the border sank in.

Finally, Elle nodded. "Stay where, though?"

"I have an idea," I told her. "It's not going to be easy, but it will be better than this."

Without hesitation, Elle nodded again and pursed her lips. "Whatever you think," she whispered. "I just—" She glanced at the sat phone sticking out of my open pack. "I know you've been trying to meet up with your friend, Ross, and—"

"That has to wait," I told her. It was a constant battle to remind myself that he and I had made a backup plan, so I couldn't completely lose hope until spring. "He wouldn't travel in this, and I was stupid to try it."

"It's not like we could've stayed in the city," she said, tucking her hair behind her ears. It was wind ravaged and wild around her face. Even with chapped lips and rosy cheeks, Elle seemed to glow in the firelight. Maybe it was her forced optimism, or maybe it was the fact that she had four kids to worry about and didn't have the option of looking back, only to keep moving forward, but I admired her for that.

For me, it felt impossible for me to move forward most of the time. Everywhere I looked—at Elle, at little Thea, at the Glock I always carried, and my hands that stacked every stone—I saw Hannah and Molly and memories that kept me tied to the past.

"We have a choice now," I told her. "There's no one chasing us. We can find a temporary home or we can do our best to chug forward."

"We stay," she said easily. "We plan and bide our time."

I hadn't expected to feel relief in her words, but I did.

As I rested against the wall, a haunting, lonely howl pierced through the wind.

"The wolves are out," Beau whispered, barely above the wind. Collectively, we held our breath to listen. So far from civilization, madmen were the least of our concerns. Nature was queen of the wildlands, and we were unwelcome.

Ensuring my rifle was loaded, I rested it in the corner of the cabin, and with an exhausted sigh, I sat down beside it. Our problems would still be there after the fire went out and the snow let up. But with the wind buffered and the sting of the cold at bay, I allowed myself to revel in the comforting heat of the shack and the crackling fire. All of us hunkered down to wait and listen as the wolves cried in the distance.

PART II

MARCH

24

ELLE
MARCH 29

Thomas came at me—eyes red-rimmed and face sweating—in the muted light of the room. The inexplicable hatred in his eyes twisted my insides, and he grabbed at my neck. His finger-nails dug into my skin as I gasped and clawed at his hold.

He was too strong—I could feel my windpipe crushing in his grasp and the blood draining from my face.

This wasn't happening—I would not die, not like this. Not at the hands of a stranger, after everything else . . .

My fear turned to rage, which fueled the burn inside me just beneath my skin.

A fiery tempest ignited and swirled through me as I willed my body to obey, my arms to lift and grab hold of Thomas's neck.

Squeezing my eyes shut, I screamed. It was satisfying, and a power both fearsome and intoxicating surged through me.

I clutched his neck harder, feeling his heart beating in the palms of my hands.

I squeezed and squeezed to prove that I would survive—that I wasn't weak.

As the struggle left his body, I opened my eyes, and I gasped. The heat drained away, a corroding terror flooding me in its wake.

Jackson's hazel eyes stared lifelessly back at me, his face red and mouth agape. His body fell limply onto mine as I tried frantically to get free.

His skin was blue. His neck was singed with impressions from my fingertips, and burnt veins spread through his jaw and up his face like a toxic leak.

He was dead—Jackson was dead, and I had killed him.

My eyelids flew open. Sweat dampened my temples despite the cool air that filled the room. Inhaling a steadying breath, I sat up in bed and peered around the room. It was just as foreign as it was comforting—the paisley wallpaper and cluttered dresser and desk. A box of someone else's things lay on the carpeted floor. It was my temporary home and I was safe in a warm bed, but in a house that held a history I would never know.

The fire burned low in the fireplace, and the candle on my bedside had long since burned out. I opened the side table drawer to grab another, but all I felt was the soft leather of my calfskin gloves and the cold handle of my gun.

Flinging the comforter back, I shoved my sock-covered feet into my slippers, and reached for the robe draped over my bed.

It had been over four months since the outbreak. I no longer kept track of the actual days we'd been in Copper River Valley, more like how many nights the six of us had made it without freezing and how many days it had been since we'd seen other people—98 and 84.

Jackson had been right. Slana—our off-the-grid safe haven in a borough northeast of Anchorage—had been mostly untouched. During our semi-short stay, we learned just how scarce everything was and what it meant to travel the distance needed to retrieve it.

Scavenging trips had to be strategically planned so that we could beat the weather and preserve fuel. Simple tasks, like brushing teeth, going to the bathroom, and bathing weren't so simple without running water or electric heat. Everything was a process. Every outing or meal was preceded by a list of rules and processes never to be broken. Generators were an extravagance we only used when necessary or when the sound could be drowned out so not to attract attention. Sometimes candles and fires felt like the last two luxuries we would ever have, and even they were never guaranteed.

Opening the bedroom door, I peeked down the upstairs hall. Shadows from the living room fireplace danced in the stairwell, and a rush of cold kissed my face. The floor creaked as I made my way down the hallway, toward the stairs.

I stopped at the kids' room and opened the door to peek inside. Sophie was asleep in one bed, Alex, Beau, and a sprawled out Thea in the other beside it. Crammed together in one room, even if it was a four-bedroom house, was better than being apart. Safety in numbers had become our second nature—to always walk in pairs and never go outside alone or without a weapon, especially after dark. *Never* after dark. The wolves liked to linger in the woods, especially at night.

Shutting the door, I continued to make my way down the staircase as quietly as possible. I wasn't sure why Jackson slept in the living room instead of the comfort of one of the beds, but he never did. Even after Anchorage and the mall—after the shack and the journey to Slana—Jackson still felt separate from us. Maybe he didn't want to get too attached because we'd be parting ways in Whitehorse, after the snow melted. Or it could've been that deep down a part of him didn't trust me. And maybe he was right not to, even if the idea of him hating me plagued my thoughts each and every day.

I stopped at the final step and eyed Jackson. He stood in front of the fire, pulling a thermal shirt over his bare chest and painted arms. He was a curiosity to me, a mystery despite the months I'd known him.

"What do they mean?" I asked.

Jackson spun around, oblivious to my standing there, and his eyes met mine.

"The tattoos." They were Haida-looking creatures with curved edges and wide eyes; puzzled together in ancient black and red symbols of a heritage I knew little about. "I knew an old fisherman in Seward who had them on his hands and up his neck." I'd never learned his name. "He would sit on the pier every morning, drinking his tea from his canteen. He was almost always the first face I saw when I arrived back at port." I smiled remembering his wide, toothless smile and sparkling jade eyes. "He told me they're sacred markings and each image means something special to the person wearing them."

"Ah." Jackson peered down at his arm, like he could see the images through his long sleeves. "Moon is the protector and guardian of people on earth. It seemed fitting when I became a trooper." He tucked his dark, longish hair behind his ears and picked his dirty clothes off the ground.

I gripped the railing. "And the others?"

"Wolf is strength and Sun is peace," he said briskly over his shoulder. "They were my wife's idea."

"You never talk about her." I'd wanted to ask him about his life so many times I'd lost count, but it never seemed like the right time.

"I know." He draped his jeans and flannel over the back of the couch. "Did I wake you coming in? I tried to be quiet—"

"No," I said. "You didn't wake me." His wife was still off limits, which I understood. I didn't want to talk about my life before, especially with him. But a part of me desperately wanted to know something that would show me who he might've been before he became the person he was now, other than a quiet, brooding protector that lost himself in a bottle of bourbon on bad days and preferred seclusion the rest.

Jackson did chores and tasks around the property, mostly planning and prepping for our approaching departure, but his mind was always somewhere else. And, where did he go off to when he was on his own? I'd never followed his trail toward the mountains. Who was I to question him when there was plenty I didn't say myself? On *my* worst days, I worried he might wander off and never come back, making me uncomfortably grateful when he returned.

"Is everything okay?" he asked, staring at me.

I stood dumbly on the staircase. "Yeah—I was just getting more candles." I continued toward the hutch on the other side of the room. Sophie and Thea had been gathering them up for me, a kindness I appreciated more than they'd probably ever know.

I slid a few candlesticks into each of my robe pockets, enough to get me through a few more nights.

"Is it the dreams?" Jackson's voice was tentative.

"Is what the dreams?"

When I looked at him, he nodded to the tapers sticking out of my pockets.

"Among other things," I admitted. "It's pretty silly, huh? A grown woman needing a nightlight."

"No, not silly." He leaned forward, his elbows resting on his knees as he sat at the end of the sofa. It was a moderately sized living room that fit the six of us well enough—a couch, recliners, side and coffee tables—but it always felt smaller when it was just the two of us alone. "We all have our own ways of coping after everything that's happened."

"It used to just be things from my past," I told him and shook my head, baffled by how different things had become. "If Dr. Rothman could see me now," I muttered.

"Dr. Rothman?"

"My therapist. She used to tell me I let the past have too much control over me. It's like I barely remember the faces that haunted me before. It's more like the faces of—" I stopped myself from admitting the full truth. I was so close, and he was right there. I could've uttered a few more simple words, liberating me forever. But I didn't. "I just . . . don't like the darkness, I guess."

Jackson's eyes lingered on me like they sometimes did, but he didn't press me for an explanation. I could always see the questions though, playing in his hazel eyes—the uncertainties behind his permanently furrowed brow, riddled with apprehension. It was one of his few expressions I could read.

Jackson wanted to ask me more, and sometimes I wished he would because he deserved the truth. But it was a well-rehearsed dance between us, the closest thing to intimacy we shared. He would nudge me with a question that I would only half answer, and I would nudge him back with another; neither of us dared probe deeper, terrified of the outcome. It was an unspoken understanding, one of many.

I closed the drawer of the hutch and turned for the staircase. Jackson sat quietly as he stared down at the sat phone on the floor at his feet.

"Will you still stay in Whitehorse if you don't hear from him?"

He peered into the fire. "Yes."

Though I assumed as much, I hated to think about us parting ways in a few weeks. No matter how much I tried to prepare myself for it, I would miss him. "This place in Whitehorse," I started. "What makes you think it's even still there? You said it's been years since you went, and with all that's happened—"

"It has to be," he said stubbornly and scratched the side of his face. His beard was a few weeks unshaven.

"Can I ask why it's so important to you?" I couldn't help nudging the line of things we didn't discuss on nights that my mind was restless.

Reluctance was Jackson's other expression I knew all too well; the way his jaw clenched and he took a deep breath before offering a vague answer. "It's where my wife and I went on our honeymoon. It's really the only thing I have left of her at this point. A memory."

And there it was—the truth—awkward only because we usually went out of our way to avoid speaking about her.

"I understand." I'd assumed it was sentimental to him, otherwise why be so dead-set on going there instead of a safe zone that boasted community and protection, a place with other children, doctors, and people of skill and consequence. "I'm glad you'll have a small piece of her back then." Maybe it would give him the peace he'd been unable to find.

I continued to the stairs. "Night, Jackson."

"Night," he said, barely audible, followed by the sound of a screw top. I told myself his drinking would only worsen if he knew the truth, and then I hated myself even more.

ELLE
MARCH 30

My back and arms strained as I split the wood that had been drying under the tarp beside the house. It felt good to be active and always moving. It kept my mind busy and my energy spent to something I could control.

Swing. Thunk.

Swing. Thunk.

My goal was a half-heap before lunch. With longer days and increasingly better weather, we were able to get more done.

Swing. Thunk.

Swing. Thunk.

Day 99 was like all the rest. Sophie woke up before all of us, her nightmares preventing her from getting much sleep, even though she never wanted to talk about what they were. I'd snuck outside to watch the sunrise, before my run, wishing I still had my Nikon and equipment to snap a few shots. Then, I ran to take the edge off, grateful to have found a way to keep the heat coursing through my veins at bay.

I'd made a few failed attempts to discern whether anyone else felt the fire in their blood the way I did, but was met with inquisitive looks and the sickening feeling to leave it alone before someone started getting too curious about my ramblings.

Sophie remarked that she wished she were always warm, because she was sick of being freezing cold all the time.

Alex joked that he often got shocked when he touched me, and that it must've been my electric personality. And if he could laugh it off, that meant he was oblivious to what I could do, and I gave up prodding for inexplicable, fire-related abilities all together after that.

No one ever questioned my gloves, adopting the false reality I was just a quirky germaphobe, one of my many lingering issues from before the outbreak, and I didn't correct them. And while I wasn't necessarily at ease with what I could do, I was more comfortable controlling it. Plus, I had little choice.

There was so much we still didn't know about the virus, including the physical changes and levels of insanity left behind in the aftermath; for all I knew I was just a little crazy, like the other, less sane survivors.

After my morning run, the kids and I ate oatmeal and thawed frozen fruit, which Alex typically threw together. Alex was used to simplistic, creative meals after a childhood of relying on his street smarts to get by. For Sophie, whose father was a chef, cooking was too closely tethered to her past, which is why I think she spent more time with Jackson working on cars and at target practice than she spent with Alex in the kitchen. I was a useless klutz when it came to the kitchen, so I stuck to busy work around the property. I did the chores I didn't want the kids to do; and Jackson remained our handyman, resident prepper, and—for all intents and purposes —our teacher.

I straightened from the woodpile and wiped the back of my arm across my forehead, debating whether or not to remove my windbreaker in the thirty-two degree weather. I already looked strange enough, manically finding backbreaking work to do, so I decided running around in a t-shirt might reach too far out of everyone's comfort zone.

Blowing a loose strand of hair from my face, I peered around the snow-covered road that stretched through Slana, barren on both sides save for a sprinkling of trees and a few commercial buildings.

The town was barely a blip on a map, but Jackson had known about the ranger station a mile down the road, and that it wasn't a big enough community to garner any attention. I hadn't seen anyone else since we'd arrived, though Jackson had been less lucky during his multi-day excursions on the snowmobile into the nearest towns and cities.

Despite the occasional excursion, we had a lot of what we needed within a two-mile radius. A general store we pilfered as needed, a mechanic shop Jackson used as a daily workshop, a clinic we'd raided during our first week here, and the solar company Jackson planned to pillage before we left. And aside from our residence, there were only a handful of other houses scattered along the road. We'd chosen one a ways down, hoping anyone who happened to stop in would scour the most convenient places first.

"We got dinner!"

I whirled around with an armful of firewood as Alex lifted his backpack from a dozen yards away. White puffs of air surrounded him and Sophie as they trekked through the snow in their puffy coats and neck gaiters. Alex had one of Jackson's rifles slung over his shoulder, which was another one of the rules when they were around town.

"Dinner *and* lunch," Sophie added as they crunched closer through the snow. She pulled her gaiter down and under her chin. "Despite having eaten two hours ago."

Alex grinned, the evergreen flecks in his eyes bright in the sunlight. "What can I say, I'm hungry again."

"Me too," I added. "Starving, actually."

Although they walked side by side, both of them smiling,

Sophie's grin never reached her eyes like Alex's did. At first I'd thought it was grief that kept her a little distant, just like Jackson, but sometimes I wondered if her withdrawal was getting worse, along with the dreams.

"So," I said, brushing the wood chips off of my hands onto my pants. "How was the market, crowded?"

Alex shrugged. "Not too bad, I had to fight a lady for the last bag of tater tots though." Alex's smirk grew big and white, and even Sophie allowed herself a genuine smile.

"Is that what's on the menu?" My stomach rumbled imagining it. "Tater tots, with perhaps a sprinkle of salt?"

"That does sound delicious, but not tonight." Alex nudged Sophie. "She convinced me to make everyone's favorite."

My stomach rumbled even more excited. "Yum, spaghetti?"

He nodded. "With garlic bread and veggies. She's going to make her dad's special sauce."

I stacked an armful of wood. "Can we just skip lunch and have dinner?" I teased.

Everything was frozen, boxed, jarred, or bagged, so I got excited when they decided to go all out and make a meal as home-cooked as we could get.

"No," Alex said. "I need to thaw the elk meat." He lifted the bag again. "I better get to it."

"Let me know if you need any help," I said.

Alex chuckled as his footsteps crunched toward the house. "I think we're good. I'd like there to still be enough food for everyone by the time I'm finished."

"I stick my finger in the sauce *one* time and you'll never let me live it down," I grumbled and walked toward the firewood stack I'd started on the porch.

"Oh, wait." I straightened. "I thought the kids were with you." I looked at Sophie, her long blonde hair hanging around her shoulders. "Where are they?"

She shrugged. "With Jackson at the shop, I assume. We were

putting fuel stabilizer in the carriers when Alex said he was going to the store. I needed to pick up a couple things, so they stayed with him."

"You make more trips to the store than any of us," Alex said. "What could you possibly need so much of?" He nodded to her backpack.

"Tampons," she bit out, the way awkward teenagers do. "Would you like to see?" She lifted her pack.

His eyes widened and he hurried into the house.

Rolling her eyes, Sophie followed after him.

"I'll tell Jackson to wrap things up in time for lunch."

"Okay!" Alex called and Sophie closed the door to keep what little heat was in the house inside.

I circled back for another armful of wood. If Beau and Thea were with Jackson, it meant they would be covered in grease by the time they got back to the house. After stacking one more armful on the porch, confident I'd gotten a decent amount of energy out for the day, I trotted down the front steps and headed down the road to the mechanic shop.

I followed little footprints trailing behind bigger ones and smiled to myself. Even if Jackson wasn't very paternal, the kids liked him. Thea especially, who liked to ask him weekly if he was going with us to Hartley Bay, as if she thought he was going to change his mind.

Mixed among their trail, I noticed another set of prints in the snow and I paused mid-step. Animal prints—wolf prints, specifically. Jackson had pointed some out to me twice before. At first, I thought they were old, but that the prints were in the neighborhood at all was unnerving. Feeling a niggling unease, I jogged toward the shop. Jackson would calm me down by reassuring me they were old, then he'd chide me for not listening when he was teaching the kids about game tracking. He'd say I was completely overreacting, and I'd feel foolish and all would be well with the world. I hoped.

A couple minutes later, I skip-walked through the abandoned junkyard of cars next to the shop and walked in through the roll-up doors, stopping to catch my breath.

"Hey," I said, my footsteps echoing in the warehouse.

Jackson straightened from bending a piece of metal in a clamp, his nose red and icicles on his mustache. I tried not to smile as I glanced around for Beau and Thea. "Where are the kids?"

Jackson only stared back at me and if I wasn't mistaken, his eyes were too glassy for this time of day. He peered around. "They went to play. They're probably building a snowman or something."

"Or something?" I turned on my heels, scanning the snow-covered parking lot. "Jackson, I saw wolf prints out there." I peered out at the empty streets beyond the shop. Slana was a sprawling, wannabe town before, but it had become a vast desert of white, with hiding places and dark corners everywhere. There were no fences to keep things in or out, and no noise to scare predators away if they got curious or hungry enough.

"Thea!" I called, heart pounding in the onslaught of dread.

"They didn't just wander off," Jackson uttered behind me, but I called for the kids again, and when they didn't answer, I flung open the side door to the other side of the building. "Beau—" I stopped in the doorway. Beau and Thea were sitting on a felled tree trunk, staring into the distance. "Oh, good." I was about to sigh with relief, when I saw two wolves standing in the woods a couple yards from them.

"Wolves! Jackson—" I ran toward the wolves on instinct, my arms flailing, hands clapping as I shouted as loudly as I could to scare them away. Despite the potential for my plan to go terribly wrong, the wolves retreated deeper in to the trees.

"Thea, Beau—come here," I ordered, my eyes never leaving the tree line.

"Beau," I said, reaching for his hand as I pulled Thea against me and hurried back to the shop, their little legs struggling to keep up.

Jackson stood tall and formidable with his rifle, but it was too late. The wolves were already gone, no thanks to him.

When we were safely inside, I crouched down to look them in the eyes. "Never wander off on your own again," I told them. "Do you understand? You know how dangerous it is out here—how many bad people there are, and those wolves are hungry. Do you hear me?" I could finally see the fear registering in their wide eyes.

"Do you hear me?" I said more calmly.

Thea's lip trembled, and she nodded, then Beau dipped his chin, if a bit reluctantly. I pulled them both against me and squeezed them close.

"I don't think the wolves would've hurt them," Jackson said.

I jolted up and whipped around to face him. "Oh really? And that was a risk you were willing to take? Wild animals—pack animals that hunt—hanging around the kids. You don't think that's something we should be a little worried about?"

His lack of concern made my blood boil. "What the hell were you thinking, Jackson, letting them go off on their own like that? We've survived flesh hungry lunatics, a fucking virus that killed just about everyone else, so wolves are no big deal?"

When he said nothing, I took a step closer. "You're drunk aren't you?" Shaking my head, I took Thea and Beau's hands in mine. I already knew the answer. I could smell it on him and see the blur in his eyes, even if he thought he was an expert at hiding it.

"I'm not one of the kids, Elle. You don't get to scold me."

I didn't care if his voice was loud and angry. I glared back at him. "Then stop acting like a mopey teenager all the time."

"Hey!" he shouted. "I didn't ask for this." He pointed to the kids and then to me. "I didn't ask for *any* of it. I said we could travel together, I didn't say I would play house with you."

"Play house?" Unsolicited tears burned the backs of my eyes. "You're such an asshole."

"That's right, I am. I told you from the beginning I was no role model, and you still came, so screw your self-righteous bullshit."

I nodded, too livid to say anything else, and too wounded by how easily he could disregard us.

"Come on you guys," I whispered to the kids. It was all I could manage.

Thea and Beau looked up at me, then back at Jackson, but they didn't protest as we marched back to the house.

Before Anchorage, I'd never hoped for anything. I lived in an existence where life sucked and you did what you could to get through it with a scrap of sanity. Now, hope was like a drug I couldn't shake, and I needed to come to terms with reality, not what I hoped would happen.

I couldn't worry about the kids, myself, *and* Jackson on top of everything else. Once we got to the Yukon, we would go our own way without looking back, it would be for the best.

I repeated it over and over until I believed it was true.

26

JACKSON
MARCH 30

Months ago, I felt like a shit stain on God's boot heel and I'd wanted to die. Hell, I thought I *was* dying. But here I am.

The edge was a precarious place. If you paid too much attention to everything in front of you, you risked the view, but ignore the dangers and you could fall. If your intention was to fall, like me, the catch was whether or not you could.

I had my days, days where I couldn't imagine going any further, but there were better days when the void without Hannah and Ross, the memory of Molly, and even the knowledge that my dad was no longer breathing, could be tempered with a little help to dull the pain.

With Ross alive, it had felt like I had a purpose. Someone to wade through the fallout with; someone to commiserate and figure shit out with, after it all fell apart. Without him, I was alone, or at least I would be eventually, and it was a daily struggle to remember why being alive was considered lucky.

Especially when Thea looked at me. Her big brown eyes held a thousand questions and possibilities, and it was impossible not to wonder and imagine what could have been, even if I knew being stuck in the past was making everything worse. I didn't want to forget though. Why would I?

The longer it took for Ross to call me, the easier it was to assume the worst, even if a voice in the back of my mind kept telling me he was still alive. Ross had always had my back and I always had his—he didn't know how to fail at anything, which helped prevent me from a complete tailspin. But time was corrosive, and it was hard to find the smallest remnant of possibility amongst a minefield of shrapnel. It grew harder to breathe. Especially the longer I was with Elle and the kids, and all that I tried to keep close drifted further away.

Slogging down the abandoned road toward the house, with toes numb in my boots, I inhaled the harsh, cold air and peered into the utter darkness. There were no stars in the sky and gratefully there was no wind either. All I had were my thoughts and the sound of my shoes crunching in the snow.

Arctic nights had a scent: the sharpness of evergreen and a freshness so pure and indescribable, it numbed the inside of your nose and lungs with each inhale. I'd come to appreciate it while the others slept, a routine I'd fallen into each night. A walk—or trudge in some cases—and occasionally a half-bottle of whiskey.

There was a reason I hadn't taken a drink in eight years, until the night I did. But I never wanted to think about that night again. And yet, that's the thing about haunting memories, they were like shadows; they moved around, impeding your view. Other times, light warmed the dark places and basking in it felt like a betrayal. Elle, Alex, Sophie, Beau, and Thea were not part of my life before and the memories I cherished, they were part of the reality, and it felt wrong.

Tonight, my bottle remained heavy and untouched. I resented Elle for making me feel guilty when I'd promised her nothing.

I stopped in the driveway and peered up at the house. I sometimes wondered about the family who'd lived in it. They weren't here when we'd arrived, but all of their things were—two kids and a father, from what I could gather. Had they built their home in a conventional neighborhood, it would look like any other house with windows and doors weathered by time. But in Slana, with only a handful of houses scattered across acres of woods, it stood out from all the rest. Five hearts beat inside—people I'd known for only a fraction of time compared to those who were gone forever; strangers in the grand scheme of things. And yet I was with them.

Shaking my head, I walked to the back porch. When my mind was clear, it wandered, asking questions I couldn't answer. Were we alive because of our genetic makeup? Was it pure luck? Or was it some form of twisted fate that two siblings survived when none of the rest of us had family left? Were those who died the lucky ones, or were we? If Hannah had survived, would she be like me, or like the woman at the outpost who'd lost her mind and lived off human flesh? Nothing was certain, everything felt wrong, and I was tired of feeling lost.

One of the wolves howled off in the distance, and as I opened the backdoor another howled back in answer. I peered behind me, out at the mountains surrounding us. Packs hunted together; they protected one another. I couldn't protect my wife and child, so how would Elle and the kids be any different? I didn't want the responsibility, and as hell-bent as I was to drink the bottle in my hand to prove it, I hadn't taken a single sip.

The floor creaked as I made my way through the house; through the kitchen that rumbled with voices when everyone was in there together, into the living room where everyone nestled in and kept busy in the evenings until bedtime—everyone but me.

We'd been preparing to leave since we arrived, knowing the day would come when the snow would stop falling and the ice would melt. I could leave tomorrow and Elle and the kids would have what they needed to stay here a while longer, and what they'd need for their journey to British Columbia. The Explorer was running again, and they would be okay without me.

I lifted my rifle strap over my head and leaned my gun against the mantle. I didn't bother lighting a fire or taking off my boots and jacket as I sat down on the sofa in the darkness. If I was lucky, I might get a couple hours of sleep, but I doubted it.

Sometimes Hannah was in my dreams. Sometimes I saw Molly and got to hold her in my arms again, chubby cheeks rosy with life. Other times I was burying them in the cold, hard ground. Every dream ended with an aching loss, but I would awaken to a house teeming with life. Like grief, sometimes it overwhelmed the senses.

I closed my eyes, imagining a life where I slept in silence and woke up to it, too. If I left, Beau would wonder where I was when he came downstairs to help me with my morning call to Ross, which would inevitably go unanswered. Sophie might make an entire pot of coffee, not realizing I wasn't here to drink most of it.

What had I been thinking, letting the kids play with wolves? I had been so certain they were fine, and it was beyond careless. Elle wasn't just furious with me, she was disappointed. But along with fury and disappointment, her green eyes had glistened with fear, and I hated that it was because of me.

I scrubbed my hands over my face, wanting to laugh at the irony. Every reason I needed to go my own way was exactly why I wanted to stay, and I had hours yet to think about it.

27

ELLE
MARCH 31

I relied on the sharp sting of morning air in my lungs and the chill it left in its wake to keep me going. It wasn't just a salve that soothed the fire, but a welcomed burn in my muscles that made them ache with exhaustion; I felt like at least one thing might still be in my control.

"Life's harsh, Eleanor," Jenny used to tell me. *"Hoping and wishing are pointless. Suck it up and do something instead."* That was the last thing she said to me before she ran away ten years ago.

In my youth, I thought her *advice* was simple cruelty, and yet those same heartless words continued to pop into my head, and I wished she were here to say them again. To help me feel stronger in each moment of weakness.

I pushed harder through the snow, running until my thighs and chest screamed for me to stop and I felt the fire subside. But I wasn't running only for temporary relief; I ran for clarity. I ran to expel the gnawing uncertainty of what the next twenty-four hours would bring.

I hadn't seen Jackson when I woke, but that wasn't entirely unusual. I wouldn't be surprised if he left in the middle of the night, though, either. He wasn't a man of many words, and it would've been easier for him to leave that way.

My eyes watered from the cold and the house came blurrily into view. Out here in the remote villages there was nothing. There was no help if we needed it, but no lunatics either. At least none that had found us yet. Slana's seclusion and proximity to our final destination was why Jackson chose to make it a temporary home.

House, I corrected. It wasn't a home, and we weren't a family, at least not one that included Jackson. Imagining my life without the kids seemed impossible, after only four months. For Jackson, I knew it was different. As much as I wished things were the way I wanted them to be—neatly wrapped and packaged with a post-apocalyptic bow—they weren't, and Jackson didn't owe us anything; he'd promised us nothing and yet he'd done so much.

It wasn't Jackson I was disappointed in, despite what I told myself. I just wanted a partner in all of this. An equal and friend to help me manage this new life with four kids so I wasn't in it alone.

Suck it up. Jenny's voice was still clear as day.

I slowed as I made it to the front porch, stopping just shy of it. My chest was so tight from exertion and cold, I had to drag in every breath just to fill my lungs. Hands on my hips, I paced the driveway and took stock of what felt like a single spark inside me. It was nice to feel more in control. I considered experimenting with it, but what if I couldn't stop? What if exploring it unraveled what little control I had over it—the control I worked so hard to manage? I imagined the floodgates opening, the potential of what would follow scared me most of all.

I turned on my heel and nearly walked into Jackson. "Geez—"

"Sorry," he grumbled and fiddled with a case of batteries in his hand. I hadn't heard the crunch of his footsteps in the snow with my heartbeat racing in my ears. "I wanted to catch you before you went inside."

I wiped my brow with the back of my hand.

"About yesterday," he said, looking up at me. His eyes were warm pools of uncertainty and sincerity.

"No, Jackson. You were right, you didn't ask for any of this—"

"Neither did you."

His words surprised me. "You're right," I said quietly. "But it's different for me. I want to help them, and I—I know it's not your problem."

"Elle, will you stop pretending you don't think I'm an asshole for a minute so I can say something?"

"I don't think you're an asshole," I said, pulling in another breath. I brushed the loose tendrils of hair from my face. "You've already done so much . . ." I shook my head, glancing everywhere but at him.

"Elle." His voice was more commanding than I expected and forced me to look at him. "I didn't mean what I said yesterday. Whatever shit I'm dealing with doesn't give me a free pass to be a dickhead. I don't mind watching the kids."

I nodded, uncertain if this was an apology or something more.

He dropped his hands at his sides. "I was going to leave last night," he admitted.

"Oh?" Blinking, I stared at him. That he'd actually considered leaving didn't surprise me but it did make me sad. "Why didn't you?"

He shrugged. "Because I'll have the rest of my life to be miserable and alone. I can hold out a couple more weeks until you guys head for Hartley." The chestnut and green flecks in his eyes were so crisp in the sunlight they reminded me of the rich hues of the forest reflected on a still lake in summertime. "I wanted you to know I'm sorry, and I won't be drunk like that again." His brow crinkled like usual, and he looked down at his hands. They were rough and battered and stained. No one could ever fault him for not pulling his weight and giving it his all, even if emotionally he was a mess. "Believe it or not, I wasn't always like this."

"I believe it," I said easily. "There are a lot of things I didn't use to be either." A liar was one.

His eyes met mine, and a silent understanding passed between us.

I was grateful he'd stayed, and relieved to know he wasn't so different from the guy I thought I saw in him, even if that would only make things harder in the end. I had a partner again, for now.

"I left you coffee," he said, and the tension between us dissipated in the brisk morning air. "It's getting cold."

"Buttering me up, huh?" I smirked.

Jackson's mouth quirked in an almost-smile, which I didn't get to see often enough.

He nodded to the mechanic shop. "I'll be loading things on the trailer, if you need anything."

I nodded and shoved my hands in my back pockets as I watched him walk down the road. He was wearing clean pants and a jacket I hadn't seen before, one that wasn't covered in grease. Before hope could weasel its way into my thoughts, I headed into the house. I just needed to let things be as they were without over-thinking it. And I was resolved to do so.

Walking through the door, I stopped in the entry and smiled again. The whiskey bottle beside the couch was full, and my heart swelled more than it should have. Maybe things would be different. And just maybe, he would decide to stay.

APRIL

28

ELLE

APRIL 8

Our routines had become less rigorous as spring set in. We no longer raced against days with limited sun, and there was an unexpected excitement in the air. In a matter of days, we'd head to Hartley, where there were other survivors like us. And, unlike myself who always hated birthdays, Alex was a different story.

He'd been keeping track of every day in the beginning, waiting for his eighteenth birthday so he could be his own man, exiting a system he never asked to be in to begin with. But the longer the power remained off and law and order went ungoverned, his excitement to turn eighteen waned, openly at least. Alex no longer had to worry about the foster care system or what freedom would look like, he already had it, in a manner of speaking, anyway.

I'd been tracking his birthday ever since. Just because I wasn't a fan of mine, didn't mean we couldn't celebrate his.

"What are y-am-es?" Thea stared at a can further down the aisle.

I dropped the last three cans of pink salmon into my bag to add to our trip inventory. I wanted to make sure we had enough food to last us a few months if possible, since life in Hartley was a giant question mark.

"It's *yams,* stupid," Beau corrected.

"Hey." I nudged him. "Give the girl a break, would you? She's learning how to read." From time to time, Beau forgot he was three years older than her.

"Yams are like potatoes," I explained. "But they're sweet."

"Like candy?" Thea chirped.

Beau rolled his eyes, but I didn't take it personally. "I'll get the crackers," he grumbled and went down another aisle to mope. Nine was an age of impatience and confusion, I realized, or maybe it was just Beau adjusting to all he'd been through.

"Yummy." Thea eyed the purple label. "Can we have *these* for dinner? They would be good with our casserole," she explained.

"Would they now?" I chuckled. "Okay, put two cans in your bag."

She dropped the cans in with an oomph, weighing her bag down quickly so that it just brushed the floor.

"Beau," I called, peering over the shelf into the other aisle. His blonde head hovered by the cookies. "Grab Oreos for Alex, would you? The doubled-stuffed kind. We'll give them to him with his present." I couldn't let Alex's eighteenth birthday come and go without celebrating it. We still had a couple days, but I'd been preparing for it for nearly a month. It was the perfect excuse for everyone to focus on something other than packing and what was to come. Plus, it was time to have a little fun.

"Okay," he grumbled. Beau didn't do well when he wasn't busy with purpose, like the rest of us, and with Alex, Sophie, and Jackson working on the snowmobiles to take to Whitehorse, he was stuck with me and Thea.

The three of us continued our perusal of the market, each with a list of items to fill our bags with. It was a mundane task, but a necessary one, and it passed quickly. The market was neither large nor fully stocked, not like a grocery store would be, but it had fed us well over the past few months and I'd stocked up plenty of the necessities, should something unexpected happen.

"Do you think he'll like his beanie?" Thea asked, dropping a package of gum into her bag. She looked up, found me watching her, and grinned.

"You can have gum," I told her. "Just don't get it in your hair or we'll have to cut it off."

Her eyes widened, big, round, and brown like saucers.

"Would you like it if Alex made you a gift?" I tugged gently on one of her braids.

She nodded.

"Then I think he'll love the gift you made him, too." We'd tried our hand at crocheting, and while it was a work-in-progress, it would serve its purpose and keep Alex's head warm. "Go grab a package of toilet paper to take back with us, okay? Then we're heading out."

Thea skipped down the aisle happily and disappeared around the corner. One saving grace in so much change was the cost of living. It was low and there were never any checkout lines. I would have needed a second job just to buy enough TP and paper towels for a family of six before the outbreak. And more time in the day to shop for it.

I made my way down the shampoo aisle and plopped a few bottles into my bag. Plumbing, on the other hand, had proven less convenient. The lack of electricity and frozen water pipes had become a major issue, making hot showers a thing of the past. No one wanted to bathe in cold water when it was already freezing outside, except maybe me sometimes. A lukewarm birdbath was all we could manage on most days.

"Come on, you two. Let's head back before the sun sets." It grew exponentially colder as the sun dropped behind the horizon, and the wolves had been coming out earlier—howling throughout the night. Whether it was because of spring or the scent of children, their nightly howling contest became more incessant, making me uneasy.

Beau made his way past me and out the door, his canvas bag full and heavy over his shoulder. "Set your bags on the sled. We'll pull them back to the house."

While the Explorer would've come in handy for our two-mile trip, I took every opportunity I could to keep moving and save fuel. The kids seemed to have an endless well of energy like I did, so I used them as an excuse to go for as many walks as possible.

I dropped chocolates and marshmallows into my bag at the last minute, assuming s'mores would do in place of a birthday cake since we didn't use the oven, then I shut the door to keep the weather and animals out in our absence.

The distant sound of snowmobiles caught my ear, and, shielding my eyes with the cup of my hand, I peered down the highway. Had both snowmobiles not been completely white, I would've been apprehensive, but I recognized Jackson's height and Alex's mohawk helmet immediately.

"Looks like they're working!" Beau practically jumped with excitement as they drove closer. Snowmobiles were somewhat of a surplus supply in these parts, a necessity for winter travel, yet finding ones that actually worked proved more difficult.

"Maybe they'll take you for a ride now that they're working again."

"That's okay, I need to pull this for you girls."

"Oh, really?" I asked, more than happy to have him do all the work if that's what he wanted. "You don't think Thea and I can handle it?"

Beau shrugged. "Jackson wanted me to be helpful," he drawled.

Alex and Jackson slowed the snowmobiles as they pulled into the parking lot, winding them down a few yards in front of us.

"We got you something," Thea sang, looking at Alex conspiratorially.

Alex removed his helmet. "You did? What for?"

"Your birthday, silly." She giggled.

"Will I like it?"

"Yes!" she chirped with an enthusiastic nod.

Alex winked at her then looked at me. "We're going to take the machines for a spin and get some target practice in before the sun sets."

"Really?" Beau yipped. "Aw, can I come? Please?" Beau looked at me, but I deferred to Jackson. He was the one who'd issued the help-the-girls order.

Thea skipped up to Jackson and opened her bag to show him Alex's surprise Oreos. "Yum. That's the good stuff," he said.

She put her finger to her lips.

"If Jackson says it's okay to go, Beau, then it's fine with me."

He ran over to Jackson, who was hulking compared to Alex's thin frame on the snowmobile beside him. "Can I come with you?" Beau asked. "Please?"

Jackson looked at me askance, and I gave him a consenting nod. "He was very helpful today," I assured him.

"All right bud. Put this on first . . ."

"Do you guys want to come?" Alex asked, glancing at me and Thea. "We can come back for the food. That way you can get some shooting practice in."

"Are you kidding, Elle's a better shot than all of us." Jackson winked at me.

"Ha, that's a lie. But I'm okay for now. What about Sophie? I thought she was with you guys."

Alex couldn't hide the downcast expression that washed over him, but he tried to shrug it off. "She said she had stuff to do."

"When people get secretive around birthdays, it's best not to ask too many questions," I told him. I wasn't sure if that was Sophie's excuse, but I thought it might make him feel a little better.

He smiled, but it wasn't real, not the heart-stopping smile I knew he had in him.

"Okay, well you boys have fun. Hit all the targets and be safe."

"But I want to go too," Thea whined.

"Yeah, you need to work on your aim," Beau said, climbing on the back of the snowmobile.

"Nuh-uh!" Thea taunted.

"Yeah-huh—" Beau froze when a snowball hit him in the helmet.

"See," Thea taunted. "I'm a better aim than you."

Beau swung his leg over and climbed off the snowmobile, breaking into a run after his sister. She shrieked and threw a wad of snow at him, hitting him in the shoulder, and he stumbled back.

"Oh, damn!" Alex hooted as they went at it, the two of them throwing half formed balls of snow at each other. Within seconds, Alex joined in, the three of them having an all-out snowball war.

Thea ran toward me and I began to back away. She ran behind my legs, her head butting into my backside as she tried to shield herself. "Hey—don't bring me into this!" I shrieked, and moved out of the way too late. Snow hit me in the leg and I spewed empty threats as the kids ran the opposite direction.

Jackson climbed off his snowmobile and came to stand beside me, both of us amused as we watched the kids play like normal kids used to. "So much for target practice," he mused.

"What do you mean? They're practicing as we speak."

Jackson glanced at me, then out at the kids. "Whatever you say."

I gave him a nudge. "Trust me, this is more important right now," I told him. I swooped down and grabbed a handful of snow.

"Don't throw that at me," he warned. "I'm serious."

"Yeah?" I took a few steps away, putting plenty of distance between us.

"I'm a really good aim," he answered. "Seriously. You'll regret it."

Even if I did regret it, it would be worth it to see Jackson actually smile. Balling the wad of snow in my hand, I chuckled as he shook his head in warning.

"Don't do it, Elle."

Eagerly, I tossed it at him, hitting him directly in the face.

My hand flew to my mouth as the snow fell in chunks from his beard. "I swear, I was aiming for your chest."

The longer his head continued to shake the more nervous I became.

"Jackson—I didn't mean to hit you in the face."

"That's what they all say," he said and crouched down to grab a handful of snow. "I'm glad your shooting aim isn't as bad as your throwing arm," he jested.

And with a rumble of laughter in his chest, Jackson threw a snowball right at my stomach and the game was officially on.

29

JACKSON

APRIL 9

"This is Huck Fulton from Hartley Bay for the daily broadcast." Fulton's voice was lower than usual and seemingly deflated, but still grating over the radio against my pounding headache.

"It's been a few days since our last broadcast, due to radio transmission issues. Having since found a cache of military radios, we're back to broadcasting. That being said, are there any electrical engineers out there interested in joining us?" He laughed, though it sounded more brittle than amused. "Today, I'm happy to report that we haven't seen outsiders in nearly two weeks, which is fortunate . . . and troublesome. We're still in need of another doctor after the militants robbed our scavenging party just outside our walls three months ago. We lost Doc Chin in the raid. Without giving too much away, we learned our lesson and we've become more strategic; it's been quiet, though, ever since. As always, I urge survivors to come this way, especially if you have any medical skills. We're nearly a hundred strong and could use your help. We have weapons and plenty of food, and in the months since the outbreak, we've been able to find a semblance of community and a new normalcy within our walls."

I glanced up from my maps of Canada fanned out across the table to Sophie. She sat on the couch, listening intently to the broadcast. I wasn't sure why, but she seemed less eager to go to Hartley the closer the time came to leaving.

Alex sat with Beau on the floor, staring at the radio as well.

"As long as you're willing to pitch in, we'll find a place for you," Huck Fulton continued, then he rattled off their coordinates as he always did.

"Who wants snacks?" Sophie asked, uncurling from the couch.

Thea jumped up from her book organizing on the rug in front of the heater. "I want the circus cookies."

"Come and get them then." The two of them disappeared down the hall.

Alex and Beau were oblivious to snacks as they cleaned the rifle I'd lent Alex for target practice the day before. His thoroughness and attention to detail made me proud, and while Elle was capable of protecting them, it never hurt to have someone to share the burden with, especially once I was gone.

I took a gulp of water from my thermos. Being cooped up indoors during a whiteout was different when you were stone-cold sober; everything was borderline distracting, and the heater was turned up so high, I thought I might melt, but I wouldn't say anything. It was an extravagance for the kids, one they rarely enjoyed.

I angled the lamplight on the card table and zeroed in on my maps as the clan stirred around me. Focus was something I was fairly good at, I was just out of practice.

"Don't tell Elle I gave you cookies, Thea," Sophie said as they walked back into the living room.

"I heard my name," Elle shouted from her room upstairs, and Thea's eyes widened.

Shoving another cookie into her mouth to get rid of the evidence, Thea wiped her hands on her pants, checking for crumbs before she grabbed one of our Alaska survival books and flipped through the pages.

"Here," Sophie said, handing me some jerky. The circles under her eyes were darker than usual, her demeanor more withdrawn.

I reached for the jerky. "Thanks—"

She bypassed me and set the rest on the table, her eyes shifting away from mine just as quickly. "Sure."

I must've looked more haggard and harried than I thought if I was scaring the kids now.

"What are those?" she asked, pointing to the dots on the map.

"More squatter shacks, in case we need them."

She looked at me, incredulous. "I thought we were waiting for spring so we don't have to worry about hiding out? It's only a day's drive."

"A lot can happen in a day," I explained. "You know that."

I didn't have a good feeling about leaving Slana; it was a combination of a lot of things. I didn't know what I would find in Whitehorse, or if I'd meet up with Ross again. And Hartley Bay claimed to be safe, but they'd had enough hiccups outside their walls to make me wonder what their definition of safety was and how, exactly, they could guarantee something like that.

"Which route are we taking?" Sophie pointed to two different paths.

"I haven't decided."

She sat down in the chair next to me. She'd been eager to learn more about cars and how things worked, so her interest didn't surprise me, even if I was still trying to figure her out. Beau and Thea were easy—kids who bickered, asked a lot of questions, and had a hard time sitting still. Alex was equally straightforward with his street smarts and innate will to survive. Elle was a mama bear when it came to the kids, even if she was still trying to figure out her place with them; they'd pretty much become her life now. But Sophie was struggling, and while I was struggling too and could understand why she would be, I wasn't exactly sure *what* she was struggling with. The loss of her family? All the horrors she'd seen? Did she not feel like she was part of the team? Every time Elle or Alex tried to talk to her, she brushed them off. Whatever it was, I worried about the toll it was taking on her.

"Want me to help you decide then?" She leaned onto the table, studying the map closely.

"Sure." I sat back, arms crossed over my chest. "A straightforward route on the highway would be fastest, but it would also expose us and everything we're hauling with us—the trailer and supplies, food, a snowmobile, that sort of thing."

Her gaze shifted from the map to me. "You're worried about other survivors stealing from us?"

I nodded. "Or worse. We're not the only survivors with a plan like this, either, at least it's not likely. Especially with the announcements continuously circulating about Hartley. People will be heading there, especially with the weather changing."

"And the other route, it follows the river?"

"I figure it'll keep us off the roads. We'd need to get more snowmobiles, though. We'd be close to a water source—"

"But have to brave the elements," she finished for me.

"Yes, hence the squatter shacks. The weather is getting better, but it's still Alaska, so nothing's certain."

"And the wolves have been out in force," she added.

"And that." I scrubbed my beard and sighed. "Like I said, I haven't decided."

Sophie stared at the map, her gaze tracing the curves of the river. "It seems so easy on paper."

"It sure does," I mused, eyeing the journal her hand rested upon. "You look like you've been doing some planning of your own."

Sophie blushed and picked up her journal. "My favorite subject in school was biology—well, science in general. When you were telling us about beard lichen and where to find it, I was thinking I should write that kind of stuff down—for when you're not around anymore, I mean."

She'd been listening more than I thought she was, and it made me feel a little bit better about separating in Whitehorse.

She opened her journal and showed me a sketch of a spruce branch draped with lichen. "I wrote down all the things you said we can use it for."

Versatile: Dye, deodorant, toothpaste, salves. Her notes were written in big round letters across the bottom of the page.

"Does it look right?" The sketch was long and stringy, just like an old man's beard. "I know all lichen looks similar, but I figure I should be as specific as I can, in case Elle or someone else needs to reference it, they'll know what they're looking at."

"I think it's great." I was actually awed by how much work she was putting into her journal. "And all this time, I thought you'd been writing about boys. You have your own survival guide in here."

Sophie closed her journal. "How do you know all this stuff anyway? I mean, is it all from your job or . . ."

"My mom," I told her. "A lot of it is at least. She taught me about nature and the ways of her people before she died. They used to live off the land, so it was all second-nature to her."

"And you remember it all?"

"No. But it helps that I've had to use some of the knowledge she gave me over the years through my work. There are things I've forgotten, but there's a lot that's stuck with me, too."

The stairs creaked as Elle came down, something draped over her shoulder. "Finished," she sang victoriously.

"With what?" Thea sprang up from the floor.

Elle grinned, pleased with herself, and held out a net of black string. "It's for fishing, catching, trapping, strapping, lugging . . ." She appraised one of the knots more closely and shrugged. "Not too shabby for my first time."

"I was wondering what you were doing up there." I pushed my chair out to stand. "May I?"

With a nod, Elle handed me her pride and joy. The net was taut and lightweight, perfect to put in one of our packs in case of an emergency. "This is great." I handed it back to her.

"I want to make one!" Thea chirped, jumping in place as she craned her neck back, peering up at us. "Please?"

"Sure you can." The corner of Elle's mouth lifted, along with an amused eyebrow. "You can use my pile of practice knots to see what not to do." She tickled Thea's neck, making her giggle.

Elle winked and handed her the net.

I liked it when Elle winked. It reminded me that not everything was always so bad, which I forgot sometimes. It was that forced optimism she had that I'd grown to appreciate.

"I want to see," Beau said, plodding over. He gave the net a once over and nodded in approval. "It looks pretty good," he said. "You definitely got better at it."

Elle pushed his shoulder playful. "Thanks, bud. It was a lot of effort. You left me high and dry up there."

"I needed to help Alex clean the rifle."

She brushed Beau's blonde hair from his face. "It's sort of a one person job anyway." Her stomach rumbled, and Thea giggled again. "I guess I'm starving," she said. "Anyone else want lunch?" Elle glanced around the room.

"Yep!" Thea shouted and zoomed past me, practically pushing me out of the way. I backed up, knocking into Sophie.

"Shit. Sorry—" I reached for her arm as she lost her balance, but when I touched her, she shrank away. Immediately, I let go. Sophie took a faltering step back and her wide eyes shimmered.

"Did I hurt you?" I asked, worried I'd grabbed her too tightly.

Her cheeks reddened and her gaze darted toward the stairs.

"Soph?"

She took another step back. "Yeah, I'm fine." She looked

fearful and brokenhearted at once, and a concerning ache filled my heart. "Just, please, don't touch me."

I nodded, uncertain what else to do, and she hurried up the stairs, to her room. When the door clicked shut, I fell back into my seat, my heart thudding and my hands clenching. I'd seen that cowering look from other woman a few times before.

For the first time, I was grateful so many people were dead; the chances were good if someone had hurt her, that bastard was one of them.

30

JACKSON
APRIL 10

S tanding at the workbench in the warehouse, I stared down at
my chicken scratch.

Recalculate fuel supply.

Sat phone battery replacement.

Check solar warehouse for generator parts.

Replacement snowmobile clutch.

AA, D Battery stock for scanner and CB.

I skimmed the list, trying to remember what else I'd wanted to
get done before we got back on the road. The time was nearing,
quickly, and I didn't feel as ready as I'd expected to.

Rifle for Alex.

I picked up the hardwood bolt-action rifle from the worktable,
appreciating its weight in my hand. It was lighter than a shotgun,
perfect for hunting, and with the strap it would be easy enough to
carry with him wherever he went.

The new world was a savage place and Alex was ready for his
own gun. He'd proven that much in the last few months. Sophie
had wanted to learn initially, was even pretty good at it, but she'd
stopped joining us as the months went on. With the ice melting,
predators were on the move, hungry and hunting, but it was the

human variable I was most worried about. With Alex's hard work, a gun would become an extension of him easily enough, and would help ward off anyone who might consider taking advantage of them in the months to come.

I set the rifle down and tugged my fleece cap off, rubbing my fingers through my hat hair. Even without a day job, ticking clocks, and everything scheduled out on a calendar, time was flying by. It was hard to imagine what I'd be doing another four months from now, and with whom.

I peered out the window as the sun sank behind the white-capped mountains to the east. Taking a deep breath, I inhaled the sharp scent of gun cleaner and lubricant. It was familiar and teth-ered me to my past life, which was slipping further away from me each day.

With one last thing to do before I called it a day, I grabbed the handheld radio off the worktable, already programmed on Channel 07, and turned it on. When there was no sign of Ross, I scanned the other channels, waiting for the static to fade and his familiar voice to come over the airwaves. There was only static. He wasn't likely close enough, but I had to try, daily. I tried to call him on the sat phone, but that went unanswered as well.

"Fucking Ross." I shook my head. Where the hell was he? He was a state trooper in one of the darkest, coldest, most dangerous cities in the United States, a damn Eagle Scout and infantryman, for God's sake, and the only family I had left. I refused to believe he was dead. Yet the relief I'd felt seeing him alive had become a distant memory, and I struggled to hold on to it.

I turned off the generator and charging cradle, double-checked that the ammunition and weapons from our afternoon target prac-tice were locked away, and made my way for the door. I could feel the onslaught of nighttime temperature as the sunlight dimmed and caused me to uncurl my woolen collar up to my ears. Slinging my rifle over my shoulder, I headed for the house.

It was a short walk down the road, but provided some calm

before the storm. The second I stepped inside, the house would be full of noise. That was still hard sometimes.

I ran my hands over my face, feeling the effects of ten days without a drink. The past four months hadn't been a complete drunken blur, but I'd definitely had my moments. And it was hard not to crave the numbness that dulled my mind when it was too restless for its own good.

The door opened as I walked up the porch steps, and Sophie stepped out. "Oh, hey," she said.

"Hey."

She barely looked at me as she dumped a bucket of dirty water into the snow.

I held the screen door open for her. "Hey, Soph, I'm sorry if I made you feel uncomfortable yesterday or—"

"No, it's totally fine." She rolled her eyes, forcing a smile. "I was just being weird. I haven't been sleeping and—it's okay. Seriously."

Before I could ask her anything else she turned back into the house. "Dinner's just about ready. You better get cleaned up." Sophie picked up a couple of empty glasses from the coffee table and placed them in the bucket, her long blonde hair swinging against her back as she straightened. "You're in for a treat," she said, turning for the kitchen. "Elle and I made something special tonight, for Alex."

"Should I be afraid?" I joked. Elle being in the kitchen had resulted in a few questionable meals.

"Don't worry, I supervised," Sophie said, flashing me a real smile this time.

Maybe I had been completely off the mark yesterday, and it *was* a teenager thing, or hormonal. My gut told me that wasn't true though, and shaking my head, I stepped inside. The scent of garlic and something sweet hit my nose, and the sound of children laughing in the kitchen and pots and pans clanking together filled the house.

I divested my coat and cap and hung them on the coat rack. Then removed my rifle and leaned it against the wall by the door. Thea and Beau had seen what guns could do first-hand, I didn't have to worry about them getting curious. I didn't have many rules, but not touching the guns was one of them.

On cue, the kids chirped and bickered in the dining room as I made my way in.

"Okay," Elle said. "It's time to play the giraffe game while we finish getting everything ready for dinner. Get in your seats."

"What's the giraffe game?" Beau asked.

"Yeah," Thea echoed. "What's the giraffe game?"

"Well, think about it for a minute." Elle winked at me as I walked in. "What sounds do giraffes make?"

The room fell silent as the kids sat thoughtfully in their chairs.

Elle hustled around the kitchen. "Pot holders . . ." she said, peering around. "Ah-ha." She blew a loose strand of hair from her face and lifted the casserole from the counter. Her verdant eyes flashed to mine as she headed to the table. "How is it you're always just in time for the food?"

"My stomach knows," I told her.

"Sophie," Beau said. "What sound does a giraffe make?" His brow furrowed deep with thought.

"You know, I don't know," she said. "But think a little longer, you'll figure it out."

I sidled up to Elle at the counter. "What sound do they make?" I whispered.

She shrugged. "I have no idea, but I figured it would keep them occupied for a few minutes." She smiled, her full lips exposing white teeth. I liked Elle's smile.

"Aren't you clever," I muttered and washed my hands in the wash bucket. The water was beyond cold, nearly freezing, so I lathered them up, dipped, and dried them as quickly as I could.

Elle took a collection of water glasses to the table. "I can't open this," Thea said, trying to hand her something.

"Ask Jackson, Thea. My hands are full."

Thea climbed out of her chair and walked over with her hand outstretched and an inquisitive look scrunching her face. She offered me a mangled Band-Aid wrapper with a pink cartoon panther on it. "I can't open this," she said. Her big, brown eyes were expectant, and my heart squeezed. "Can you help me, please?"

I cleared my throat and took the wrapper, tiny in my hands, and peeled it open. Then, Thea held up her middle finger. "I have an owie."

It was the smallest prick of red—I could barely see it. "What happened?"

"I was getting sticks for the fire with Beau and got a splinner."

"A splinter? Well, did you already get it out?"

She shrugged.

"Maybe you should get it out before you put a bandage on it." I glanced at Elle, knowing she was better at these things than I was.

"There are tweezers in the bathroom," she said, her eyes glinting with amusement. "In the medicine cabinet."

"Will you get it out for me?"

I looked down at Thea's freckled cheeks, rosy with warmth. Her big brown eyes stared innocently up at me. She was a cute kid, I'd give her that. "Let's do it quick. It's time for dinner."

"Okay." She took my hand in hers, the way Thea randomly did sometimes, and I nearly stumbled. It was small and precious, and she squeezed my fingers as she peered up at me.

I nodded to the bathroom. "We need the flashlight," I told her. "So I can see better."

Thea pulled a small one the size of a key chain from her belt. "We can use mine," she said, taking her hand from mine so she could click it on.

"You have a tool belt?" I hadn't noticed it underneath her over-sized sweatshirt, or maybe it was because until recently, I hadn't wanted to notice things.

Thea tilted her head, absently studying her finger.

That was what life had become for a six-year-old kid—utility belts with survival tools—so she could go about her normal day.

"It's the perfect size for you," I mused. "Where did you find it?"

"Elle got it for me at the tool store."

I grabbed the tweezers from the medicine cabinet and sat down on the toilet lid, closer to Thea's height. "Does your brother have a tool belt too?"

"Yep. We have the same one, but he hides dog treats in his. I don't do that."

"Really?" I lifted her small finger closer and looked for the tiny splinter in the middle of a tiny red dot. "Why does he have dog treats?"

"In case the wolves come closer," she said.

I looked at her, eyebrows raised in warning. "You stay away from those wolves, Thea. Both of you. Okay?"

She stared at me, then nodded, hesitant.

"Promise?"

She licked her lips, taking too much time to answer, but finally she did. "I promise."

I eyed her a second longer, then squinted at the tip of her finger. After my third attempt, I plucked the splinter from her finger, earning an "ouch" but I didn't have time to apologize before she pressed her hurt finger against my lips. "Will you kiss it?"

I blinked. I must have done something resembling a kiss because she grinned gratefully, shouting a thank you as she skipped out of the bathroom, taking her tiny flashlight with her. I blinked again, took a deep breath and put the tweezers away in the darkness. Kids were an emotional whirlwind, I'd decided. And being around Thea warmed my heart and made me miserable at the same time.

Clearing my throat, I went back into the dining room to join the others. Thea settled back into her seat beside Beau and handed Elle the bandage wrapper.

"You got her splinter out." Elle glanced at me from the end of the table, smiling as she fumbled with the bandage wrapper. "I didn't know you had such advanced medical skills," she teased and wrapped the Band-Aid twice around the tip of Thea's finger.

"Well, troopers get a lot of owies in the field," I told her.

"Ha. I bet you did." With a sigh, she surveyed the table. "Beau, will you do the honors, please? It's officially getting dark in here." She handed him a lighter. It was a grown-up task he took seriously, and he leaned forward carefully and flicked the lighter on.

"Did you see giraffes when you were a wildlife trooper?" Thea asked. "Do *you* know what sounds they make?"

"No, no giraffes," I told her. "Mostly bears and moose."

"There aren't giraffes in Alaska, stupid," Beau said, holding his mouth just right as he lit the tapers in the candleholders. The entire table began to glow.

"We're not using that word, Beau, remember?" Elle chided.

"Sorry," he grumbled and sat back down in his chair.

"Good job," Elle said, admiring the candles. "High-five."

"It looks like you've outdone yourself tonight," I told her, eyeing the dressings on the table: a vegetable medley, a basket of garlic bread, a casserole baked golden-brown, yams, and even a pecan pie. She set crystal goblets out, even for the kids, making the table sparkle in the candlelight.

"As Alex would say, it's all about the frozen section." Elle was good at playing off her hard work. But she'd put a lot of thought and effort into the dinner, wanting it to be special for Alex's birthday. And she wasn't much for cooking, so the effort was all the more noteworthy.

"Good job supervising, Sophie," I told her.

She grinned, knowingly.

"Alex told us about a casserole recipe his grandma used to

make—" Elle started, then she paused. "I just hope we did it justice." She eyed the dish skeptically.

"It will be perfect," Sophie reassured her, laying a clutch of extra napkins on the table.

Elle pulled her chair out from the table and nodded for me to sit down in mine.

"I found some," Alex said as he stepped out of the walk-in pantry. He lifted up two dusty bottles.

"What is it?" Thea asked.

"Sparkling cider. I had it once when I was a kid. I think it was at Thanksgiving or something." Alex didn't talk about his family all that much, but I got the impression family gatherings were rare occasions. What I did know was he could boost cars and had a decent-sized scar on his right temple from who knew what, and more than anything, he was kind and grateful; he was always thanking me for teaching him how to do things big and small, like build a proper fire and keep a gun from freezing.

"Sparkling?" Thea said with awe. "Like soda pop? Can I have some?"

"It's better than soda, and I'll pour," I told them, unscrewing the cap.

Once everyone had a glass of something, Sophie lifted her fancy goblet. "To Alex," she said. "A great partner in crime and . . ." Her light-hearted words became heavy. "I don't know what I would've done without you." She said in more of a whisper.

Alex nudged her arm with his elbow, smiling bashfully, but Sophie's smile faltered and she quickly leaned away.

"Sorry," Alex said, and took a drink from his glass.

That was the second time Sophie had shied away from some-one's touch—a male touch, as far as I could tell. But she smiled it off again. "Happy Birthday, Alex!"

I looked at Elle; she had to have noticed.

"Yay, Alex!" Thea cheered. "Happy Birthday!"

Elle echoed the sentiment, but her perplexed gaze finally met mine, and I could see her worry too. Now wasn't the time to discuss what had just happened, but at least I wasn't the only one.

31

ELLE

APRIL 10

We sat at the firepit behind the house, watching the northern lights sailing across the sky, our marshmallows toasting in the hot flames of the campfire. It was nice to enjoy one of the few harmless Alaskan wonders. It almost felt like things were normal, or as normal as they could be.

Sophie stared into the flames, watching them dance. I wanted to ask her about what was going on with her tonight at the dinner table, but we hadn't had a minute alone. Something was wrong— we all knew it—and it was getting worse. She woke up each morning earlier than the last, and retreated to her room almost immediately after dinner to work on her survival book, or because of her menstrual cramps; it was always something.

As withdrawn as Sophie was becoming, I began to wonder if she was depressed. The more I watched her, I began to recognize a familiar look of fear in her eyes—and that's what worried me the most. I knew that fear; it was haunting and made you desperate. What was Sophie so afraid of?

Her sapphire gaze met mine across the fire, and she straightened in her Adirondack. "I'm getting tired, Thea. Are you ready for bed?"

Thea licked the chocolate off her fingers and shook her head as she sat back in her seat, yawning. "No." It must've been nearly ten o'clock.

Beau was already curled up in his chair next to Alex, trying and failing to stay up past his bedtime with the rest of us. And Jackson . . . I peered around at the darkness and then at the back-door. I wasn't sure where he'd run off to.

"Thank you, Elle," Alex said, leaning back in his chair with his hands shoved in his pockets. "I had a pretty awesome birthday." Beau held up a corner of his wool blanket in offering, but Alex shook his head and ruffled Beau's hair instead.

"Did you really have a nice birthday, or are you just saying that? You won't hurt my feelings." Birthdays were so personal; it was difficult to tell.

"The casserole was just like my grandma's," he said with clear sincerity in his voice. "Less burnt, thankfully. She'd forget about it warming in the oven most of the time."

"I'm happy you liked it." I smiled, admiring the affection in his voice when he spoke of his grandma. "You don't talk about her. Were you two close?"

Alex pried his gaze from the fire and looked at me. "I stayed with her in between families sometimes. I slept on her couch and she'd make me breakfast, on her good days. She had emphysema, and other health stuff." He pulled his blue beanie off his head and turned it around in his hands. "She made me one of these once too. They *evicted* me, we'll say, from a family I was living with and I had to leave it behind . . . I don't know whatever happened to it." Alex was only eighteen and yet an entire lifetime shone through his shimmering eyes.

"I'm sorry," Sophie breathed.

Alex stirred from his thoughts and looked at her. "It is what it is. I got a new one though." He smirked at Thea and tugged the beanie back over his head. He had a charming smile, especially when he was deflecting.

"We practiced first," Thea told him, yawning again.

Alex's eyebrows rose. "Did you?"

"I know," I said, "it's hard to tell."

"It's perfect. I like things that are unique."

"Ha. It's definitely unique." I watched him as he helped Thea clean off her marshmallow skewer, patient and natural at being an older brother. He had a sketchy past, exotic looking tanned skin, dark broody eyes, and a killer smile that probably made all the high school girls swoon, but he was stoic and sweet, too. He was a tough kid, and despite a life of constant disruption, Alex was solid, more than I was at his age, and I much-admired that about him.

A wolf howled off in the distance, and Thea straightened. "They're back," she whispered.

When another wolf howled in response, Beau looked at me. It was like he wanted to say something, but he looked back at the fire instead. I told myself the wolves weren't any closer than I'd heard them in the past, their howls were just louder in the still night air.

"Good thing we built a fire," Alex muttered, staring out into the darkness.

My eyes narrowed on Beau and Thea. "You two haven't been taunting the wolves, have you?" I'd heard Jackson and Thea's discussion about dog treats. "Or tried to lure them closer? They're dangerous animals, remember. You understand that, right?"

Both of them looked at me.

"That's my cue," Sophie said, unfurling her legs. She climbed to her feet.

I cleared my throat, waiting for a reply. Finally, Thea nodded. Then Beau. "We know they're dangerous," he said, though I wasn't sure he believed it. I had half a mind to start tying them up each day so they couldn't get into any trouble.

"You ready for bed yet?" Sophie peered down at Thea.

Thea scooted out of her chair in answer.

"I'll go too," Beau said, and pulled his blanket back.

They were both guilty of something, I just didn't know what.

And even if it was harmless, I needed to find out. For peace of mind, if nothing else.

Putting *discover all the kids' secrets* on my list of things to do tomorrow, I raised an eyebrow, watching them as they filed passed me, shamefaced. "Goodnight," I said as the three of them disappeared into the house.

"Goodnight," they echoed from inside the kitchen, and the back door shut behind them.

It was true, I was likely the biggest secret-keeper of all, but my secret was kept to protect them all. At least that's what I kept telling myself. I didn't want the kids getting hurt, no more than they already had been. I wasn't sure how parents did it, especially with four of them.

"Do *you* have any secrets?" I asked Alex, more rhetorical than anything.

He glanced up from the firepit. "I have a bunch," he said more serious than I'd expected. "Nothing exciting, if that's what you mean."

"No, it was sort of a joke. You don't have to share them," I said. "I was just thinking out loud."

Alex's dark eyes shifted from my face to my gloved hands, then back at my face. The longer his gaze lingered, the quicker my heart began to beat. "You shock me a lot when I touch you," he said.

I didn't think it was a question, but I wasn't sure how to respond. "So you've said."

"You don't ever feel it?"

"It's probably the gloves." I folded my arms over my lap. "Static cling and all of that." I didn't know if that was an actual thing with gloves, or why it only seemed to happen with Alex. "It doesn't hurt, does it?" I thought suddenly.

He shook his head. "It's uncomfortable, but no, it doesn't hurt. No more than pulling clothes out of the dryer."

"Oh, well, that's good, I guess."

Alex looked back into the flames, their crackle punctuating the silence.

"What about you," he started. "Do you have any secrets?"

My gaze shifted to him, tentative and curious. "What—"

The backdoor opened again and Jackson stepped out, I could hear his heavy footsteps.

"Did everyone go to bed already?" he asked.

When I peered back at him, he was a dark shadow in the doorway, then he stepped out into the firelight. His hair was loose and hanging around his face, dark and wavy. His goatee and beard still darkened his jaw, but were groomed. He'd become the quintessential mountain man, and I liked the way it looked on him.

"You just missed them," I said.

"I guess it's pretty late." Jackson walked toward Alex. "This is for you anyway," he said, stepping around the firepit. Jackson lifted the rifle strap off his shoulder and handed it to him. "Happy Birthday."

Alex's eyes opened wide, his mouth gaped. "Seriously?"

"Seriously."

"You're shittin' me." He stood up, taking the rifle in his hands like he wasn't sure it was real.

"I'm not shitting you," Jackson said, a smile in his voice. He looked at me and winked. "You deserve it, kid. You've been beyond helpful, and I know you'll appreciate and respect this."

"Aw, this is so cool. I will," he said and took Jackson's hand for a firm shake. "Thank you."

"You're welcome." Jackson came to sit in the chair beside me.

"Your gift is cooler than mine," I told him. "I'm jealous."

"What are you talking about?" Jackson shook his head. "I wish it was my birthday so you'd make me a hat."

I laughed. "Sure you do."

"I'm serious. My ears get cold sometimes."

"You already have that fleece cap you always wear."

"So, Alex already has one too."

I wagged a finger at him. "Touché."

I huffed out a deep breath, conceded my gift was a hundred times better than his, and we settled into a comfortable silence. The crackle of the fire was soothing, the rainbow of lights above mesmerizing. Sometimes I wondered how a place this beautiful could be so perilous at the same time. We'd had whiteouts and blizzards, and worried about freezing to death once during our trip, but we'd been lucky that was it.

"I'm gonna head to bed," Alex said with a long stretch. "Thanks again," He stared at his rifle, admiring it with a smile, then at us. "Tonight was fun."

"You're welcome, Alex." I tugged the collar of my coat up higher around my neck.

"We still on for tomorrow?" Alex looked at Jackson.

"Yep. When the sun comes up."

I looked at Jackson, a sense of unease washing over me.

"I'll leave you the chocolate, just in case," Alex said with a wink in my direction.

"You know me so well." I grinned. "Sleep well."

He pulled the strap of his rifle over his shoulder, and grabbed Beau's discarded blanket off the chair.

"Night kid," Jackson said, leaning forward to warm his hands over the fire.

"Night." Alex climbed the porch steps and quietly went into the house.

As soon as the door was closed I looked at Jackson. "You're leaving tomorrow?" I knew he'd planned on a supply run to Delta Junction, a town much larger than Slana, to find a slew of things on his list, especially since we were leaving in a couple weeks, but I hadn't realized he was heading out so soon, or that Alex was going with him.

"Yep, Alex wanted to go with me, get a feel for the roads and learn what to look for when you all head to Hartley. Plus, he knows cars better than I do. I could use his help finding replacement parts for the Explorer and snowmobile." He scratched his beard and leaned his head back against his chair. "I didn't think it was a half-bad idea."

"Then, what's wrong?" He seemed as excited to have Alex tagging along as he did apprehensive.

Jackson shrugged. "You mean aside from the ordinary? Nothing, I guess. I just—I want you guys to be as prepared as you can be for whatever comes next."

It was still a bit depressing to think about leaving him, but I was grateful for how much thought he'd put into all of it. "Thank you, Jackson. But we'll be fine."

His eyes drifted to mine. "I know," he said. "But you should still be prepared for the unexpected. There's no telling what might happen from one day to the next."

"Trust me, I know," I sighed, leaning my head back to stare at the sky. "I've been thinking about all the possible ways this could go wrong."

"You can't think about it like that," he said.

"No? You do."

He glowered at me, but he knew I was right. "What happened to all of that forced optimism that's so annoying sometimes?" he teased.

I wasn't sure if it was because he was leaving, Alex was going with him, or he'd reminded me that soon we'd be parting ways, but I felt sulky all of the sudden. "It's failed me tonight, I guess."

Jackson ran his hands down the wood armrests. "You'll have a tribe again soon . . . not just a band of misfits."

I sighed, strangely content with things the way they were. "I kinda like our band of misfits."

Jackson smiled. "Me too," he murmured. His voice was a baritone in the still night. "It was really nice what you did for Alex tonight, Elle."

"The kids needed something special to celebrate."

"That's the only reason?" he asked with a sidelong look. The flames jumped in the fire pit, the wood crackled. Jackson's gaze heated the side of my face, waiting for me to say something.

I picked up my cold cocoa nestled in the snow, my mouth suddenly parched. "I've always hated birthdays," I admitted and took a sip. I tried to pretend it was chocolate milk instead of clumpy, snow water and packaged chocolate powder. "They were always a disappointment."

"You didn't get what you wanted?"

I shook my head. "It's not that. Birthdays come with too many expectations—expectations that someone *needs* to care about your birthday to begin with; there's the inescapable disappointment when they don't. And you never know what strings are attached."

Jackson's brow furrowed. "There aren't supposed to be strings attached at all. Not for a birthday."

"That wasn't the case in my family." I took another sip. "I guess I needed to prove that's not true anymore."

His eyes glittered in the firelight, and as Jackson's gaze trailed the contours of my face, my insides warmed a little. A hopeful feeling that scared me burned just below the surface.

Jackson looked away, clearing this throat. "You're a good person, Elle. Alex and the kids are lucky to have you."

"Thanks," I whispered, pleasantly surprised to hear the words. Jackson didn't bestow compliments often. "I know it will be hard, but I feel lucky to have them. I failed my sister and yet, somehow, I inherited a bigger family."

"You didn't fail your sister . . ." He looked up at the sky, his fist clenching on the armrest. "There was nothing we could've done differently." He could barely say the words.

"Are you reminding me, or yourself?"

Jackson let out a deep breath. "Both."

I pried my gaze from him, and we sat in silence for a few charged heartbeats. Both of us lost in thoughts we didn't share. I thought about Jenny's last hours and I thought about Sophie's mom who died without saying goodbye to her daughter. I thought about

Beau and Thea who watched their mom kill herself by jumping out a window because she'd lost her mind. And somehow, we'd all found each other. We were all okay. When I didn't want to think about any of that anymore, I stood to put out the fire.

"You'll be okay here with the kids?"

I looked at Jackson, waiting for him to continue.

"While I'm gone, I mean. Since Alex is leaving with me, I want to make sure you feel comfortable."

I didn't feel comfortable with it, not because I didn't think I couldn't handle the place for a couple days on my own, but because I knew what would come after they returned. "We'll be fine," I promised. "Besides, I need to get used to running things on my own anyway. Soon I won't have a choice."

Jackson blinked, opened his mouth to say something, then stopped. For a moment, I thought he might invite us to stay with him in Whitehorse, but then he conceded. "I guess you're right."

Nodding, I exhaled my unwarranted disappointment and shoveled a pile of snow onto the fire. "You've got a long day tomorrow, you better get some sleep."

32

ELLE

APRIL 11

Thea and I hung laundry on the line outside the house, enjoying the sun on our faces and the woodpeckers looking for grubs in the early afternoon. Like last night, the skies were clear, and despite the cool temperatures, the sun was warm, a welcome break from the clouds and cold.

"Do you think Alex and Jackson are on their way back yet?" Thea asked, clipping her seventh clothespin on her jacket.

"I don't think so. They're staying in Delta Junction for a couple days." I put my hand out. "Can I have another pin please?"

She scooted closer, her boots like miniature plows in the snow. She stuck her chest out so I could remove a pin from her jacket.

"This wasn't what I had in mind when I asked you to help me," I muttered, and as Thea often did, she giggled in reply. "Will you at least hand me the rest of the wet socks from the basket?"

"Yep!" she tweeted with a bounce.

"Thank you—"

"Elle . . ." Beau said tentatively as the front door opened. He stepped out of the house, the hinges squeaking as the door swung shut behind him.

"Yes?" I glanced over my shoulder. "You're letting all the heat out, bud." He balled his hands in front of him and he glanced into the house. His chest was heaving like he was going to cry.

I dropped the socks in my hands. "What is it?" I walked toward him.

"Something's wrong with Sophie. She won't stop crying."

I took Thea's hand. "Come on, let's make sure she's okay." I already knew she wasn't. Sophie wouldn't even come out of her room this morning for breakfast.

I hurried into the house. Letting go of Thea's hand, I swung the door shut, and ran up the stairs. I could hear Sophie's body-wracking sobs from the hallway and opened the bedroom door.

"Soph?" I stopped in the doorway, taking the sight of her in.

She looked broken, completely undone. Her face was blotched with red, her cheeks wet with tears as she shook her head.

Taking an urgent step forward, I kicked her backpack, hearing a familiar sound. I looked down to find a pill bottle. I reached for it, finding another one beneath it. I grabbed that one too. *Sleeping pills?* I turned one around so I could see the front of it. "Modafinil . . ." I looked at her, blindsided, though I knew I shouldn't have been. "Sophie—"

"I can't do this anymore," she mumbled through a thickening sob.

Can't do it? The entire world seemed to stop. "Soph." My voice was less than a whisper as I climbed onto the bed next to her. "What does that mean?" I reached for her, wanting to comfort her.

"You don't understand!" she cried pulling away from me. "You can't touch me—no one can touch me."

"You're right, I don't understand," I pleaded, searching her face. I trembled beside her with fear and uncertainty. "What happened?" I stared into her muddy blue eyes, bloodshot and heavy with exhaustion. "Please, tell me what's wrong."

"I can feel it, inside me—in my head," she cried. "I see it when I close my eyes—"

"See *what*? I can't help you if I don't understand." I couldn't help the desperation in my voice, the rising panic. Deep down I think I knew what she saw, what she felt. Fire, like me. "What do you see?" I repeated. I didn't recognize my own voice—the unbridled fear, the shock. "What do you see?" It was a tentative whisper this time, horrified by what she might say next.

Sophie inhaled, a jagged, rough sound that tore at my heart, and she looked at me. "Everything." She balled herself against the wall, desperate to be left alone.

My vision blurred with tears and I ran my fingers through my hair. "I don't know what that means, Sophie." I felt helpless as her body quaked, and there was nothing I could do.

"I *know*," she bleated and looked at my gloves. "I saw it this morning when you came to check on me. I know why you wear them every day and what you've done."

I nearly fell backward. "You . . . *saw*?" My head was shaking of its own accord. That made no sense. I couldn't see things; I could only feel the fire. I could only feel the unquenched ache deep down.

"I've seen it all," she whimpered, closing her eyes. "Like your fire burns inside you, something twists inside when people touch me."

"Sophie . . ." I had no words of reassurance. All I could do was gape at her and stare at her hands and her sleeve-covered arms. "Touch?" It was only a breath of a word, but all I could manage. I couldn't imagine the implications of what she was telling me, but I could see her hopelessness like it was my own. "You don't feel the fire?"

"No," she said, sniffling. She blinked with swollen eyes. "I only feel what you've felt, I see what you've seen." Remembering my fear and my pure will to live no matter the consequences, I knew exactly how terrified she must be of me.

Finding my voice, I forced myself to gather my wits and be strong for her. I balled the blankets in my hands to keep them from shaking. "I would *never* hurt you, Sophie," I rasped, barely able to speak. "I promise you. I would never hurt *any* of you." But just like Sophie knew what I'd done to Thomas, she knew I couldn't promise something like that either. I hadn't realized it until now myself. I could promise nothing because I knew nothing.

"Please don't be afraid," I implored.

But Sophie was a million miles away, staring through me, at nothing. "I'm not afraid of you," she breathed. "But I don't want to feel any of it anymore." She swallowed thickly and her chin trembled. "I know how Alex got the scar on his eyebrow. I know what it felt like to be shoved through the glass." Each word was frail but the weight was heavy. "Jackson and the baby . . ." She ran her hands over her face and through her hair, swallowing her sorrow as best she could. "I don't want to see it anymore. I don't want to feel it—" She broke into sobs again.

Thea whimpered behind me, Beau whispering weak reassurances the way big brothers do, but I couldn't think of them. I could only see Sophie. Broken and lost, the way I'd been. I didn't understand any more than she did.

I inched my hand closer to lean in and she stiffened. "Don't touch me, I only feel it when people touch me."

"I won't touch you," I promised. "I just want to understand." For months I'd been hiding the strange thing inside me, and for months I'd thought I was the only one. "How long have you been seeing these things? I mean, you should've told me, I would've understood. I would've tried to help you—"

"They were dreams at first." She brushed the sweat-dampened hair from her face. "Then, I thought I was imagining them sometimes." She looked at the pills on the edge of the bed. "But I can't stop them anymore." Her voice was rising again, and she buried her face in her hands. "I just want it to go away . . . I thought it would go away . . ."

"We'll figure something out," I told her. "We'll talk to the others—we'll figure it out together."

Sophie looked at me, knowing all too well what that meant for me. I would have to tell Jackson what I'd done, and everything would change after that. I hated the reality but there was no other choice. Not anymore. Sophie was changed, I was changed—all of it was impossible. Maybe he would understand that, even if he could never forgive me for lying to him.

"We'll tell them, and we'll figure it out," I repeated, and remotely I thought we couldn't be the only ones. I hedged toward the edge of the bed. "Soph, do you hear me? We will." Fire and telepathic memories—no, feelings *and* memories—were different, but in my gut, I knew it wasn't a coincidence that she'd suddenly become psychic, not when my own physiology differed so greatly from before. "These are impossible things," I whispered. I couldn't wrap my mind around it. "If I would've known, I would've been more careful around you, we all would have."

I felt naked sitting beside her, a thousand question marks floating in the air between us. There were things I never allowed myself to think of, memories from my childhood I prayed I'd forget. Did she know them too? "Every memory? Every feeling?" I hated to ask, knowing what it cost her to think about all of it, but I had to know. Even if I understood she needed space to process her own feelings instead of ours.

"Every feeling of every memory I've seen, like I was there." She nodded to the pill bottles. "I thought sleep would help, and when it didn't I *wanted* to stay awake." She gritted out angrily.

"Jackson and Alex are gone," I said, trying to think it all through. "We won't touch you—you won't have to worry about that right now. You just need rest." It was another plea.

I looked at Thea and Beau, both of them frightened, eyes wide with worry as they clung to one another. They didn't need to know what we were talking about to understand the toll it was taking.

I climbed off the bed and I crouched down in front of them, tears streaming down my cheeks. I wiped them hastily away. "Sophie will be okay," I told them. I reached for Beau's hand, and then I reached for Thea's, clasping their fingers in mine. "Sophie and I," I told them. "We haven't felt the same since we were sick." I didn't know how to explain it to them. "Do you feel different?" I asked, reminding myself we couldn't be the only ones.

Thea shrugged.

"Do you feel it inside of you?" I tried to explain. "Something different, something scary?"

They both glanced between us, eventually shaking their heads, and I sighed with relief.

"We should give Sophie some space—"

"No," she said. I turned around as she wrapped her arms around her knees, laying her head down. "No," she repeated, so quietly I barely heard her.

"Are you sure?"

She nodded with a sniffle.

Beau led Thea to the bed, her hand in his. "Are you going to be okay now?" he asked. While he'd been strong and brave for his sister, I could see the damp skin beneath his eyes.

"I'll get better," she lied to him, patting the area of the mattress beside of her. "You can sit with me." I wasn't sure if she believed that, but I hope she did.

Beau climbed up onto the bed, sitting up against the wall next to her. Thea climbed up into my arms and we sat wrapped together on the edge.

"What's wrong with her," Thea asked, nuzzling into me as she rubbed the tears from her eyes.

"She's sad," I explained. "And afraid."

"Why is she sad?" Thea's little hand inched closer to Sophie, like she wasn't sure she was the same person but desperately wanted her to be.

"She's sad because we're sad."

Thea and Beau looked at me. I knew it wasn't as simple as that, but if Sophie could feel our fear and sadness, she could feel our happiness, too.

"I have an idea," I said, scooting further onto the bed, with

Thea wrapped around me. "Why don't we take turns sharing our happiest memories? Wouldn't that be nice?"

"I have a lot of funny ones," Thea admitted.

"Good, then why don't you start?"

"Okay, well," Thea began, and she looked at Sophie. "The first time I ever got a kitten, I named him Arnold, after my grandpa . . ."

Sophie's gaze drifted to mine and she mouthed a thank you.

I nodded, just happy to see the tears had stopped, but my mind wandered. If Sophie knew what I could do, she would know what others were capable of, too. It was a conversation for later, but either way, I knew the next time I saw Jackson would likely be the last. When he returned, I would finally tell him the truth.

33

JACKSON
APRIL 11

The roads were still covered in snow as Alex and I drove to Delta Junction, but the snowplow hitched to the front of the truck helped us make decent time. With more daylight came more sunshine and a bit of warmth to take the sting out of the air. The snow became more compacted and drivable, adding a bit of ease among an unending list of all that could potentially go wrong. So, as the city came into view, I let out a relieved breath and glanced at Alex, dozing in the passenger seat.

"We're here," I said, slowing the truck just outside of town. I pulled the Tacoma off the road and into the tree line. The truck was Ross's baby, souped up and weatherproofed, but the deep purr of a MagnaFlow exhaust echoing through town was the last thing I needed.

"Do you think anyone's here?" Alex asked through a yawn. He'd woken up even earlier than I had, after Sophie's early hour roaming through the house.

Peering out at the neighborhoods and buildings surrounding the outskirts of the city, my gut instinct was to tell Alex no, I didn't think anyone was there, but instincts could be wrong, and our luck would likely lead to a big, fat yes.

"I guess we'll find out," I muttered and pushed the driver door open, then climbed out. "We've got four or five hours of daylight left." I stretched, squinting at the snow-topped roofs that glistened in the sunlight. A hawk's cry met my ears as I surveyed the cotton-wood and birch trees surrounding the town. Everything seemed quiet, but we'd find out if that was true soon enough.

"Let's get our things and make our way to the airlift first, it's closest. They'll have the medical supplies we need there. Then we can decide where to hit next."

Alex heaved his backpack on. "Where will we stay tonight?" He closed the passenger door and walked around the front of the truck. He scoured our surroundings, gaze darting in all directions. I wasn't sure if he was anxious or just curious. Or, maybe he was excited.

"We'll look for a lodge to stay at on the way, something on the outskirts."

I lugged on my pack and checked my compass, ammo, and secured the knife in my boot, the pistol in my belt, and the rifle on my back.

Alex did the same, patting himself down as he took stock of the knife clipped to his pocket, the rifle on his back, and the array of tools clipped into his utility belt. He looked legit in his cargo pants and long sleeves. With the weather mellowing a bit more, thermal layers sufficed without the bulk. Add the muted brown and green shades of camo, and Alex would look like he was ready for hunting season.

"Bear spray?" I asked.

Alex grinned easily, per usual. "You never know." A white puff of breath filled the air as he chuckled.

"Isn't that the truth," I muttered, and nodded toward town. "Shall we?"

Alex fell into step beside me as we followed the road. There were bird and fox prints, even caribou beginning their trek for calving season, but there were no shoe prints or visible predators to be worried about. The tension in my shoulders eased a little as our boots crunched through the snow, almost echoing in the still air.

"If the weather stays this nice," Alex said, "we might have a decent trip."

"Don't jinx us, kid. That's the last thing we need."

He grinned. "What's a little more adventure?"

"Trust me, there will be plenty of it to come, and you might change your tune then." I pulled my rifle off my back. "In fact, grab your gun. Keep the safety on, but hold it. I want anyone who sees us to know we're armed."

"Have you run into any survivors on your other scavenging trips?"

I nodded. "A couple, but I've stayed out of sight. I've only gone on two though. There's not much in the way of supplies in these territories, things get airdropped more often than not, and since that hasn't been happening, any sane survivors would hunker down and wait for winter to pass, like we did. Now, though, would be the time they'd come out, like us, and I don't want to take any more chances than we have to. There are only six people I trust, you guys and Ross, everyone else is dangerous."

I pulled my sunglasses down off my head, covering my eyes. The sun glared off the snow-lined gutters, nearly blinding me.

"Did anyone ever shoot at you—when you were a trooper, I mean?" Alex whispered.

I glanced at him. He was alert, his eyes scanning the street and toward town. I thought back to the meth lab I'd stumbled across, one of a few I'd found by my fourth year on the job. An addict in need of a fix had nearly blasted me; I'd ruined his score by showing up in the dead of night, out in the middle of nowhere after someone in the house called in an assault and battery charge. "Yeah, but only once, and Ross had my back."

"You worked together?"

"We worked similar shifts." I surveyed the sporadic businesses lining the side of the road, mostly warehouses and junkyards, a sign shop and mechanic garage situated between them. "If Ross was in the area, he'd show up if I needed backup. I did the same."

"Sounds gutsy, pulling a gun on you. I've had a few run-ins with the cops and some of them even I thought I could take. But you—you're a pretty intimidating guy. I wouldn't mess with you."

I chuckled. "A few run-ins, huh?" I glanced at him.

"Petty stuff, mostly."

I stared at Alex, waiting for him to elaborate. He pulled his weight and helped out far more than I'd ever expected an eighteen-year-old to, but he never got personal, which I understood, but that didn't mean I wasn't curious.

"Vandalism," he offered, and grabbed a couple of pieces of jerky from his pocket. He handed one to me, but I shook my head. "Burglary—but that was some bullshit," he added. "I knew the guy whose house I was in, he'd just double-crossed me." He tore a piece of jerky off with his teeth. "The charges didn't stick, thankfully. I had enough incriminating crap on him, they didn't care about me."

"Sounds like you had shitty friends."

Alex squinted down the road, a white puff of breath floating in the air as he exhaled. "They weren't really friends, just guys I knew. Sometimes you don't have a choice, you know?"

I understood what he meant. It was one thing to be given opportunities and make the wrong choices, but to have none to begin with, as I'm sure Alex often dealt with, your only choice was to take the lesser of the evils.

He looked at me like he thought I had a speech coming. "I've been a drunk most of my life. I'm not one to pass judgement. Besides, if bureaucrats still ran the world, your record would've been clean as of yesterday."

The corner of Alex's mouth quirked up. "I guess you're right."

After a few seconds, he said, "You know, you're not so bad for a cop."

"Thanks, I think."

Alex nearly snorted. "You're welcome."

A flagpole came into view. A dark blue flag with gold stars hung as the state symbol at half-staff, just like I'd seen on most flagpoles since Anchorage. It was a tribute from all the dying to the already dead, and they would likely hang that way forever.

"Do you want to check this high school?" Alex stared at it, uncertainty in his voice. It was a sprawling tan building with light blue trim that looked untouched from the outside. "They'll have a nurse's office. Maybe something we can use in the science class."

I beamed with pride. "You know, I never would've thought of that." I stepped aside. "Lead the way, hotshot."

Alex took a deep breath as we crossed the street. The baseball diamond was mushy, the batting cages wet with melted snow.

"Did you like your job?" Alex tore off another pieces of jerky. "It's one thing to be a street cop but out here . . . it's gotta be rough, but it probably has everything though—the adrenaline rush, the brotherhood, the *prestige*."

"Oh, and suddenly you care about prestige?"

"Definitely not. But the comradery sounds nice." Alex shrugged like he didn't care one way or the other, but I knew better. Everyone liked to feel like they belonged, and being a trooper made me feel like I was part of something bigger than myself.

"It was. Comradery was probably the main reason I lasted so long," I admitted. "But it wasn't exactly like they made it out to be in the recruitment commercials either. It was a lonely job too, kid. It's not all honor and bravery and saving the world one kitten at a time. But yes, it was all worth it. Not only did it give me a purpose I didn't know I needed with a group of guys I could count on, it pissed my dad off, so it was a double win." I squinted toward the side entrance, watching for movement in the fenced in courtyard still covered in snow.

"What did your dad want you to do?"

I looked at the giant husky emblem on the side of the building. "Dog mushing."

Alex laughed. "That's kinda cool. You didn't want to? I'm trying to picture you on the back of a dogsled."

Eyebrows lifted, I glanced at him. "What's with all the questions?"

"I don't know, just curious."

As we reached the door, I put my finger to my lips. Alex nodded and pulled his rifle closer. I didn't hear anything as I leaned in, but that meant nothing. I reached for the handle and slowly turned it, trying not to make too much noise as I gripped my rifle more tightly with the other hand.

The door was unlocked, which wasn't surprising given how suddenly the virus had happened, and I opened the door as quietly as I could. While the air outside was brisk, inside it was stagnant and almost humid.

The hallways were empty and there were no sounds or noticeable movement.

I motioned for Alex to check the office area while I headed down a hall of lockers, toward the classrooms. Luckily, movement in a place like this would echo; alerting us to anyone who might be inside. Unluckily, it would also echo our footsteps and give us away.

The office door squeaked open behind me and Alex froze, peering inside before he stepped in completely.

I continued down the hall. The walls were dressed with colorful banners. Bulletin boards were cluttered with hockey game schedules and haphazardly hung flyers with club announcements and the January production of *Fiddler On The Roof.*

Walking through a place so silent I could hear only my own breath, and my boots against the linoleum made the hair on the back of my arms stand on end. The halls were once teeming with voices but they'd never be full again. It was one thing to think about billions of people dying; it was a gargantuan, sweeping number that painted an extraordinary picture. But thinking about the individual lives that ended in a matter of days and hours felt heavier than a simple number, even one so immense.

These kids were complaining to their parents about homework and planning what to wear and who to ask out for the Turnabout. They'd had grueling hockey practices and tests to study for, and all their sleepless nights and worrying was inane. Every argument with their parents was wasted breath, just like my arguments with my father had been. Neither of us got what we wanted in the end. We'd resented each other all our lives, and it was all for nothing.

Alex walked up behind me. "One body in the principal's office," he said, swallowing thickly. Though I wished I could protect Alex from seeing dead, decaying bodies, it would only be a disservice to him.

I patted his shoulder and peered in through the window of a closed classroom door. Math formulas I didn't understand were scribbled on the whiteboard, and I kept walking. "They must've cancelled school," I whispered, looking in through another window. There weren't bodies everywhere, like I'd expected.

Alex looked through a door window across the hall. "Hey look," he said, opening it. I strode across the hall and stepped inside behind him, stopping in the doorway. Alex and I both stared at the whiteboard. "It must be a science class or something." He glanced around the room and nodded to the periodic table across the back wall.

But it was the whiteboard that interested me. The sketch of a virus and its host with words, most of which I didn't understand, scribbled around. *Nucleoside. Darwinism. Quasispecies.* I lifted a Genetic Mutation handout left on one of the desks.

Reassortment*: responsible for major genetic shifts in the history of the influenza virus. Pandemic flu strains are caused by* *reassortment between different viral strands, avian and human, for example. H1N1 virus responsible for the swine flu outbreak was the result of an unusual mix of swine, avian, and human influenza genetic sequences. Ever-changing viral sequences lead to new or revived diseases, as well as natural selection.*

I'd never been an A student, and science definitely wasn't my strong suit, but Sophie liked it. I folded the handout and slid it into the textbook on the desk.

"Sophie's going to geek out over this," Alex muttered, and he followed me out the door. I set the textbook in the hallway to grab on our way out, and continued down the hall.

Alex and I moved in tandem toward the other end of the school; Alex continued to check the right and I checked the left.

"Look, a vending machine," he said. "We could take a treat back for everyone."

"On the way out," I told him, eyeing the walls of an open class-room. "Make sure we remember to grab a Milky Way for Elle," I said absently and stepped inside. Photos of students lined the walls, candid shots of them huddled around lab tables and posing with teachers. There were action shots of hunter green and off-white uniforms with hockey sticks in the air mid-motion. The entire room was a time capsule, and for the first time I considered what the footprint of our existence would look like in ten or twenty years.

Someone had written a production timeline on the whiteboard, and the yearbook was slotted for print this month.

I eyed a camera on the teacher's desk, wondering what photos were still on it.

"Jackson," Alex hissed. I glanced behind me as he walked into the doorway. "I found the nurse's office. It looks a little ransacked."

I spun around and followed him out into the hall, rifle in my hands, and waited for him to go in. Alex was cool and collected as he made a sweep of the room, and I followed in behind him. The room was tiny—large enough only for a cot, a stool, and a cabinet of supplies for the typical fever and sore throat.

Wrappers and torn boxes filled the wastebasket, shelves were disorganized, and a tan blanket made the cot look like someone had slept in it. The supplies weren't as ransacked as I'd expected, but they'd definitely been gone through and some of them used.

Some over-the-counter antacids and anti-inflammatory bottles were open, and a disposable thermometer was out on the counter. The common flu they'd prepared for hadn't been so typical in the end, though. None of this had helped them.

"Get the first aid kit, and the disposable thermometers," I told him, eyeing what was left on the shelves. I grabbed suture scissors, gauze, and a bottle of Advil and put them in my backpack. I smashed open a locked cabinet to find the special and more urgent treatments. Fortunately, none of the kids had chronic ailments or allergies I knew of, but I grabbed the two EpiPens, sample inhalers, and what I thought might be the nurse's pain pills. It wasn't a lot, but it was better than nothing.

In all of our commotion, we heard a crash carry down the hallway from somewhere in the building, and Alex and I froze. I listened hearing nothing more, but it was time to move. Swinging my rifle around to my back, I pulled my Glock from my holster. I nodded for the door, then swept the hallway again.

There was a snarl in the distance—an animal's. I wondered if Alex's bear spray might actually come in handy as I turned the corner, met by a wall of windows that faced a courtyard. The scattered lunch tables were peppered with snow, and a dog's wiry tail wagged as he tore at a mound in the snow. The dog jerked again, catching a brown tweed jacket in its mouth.

I held up my hand as Alex came up behind me. As the dog tugged, the body moved into view, and I turned away.

I could've scared the scavenging dog away, but there was no point. These people had been dead for months, and their ice capsule was melting. Soon every animal, both wild and once tamed, would know it.

Alex didn't ask questions as we turned and headed back the way we came. "Let's gather our things," I told him. "We've still got a lot of ground to cover."

34

ELLE

APRIL 11

T *he "constructive web" consists of strands that represent*
pathways of child development . . .

Candlelight flickered across the page as I scrolled through the developmental science book I'd found in the bookcase. Scouring the house for anything and everything that might be useful in understanding what was happening to us, especially after what I'd learned about Sophie.

. . . responsiveness to emotion and a support system deter-mined by a child's capacity for resilience. All of which depend on a variability in sequence, synchrony, and developmental range. Some children are more responsive and can process what others cannot. Many children can "bounce back" because their "constructive web" is still being developed.

I considered the way a rubber band twists and bends under pressure. Then about Beau and Thea, who both survived the same outbreak, yet had no symptoms—Sophie had felt nothing from them or Jackson. No strange powers, anyway. Why were they different than us—why had my own twin with the same DNA died and I hadn't?

Broken down even further, why were some of us still alive

while others weren't? Even strong, young, healthy people hadn't made it. If we couldn't even answer that, then the rest would be impossible. Could the powers be gender or age related? Were the lunatics that walked the streets a sign of what might happen to us in time? I didn't feel like I was losing my mind, yet. Especially knowing I wasn't the only one who was different.

I pulled the glove off my hand and stretched my fingers. Physically there was nothing wrong with my hands, but I could feel it inside. And if the coastguardsman or Thomas—or any other crazy son of a bitch—could've done what I could do, I would probably be dead.

I closed the book and leaned back in my chair. Sophie and I could do impossible things, but the madmen we'd run into seemed to live on unchecked, instinctual human needs, not any type of power. What did Sophie and I have that no one else did?

Nothing in an old science book would explain what the hell was going on. Exhausted from thinking about it, I dragged my hands over my face. The warmth of my fingertips against my skin was a pleasant change to the soft leather that had become an extension of me. I stared at my fingertips, seeing what I've always seen. Hands that had snapped thousands of photographs, adjusted shoulders, and fluffed hair. They'd nearly frozen in the snow waiting to capture the perfect sunrise over Harding Icefield.

Now they did otherworldly things, and the idea weighed heavier on me than usual, as it often did when I was alone too long with my thoughts.

"Elle?"

I spun around. Beau stood at the bottom step, his hair mussed from sleep.

"What is it, bud?" I grabbed a blanket from the couch to wrap around him. "Bad dream?" I knelt down in front of him, careful not to touch his skin as I realized my gloves were on the table.

He shook his head. "I have to tell you something," he said.

"You do?" After what had happened today it could've been about anything. "About what?"

"It's about Thea."

A distant sound caught my ear, and I shot to my feet. It was an engine, a truck—a big one. It rattled and rumbled, much larger than the Tacoma.

"Beau," I whispered as it drew closer. "Go upstairs. Put out the fire and wake the girls—be quiet, okay?" I looked from the door to him. "Stay in the room and don't come out. I'll be up in a minute."

All remnants of sleep were gone, and fear quivered in his blue eyes. He wanted to protest, I could practically see the words forming on his lips, but he did as I asked and scurried up the stairs.

I stared at the front door afraid to breathe. It was likely the people outside had already seen the smoke from our chimney, but I grasped at a shred of hope they hadn't.

Blowing out my candle, I hurried to the window and pulled back the blackout drapes. The night was clear. The moon cast a blue sheen across the snow, and I could make out two human outlines a few buildings down. It most definitely wasn't Jackson and Alex. Both silhouettes were those of men, big men, and they were searching for something. Another man stepped out of the shadows and stood a dozen yards down the street from the house, facing me, like he could see me through the window. The familiar heap of dread settled in my stomach.

They'd come with mal intent. The man's grin spread from ear to ear, just like Donahoe's had at the bus depot. The hair on the back of my arms and neck rose, and a sickening chill shot down my spine. They were crazy.

He eyed the house, appraising it. Wondering who was inside. Looking for a way in. Plotting. Planning.

Mind whirling, I grabbed all the coats from the rack and ran up the stairs, taking the steps two at a time until I was in my room. My pistol was in my hand in seconds, and I ran down the hall to the kids' room. It smelled of fire smoke, and the three of them were awake.

"Soph," I said, urgent but quiet.

"What do they want?" she rasped, as I shoved the jackets at the kids.

"I don't know, but I need you to be calm and listen okay?"

She nodded warily, her eyes opening wide and saucer-like in the moonlight.

"You know where the shotgun is. Get it. Load it—I want you to arm yourself and put on your jackets because we will have to leave." I looked at the three of them, needing them to understand. "Grab your bags, and when you have your things and the gun, I want you to barricade yourselves in this room until I come for you."

I wasn't sure if Sophie was nodding or shaking.

"Sophie—"

"I got it."

"Soph," I said, willing her to hear the gravity in my voice. "If something happens to me, you take the kids down, over the balcony—be careful—and take the Explorer straight to our meeting place, okay? Jackson will know to look for you there."

"Elle—"

"Please, listen." We'd discussed it all before, but in the moment's urgency, I needed her to focus. "Follow the map, just like we've gone over and over. It's imperative, Sophie. It's the only way Alex and Jackson will find you."

She nodded again, her eyes glistening, and my throat tightened. On light feet, she ran out of the room for the shotgun and I hurried to the window, peering out at the road. The man was still standing in the middle of the street, staring at the house. What the hell was he doing?

Suddenly, he disappeared into the shadows. "I know you're in there!" he shouted. "I could smell you a mile away."

"Get your boots on," I told Thea, whirling around. "Soph," I bit out as she ran back into the room, gun in hand. "Keep that gun fixed on this window and shoot any of them that come into view." I didn't know what they were planning but a slug to the leg or chest would slow them down enough for me to get a decent shot.

Her eyes widened, but she nodded without hesitation.

I ran down the hall and descended the stairs, using the kids' terrified whimpers to fortify my resolve to kill the motherfuckers who'd clearly come to taunt us and then do worse.

I needed my eyes on them first, if I had any hope of taking them down. I snuck out the back door, quiet and careful, and rounded the house, listening for the approaching sound of footsteps in the snow.

It was biting cold out, but I barely noticed as my body felt aflame with adrenaline.

The men laughed beside their trucks as if they didn't care if I knew where they were or if I could hear them. It was likely a trap, and I refused to take the bait. Using the station wagon in the driveway, blanketed in months' worth of snow, and the foliage grown in around it, I hid from view and held my breath to listen.

"You can go back and tell the others about it," one of them muttered.

I could barely make out their outlines through the trees. It wasn't enough to get a shot without having to leave the cover of the station wagon.

"There are women in there, and children." Mr. Smiles stepped out of the shadows again, closed his eyes and inhaled. "I can smell their fear."

"Yeah, but how many are there?" whispered another. "You almost got us killed last time. That old woman was armed—"

"This is different," Mr. Smiles' voice was low as he peered around. "There's a weak one—sick maybe. And the children . . ."

"And a pissed off mother," another bit out. "You're going to get us killed, Tommy."

"Not if you stop them first," Tommy bit out. "We're here to

practice, so fucking practice—use your senses and stop being a little bitch." He smacked the man upside the head.

Senses? Like *powers*? My worst fear assembled before me: insane wielders of inhuman powers hunting for victims, ready and willing to use them, even on children. But in this scenario, I wasn't helpless. In fact, I was fuming, loathing every crazy asshole left in this world, wanting them to burn.

The anger stirred, vehemence stoking the flame.

I needed the rest of the men to step out of the shadows so Sophie and I could take our shot.

"How many of them are there?" One of the men rasped. I could see pacing shadows through the trees and hear the uncertainty in his voice. Tommy's flunkies were wobbling and I could use that to my advantage.

Tommy shook his head. "I don't know."

"Why don't you come and see!" I said as loudly and confi-dently as I could. "We won't hurt you."

Tommy's sneer was visible in the moonlight, and his eyes glis-tened as he searched the outline of the station wagon for me. "I wondered why the scent grew stronger."

That he could smell me made my skin crawl and the burn in my veins turned to a boil. "If you drop your weapons we won't kill you," I lied.

Tommy held up his hand as he slyly motioned for the others not to move, then he stepped back into the shadows with them. "You promise?" he asked, and I could hear the smile in his voice.

That was one thing I was learning about the crazy survivors; they tended to think they were so smart, but were overzealous and that left room for error. The people in the bus depot had been the same way, and all it took was a little unexpected disorder for them to lose their footing.

"Of course I promise."

I heard him inhale, in an exaggerated manner, like he wanted me to know what he was capable of.

"You're not like the others," he realized.

I wasn't sure what that meant, but I used it to egg them on. "Is that why you're hiding in the shadows, because you're afraid of a woman?"

I heard the click of a gun magazine as one of the men growled. "I'm going to fucking kill her, Tom, I'm going to—"

"You're hiding like little boys because you're scared; you don't know how many of us there are. You don't know what we can do."

"The fear I smell tells me it's not much," Tommy bit back.

"Then, come closer—"

"How about I shove my pistol in your mouth, bitch, and shut you up!" the aggressive one shouted.

"Get your shit under control, Bill," Tommy ground out. Low voices were pointless on a still night. "You hear me? Your strength is no good if you get shot in the fucking head." There was a rustle, and while I couldn't see what they were doing, I didn't care.

Strength. Smell. Whatever their abilities, I wasn't waiting around to find out what they could do. Without hesitation, I aimed through the trees, knowing I'd injure them if nothing else, giving myself time to get closer.

There was a creaking of a door, like they were pulling something out of the truck, planning something I couldn't see. I needed to make my move. Now.

Before I could pull the trigger, the shotgun upstairs went off, and I heard a man curse in pain as he fell to the ground. Heart pounding, I crouched and ran around the station wagon, praying I would get a clear shot before one of them did.

When I saw one of them stand up, I pulled the trigger, the man's body instantly falling to the ground with a thud.

I strained to listen over my heartbeat for movement—for noise. One growled in pain on the ground, but I heard no one else. Only two shots, and while two men might be down, there was still one unaccounted for. Hiding. On the run. Crouched in waiting for a decent shot.

I squinted into the darkness, pressed against the shadows of the trees lining the yard, hoping for the slightest movement.

Another gunshot rang out through the house, and I ran to the backdoor, not caring who could see me. "Sophie!" I screamed, and I fumbled up the steps and inside as quickly as my feet would move. My pistol was raised, and I moved so fast, I felt like I was flying. Then the kids screamed.

"Thea!" I shouted again, reaching the landing to find a lifeless man on the floor. Sophie's jacket was hanging off her arm and her shirt was ripped, but she was okay.

I leapt over the body on the floor and into the kids' room. They were crying, huddled in the corner, terrified, but alive.

They were alive.

Beau held his sister in his arms, both of them shaking as tears streamed down their cheeks.

Sophie stood facing the doorway, staring at the man's body. "I hesitated—"

"It's okay, Sophie. You saved Beau and Thea. They're okay because of you."

I dropped my gun and with shaking hands I pulled her into my arms and choked a sob. I could've gotten them all killed. "We should've gotten to the car and left," I breathed. The four of us might've been shook up, but the kids wouldn't have had to see another man killed. "We should've just left," I repeated.

Beau screamed and Sophie shouted my name, pointing behind me.

I turned around as the dead man clambered to his feet, but he hadn't been dead, the gunshot was in his leg. He had my stupidly discarded gun in his hand.

"You stupid bitch," he seethed, rubbing the back of his head. There was blood on his hand from where he'd hit the wall, I could see it on the pale paint. He glared at Sophie, then at me, limping to a stand. Sophie's shotgun was on the floor, reachable, but not without him shooting one of us first.

I stepped in front of Sophie instead; anger, terror, and hatred coursing through me like the breath that sucked in and out of my lungs. *I am not helpless*, I reminded myself. The adrenaline fed every part of me. "What the hell do you want!" I ground out.

"You to die," he said, and he aimed the pistol at me. His leg almost gave out on him, but he didn't need both legs to shoot me.

"No," I told him and shook my head. I outstretched my arms, like a protective shield.

"Next time, make sure I'm dead," he seethed, and I knew what was coming before I heard his finger on the trigger. I could feel it in my bones, the imminent future, and I would not let him hurt us.

"No!" I growled this time. Raw power whirred through my veins, and for the first time in months I gave into the incessant heat. A burning energy lit my skin, turning to roiling red flames, and the man's sneer faded.

A raging, blinding power enlivened every part of me, and without moving, I reached for the intruder with fingerlike flames. They wrapped around his neck, dropping him to the ground as his eyes bulged and he clawed at his neck. Then he began to scream.

An indescribable force leached from my every pore as the man's life force flared with desperation. I could feel his energy coursing through me, feeding the fire to blazing.

And with his final breath, the inferno was snuffed out.

Everything grew dark again, and I dropped to my knees, my chest heaved and I gasped for breath. My molten insides cooled with each pull of crisp air, and my eyes adjusted to the darkness. The man was more than dead; I scorched him nearly to ash, smoke steaming from what remained.

"Elle . . ." Beau whined. But I couldn't respond as I tried to find myself again.

"Elle . . ." Sophie said close behind me.

I peered back at their blurred visage. "Are you all right?" I croaked.

They climbed to their feet to run over, and I shrieked, backing away. "Don't—" I warned them. "Don't touch me." My body had been aflame. "Don't touch me," I reiterated, still trying to catch my breath. I stared down at my clothes, realizing they were partially singed and smelled of smoke, but my hands were my normal hands once more. I turned them over and over and I patted my chest, making sure I was in one piece.

Beau was crying behind me while Sophie tried to ease him away. "Give Elle some space, bud." I could only hear her remotely, somewhere distant, as I stared at the burnt man's remains, remembering the night I'd killed someone for the first time. This time, I *allowed* myself to feel gratitude for what I could do, even if I didn't understand it. Even if it was dangerous.

"Gather your things," I said, rising shakily to my feet. "They have a larger group, and they could be here any second. We need to get out of here."

I picked up my pistol and handed Sophie the shotgun. "You might need it." We could dissect whatever had happened later. More men would come looking for these ones. "I'll be right back."

Sophie took a hesitant step toward me. "Where are you going?"

I didn't tell her one man was still alive outside. There was no reason to. "He was right," I said as I gripped the railing to the stairs. "I should've made sure he was dead. I won't make that mistake again."

35

ELLE
APRIL 11

I brushed a loose strand of hair from my face, finally feeling the coiled tension in my body ease the further we drove from Slana. I'd changed my clothes, but my hair was a knotted mess and smelled of burnt cotton, making it difficult to lock the past three hours away somewhere deep in my mind for a little while. At least if more men showed up, we'd be long gone. For the first time in my life, I hoped for a snowstorm to cover our tire tracks.

I prayed Jackson and Alex would see our note. Jackson hadn't picked up the sat phone when I'd tried to call him. Now, it was what would happen after they saw the man upstairs that I couldn't get off my mind. Jackson would see what was left of the charred body in the hallway; he could put two and two together and would know I was the one who killed his father, and while he might not fault me for saving myself, he would hate me for lying to him. *I* hated me. He deserved the truth, and yet I hadn't been able to give that to him. It was self-preservation and selfishness, just as much as it was fear.

My gloved hands gripped the wheel, the leather protesting. Succumbing to thoughts of the unknowable future, I continued down the dark highway. The ever-present *thing* inside me had brought as much horror as it brought protection and peace of mind. Knowing there were others that could do impossible things made driving with the lights on a risk, but it was one I had to take if I would get us to our meeting point in Tetlin safely.

In our haste, we'd crammed the Explorer full of what supplies we could, and hitched up the trailer only half loaded, but we had the essentials, which was enough. It had to be.

Sophie stared out the window.

The car was awash with silence, and I cleared my throat. "How are they doing back there?" It was the first and only thing anyone had uttered since we'd gotten on the road.

Sophie glanced in the back. "They're sleeping."

"Good. But I don't know how they can sleep after what just happened."

Remembering Sophie's torn shirt, I cleared my throat. "Sophie," I said as carefully as I could. In the past twenty-four hours she'd had a breakdown, confessed her biggest secret, killed a man, and I wasn't sure what else.

She looked at me.

"Did he touch you, Soph—"

She shook her head. "I'm fine."

"That's not what I asked." I knew the look on her face. It was one of shame and disgust. Even if I knew he didn't get far, the thought of his hands on her at all made the bile churning in my stomach creep its way up my throat.

"I don't think that's what he wanted, but either way, we stopped him. Really, I'm fine, Elle. I promise." That she'd likely *seen* his intentions when he touched her might've been the worst part of all.

Thea stirred in the back seat, and Sophie leaned her head back with a sigh. "When I was little, I loved riding in the car. It was soothing. I always fell asleep. Now . . . not so much." Leaning over, she rifled through her pack and pulled out a bag of sunflower seeds. "Want some? They help me keep my mind busy."

"No, thanks." I glanced in the rearview mirror, relieved to see there was still only darkness behind us, and the faint red hue of our taillights. "My stomach's in knots. I'd probably just throw it up."

Sophie tossed a handful into her mouth, and aimed the heater vent at her.

"I wonder if I'll ever be cold again," I thought aloud.

Sophie eyed me a moment, then a slight upward curve formed on her lips. "Lucky."

I allowed myself a small smile. In a way, I guess she was right.

Sophie brought an empty water bottle to her mouth and spit in a few shells. "Hey, Elle? He said he could smell us."

My jaw ached as I gritted my teeth together. "Yeah, he did."

"He could *smell* us . . . That's crazy right? I mean, if . . ." She leaned her head back against the headrest. "If we can do what we can do, and we're not crazy, and he could do what he could do and he *was* . . ."

"Maybe he was, maybe he wasn't. I'm not sure how to tell who's what, fanatical or just plain mad."

"What else can people do? I mean, how much danger are we *really* in?"

Her gaze was adhered to my face, waiting for answers I didn't have.

Sophie rolled her shoulders and stared out the windshield. "Predator and prey."

I glanced at her. "What?"

"In nature, there's a balance to everything—an evolution. Like a moth with large eyes painted on its wings to scare off predators, and frogs with alluring toxic skin. Jackson said we're not the top of the food chain anymore." She popped a few more seeds into her mouth, trying to put the pieces together, but I had little insight to offer. "If natural selection reset the scales, those of us left have to find a new balance."

"You're saying what's happening to us is Mother Nature?" The thought hadn't occurred to me. "That seems a bit rash."

"That doesn't mean it's not true."

I blinked at her. "I feel like evolution takes a bit longer than a couple days of being sick with the flu."

"Mother Nature can be extreme—just look at where we live. What matters is that we're not defenseless. If the bad guys can use their powers for evil, we can use ours for good."

"Soph, we're not superheroes—"

"No, but we're different and you saved us tonight. If you hadn't fried that guy, we'd wish we were dead."

I gripped the steering wheel more tightly, hating that she had to know it was true.

"There may be bad guys out there who've become more powerful than they were before, but Mother Nature or whatever this is, hasn't left us defenseless."

"Not all of us can do this kind of stuff," I reminded her. "So how does that rate in your theory? Some of us are defenseless against superpowers? That seems rigged."

"I didn't wake from the fever like this. Maybe it takes time and not everyone knows they have a superpower yet."

"Soph, can you stop calling it that please? It's weird."

"What do you want me to call it, a *gift*?" she said dryly.

I shuddered. "No, it's not a gift."

"Then we'll stick with power for now."

I sighed, too exhausted to argue. Theoretically, Sophie's points were valid, but the *how* of it all was still a mystery. "What does that mean for you? Your superpower is to be miserable by seeing and feeling people's memories?"

"I guess," she grumbled.

I didn't want to criticize her for something completely out of her control, but if someone less obvious and sinister than Mr. Smiles had bad intentions, she wouldn't know until he already had his hands on her.

"I'm just trying to understand," Sophie whispered, her voice deflated to utter exhaustion.

"I know, Sophie. I'm sorry. I'd like to think I'm superhuman and can save the world, but it doesn't work that way. What I can do is dangerous. *I* am dangerous."

"No, you're not."

"Yes, I am."

Sophie didn't argue further and turned her attention back out the window. "Jackson will freak when he finds out what happened," she muttered.

I rested my elbow on the door and rubbed my temple. "Yes, he will." And that was putting it lightly.

"Not because of the bodies," she clarified. "He will think he failed us—he'll blame himself."

"What? No, he might worry for a minute, but he'll be occupied with other feelings, trust me."

"You don't know him like I do."

The certainty in her voice gave me pause, and I glanced at her.

"He couldn't save his wife and child, and he'll feel like he failed us too."

The last thing I wanted was Jackson to bear the weight of guilt for something completely out of his control. "But we're fine," I told her, like she could somehow channel that to Jackson. "He'll see our note and he'll know we're fine."

Sophie nodded slightly, probably just to make me feel better, but she said nothing else.

I peered quickly back at the kids, heads lobbed to the side, faces smooshed with sleep. "They're going to need so much therapy," I muttered.

Sophie chuckled, even if it was true.

I thought about Dr. Rothman. "I used to know a pretty good therapist," I said, but Sophie probably knew that already. "I'm sorry you have to know everything," I told her. My baggage was heavy and drowning, I couldn't imagine carrying the weight of everyone else's baggage too.

"Not everything, but yeah, I know about her. Sorry."

I reached for Sophie's hand, an instinctive offer of comfort, and she didn't shy away when I clasped my hand over hers. "Don't be sorry about what you can do, Soph. I wouldn't wish my bullshit on anyone. *I'm* sorry you have to feel the things you do. I honestly can't imagine."

Sophie stared at my hand.

"Sorry—" I tried to pull away, but she clasped her other hand on top of it.

"It's okay." When I glanced at her, she smiled. "It's not all bad. I see the good stuff too, it's just harder to remember sometimes." I nodded and pulled my hand away. "It's nice to have someone like you, to know how much you care."

The road blurred as my eyes began to shimmer. "I would do anything for you, Soph."

"I know. And Dr. Rothman would be really proud of you."

I blinked, licking my lips. I imagined Dr. Rothman would tell me I'd finally found my family, even if it had been in the most impossible sort of way. "Thank you." I wiped my eyes and cleared my throat.

Sophie spat her seeds into the bottle, both of us ready for a change in subject. "Let's see if there's a new transmission from Hartley," she said, and switched on the radio.

She scanned the static until it stopped at a familiar voice. I rolled my eyes, following the bend in the road.

"They're calling them safe zones," said Mr. Conspiracy Theory over the radio.

"I swear this guy is haunting me—"

"Look out!" Sophie screamed as three caribou ran out of the tree line and onto the highway.

I slammed on the brakes and the Explorer swerved. My arm flew out to cover Sophie as the car collided into one of them.

The car crunched and rolled, and everything was silent.

36

ELLE
APRIL 12

The scent of balsam and earth filled my nostrils. My head was pounding like a kick-drum in a heavy metal band, and my limbs felt too heavy to move.

I remembered the caribou, and my eyes flew open as I gasped.

"Shh. Shh." A man hummed beside me.

The world was a blur that made little sense, but I wasn't in an aluminum grave, like I'd expected. No more cold air. No more kink in my neck. I was in a bed in a warm room.

I blinked again, my heartbeat drumming as a male form stood up from his perch beside me. My breath caught in my throat as an all too familiar silhouette came to stand beside me.

I tried to shout. "Who—" My throat burned, and I nearly choked. "Who are you?"

"Shh." The man pressed lightly against my shoulders, easing me back down. "Your body needs rest," he said a little gruffly.

I shook my head, regretting it instantly, and my hand flew to my temple. A shooting pain ricocheted through my chest, and I cringed. "Ow . . ."

"Easy," he said. "You need to take it easy." His dialect was one I'd heard before, a mix of soft and hard consonants, like the old fisherman who always sat on the dock, smiling at me as I disembarked the cruise ship back home.

I blinked up at him, watching his fuzzy form take shape.

"You probably have a concussion." He had dark, wrinkly skin, a pinched mouth, and shaggy gray hair around his ears.

"Beau—Thea—"

"They're all right, Miss."

Another man with a fur cap startled me as he moved in the doorway behind him. "My wife is making them burbot stew next door."

"Next door . . ." I blinked at him, trying to piece together the forgotten moments. "You were standing outside the window—" I tried to remember. I was hanging upside down in the driver seat, and he came to get me out. "Where's Sophie?"

"Everyone is fine. A little banged up, but it looks like you got the worst of it."

Even the soft firelight seemed too bright, and I closed my eyes, willing the throbbing to go away. "There was a herd of caribou in the road . . ."

"I know, Miss," he said as he stepped further inside. "One of them didn't make it, but the others took off. I'm headed out to track them now."

"Track them? Why?" I peeled my eyes open again and noticed he had a rifle in his hand.

"There's no sense in lettin' good meat go to waste."

Caribou. After everything else, I hit a fucking caribou? We'd almost died. Again.

Unbidden, tears burned the backs of my eyes. "The kids," I said. "I need to see them."

"Of course," the hunter said, and the floorboards protested as he turned to leave. "I'll send them in." There was a gentleness in his voice that made the tears form faster.

"Who are you people?" I asked with a tremulous breath. I stared between the old man and the hunter at the door.

"I'm Del," the hunter said. "This man here is my father-in-law, Took. We heard the accident as we were packing up to go out ice fishing. We brought you back to our place on Mentasta Lake, just outside the village."

They were Athabascan, natives to the land and subsistence homesteaders, which accounted for the Moon Totem around the old man's neck. They could've hurt us if they'd wanted, instead I was in a warm bed with a fire burning in the stove and incense in the air.

"Thank you," I heard myself say, though my voice seemed far away. I wiped the moisture from my eyes, registering how strange my hands felt, then horror shot through me. I stared at my naked fingers. "Where are my gloves?" I croaked. "I need my gloves—"

"Miss—"

I gripped the blankets between my fingers, ignoring the ache in my wrist. "Where are they?" I grimaced as a sharp pain shot through me. I would get up if I had to, and the old man knew it. His eyes widened, and he leaned over to a small table against the wall and handed them to me.

I pulled them over my fingers. "You don't understand," I said in a rush. "You don't understand." I ignored the pain in my side and my chest—in every tiny movement. "Please," I pleaded, barely able to keep myself together. What if they weren't kind, what if this was all a ploy I couldn't make sense of in my fuzzy state? What if the kids weren't really okay? "I need to see Sophie." It was the only way I could be sure she and the kids were safe—that these people were trustworthy—before I lost the last shred of control I had left to hysteria.

"I'll get her," Del said, more apprehensive than kind this time. With a final exhale he disappeared out the door.

"Can I continue then?"

"What?" I looked at Took.

"I need you to look at me," he said, grumpier than before.

I did as he asked, and followed a barrage of requests: look to the left and to the right; let me know if you feel nauseous or dizzy; take a deep breath. And when I winced, Took nodded and leaned back in his rickety, old rocking chair. "It's as I suspected."

"What is?"

"You have a bruised rib, or maybe it's cracked, and a strained arm too, by the look of it. I don't think it's broken though. And you likely have a concussion." I didn't argue with him. My chest, my arm, my face and head . . . They all ached.

"May I touch you?" he asked. There was a sass in his voice I appreciated; even if he was irritated, he was at least being rational. "I need to wrap your wrist before you make it worse." He practically glared at me, and I felt my cheeks redden. I peered down at the quilt clenched in my hands and let go.

I nodded.

"Now," he said evenly. "Can I fold your glove down so I can finish with your wrist?" He was beyond exasperated with me.

"Uh, yeah. Sure." With rough but steady fingers, he folded the hem of the glove down and rubbed a salve around my wrist. It was mentholated and cool against my skin, and smelled of dirt.

"What is that?" I asked.

"Birch sap, to help with the swelling," he said, wrapping a bandage around it.

I peered around the small cabin, the size of my room back in Slana. There was only a single window, covered with a gray-and-black fur. Light from the wood-burning stove flickered against the walls, and a candle burned in an old coffee tin on the table beside the bed.

I wanted to believe these were good, honest people who wanted to help me, but a whisper in the back of my mind kept saying, *what if?*

Took sat back in his chair, putting the lid on the salve.

I flashed him a sheepish, tentative smile. "Thank you."

He nodded but watched me with shrewd, gray eyes. He was as

leery of me as I was of him. I probably seemed psychotic after my outburst with the gloves. It was for his own good though.

"Can you tell me how long I was asleep?" My head was too muddled to tell.

"A couple hours." He poured me a copper cup of water and set it on the side table. "You should rest." He got up and stretched his back, clutched the salve in his hand, then went to the door and stepped out. Daylight filtered inside, cold air came with it, and I welcomed the reprieve. Then Took closed the door, shutting me inside again.

Leaning back against the feather-stuffed pillow, I took a deep breath and peered around the small wood cabin, devoid of any frivolities. The only thing that hung on the wall was a realistic sketch of an owl. A walking stick was propped up next to a patchwork leather jacket, hanging on a hook by the door, and snow boots were discarded beneath it.

The only other furniture was the small table, which had the candle and the cup of water. The table could fit no more than a book, and a trunk sat at the foot of the bed, resting on a pinewood frame. A quilt and blankets of fur were draped over me.

As carefully as I could, I peeled one of them off with a shaky arm. The cabin was well insulated, I'd give them that, and the longer I laid there, listening to the roar of the fire, the heavier my eyelids became.

I pressed my fingers to my side and then to my chest, wincing as I tried to figure out where it hurt the most. My chest and my side. My head. *Everywhere*, I decided.

The door creaked, slowly at first, and my eyes flew open. Sophie poked her head in, and when she saw me, she smiled and opened the door wider for Thea and Beau to come in.

I exhaled every ounce of tension in my body at the sight of their smiling faces.

"You're awake!" Thea chirped, and she skipped over. She had a butterfly bandage on her left cheek.

"You—" I winced, moving too quickly to sit up in bed.

Sophie reached for Thea's arm before she got too close. "Del said to be careful," she reminded her. Regretfully, Thea stopped short of jumping up on the bed.

"Oh, I'm okay, just a little tired," I told them, overjoyed. The scratches and bumps on their faces could've been so much worse.

I absorbed the sight of Beau and Thea, both in one piece, then looked at Sophie. Each of their expressions were soft with affection not fear, and my eyes filled with tears. I covered my face and shook my head. How was it possible that things had gone from bad to worse in a matter of hours? "I can't believe that happened," I said, voice trembling.

"It's okay," Sophie said, sitting on the edge of the bed. "*We're* okay."

"The car's screwed," Beau added, and I huffed a quick laugh.

Thea glared at him. "That's a bad word."

Beau rolled his eyes. "Whatever." If they were bickering, they really were okay, and I nestled a little deeper into the bed.

"Jade is really nice," Thea said. "She's making lunch, and we can stay here as long as we want."

I glanced at Sophie. "Are you certain?"

She tilted her head and tucked her hair behind her ear. "Yes, I'm certain. They're all very nice."

"Took is funny. He's just like my grandpa," Thea said. "He makes funny duck noises."

Beau rolled his eyes. "He doesn't look like Grandpa. Grandpa isn't Inuit."

"Yeah-huh!"

"No, he's not. You're such a liar—"

"Okay you guys," Sophie interrupted and she shooed them away from the bed. "Let's let Elle get some rest, okay?"

"I can't rest," I said, wincing as I flung the rest of the covers back. "We need to figure out how we'll get back on the road. Jackson and Alex—"

"Elle, please. We'll figure it out, but you can't fix this right now—you look like you're going to pass out."

My pain tolerance was high, but between my head and the fact it hurt to breathe, I knew she was probably right.

"Alex and Jackson won't be heading back until tomorrow, anyway. They won't know anything's happened. You have time to rest."

Each breath was a sharp twinge, and I knew the pain meant one thing: I was useless for now, and I had to trust Sophie's judgement. "Okay," I said. "I'll try."

Sophie stood up to leave.

"Elle," Beau said, excited. "They have a real bow and arrow. Del said he might teach me to use it if you say it's okay."

"Guys, come on," Sophie ordered. "We'll deal with that later. Elle needs to sleep. We'll bring her some soup when it's ready."

"That would be great, thank you." I had no appetite, but I welcomed any excuse for them to come back and reassure me they were okay.

The kids turned on their heels, the knitted ball at the top of Thea's beanie shaking with each step as they made their way to the door. Sophie turned back to look at me. "We'll be back to check on you in a little while."

I nodded, beyond grateful for her. Then, the three of them were out the door, clicking it shut behind them.

I stared up at the birchwood ceiling as the light from the stove flickered across it. How long did a busted rib take to heal? With my luck, months. After I got some sleep, I would walk back to the Explorer and get the satellite phone. I would call Jackson, they would find us, and we'd figure it out together.

With that comforting thought, my eyelids drooped lower, and I fell back to sleep.

37

JACKSON

APRIL 12

The sun sank behind the mountains and the sky grew darker as we settled in for the final stretch back to Slana. The trip was successful with no run-ins to speak of. In the scheme of things, the hungry dog didn't count. We'd gotten what we needed and were out faster than I'd expected, which meant we'd return to Elle and the kids a day early.

The trees passed outside the window, dark shadows in the inky sky.

"Jackson," Alex said, he'd been quiet for the past couple hours.

"Hmm?" I glanced in the rearview mirror to find a stretch of snow and nothing more.

"Have you felt weird since you had the fever?"

I glanced at him. I'd felt a whole mess of things since the virus. "Just about everything is weird these days."

Alex stared out the passenger window, quieter than usual.

"What's on your mind, kid?"

He shrugged, though it was obvious it was weighing on him. "I haven't said anything because I don't actually know what it is, but, sometimes I wonder if something is wrong with me."

It felt like we were heading into a discussion I was ill-equipped to handle, but I had little choice. With a quirked eyebrow, I looked over at him. "What do you mean?"

"Sometimes, when I'm around Sophie, I feel strange things—"

"Wait—aren't you old enough to know about boys and girls and—"

"What? No—I mean, yes, I am." He shook his head. "I'm not talking about sex."

I silently thanked Mother Nature that puberty hit before eighteen.

"It's a charge . . . it's kind of indescribable, I guess. I've gotten it around Elle too, a couple times. It's different around both of them, but the same too."

"A charge? What, like static?" I switched the headlights on as the road grew darker in the failing light.

He shook his head. "It's fucking weird, like I said. It's not all the time, but it makes me feel powerful and full of energy, like I need to do something with it."

"Like what?"

"I don't know." He crossed his arms over his chest and leaned against the window. "I sound crazy."

"Alex, I'm not sure what—" I leaned forward, looking out at a large dark mass on the highway ahead.

Alex braced the dash. "What is that?"

"It looks like . . . a trailer and—" Dread washed over me. "That's the Explorer." I sped up only to damn near slam on the brakes as we came up to the overturned car and the trailer.

"What happened?" Alex shouted, jumping out of the truck.

I grabbed my rifle and jumped out after him, running to the busted windshield and the crunched metal. Icy fear shot through me, and I gripped my gun so tightly the foregrip creaked in my hands. A few boxes and bins scattered the ground; the snack box with Thea's smiley face sticker was dumped all over the road.

I stepped over the trailer hitch and hurried to the driver side.

The door was open and drag marks overlapped footprints in the snow. The Explorer was empty.

"Where are they?" Alex ran his hand over his head and peered around the dark road and the surrounding forest. "What the hell were they doing out here?"

My mind spun as I tried to understand. It was too early in spring to pull the trailer, Elle knew that, yet she'd packed everything and headed northwest.

Alex stood a toppled gas can up. "They had extra fuel—do you think they were going to the meeting spot?"

"Yes, but something happened." I peered around at the wreckage. And now they were gone and there were traces of blood in the snow where I stood.

"Elle!" I shouted, glancing into the tree line. She could've dragged herself into hiding, or the kids. "Elle!"

"Jackson," Alex hissed from the front of the car.

I shined my flashlight down at the caribou tracks, there were several, and there was blood. A lot of blood. The pieces began to fall together. It was what happened after the accident that worried me.

I spotted snowmobile tracks a few yards out, barely illuminated by the Tacoma's headlights, and my gut twisted. She hadn't loaded the snowmobiles, and the tracks were fresh. "Alex, we have to find them," I said low and calm. "Get your gun."

38

ELLE
APRIL 12

When I woke, it took a split-second to remember where I was, but the instant I tried to move, it all came rushing back. The room was as it had been before, only this time, my boots and snow coat were at the foot of the bed, along with my gun in my hip holster.

I lifted myself up from the bed with my good arm, though it felt just as banged up as the other. I grumbled to my feet, wincing and irritated that I'd gotten myself into this mess, but eventually I was sitting up, trying not to breathe too quickly and too deeply, knowing it would hurt.

Standing, I reached into my back pocket, and I let out a breath of relief as I pulled out my sister's note. It was folded in half, but still here.

The sound of silence will set you free. In the silence there I'll be.

Though I'd read it a dozen times, chills raked over my skin as I read the second sentence. *In the silence there I'll be.* Though I knew it was impossible, it seemed as if Jenny had known the end was coming, that maybe in some way, we'd find our way back to each other somehow. It was eerie to imagine her curled up on her couch writing it while death loomed in the future; it was a future in which the world was silent and all I had left of her were these words, making her more present in my life, dead, than she ever was alive.

I didn't have the bandwidth to think about it; Jenny's riddle would have to wait.

Painstakingly, I pulled my boots on over my socks, forgoing the laces since my wrist was still tight. Though Took had been right and sleep had made my mind a bit clearer, my chest was killing me. I winced with each movement and prayed bark salve wasn't his only remedy. I knew subsistence living meant removal from society, forgoing the daily conveniences of modern day, but did that include absolutely everything?

I clipped on my hip holster, saw a clean thermal shirt, but stayed in my dirty clothes, torn sleeve and all. The sooner I could be functional again, the better, but clean clothes seemed too ambitious just yet.

Foregoing my jacket, since I didn't need it anyway, I eyed a large folded cloth on the side table that would come in handy if I remembered what Jackson had taught me. I had a sneaking suspicion my generous hosts didn't have pain killers readily available, and the pain could use a little numbing.

I took the cloth and made my way to the door, grateful my sprain and hurt rib were on the same side so I was partially operational.

Shockingly, the tingle in the tips of my fingers hadn't returned since Slana, but I told myself it didn't matter. I had plenty of problems to figure out without adding Sophie's superpower theory to the mix.

The crisp evening air hit my face, sending chills over my skin, as I stepped outside. It felt refreshing after being cooped up inside, and I welcomed it in my lungs.

Using the porch rail, I lowered myself down to sit on the step as slowly as possible, careful not to make any sudden movements.

I reached my good arm out and scooped up a handful of snow to wrap into an icepack. The idea had been well thought out in my head, but I could feel the sweat beading on my brow as I tried to face the smarting pain that followed.

A dog yipped at the edge of the homestead, and I looked up to find I was being watched. A husky sat on the roof of his doghouse, his white and black-splotched head tilted to the left.

"I'd like to see you try it," I muttered, pressing the cold pack against my side. I felt instant relief, though I wasn't sure how long the ice would keep against my skin.

Letting the cold seep into my side, I peered up at the night sky. The moon was nearly full, lighting the path between the cabin I was in and the larger, main cabin. Took and Del had their own little compound here, an acre or so at least. What looked like an outhouse was set further into the trees, and a couple weatherworn sheds created a semi-circle around the perimeter. Pines and spruces sprinkled the property in between, and a truck was parked under an awning to my left.

As I trudged my way to the bigger cabin, I passed piles of wood stacked against the sides of each building, protected by more awnings that looked like they could use a little maintenance but served their purpose all the same. A narrow, aluminum-sided struc-ture was nestled between the two outbuildings, and I could imagine the racks of meat hanging inside, in fact, I could smell them. There were no fences to speak of, but I assumed the dog served as their security guard.

I'd never met anyone who lived on the land the way these people clearly did, and as apprehensive as I was about it, it was comforting in a way, too.

I stopped at the porch where The Ranskins was carved over the cabin door. Pots and pans clanged inside, amidst the tittle-tattle of the kids. With a tummy full of butterflies, I lifted my hand, prepared to knock, but hesitated. Knocking seemed strange knowing the kids were inside. Slowly, I turned the handle and opened the wood door.

Heat immediately pressed against my face, dense in the confines of the house, and the savory scent of food filled my nostrils.

"—mix it with potatoes. Everything is better with potatoes, they absorb so much flavor." An older woman, probably in her fifties with white hair knotted at the back of her neck, stood beside Sophie. The kitchen was just a nook in the far corner of the cabin, barely large enough for two people—but Jade didn't seem to mind sharing. They stirred their respective pots at the two-burner wood stove, conversing easily, with their backs to me. They looked like they belonged there together—grandmother and granddaughter. There were two shelves with plates, cups, and cooking utensils; some of them looked metal, but they were mostly wood.

"Alex is the one that likes to cook the most," Sophie told her.

I glanced up at the darkened loft above, then at the table where Beau and Took sat tying knots into a thin rope; then at Thea, curled up on what looked like a futon—small and functional for a mid-size cabin—flipping through the pages of a sketchbook twice as large as her lap. A large, soft-looking fur draped the back of the sofa, part of it covering Thea's little legs. She noticed me first from her perch on the couch. "You're awake!"

As everyone looked over, I closed the door behind me.

"Elle," Sophie said, and the older woman's eyes opened wide.

"Oh, dear me. I thought you were Del come back." She laughed nervously and hurried over, wiping her hands off on the corner of her dirty, cream-colored apron. "Elle, dear, it's nice to officially meet you." The smile in her eyes was warm and welcoming, and I tried not to stare at the vertical lines tattooed from beneath her lip, down to her chin. "I'm Jade, and this is my father, Took."

"We've met," he grumbled.

"Don't mind him," Jade said, waving his gruffness away. "He's harmless."

I nodded, sensory overload making it difficult to focus while the noise and scents registered. "It's nice to meet you." I smiled to be polite, but I couldn't help but wonder why they were being so kind. Either they hadn't come across any crazy people or they simply didn't care, and both were equally curious.

"We're having dinner!" Thea clapped the sketchbook shut and scooted it to the side.

"Dinner, huh?" I tried to smile, but my gaze got away from me, sweeping the rest of the room, like I might find more answers.

Books were stacked beside the couch, snowshoes and walking sticks mounted on the walls. Baskets hung from hooks on the ceiling, using every space so that the place was practically full. And then I realized five faces were appraising me.

"It's just about ready," Jade said. "You must be starving. Why don't you grab yourself a seat at the table there? My dad will help you—Dad, get Elle a chair, would you? Just move that laundry to the loft for now. I'll worry about it later."

"Uh, thank you, very much, but we really should be on our way."

"Nonsense, where will you go? It's dark and Del told me about the car." She sighed regretfully. "Besides," she said, wiping her brow with the back of her hand. "You still need rest and Sophie has made enough potato soup to feed an army." Jade smiled, winking at Sophie, like they'd known each other for years.

I glanced around at the kids, settled and entertained like they were visiting their grandparents for the evening. "You've already done so much, I don't want to overstay our welcome. After dinner—"

"Oh, it's no trouble at all. The truth is, we don't get visitors, and my son moved into town a couple years back. He comes around only a few times a year, though Del sees him regularly during the spring. That's a long way of saying, I enjoy the company," she finished, her smile broad and reassuring.

"Oh, okay," I said dumbly. It was like I'd walked into the Wilderness Family and I was only a viewer.

"Elle! Come see the new knot I'm learning." Beau waved me over. "Look." He held it up. "This one's hard."

"It *looks* really hard. What's it called?"

"It's a Car—" He looked at Took.

"Carrick Bend—"

"Carrick Bend," Beau echoed, chest out and proud. "It's a cargo net, sort of like the one you made."

"It's better than the one I made," I muttered. "It will be really useful. You'll have to show me later."

"I don't know if I can, but I'll try."

"Let's clean this up before Jade has a conniption," Took mumbled, gathering the thin rope into his hand.

Beau frowned. "A what?"

Took glanced from Jade who was oblivious to his mutterings, then back to Beau. "Nothing." So, Took was ornery and not just with me. I liked it.

"Look." Thea grunted as she lifted the sketchbook, it teetered in her hands as she strained to hold it out to me. "Wow," I breathed, and noticed a large *J* at the bottom of the sketch.

"Jade did them," Thea explained. She stretched her legs out, barely able to rest her feet on a giant tree stump that served as the coffee table. "No feet," I whispered with a frantic glance toward Jade.

Thea looked sheepishly at Jade, who was busy unstacking bowls for Sophie, and let her feet fall.

"Dinner's ready!" Jade announced. "Everyone grab a seat at the table. Sophie and I can take the couch."

I claimed the chair Took set out for me and anxiously waited for a steaming bowl of potato and leek soup, I could see the root ends discarded in a basket on the floor by the sink. I'd never had it before, but my mouth watered for it all the same. I hadn't realized how hungry I was.

"Did everyone wash their hands?" Jade draped a rag over her shoulder.

"Yes," Beau, Thea, and Took said in unison.

"Oh," I said, glancing at my gloved fingers. "I didn't."

Jade waved my concern away and grabbed a ladle from the utensil bin. "You didn't have a compost fight today, like some people." She waved the spoon at Took.

"What?" he grumbled. "It was for the kids. They had fun."

"Hmm. Sure." Despite her reprimand, she seemed happy to have all of us around, which made it feel like we were less of an inconvenience as I took some time to figure things out.

"Dad?" Jade said, handing Sophie the ladle to finish dishing up the soup. She walked over to the window and peered out at the dark sky. "Del should've been back by now. Will you see if he's out in the shed and bring him in for dinner?"

"Don't let anyone take my seat," Took told Beau, and he slid out of his wooden chair with a grunt and reached for his jacket on an iron hook by the door.

"I won't." Cold air fanned through the room as Took opened and then shut the door.

Jade sat a bowl of soup in front of me. "My husband gets so caught up dressing the meat after hunting, he loses track of time. Always. He'd likely be out there all night, the best cuts strung and hung up before morning."

The caribou, I remembered. Del had gone to salvage the meat. "Did he find them, then?" I asked.

"One died," Sophie said, setting a stack of napkins to the table. "He went for the others though." She inched my bowl closer to me. "Don't be scared," she said with a sly grin.

"Yeah, yeah. I didn't help with it, so it's edible." I knew the schtick. With feigned annoyance, I shook my head at her.

"You like to cook?" Jade asked me, and I nearly laughed.

"I like to, but apparently I shouldn't," I told her.

Jade's smile widened as she set another bowl on the table for Took. "It only takes a little practice," she said.

Shutting my eyes, I inhaled the scent of onion and pepper, and every other good thing inside. "It smells *amazing*."

Sophie set a bowl in front of Beau and he leaned closer to smell it. "Is it fish again?"

"It's potatoes and leeks," Sophie told him. "And yes, there's fish, so hush." She nudged his shoulder with a warning glare and walked back over to the stove.

Finally, after soup was served and water glasses were filled, Sophie sat down on the futon with her soup. "It smells okay," Sophie said, clearly surprised, and a little relieved.

"It's heavenly," I told her, swallowing my first bite. It left a garlicky singe on my tongue. "Hot but heavenly."

"It's Dad's favorite," Jade said and pulled her apron off over her head. "Though he'd never admit it."

Jade walked over to the window, peering out at the darkness.

"What about you, Jade?" I asked. "Are you going to eat?"

"Yes, but I'll wait for Dad and Del to come in." She waved for me to eat. "Go on, no sense in it getting cold."

Though I felt bad eating without her, I was too ravenous to argue and took another bite. I could see why the kids were so at ease here; Jade made it easy to relax and feel welcome. So much so, I momentarily forgot the guys would be looking for us come tomorrow morning. As I sat there examining every part of their modest home, I envied their little piece of wilderness. I knew it was endless work, but it was theirs.

Jade rubbed her arms and pulled the drapes closed. "I think it's time to replace the window." She smiled and finally sat down on the futon by Sophie. "As much as we try to live on our own, I'm getting too old to be cold all the time." She smiled, a kindness exuding from her that made me feel like I'd known her longer than mere minutes.

I swallowed another spoonful of soup and shut my eyes.

"Well, Beau, you're my greatest critic. Tell me, how do you like it?" Jade asked, sidling up next to him. Her eyes widened at his half-empty bowl.

"It's good I guess," he said.

Jade rumpled his hair and chuckled. "Good then. Now Sophie can make it for you."

"If I can remember." Sophie glanced at me. "Maybe I should've been writing this down."

Jade waved her uncertainty away. "I'll get you the recipe before you leave. Sarah, Jet's wife—that's my son—she caught on quick though, you might not even need it. Last I heard she'd even spruced it up, and it's one of Jet's favorite dinners."

"Where did you say they lived?" I asked.

"Delta Junction, it's a few hours away." She sighed. "I know it's not far, but when you don't get out much, it seems like the other side of the country." She sat on the couch and crossed her legs. "He moved there probably five years ago now. He met Sarah in town, and they fell in love. She's a good girl, and they have a lot of things in common, but subsistence living isn't one. Her father's got a welding shop in Junction, so that's where they settled."

She stared down at her fingers, turning the band around and around on her finger. She clearly missed her son, and like Jackson survived his wife and child, I couldn't imagine how hard it must've been for Jade to lose Jet.

She cleared her throat. "He doesn't get out here much to see us anymore."

I swallowed another spoonful and licked my lips. "So, he survived then?" Del, Took, Jade, *and* her son? While it was beyond fortunate for her, it seemed startlingly unfair in the scheme of things when I thought about all four kids and the parents they'd lost.

Jade's brow furrowed. "I'm sorry?"

"He survived the outbreak," I clarified. "You said he doesn't get out here much *anymore*."

But the lines in Jade's brow furrowed deeper, transforming her entire face from one of openness to desperate concern. "I'm not sure I know what you're talking about."

I looked at Sophie who seemed as confused as I was. "From the virus outbreak," Sophie said.

I shook my head. "We'd just assumed—"

"Assumed what?" Jade said. Her question teetered the sharp edge of panic.

"I told her about the men at the house—that we were attacked," Sophie said, frantic. Her eyes shimmered and her cheeks reddened. "But I didn't bother to mention . . ." *What they were capable of or how.* And why would she have? It seemed impossible that Jade *didn't* know about the outbreak.

I swallowed a thick, suddenly nauseating mouthful of soup, uncertain what to say next. "Last December," I started as calmly as I could, "the H1N1/12 virus that ravaged the lower forty-eight before it made its way here . . . People got very sick."

Faintly, in a thought I pushed as far away as I possibly could, I began to worry Jade *was* crazy, and I'd made a dire mistake in letting us stay here. "We've all lost our families," I told her, measuring her every move as her eyes searched our faces.

Jade's uncertainty hardened, her gaze darting between the kids and me. "Is this a cruel joke?" she rasped, and there was no mistaking the distress in her voice. She wasn't crazy—she was clueless.

My heart hammered with uncertainty, and I paled. "We would never joke about this." I dropped my spoon into my bowl and faced her fully. "We were all sick," I told her, hoping that something might register in the gray depths of her eyes. "We all lost our families. We were strangers four months ago."

Jade scooted to the edge of the futon, searching our faces for the truth. Beau and Thea—all of us—stared at her, just as perplexed as she was.

"You don't get visitors," I breathed. It was a realization I couldn't believe I hadn't thought about until now. Being holed up here all winter, they had no reason to go anywhere. Incredibly, they didn't know about the virus at all, and miraculously they'd never been infected. With no television and no visitors, how *could* they have known?

My mind ticked through the possibilities of what that meant exactly. How many others like them were there? What did that mean for their physiology, and how did that play into Sophie's theory? Most importantly, were we contagious to them? I nearly choked on the thought, and the dread whitening Jade's face was enough to send everything I'd consumed back up again. There was a more delicate way to explain what had happened, but it was too late.

"Jade," I rasped. "When was the last time you saw your son?"

Her brow lifted and her eyes widened. "What?" She stood up as the panic set in. Her chest rose and fell, and she clasped her hand around the base of her throat like she was trying to hold back a scream. I could imagine the lump moving up her throat and the racing of her heart in her ears as she felt the weight of my words and thought of her son. It was how I'd felt when I thought I would die. It was how I'd felt when I thought my sister would die. It was how I'd felt many times since.

She hurried to the door and reached for her jacket. "Del!" she shouted, flinging it open. She stopped on the porch, unmoving.

"Jade!" I lunged to my feet, pain biting through me, but it didn't matter. If I'd given her a heart attack, I could never forgive myself. Wincing, I hurried out the door after her. "Jade, I'm so sorry—"

Del stood in his coat with his rifle in one hand, pulling a sled loaded with frozen meat behind him, like he was only just coming home.

"Where the hell were you?" Took complained as he came out of the shed across the yard, stomping his way across the snow. "I thought maybe you'd snuck off for a cigar without me—"

An engine rumbled in the woods behind us, and I turned around to see the snow plow jostling back and forth as the Tacoma rolled to a stop beside the cabin.

"I think I found your friends," Del said, meeting my gaze. "I should say they found me."

39

JACKSON
APRIL 12

D el had told us Elle and the kids would be here, and while I strangely thought I could trust him—I *needed* to if we had any hope of finding them—I was reluctant. Crazy people went to great measures to get what they wanted, they'd proven that time after time. Somehow, I thought Del was different though, and the instant I saw the smoke from the cabin chimney, I instinctively knew he was.

Alex jumped out of the truck before I'd brought it to a stop outside the settlement. I reached for the door handle as an older woman hurried, almost frantic, from the porch to Del. When I noticed Elle, standing just outside the doorway, it gave me pause.

Del had been telling the truth. She was alive like he had promised, looking at me. Her gaze was as expressive as always, wild and wide and shimmering. She chewed on her bottom lip—like she sometimes did when she was lost in her darkest thoughts—and I hated myself for not being there to protect her and the kids. The scratch on her cheek was an angry, taunting gash. Her ponytail was crooked and her long-sleeve shirt was torn, but she was standing there in one piece, practically glowing as the light spilled through the doorway behind her.

Letting out a ragged breath, I scrubbed my hands over my face, braced myself for whatever came next, and flung the door open as the fear finally subsided.

The instant I stepped out of the truck, Elle came closer and began to sob. "Jackson, I almost killed them," she cried. "I almost killed the kids. I'm so sorry—"

"Shh. You guys are okay." I wrapped my arms around her, feeling her flinch. As I let go, she gazed into my eyes and searched my face for only a second before grabbing desperately onto my jacket—balling it up in her fist—and she cried.

She was warm and solid, a fireball nestled against my chest, and a sense of calm came over me in a way I'd never felt before. The tension eased from my shoulders and I rested my cheek against her head.

"I knew we had to get out of there," she said in a rush. "I knew they would come back if we stayed, but the caribou—I didn't see the caribou . . ." Her words choked away as she tried to catch her breath, and like a bullet casing dislodged from its chamber, my calm spiked to a stomach-churning dread.

I looked down at her. "Who would come back?"

Elle blinked and swallowed, then she pulled away. Her wet eyes were shadowed and tired. "You didn't go to the house?"

Slana? Hesitant, I shook my head.

Elle stumbled backward. The relief in her eyes was gone. Her expression drawn and her chest heaving.

Why was she pulling away? "What happened, Elle?" I took a step closer, desperate to know what she wasn't saying.

"There were men," she said. "Three men who came. We're fine and they're dead, but"—she shook her head—"they said there were others. So, we left."

Breath wouldn't come quick enough and the implication of her words fell over me with a wave of hair-raising unease. "What men, Elle?" I took a step closer. "What did they do?"

She shook her head and wiped the tears from her eyes. "Nothing," she said, reluctant. I waited impatiently for her to continue. "Jackson, we're fine. Sophie and I shot them. You'd be proud of her, actually." She said it lightly, but those tears were not for nothing. There was something she wasn't telling me. "They didn't hurt us," she reiterated, but her eyes shimmered as she stepped closer, searching mine as if she struggled for the right words. "But they *were* dangerous, Jackson. They could do things—"

"—have to check on him!" Del's wife shrieked, staring up at him, and her hands flailed in desperation. "We have to know!"

Elle wiped the tears from her cheeks. "They have a son in Delta Junction," she explained. "And they didn't know about the outbreak, until now."

"What?" I looked at the old man standing in the doorway, peering out at the couple as Del pulled his wife into his arms. "How could they not—" But I already knew the answer. They'd carved themselves a place so self-sufficient they were cut off from the world, and the turmoil that came with it. Like our world had fallen apart months ago, theirs was only beginning to crumble.

After all they'd done for Elle and the kids, I took a step forward. "I'll take you to Delta Junction," I told them, glancing at Alex and the kids huddled in the doorway. "We just came back from there." They didn't know what they were up against, and after what had happened to Elle and the kids in Slana—whatever it might've been—I wouldn't let Del take any chances.

The man and woman looked at me. Tears filled her eyes and worry creased his brow.

"You helped my family, I'll do what I can to help yours."

40

JACKSON
APRIL 12

lex, Del, and I drove nearly the whole way in silence. It felt necessary after we'd dropped a bomb on them, potentially shattering their world. Del's attention was fixed on the long stretch of white that covered the road, lit only by the headlights of his old, clunky Dodge. We'd already plowed a path, which helped us make decent time.

Although I'd offered to drive, Del had needed to do this on his terms and in his own way. I'd thought about bringing two vehicles in case we needed room for one more, but I knew it was unlikely, and false hope wouldn't do Del or his wife any favors.

In the silence, my mind turned Elle's words over and over. There'd been a lot going on, a flood of high emotions and urgency as we loaded up to leave again. But what Elle had told me was enough to make the apprehension I'd already felt triple, and Slana had become a looming question mark I needed to know more about, though I feared the answers even more.

"They're not just crazy anymore, Jackson. They can do . . . un-natural things."

Yet when I'd asked her what they could do, she wasn't entirely certain.

"One of them said he could smell our fear, but I—I don't know about the others."

It was the way she'd grabbed my arm as I turned for the truck, the way she'd refused to let go until I acknowledged the heaviness of her words, that stayed with me most.

"You have to be careful."

I was certain Elle knew what she'd heard, but in the height of the moment and as crazy as the men clearly were, it could've been a group of sick fucks taunting her and the kids because they could. What weighed on me the most were the tire tracks we'd left behind for them to follow to begin with. I'd led the men right to the shop and respectively to the house, and I hadn't been there to protect the four of them. It gave me some comfort to know that Elle and Sophie didn't need my protection, but not enough.

Del grabbed the empty can from the cup holder attached to his dash and spit into it. He was like an old cowboy, but instead of living out west he was here, in the wooded mountains of the arctic.

"Birch bark," he explained, and looked at me sideways. "I chew when I'm restless. You want any?"

I knew birch wood and spruce gum were used a lot in the wildlands but seeing it used as a replacement for chewing tobacco was a first. I shook my head. "Thanks though."

"Suit yourself."

Alex dozed in the center seat, his head lulling back in exhaustion. I didn't blame him. Part of my mind longed for a glimpse of sleep, but I knew it was a long time coming yet. It felt more like a week had passed rather than a single day, and I'd been feeling the effects for hours now.

I stretched my legs out as much as I could, trying not to get too comfortable in the truck's warmth.

"So," Del said, clearing his voice. It was rough from disuse and maybe a little apprehensive. "The whole world, huh?"

"All of it." It still sounded fictional, saying it out loud.

"What else do I need to know about it?"

How did one explain the downfall of humanity on a global scale and the aftermath that followed, when all that likely mattered to this man was finding his son? "It mimicked the flu, or maybe it was the flu"—I shook my head—"I don't know. But, there was a rumor it was a government experiment gone wrong, and another that it was some ancient virus unearthed by climate change. If that'd been the case, I doubt the biggest outbreak would've been in New York so early on."

"There was never any explanation then?"

"Not yet." There was no one left to figure it out, which stirred deeper concerns the more I thought about it. "It was too late by the time they realized how bad it really was." I remembered the first day I'd heard about it on the news, and all I could do was shake my head, grateful we were in the middle of nowhere and not some metropolis. A lot of good it did us. "So much for innovation in the twenty-first century. Science couldn't even save us."

Del glanced at me. "Maybe that's what caused it."

Damn. He was probably right. "I wouldn't be surprised."

"At least your family survived, it sounds like that's more than most can say. How did you manage that? Did you have a bunker?"

"No, I'm not a prepper. And I did lose my family—my father, my daughter, and my wife."

Saying it out loud for the first time was like sticking a dull blade through my heart and cutting me through. The hurt hadn't gone away even if it had become easier to push away.

"I should prepare myself for the worst, is what you're telling me?"

His son was either dead or alive, and if he were the latter, he would not be the same person Del remembered. If he had been, he would've come home. "If Jet is alive, he'll be different. You should prepare yourself for that."

The truck bounced over the uneven snow, and Alex swayed in his seat beside me.

"Del," I started, fearing my concern had come too late. "We

haven't met people like you before, people who never had the virus. While I assume it's come and gone like the fever, having run its course, I don't—"

"Know if you're contagious?" he asked. There was no censure in his voice and no fear, like he'd already thought it through.

I nodded.

"If you are, it's already too late," he said. "And if we find Jet and bring him home, well, we might get infected that way too. I'm not sure there's a way around it at this point. There's no sense in dwelling on it."

In a way he was right, there was nothing we could do now. The kids had settled into their home, and Took, at least, had touched Elle's blood while dressing her wounds. I ran my hands over my face, rubbing the feeling back into my skin as numbness to all of this set it.

The outbreak had transformed the world—I could feel it in the silence, a void unlike anything I'd ever experienced. The more I thought about what Alex had said, the more I realized he was right. You could feel a charge around survivors—an energy—if you stopped to notice it. You could practically feel what was coming, good or bad.

"It makes sense," Del said. "Elle not being their mother," he clarified. "I thought she looked too young, but you never know these days."

"She found them in Whitely when she was looking for her sister. They all lost their parents."

"It was good of you to take them in."

"That was all Elle," I told him.

Del looked at me then peered out at the passing Delta Junction sign on the highway. Slow driving made for a long night, especially with uncertainty as to what awaited us, but we were close, and I hoped whatever we found gave the Ranskins some sort of peace.

"You know," he said. "When I first met Jet, he was a punk kid who was giving his mama a rough time. I knew it was because his father never treated him right, always drunk and belligerent, but I liked to think he was a decent kid under all the hurt."

"I didn't realize he wasn't your son."

"Oh, he is. That's how it works, you know? They wiggle their way into your life. It starts with seeing a spark in them you haven't noticed before, and maybe no one else has either. You see something that makes you want to work for it and somehow you build a friendship and a bond you never expected. Jet was never my son by blood, but we were closer than he ever was with his birth father."

Unexpectedly, I became acutely aware of Alex sleeping in the seat next to me. In my thirty years, I'd swayed between wanting children and not. Hannah changed all of that, and yet even now that she was gone, I could still imagine a relationship close to that of a father and son with Alex, which scared the shit out of me.

I looked at Del. "Were you a family friend or something?"

"I was Hank's best friend, and I watched the way he treated his family, maybe I even felt a little guilty for not stepping into their turmoil more while he was alive. But Jade has always been a good woman, and deserved someone to cherish her and her kid, and after twenty-three years . . ."

Del turned at the exit sign and onto the main road, passing the high school Alex and I had scavenged only hours ago. "Sometimes families have a way of forming, even if we don't think we need or want them."

The kids, Elle, and I had never planned on staying together; it was something we agreed early on. But I knew saying goodbye would be challenging, it was part of the reason I'd wanted to stay detached for so long. But growing closer or not, Hartley wasn't the place for me, I could feel it in my bones. "Elle and the kids are going to Hartley Bay," I told him. "There's a safe zone there, with a community for the kids, and safety . . . It will be the best place for them."

Del looked at me as he turned down a side street. "Will it?"

Scratching my jaw, I stared out the window. As we drew closer to the buildings and neighborhoods, I nudged Alex awake.

"You should park out here," I told Del. "Before we get too far into the populated areas."

"Why? We're still a good mile away from Jet's place."

"If anyone *is* here, we don't want them to know we're coming. Trust me." While Alex and I had already swept parts of the town, that didn't mean there weren't survivors somewhere, and after Elle's concern, we couldn't be too careful.

Del's face was expressionless, but fear was a black glimmer in his eyes, illuminated by the truck's dimly lit interior. He nodded, and drove a bit further up the road before pulling over under the cover of an empty carport.

I took my fleece cap off and ran my fingers through my hair. I wasn't sure I was ready for whatever we would find, let alone what Del would have to go through, but it was inevitable. And in a way, I knew Del was lucky to be with us instead of stumbling into the unknown completely blindsided.

"We go in on foot, take our weapons, and stay out of sight as much as we can," I told him and glanced at Alex. He already knew the drill.

With a nod from Del, I got out of the truck, Alex sliding out behind me, and we wrapped ourselves as best we could against the midnight cold.

When Del was ready, the three of us made our way into town against wind that felt more like razor blades. We didn't talk or stop for a break. We stuck to the shadows and paused every now and again to watch for movement or lights in windows, and to see if any smoke billowed from chimneys. We listened for sounds that carried in the increasing wind, but other than Mother Nature's nighttime fury, the coast was clear.

There was barely enough moonlight to see as it disappeared behind the clouds, but we made do; only using our flashlights when we needed to. Cars were partially buried in snow, some of them abandoned in the middle of the street—the passengers, human icicles inside—but Del didn't stop to look, and neither did we.

Homes and businesses had icicles hanging from the eaves, and not a person stirred as we made our way down a side street into a sparsely established neighborhood. It didn't look like one might expect—like a city that had been looted in the aftermath of the outbreak. Instead, it felt like the small town was only sleeping, under a dark and dangerous spell.

Del stopped at the street corner and peered around, not panicked like he was looking for something, but like he was taking it all in. Del was seeing the world as it was for the first time, and I could imagine the reality of it all settling in. If he couldn't quite grasp what I'd been telling him before, he understood it now.

He tugged his neck gaiter down to speak. "It's the last one on the right," he said into the wind, pointing down the street. He pulled his face protection up again and led the way.

Alert with our weapons in hand, we made our way down the abandoned street. Alex was cautious but walked with confidence. He held his gun like he'd been on a rescue mission a dozen times before. It was a welcomed reminder he would do well once I was gone.

When we reached Jet's house, an old 4Runner was parked in the side driveway, nearly covered in snow that slid from the rooftop. The 4Runner hadn't moved in months, and like the other houses we'd passed, the drapes were drawn and everything appeared dark inside.

Del tried to turn the front door handle first, but it was locked. "I don't know where he keeps his spare key," he admitted.

"We'll find a way in," Alex said, and he headed around to the back of the house, Del and I following behind him.

Del knocked on the sliding glass door and peered inside, through the open blinds into the darkness. No candles flickered and

Jet never came, and soon my unease turned from apprehension about what we might find to a sadness that seemed to settle over all of us.

Alex gabbed a shovel leaning up against the side of the house and offered it to Del. It would be the only way in, Del knew that much.

There was a thunk and a crash as the glass fell inside onto the linoleum floor. "Jet? Son, are you in here?" Del stepped through the glass and Alex lifted his rifle as he walked in behind him. My eyes shifted around the backyard, wondering if neighbors or anyone lurking nearby might've heard us. The wind was loud enough to muffle the sound and arrowlike spruces surrounded the whole backyard, encapsulating it in a winter wonderland that showed no signs of melting anytime soon.

Glock in my hand, I followed them inside, bracing myself for whatever Del would find next.

"Son?" Del's hunting rifle hung at his side as we swept the galley kitchen with our flashlights; followed by the adjacent living room, which looked forgotten.

Resigned, Del made his way down the narrow hallway, passing a bathroom that had a pile of towels and clothes on the floor, and toward a bedroom.

The air was frigid, like the ice itself had seeped inside and clung to the walls, and my breath was a white puff in the darkness.

Del stopped in the bedroom doorway, and Alex and I hung back, giving him all the space we could. A few breaths passed before Del stepped into the room, and reluctantly, I crept forward to ensure the room was clear. It was, save for a bearded man tucked into his bed, like he'd fallen into a frozen sleep, and the mound covered in a sheet beside him.

Del stood at the bedside, staring down at him. "He was lucky then," he croaked. Del crouched down, hesitantly resting his hand over Jet's, and I backed out of the room, leaving him with his grief.

A quiet Inuit prayer I'd heard only once reached my ears as I headed down the hallway, toward the back door. As the words rolled off of Del's tongue, they soothed old wounds and stung others still too raw, and I was grateful Alex didn't follow me.

Del's son had died peacefully in his sleep, but Hannah's final hours were more gruesome than that. I tried not to think of her terror as her murderer pointed a gun at her after she'd fought so hard to save herself, and I tried not to think about her pain as she bled out, or the heartbreak she felt knowing her daughter was dying. I tried not to remember either of them the way they were the day I put them in the ground, but it was impossible, and while Del mourned his son, I mourned my family. I mourned the mother I'd missed most of my life, wishing she were still here to offer words of wisdom when I needed them most. But she was gone, they all were, and I felt the loss as keenly as ever.

I let my sorrow consume me as I stepped out into the cold, bleak night. When we returned to Jade and the others, we'd put on a brave face and be strong again.

41

ELLE
APRIL 13

Sophie, Thea, and Beau were asleep on the same bed I'd woken up on earlier, swathed by the heat of the fire burning in the stove and the blankets tangled between them.

The guys had been gone for nearly six hours and still hadn't returned. I'd offered to wait up with Jade, but she insisted I retire to the cabin with the kids. Granting her privacy while she waited in a state of grief and aching uncertainty was the least I could do. I'd upturned her world in a single, thoughtless sentence: "So, he survived then?" The answer, I assumed, was no.

But the hours felt like an eternity, one impossible to sleep through despite how many times I commanded myself to close my eyes and count sheep instead of regrets. My body ached with exhaustion and my mind was heavy, but none of it mattered. Jackson hadn't known about Slana when he'd arrived, which meant he didn't know what I had done to the man in the hallway.

From my pallet of sleeping bags on the floor, I stared up at the wood-slatted ceiling. It hurt to breathe, and it wasn't only because of my sore body. I'd prepared myself for the probability that Jackson would come to make sure we were okay, because that's the kind of man he was, and then he would leave barely able to look at me for what I'd done. The fire was something that might frighten him but it was out of my control, the lie, however, was a betrayal no one would easily forgive.

When he'd stepped out of the truck, I'd braced myself for coldness and anger, but the worry in his eyes, the fear on his face . . . I'd thought for a flickering moment he didn't care about any of it as long as we were okay.

But he hadn't even known. Any of it.

Whatever I felt in that knowledge wasn't relief. If anything, the weight of my secrets now felt heavier and graver. He had been relieved to see someone he only thought he knew.

I looked at the kids, bathed in the soft glow cast through the door of the stove. Sophie's brow was lined with discomfort as she dreamed and I wondered if it was my haunting memories she saw tonight or someone else's. I needed to help her. And I had to tell Jackson what was happening to me and to Sophie. And I had to tell him what I'd done to his father.

With my better arm, I manhandled the pillows underneath my head, trying to prop myself up more, when I heard Del's truck coming toward the house. A flutter of nerves followed. The truck doors shut and the tailgate squeaked open, and after a few minutes of murmurs, I heard the tailgate slam closed. They'd found Jet, apparently, and it didn't seem like he'd made it.

I squeezed my eyes shut and my heart broke for Jade. She'd been so kind to us, and what had been open smiles and warmth today would be sadness in the morning.

The cabin door creaked open and cold air whizzed into the room. Jackson's heavy footsteps preceded his shadow, followed by Alex's, and then they shut the door quietly behind them. It felt as if the air was being sucked from the room and my heartbeat trembled with the urge to blurt the truth, though I thought it better to pretend I was asleep.

I glanced up at their darkened forms. "The folding cot is for you, Alex," I whispered. Apparently my decision was to do neither. "And your bag is next to Sophie's at the foot of the bed."

He nodded and mouthed a thank you.

Closing my eyes, I draped my arm over my face to give him a modicum of privacy.

With no downstairs couch to sleep on or separate room to remove himself to, I wondered if Jackson would lie on the pallet beside me, or if he'd disappear somewhere, like he usually did when he wanted time to himself.

Alex rustled into his nightclothes. A strong gust of wind wracked the side of the cabin, making it creak. I wasn't cold, but the impending *what next* was a deep-rooted chill, and I pulled the blankets up higher around my neck. When I heard the squeak of the cot, I opened my eyes. Alex was settling in beneath a blanket, facing the wall.

Jackson crouched beside the woodstove, warming his hands. He looked at the kids then down at me.

"They're zonked," I reassured him.

He turned the handle and opened the stove. I could feel the distance, thick and gravid between us, even if he crouched only inches from me. "You should rest," he said, and reached for another log to throw on the dying flames. "The sun will be up soon, and we need to gather our things from the Explorer."

"I know," I told him, wishing he'd take his own advice and let his mind rest for once. "But, I need to talk to you about something." Now wasn't the time, there would *never* be a good time. But he needed to know.

"Elle," he said. My name was a heavy, quiet breath. "Can it wait until tomorrow?" I could only imagine what they'd found in Delta Junction, but the toll it took on him was palpable.

"Of course," I whispered.

Jackson closed the stove and brushed his hands off on his pants as he stood up. He removed his hat and jacket, and cold air wafted off of him, carrying with it a scent I recognized as his own. Wood smoke, earth, and whatever it was about him that made him formidable-stoic-alluring-Jackson. He removed his boots and stretched out on the pallet beside me.

"How's Del?" I asked. I knew he was grieving, but it was one thing to mourn someone you love and another to find their dead body.

"Grateful it wasn't worse, I think." Jackson's voice was soft despite its deepness, and he pulled a sleeping bag half over him, like being warm was only an afterthought. His clothes rustled. Our shoulders touched, but barely as he ran his hand over his beard. Finally, he let out a deep breath. "Don't let the kids go into the garden shed, okay?"

I turned my head to look at him, watching the way his eyelashes fluttered with each thoughtful blink. "Okay."

Jackson met my gaze. In the silence, I could almost feel it, hot and prying me open, searching for something, even if I wasn't sure what.

I swallowed, and his eyes shifted down to my mouth and neck, then he looked away. "I'm glad you're okay," he whispered.

"I'm glad you're okay too." Tears blurred my eyes. I wanted to say everything and nothing at the same time because tomorrow everything would change. But within moments his breaths slowed and deepened, and Jackson fell asleep.

42

JACKSON
APRIL 13

While Jade prepared her son's body for burial, the five of us, minus injured Elle, made our way out to the overturned Explorer and trailer on the highway. Not only did we need to gather our things and inventory what we'd lost, but we needed to get the trailer off the road and out of sight from unwanted eyes. If what the Slana visitors had said was true, and there were more men somewhere close by, we didn't want them to find us, or the Ranskins, and we'd made it easy with all the tire tracks in the snow.

Alex and Sophie manned Del's snowmobile, pulling an empty sled behind them, and I drove Thea and Beau in the Tacoma.

"Do you think someone took our stuff?" Thea asked, sitting straight and alert in the back seat. Her little head shifted back and forth as she glanced between the windshield and the passenger window.

"Who would take our stuff?" Beau quipped, throwing his hands up like he couldn't believe she was even thinking it.

"Wolves," Thea retorted. "They could take our food."

"That's true," I told them. "If any animals smelled the food in the bins, they might have figured out how to open them. The food may be gone."

Thea's eyes flashed wider. "What will we eat then?"

"We'll find more," I told her. That was the least of our problems right now. While grocery stores weren't exactly accessible out here, whatever stores we found would likely be stocked with enough food to tide us over. It was finding another weatherproofed, working vehicle that had been on my mind. With Elle injured, things would progress more slowly than usual.

I'd always known she'd done a lot managing the kids, but in the time it took to give herself a sponge bath and change clothes with her one good hand, Sophie, Alex, and I got the kids their breakfast, dressed, and out the door so that Del, Jade, and Took could deal with their family business.

Besides gathering our things and restocking the supplies we were missing, we needed to find another vehicle large enough for five that could also carry most of our necessities, before we overstayed our welcome.

Elle was in pain. We could all see it plainly on her face, even if she thought she could hide it. And, with everything there was to do in the shortest amount of time possible, the next day or two would be arduous. Assuming we even had that long. At any minute the Ranskins might decide their generosity had run its course, and it was time for us to leave.

"Are we going to have a funeral?" Thea asked. She was full of questions. That was her *thing*, I realized. Thea didn't care what was happening as long as she could play in puddles and ask as many questions as she wanted. She was curious and Beau was a thinker. Beau liked to roll his eyes and be part of the big-kid action. He was observant, and I often wondered what gears were turning in that little head of his. I didn't have to wonder with Thea. Ever.

"Well?"

"Well, what?" I glanced at her in the rearview mirror.

"The funeral . . ." she reminded me.

"Yes, there will be a ceremony for Jet," I told her. "Later this afternoon, after the sun goes down."

"Did someone kill him?" Thea asked quietly. Worried. Sad. Her mind went there first, which was a reminder of how much these kids had seen. They related the world to violence now, and the trooper inside me felt like I'd failed them in some way.

"No one killed him," I said softly. "He died peacefully in his sleep."

"From the fever?"

I nodded.

She was quiet and introspective for a few breaths, like her brother, then asked, "Why didn't we die?"

Both Beau and Thea looked at me, curiosity widening their eyes. I'd seen it before when they asked if we were their new parents. I had let Elle take that one and buried myself in a bottle of bourbon. We definitely weren't their parents and never could be, but without a better adult figure, it was up to me to explain things to them the best I could, even if I didn't have all the answers.

"I don't know," I told her. I thought of the science book I'd brought back for Sophie, making a mental note to give it to her once we were back at the cabin. If Sophie could come up with even a general hypothesis, it would be something to help us make sense of things. For now, the truth was like a gray fog over a bridge we had been forced to cross, uncertain what had happened between one end and the other.

"I'm sorry, Thea. I don't know why some of us died and some of us lived."

"We're just lucky," she told me, and her words gave me pause.

Were we lucky? The past four months had been tough, straight up misery at times, and the past couple days had been a torrential shitshow. But we were alive and somewhere safe. We'd found each other, which felt like a miracle. "Yeah," I decided. "We are lucky."

I brought the truck to a stop a few yards shy of the Explorer and looked at the kids. "All right, ready for Operation Clean Up?"

Thea and Beau lifted two canvas bags each to fill with whatever they could. "Yep!"

"Be careful of . . ."

"Broken glass," they said in unison.

"And?"

"If we find your popcorn, make sure we give it to you, not Elle," Beau muttered.

"You got it. Let's load up what we can."

Alex brought the snowmobile to a stop beside the truck and he and Sophie climbed off.

"Got it?" I asked, turning in my seat as Thea struggled with the door handle.

She grunted in reply, and Beau, ever the older brother, reached across to help her open it, then they both jumped out of the truck.

I opened the driver side door and watched as the kids ran over to Sophie and Alex.

"Okay," Sophie said and clapped her gloved hands together. "Ready? We're going to see who can gather the most food and supplies first. Winner gets some of my Skittles."

Sophie was clearly feeling better than last I saw her in Slana. I wasn't sure if it was the near-death experience, or the fact that she'd proven to herself she could shoot someone if she needed to, but she seemed less cagey, even if she still kept her distance. I still knew little about the Slana story, and what had happened with the men. But I had a sickening suspicion that's what Elle wanted to talk about last night. Her face had said it all, and I was scared. I didn't want to hear what those men had done; I didn't want to feel worse than I already did for leading them right to the front door, even if I knew she'd gotten the kids out safely.

I climbed out of the truck and shut the door, rifle in hand. The cold air was always welcome, especially in the morning, and I took a deep breath. The sun was out, the sky was clear, and I was glad to know we'd at least have a beautiful day to get a lot done.

Scanning the tree line and the road for anything amiss, I made my way around the perimeter. I wanted to find out which critters had been in our backyard overnight, and if it was only the animal kingdom I needed to worry about.

I followed the patterns in the snow, noting the ptarmigan and fox prints, as well as a tattered bag of bread a dozen feet from the crash site. If frozen Wonder Bread had been the only casualty, I was okay with that.

The caribou prints were still fresh, as was the snowmobile path from Del's impromptu hunting after the accident. Other than tire tracks I felt safe assuming were from the Dodge and Tacoma, it appeared no one else had been on the road, which was one less thing I had to worry about, for now.

"My first bag's full!" Beau announced.

"Mine too," Thea said as she bent over to grab a box of crackers to shove on the top.

"Set them on the sled and fill up another one," Sophie instructed as she crouched beside the medical supplies, sorting through what remained.

"Beau, I need your muscle," Alex called. "This camping gear is heavy."

Beaming with purpose, Beau handed Thea his bag and headed over to help.

All of them were busy at work without a single complaint, and even if I was still getting to know them, it was sad to think I'd wanted nothing more than to be their travel companion in the beginning. Now, I couldn't imagine the next five months without them.

I tried not to think about it and stared at the Explorer. We had our work cut out for us, that was for sure. Staring at the dented hatch, I wondered what it would take to get it open and unload the rest of our things, when I noticed a pad print with four claws beside my boot. While I wasn't generally afraid of wolves, knowing they weren't exactly man hunters by design, their constant presence was beginning to change that.

I followed the trail a few yards north and then back again before they wrapped around the other side of the vehicle. There were claw marks in the snow, near the back seat where either Thea or Beau had been sitting, like the wolves had been trying to get in or get something out—possibly food. I might not have given it another thought, had my instincts not screamed at me that something was glaringly wrong.

43

ELLE
APRIL 13

While the others were at the road gathering our frozen belongings, I straightened our little living space the best I could, smoothing out the fox fur blanket that covered Took's bed, doing a slow, awkward side bend to pick up Beau's socks half-hidden beneath the bed frame. It was only a matter of days, maybe even hours before we would leave, and with our few belongings already packed in our bags, it was difficult to find something to do. Bothering Jade or Del while they were in mourning wasn't an option.

And even though I missed the chatter of the kids, I was relieved Jackson was gone. It was easier that way, for now. We would talk, eventually, but it was a matter of timing again, for the Ranskins' sake this time. We'd already caused enough upset to last them the rest of their lives.

Fresh air. I needed fresh air and sunshine. There had to be a scientific study published at a college campus on the California coast somewhere about the healing powers of sunshine, or maybe that was just wishful thinking. I doubted it could heal sore bones, but it might help ease my mind a little.

Stepping outside, I turned my face to the sun and closed my

eyes against its bright rays. I inhaled the morning air, willing it to seep as deep as possible into my lungs. The warblers chirped, the pine trees rustled in the light breeze, and my hands flexed at my side. It was a beautiful day, and yet it was too quiet—I was stewing. I couldn't run to expel nervous energy or help the crew clean our supplies from the road. It felt like I couldn't do anything worthwhile at all, but I was determined to find *something*.

The Ranskins' dog yawned and stretched in his kennel; his tail wagged when he noticed me. With an excited yip, he paced back and forth, looking at me like he was waiting for me to do something. There had been little opportunity for casual conversation, so I hadn't learned his name. He was gray and slender, with a thick fluffy tail and white markings around his mouth.

The closer I drew to him the more excited he became, and when he nudged his empty bowl, I began to understand. "Ah. It's breakfast time. I'll see what I can find." I wasn't familiar with the property, aside from what I'd seen walking from one cabin to the other, but finding the dog food seemed easy enough. It would be stored somewhere indoors, or in a bin—safe from critters.

Veering away from the shed I knew held Jet's body, I headed to the shop where I assumed meat and other foods were stored. It was heavily latched with reinforced metal siding, enough to make it more bear proof than the rest.

As I passed the smokehouse, I made a mental list of other tasks that might be helpful, which included checking the embers that smoked inside and pulling the laundry down from the line to fold if it was ready.

I reached for the shed door, realizing the latch was already open, and heard a loud thwack, followed by scraping. Though I thought I should probably turn around so not to intrude, curiosity outweighed my uncertainty and I creaked the door open to peek inside.

The shed was the size of a three-car garage with a workbench along the back wall and a large table with stone slabs in the center.

Blood stained the wood paneling around it, but it was too cold to smell anything other than the tang of metal that bolstered the building and the scent of damp earth.

Took stood at the worktable, cutting up caribou meat Del had brought back with him.

"Have you ever killed and prepared your own meat before?" He barely lifted his gaze to look at me.

"No," I admitted. "I haven't." I hadn't realized he'd noticed my snooping.

He tossed the strips of meat into a container and lifted what looked like an entire side flank from the workbench behind him onto the cutting board. Thwack. He chopped the flank in half. Took managed it effortlessly despite his age lines and peppered hair poking out from beneath his cap.

"Well, I guess I've *killed* my meat before," I teased, somewhat abashed by my horrible joke. I cleared my throat. "But I've never prepared it, no."

"It's satisfying—you might like it."

"I can imagine." And I *could* imagine. Out here living was about knowledge, hard work, and patience, and with those three things I would never have to worry about having enough food or providing for the kids. We would be safe, and secluded too.

I peered into two buckets of entrails set off to the side on the floor and tried to remember it was sustenance, not disgusting. The look of raw meat was one of the items I'd have to add to my list of shit to get used to.

"Do you know what a caribou flank would cost at a butcher?" Took's gaze shifted to mine again. I'd assumed he was being facetious, but he seemed more inquisitive than glib.

"A lot?"

Took shrugged. "No clue. I've never had to buy one."

"Touché," I said with a quirk of a smile, and I stepped further inside the shed. If he was talking to me, my presence must not have been wholly unwanted. "Can I help you with anything? The rest of the gang went to get our supplies from the road. I'm in the market for some chores." I held my palm up to add, "I should preface that I'm not good for much."

Took lifted an eyebrow. "Restless already?"

"Pretty much. I'm one of those people who needs to keep busy. Ever since—" I stopped myself before I could put my foot too far into my mouth. The outbreak was probably like a fresh, gaping wound to them because it was all so new. Took didn't need reminding.

He tied a strap of leather around a caribou thigh. "The sickness," he finished for me. "You might as well say it." He hefted it up, sidestepped me, and headed out the door.

"Okay . . . Well, ever since the outbreak, it's unnerving to be idle." I followed him out to the smokehouse, our feet crunching in the snow—still thick in the woods despite the warming days. "You think you won't survive the illness, then the next thing you know you're just trying to stay alive. Even in Slana we spent our time stocking up on food and supplies, preparing for whatever comes next. So, being busy keeps me focused."

Took glanced over his shoulder, his gaze meeting mine. "A restless mind is a restless soul." He pulled the knot on one cross-beam tighter, stringing the meat up, causing it to swing.

I reached out to steady it. Took was right about that. Restlessness felt more like a disability or a disease, difficult to treat though I'd been trying different remedies for months.

Once Took was satisfied the meat was secure, he turned around, gaze fixed on me. He was a little taller than I was, maybe five-eight or five-nine, and reminded me of my old friend, the fisherman. He had baggy, all-weather trousers on and a trench coat of sorts that looked waterproof, maybe easy to clean after a day butchering meat. "It is a test," he said, walking past me and out the door.

"Yeah, another one," I muttered with a humorless laugh.

Took turned to me. "Everything is a test," he said in earnest, and my face flushed. He lowered a bushy gray eyebrow, and I realized he was referring to himself too, to the turmoil his family was facing. I could see the truth of his words in his eyes, both shimmering and stark. "It's all part of change—even if it's difficult. It's a natural part of life."

I wasn't sure how natural the outbreak was; but he was right. Nothing was certain and change was inevitable, no matter how big and small. No matter how heartbreaking.

"I'm sorry, Took. That was insensitive. We've turned your world upside down—"

"You should never be sorry for telling the truth," he said, pointing at me with a dirt and bloodstained finger. Although he was adamant, his voice was soft. "If you hadn't showed up, we wouldn't have a month's worth of caribou meat." His head tilted ever so slightly and I saw a satisfied twitch in his dark, gray eyes. They were silvery pools of wisdom, just like his daughter's. "Everything happens for a reason. *You* are here for a reason."

For a man who had to give up his house for us to stay in, watch his daughter grieve for her only son, and mourn Jet for himself, Took was less cantankerous than usual. "Thank you."

"What are you thanking me for?" he grumbled, and continued to the shed. And just like that, grouchy Took was back.

"I'm thanking you for putting things into perspective." The wood smoke clung to my clothes and hair as I stepped inside behind him. As bad as I felt for the Ranskins, I knew Took was right; they may or may not have ever known what actually happened to Jet, or anyone for that matter.

With a grunt, Took hefted one of the buckets of entrails onto the worktable and began picking through them, sorting the meaty bits from the rest.

"What are you going to do with those?"

"Save some for fish bait and trapping. It's time to start stocking up for winter again."

"Already? There's never a dull moment living out here," I mused, but it was admiration I felt.

"Each season brings with it new tasks that need to be done. This month the salmon and waterfowl are rampant and we need to stock up before they've moved on to their next stop." He looked up at me and nodded to the door. "Did you see the pot warming on the embers in the smokehouse?"

I nodded.

"Can you carry it?" He glanced at my rib. The pot wasn't any bigger than a teakettle so I nodded. "Good. Take it to Jade, she's in the garden shed."

I nodded because I couldn't say no, but I wasn't sure she'd want me in there.

Took handed me a thickly folded cloth and nodded for the door again.

"Oh, the dog . . . he's hungry."

"Yeah, Koda's always hungry. I'll take care of it. Go on now," he urged. "Jade could use a hand, and since you've only got one to spare . . ."

I couldn't help but smile and hurried toward the smokehouse. Took had made a joke, a pretty funny one at that. But I did what I was told and picked the pot off the embers with the folded cloth, feeling the weight of the water in every part of my body as it protested.

With a deep breath, I squared my shoulders and steeled myself for what awaited me in the garden shed. I knew Jade was readying her son's body for burial, something that felt especially intimate.

Hesitant, I stopped at the door and tapped my knuckles on its rough surface. I'd grieved for my sister's death and for a life I hadn't appreciated to the fullest, but I'd never grieved for a child. I wasn't sure what state I would find her in, but I got the impression Took didn't want her to be alone.

"Jade," I whispered through the wood door. Some sort of steel protected the seams in the door for better insulation, and I assumed it was warmer inside.

Jade remained quiet, and I thought maybe she'd returned to the house, but when I creaked the door open, she stood on the far side of a wooden table. Mechanical parts were stacked beneath its thick legs, and plants and burlap bags with bulbs poking out of them hung in clay pots on the walls. Soil dusted the ground, and it looked like the space might have served as their garage too.

Her son's body lay out on a blanket of caribou hide, wrapped in another blanket from the waist down. Jackson said they'd brought his wife, Sarah, back too. I didn't see her in the room, but I wasn't going to ask where she was either.

I cleared my throat. "I'm sorry to intrude," I whispered, stepping inside. "But . . . I have the warm water." Jade brushed Jet's black hair out of his face as one of her tears dripped onto his shoulder. She didn't acknowledge me—I wasn't sure she even processed my being there—but she needed the water all the same.

Uncertain where she wanted it, I placed the pot on the table by the crook of his neck.

Like Jade, he had a tattoo, but not dashes on his chin like she did. A black and red Haida moon wrapped around his right shoulder, glistening with Jade's tears in the sunlight. It was similar to the totem around Took's neck. *Guardian and protector of the people of earth.* Jackson had the moon tattoo on his arm as well, and while he was very much alive and virile, it seemed unfair that Jet hadn't made it too.

I tried to reconcile the way Jet looked now—discolored but not dead-for-four-months decayed, like he'd been preserved in an ice tomb—and how he might've looked before.

Jade stared at his face, her eyes red-rimmed but bright gray wells of sadness in the sunlight. I was about to leave her to mourn when she said, "When he was a boy, he loved ice fishing." She looked up at me, as if a thought struck her. "Have you ever been ice fishing?"

I nodded. "Once, when I was nine."

"With your father?"

"Yeah, something like that." Dr. John was the closest thing I'd ever had. At some point I had to accept it.

"Jet loved it. Del and I thought for sure he would be a fisherman one day." A small smile curved the corner of her mouth as she looked back down at him, seeing the boy he'd been instead of the lifeless man he was. "Can you hand me one of those rags, please?" She pointed to the shelves in the corner behind me where three of them were folded and stacked.

I handed one to her as she poured water into a ceramic dish resting on a shelf behind her. She replaced it with the pot on the table by his shoulder and dipped the cloth, testing the heat of the water before she submerged it completely. Unrushed and thoughtful, she began to wipe his body. Back and forth. Gently. She ran the rag over his cheeks as if she were bathing a small delicate child. A trail of steam followed each careful stroke.

"Is there anything I can do to help?"

Jade's head drifted to the right and then the left as she memorized the curves of his face. He was a handsome man with narrower features than Jade had and closely shaven, black whiskers on his face.

"After I had Jet, I thought I might want to have another child, until I saw what kind of father my husband was." There was a sadness in her voice I understood. A longing, like I often longed for a real family in my childhood. "I wanted Jet to have someone to play with, but it never worked out that way. There were other children in the village back then, but I know he grew lonely sometimes. Especially after they all moved away, lost to the changing world of convenience. I didn't begrudge any of them, but Jet did, I think."

She dipped the cloth into the warm water again. "When you live out here, it's easy to keep busy, but the quiet hours are harder for some; Jet struggled with it, I think that's why he moved to town with Sarah. He liked the noise and the city." She talked about her son with a lilt of joy in her voice, a contentment I was grateful she had. "He thought I was so silly for calling it that, the *city*. It always felt big to me, I think that's why I never went back."

A bird whistled outside the shed, and Koda's excited yelp ricocheted between the outbuildings, but Jade was lost in a world where her son was alive and happy memories made her eyes smile. "I've always liked the quiet. It brings me peace, something that Del realized a long time ago. It's why he's never made me leave." She glanced at me. "He moved out here just before my husband died, you know? He had a ranch back in Oklahoma, came here on a fishing trip, my husband was his guide, and Del never left. Jet and I were lucky for that." Her eyes shimmered as she submerged the rag in the water again and wrung it out. "You find people in your life when you need them," she said. "That's something I've always believed." She looked up at me again, her gaze lingering this time, and what looked like gratitude pulled at her cheeks as another small smile twitched into place.

Jade's sincerity made my chest ache. She was right, we'd needed them in more ways than one, and they'd needed us in some strange way too. It was a fate I could feel, even if I couldn't quite understand it.

With a deep sigh, Jade took Jet's hand in hers.

"Will you bury them today?" I asked.

"Tonight," she whispered, running the damp cloth over his fingers. "When the lights dance in the sky."

44

ELLE
APRIL 13

We stood, nine strong at Jet and Sarah's graves, protected beneath a towering spruce in a quiet forest. Only the sound of a soft wind blew through the boughs above, and though the sun had long set, the snow sparkled in the dancing lights illuminating the sky. They'd always felt like an earthly wonder, but tonight they were more than that. The northern lights were vibrant with life and hope.

Jet's wrapped body was barely visible as Del and Took placed the final two stones over his grave, a fortified protection from the elements and the wildland creatures above the frozen earth.

Del stood beside Jade and took her hand in his. She squeezed his fingers before she took a step closer to the grave and placed a bear figurine on the headstone.

We stood in a quiet semicircle of grief and sadness. The biting cold breeze stung my over-warm skin. Cold puffs of white comingled between us, and Jade let her tears fall silently on his grave as she said her silent goodbye.

Del bowed his head, as did the children, Thea taking Jade's hand in hers as she peered down at her little snow-dampened boots. Then Jade closed her eyes and began to sing.

It was a whisper at first, words I'd never heard but that were more beautiful than anything ever spoken. Sounds so celestial they evoked a calm unlike anything I'd ever felt. As her voice grew louder, I recognized the tune and my eyes blurred with tears. She was singing "Amazing Grace."

Jackson glanced from Jade to me, surprise filling his eyes. The more he listened, the more the permanent crease in his brow softened. I wanted to know what he was thinking, almost yearned to, but when he peered up at the lights, so did I, and I imagined a life where all things could be so breathtaking.

"Dance with the spirits, my son," she whispered when she finished, and a strong gust of wind blew through the forest, sending Jade's fur cape flapping in the breeze as she kissed her flattened palm and bent down to place it on a stone for a final time before she joined us in the semicircle again.

Thea did the same, reclaiming Jade's hand again, and we all stood in respective silence, taking in the beautiful lights that shimmered above us, clearer than they'd been on any night before.

"He will live with the spirits now," Jade said, peering down at Thea, then at Beau. "With all the souls and spirits that have come before him, animal and man alike."

Thea blinked up at the lights in awe. Beau wiped at his cheeks, gleaming with dampness, which I hadn't expected. I took his mittened hand in mine, and startled as a wolf howl sounded in the night sky, closer than I was comfortable with.

Jaw clenched and heart pounding, I peered into the woods surrounding us. The wolves were close. *Too close.*

"Come," Del said behind me. "Let's go back to the house."

"Are they going to eat Jet?" Thea whined, glancing back at Beau.

"No, sweets," Jade answered. "They can't smell him. It's too cold for that."

"Come on, Beau." I turned to leave, squeezing his hand in

mine, but he dug his heels into the snow, jerking me back a step. I grimaced and tried not to shout.

"Beau," I said evenly, "come on. We need to get inside." I'd never been afraid of wolves before, but their constant presence was impossible to brush off any longer.

Beau didn't move, acting like he hadn't even heard me. His eyes locked on the darkness of the forest, at something I couldn't see, and he wiped another tear from his cheek. "Beau, let's go pl—"

The white spruce branches trembled, and a black wolf walked out of the shadows, ice on its fur coat, twinkling from the lights above. Its head hung low, and its eyes were so yellow they were almost glowing.

"Elle," Jackson cautioned, and his looming form appeared beside me. "Let's go, Beau," he said firm but calm, his eyes never leaving the wolf.

More glowing eyes came into focus deeper in the woods as three more wolves stepped closer.

"Jackson," I breathed. He lifted Beau into his arms and took a slow step back, taking my hand in his.

We took another step back, then another, and the wolves watched us without moving as we retreated back to the cabin with the others. Beau didn't make a peep. The wolves didn't come closer. I only allowed myself to sigh with relief when Del came up beside us, rifle gripped protectively in his hand. First the wolves were in Slana and now they were here. It was growing harder to ignore the increasing draw Beau had to them—and they to him.

45

JACKSON
APRIL 13

The cabin was cramped with nine of us, and more bodies meant more heat. The kids didn't seem to mind, but I was taking layer off after layer. Elle was down to her t-shirt, though she'd kept her gloves on as usual.

I'd decided I liked that random quirk of hers; she didn't get grossed out by blood, which there was a lot of when you worked outdoors or raised kids, and she didn't shy away from hard work or uncomfortable conversations with them like I did. Elle didn't even complain when the heat was too high and she was so miserable I could see the sweat on her brow. She was selfless and seemed perfect in so many ways, the gloves were a nice reminder that she wasn't without idiosyncrasies of her own. I appreciated that about her.

"Dinner's ready," Alex announced and handed Sophie a soup bowl and bread roll to pass along. I scooted one of the tree stumps over we'd brought inside and claimed a spot next to the couch. I was a big guy, but I didn't need much in the way of comforts.

Another howl, more distant this time, pierced through the night. The wolves were persistent and still close, even after we'd moved inside. The knot in the pit of my stomach tightened as another wolf howled back.

Elle glanced at me from where she sat at the table next to the kids. The disquiet was equally obvious in her eyes, but the wolves were only one of a few topics she likely wanted to discuss. I'd kept myself busy all day, getting the food and supplies locked up in the meat shed and gathering stones with Alex for the burial. Even if it made me a coward, I still wasn't ready to know what had happened in Slana, or hear the disappointment underlying her words. *You weren't there.*

"Here you go, Del," Sophie said, handing him a bowl of soup and a warm roll as he sat on the couch beside Jade. "Caribou stew, made with ingredients from your winter garden, of course," she explained.

"And the rolls, heated to perfection, are from ours," Elle added wryly.

Del's eyes gleamed with hunger and he nodded in thanks.

There was another howl, further away this time, and though the Ranskins continued to show no signs of getting sick, I was seriously considering some animals were.

"What's Del short for?" Beau asked, turning around in his seat at the table.

"Delmont, but don't bother calling me by it," he said. "Delmont was my father, and I'm not as old as he was, yet. So, I won't answer." He slurped at his stew with a wink.

"I was named after my dad too," Beau said proudly. "But Beau isn't short for anything."

"It's a good name," Jade said. She wrapped her shawl tighter around her and nestled deeper into her spot on the futon.

"And, it fits," Sophie added, handing me a bowl of stew. Her eyes met mine, but only briefly, and she walked back to the stove. "It means handsome in French."

She'd barely looked at me all day, and even for Sophie, withdrawn as she sometimes was, it felt ominous.

"You're French?" Thea asked, running her tongue over her red lips. "Wow. That's fancy." Either Thea had been hungry enough to brave the piping hot stew, or she was more resilient than I thought and didn't care in the slightest.

"My mom is—*was*," she amended. "Or, I guess my grandma was." There was a stretch of silence as reality settled in around us again. Everyone we ever knew who wasn't in the room with us was likely a *was* now.

"Why am I not surprised you're French?" Alex smirked. His Alex-like merriment always cut through the thick tension in the room.

Sophie's pale skin flushed, and she tucked her loose long hair behind her ear and averted her gaze. I wondered if the same charge Alex felt sometimes when he touched Sophie went both ways, and I forced myself not to smile.

Sophie delivered another bowl of stew to Took, then sat at the table beside him, cramped with the kids and Elle. There were a lot of us, but we'd made it work.

"Thanks for dinner, Alex." Sophie blew on a spoonful and hesitantly took a sip.

Took sniffed the steam that rose from his bowl. "It smells edible at least."

"Oh, stop it, Dad."

I chuckled, and finally worked up the nerve to take a bite.

"It's delicious, Alex," Jade said, licking her lips. "Don't listen to him."

Alex glanced up from his bowl, broth dripping from his chin before he could wipe it away. "I hope so because there's plenty more."

Clanks and slurps and sighs filled the room as we all sat in companionable silence, appreciating our warm meal together. Elle quickly admonished the kids when they began playing with their food, and winked at them when she felt she'd done her due diligence as a parental figure, promising them a snowball fight after dinner if they kept more of their broth inside their bowls.

"What about you, Elle," I asked, growing more curious about her with every week that went by. "What's Elle short for?"

She gave me a hesitant, sidelong look, and peered around the room.

"Eleanor," she said reluctantly, and dipped a part of her roll in her broth.

"You don't like Eleanor?" Her frown surprised me.

"Who said she doesn't like it?" Del asked. "Sometimes we just like nicknames."

Elle lifted a dark, delicate eyebrow and took a sip from her bowl, contemplating. Dabbing her lips, she cleared her throat and said, "No, he's right. I don't like it."

"Uh oh," Took grumbled and sat back in his seat, settling in with bright amusement to listen.

"At least I didn't use to like it. I'm not sure I feel one way or the other about it now." She glanced between the eight curious faces staring at her. "I was named after someone I don't like all that much," she admitted.

I was expecting a funny retelling about her and her twin sister being mixed up or something at birth, not that she hated her name. But then, I shouldn't have been surprised. Elle had made it clear her life before was a dark, windy path that gave her nightmares and made her feel like she had to protect herself in order to escape. "It's your mother's name?" I couldn't help the question. I wanted to know how she'd come to be the woman I knew, purposeful and formidable and yet soft in the most striking moments.

"Yes, my mother. She left when I was little, just sort of disappeared. She didn't care what happened to me and Jenny after that." She met my gaze, a gleam in her eyes that looked almost desperate, but I wasn't sure why.

"Took was a family name too," Jade explained, breaking Elle's hold over me. "An ancestor I've never met."

I ate a few spoonfuls of stew, finally cool enough for me to appreciate while everyone else was nearly finished.

"Me either," Took said. "I heard he was a son of a bitch," he grumbled.

"Dad . . ."

I chuckled. "We've all got a few of those in our family."

"You look like a man who knows a bit about Alaskan heritage, Jackson. Who were you named after?"

"My grandfather." I wiped my mustache and leaned forward, my elbows resting on my knees. "He was a fisherman in Sitka, originally from Canada. He was one of the last people in my mother's village that still made his own boats with cottonwood he'd stripped and split."

"That's remarkable isn't it? I can't imagine having such a skill." Jade finally walked over to the stove and ladled herself a bowl of stew. "Was he able to teach you?"

I sat my empty bowl down and rubbed my hands over my thighs. Being in a confined space with everyone's eyes on me was something I was barely getting used to when it was just the six of us, but five sets of eyes had become eight.

Elle watched me, more than amused that I had taken her place in the hot seat. "No," I said. "My grandfather didn't get to teach me much of anything, not that I retained anyway. My mother died giving birth to my sister and my dad moved me to Anchorage, where he was from. I didn't learn much after I turned nine."

Jade clucked her tongue and sighed. "I'm sorry to hear that."

"I still fish with willow branches from time to time, though— just like she taught me—and I can build a screaming fire." I winked at her and smiled, proud of what I could do.

"Both are important skills if you want to live in the wildland," Del said. "Lord knows I had a thing or two to learn when I decided to stay out here. Hell, I'm still learning."

The wood in the stove crackled. Beau and Thea whispered as

they played with the salt shaker at the table, as if no one could see. Then howling punctuated the silence again.

"Maybe they want the meat in the smokehouse," Alex said, wiping his mouth with the back of his arm. Jade handed him her napkin.

"Maybe, but it's never been an issue before," Del said. "Cottonwood has a strong odor to most animals." He shrugged. "Koda will alert us if they get too close." Del was good at playing off the wolves, but I knew he couldn't dismiss them so easily.

Jade shook her head, her smoky colored eyes wary and fixed on me. "You said yourself everything was different now. The animals, could they have gotten sick?"

"I hadn't thought so, but now . . . I'm not so sure." I sighed, uncertain what to think anymore.

"It's possible," Sophie said, peering into her empty bowl. "That textbook you brought back, Jackson, listed a bunch of animals that can be infected by the avian flu, bird and mammal species."

"Del," Jade whispered. "Should we put Koda in the garden shed for the night?"

He nodded. "If it will make you feel better, we will. Just to be safe."

"We can make sure the kennel is reinforced before we leave. It shouldn't be more than a day or two. I was going to take Alex out tomorrow and see if we can find a vehicle in Tetlin, or one of the communities along the highway. We can work on a long-term solution for the kennel when we get back."

"Actually," Jade said, glancing around at all of us. "I was thinking you could stay here a while longer, for a couple weeks at least, until Elle heals up a bit more and the roads are a bit safer." She looked pointedly at Elle. "It will give you all some time to get your things in order—find another truck and whatever you need for your trip."

Elle's eyebrows shot up, then she looked at me. It was a good idea. In fact, I was relieved they'd offered. It meant we didn't have to rush to get back on the road and we could offer our help to them for all they'd already done for us.

"That's really generous of you—" Elle began.

"I insist." Jade stood up from the couch and patted me on the shoulder. "You all could use this time to regroup and rest." She walked over to the stove and set her bowl in the washtub.

"We could use the company," Del admitted. He leaned forward, swallowing the last of his soup as he glanced between Jade and me. "And the distraction."

Jade hummed as she filled the washtub with melted snow water.

I glanced at Took, uncertain what he thought about all of this. "Well?" he said, impatient.

If grumpy old Took was on board, I didn't have any reservations. I met Elle's gaze, though it wasn't as relieved as I'd thought it would be.

When she realized everyone was waiting for an answer, she smiled. "Yes, of course."

Beau and Thea shouted, "Yay!"

But I knew Elle's smiles, and while hers was big and wide, it was reluctant too. "It's very nice of you to offer. Thank you." She gathered the kids' bowls to stack on top of hers.

"Great!" Del sat back into the couch and crossed his legs with a smile. "We'll have to get some fish while you're here. Maybe show the kids what it used to be like growing up out here before everything was at your fingertips."

"*Used* to be at our fingertips," Alex muttered, and stretched as he stood, then he went to help Jade with the dishes.

"Fishing would be great." It was a pastime I rarely had time for, even before the virus, and something that always brought me a sense of peace. "It would be a nice break from all the planning and preparing for a while."

"Fishing *after* hunting," Took groused. "That herd is on the move. They will be gone soon and we could use more Caribou."

347

"Yes, after," Del agreed.

Elle walked past me, biting her bottom lip. I gently grabbed her hand as she passed. "Hey, are you sure it's okay?" I whispered.

Elle's eyes darted to mine and then to my hand on hers. She pulled her fingers from mine with just enough urgency to send a message loud and clear. "Yes, it's fine." She flashed another false smile, fisting her hand at her side, then sidestepped me and headed to the washtub.

Somehow, I'd crossed a line, and her withdrawal left an unexpected pang of hurt in its wake. Followed by a hearty dose of guilt for caring.

46

ELLE

APRIL 14

"Time for chores," Jade called as she stepped out of the house, a smile lighting her eyes. The kids and I finished donning our outdoor clothes as she slung a .22 over her shoulder. It was small but packed a mean enough punch to scare any unwanted, four-legged visitors away. Being naked of my own gun, I was relieved.

"Can't we go hunting with Jackson and Del? They probably haven't gone very far," Beau pleaded, eyeing her rifle. "Alex let me drive the snowmobile in Slana, I could take us there."

My eyes widened. "He did, did he?"

Jade chuckled. "No hunting today, Beau." She opened Koda's kennel so he could run free. His barking resounded through the air, and the grouse cackled and flit with whistling wings from their sunbathing beneath the trees.

"Besides," Jade continued. "We have something far more important to do today and it doesn't require us leaving our own backyard." She winked at me. "We're collecting wood. Now" she clapped her hands—"who's pulling the sled? It needs to be someone strong and—"

"I can do it," Beau said, trotting over to the sled leaning against

349

the side of the cabin. We'd used it so many times, dragging it over branches and rocks, I was grateful it hadn't cracked and was still in one piece.

"Thea you can wrangle Koda in," she said, handing her a leash.

"Okay!" she chirped.

The kids were more than happy to stay with the Ranskins for a while longer. I was less content, however, even if I knew it was irrational. Staying with them had the best possible outcome, but it made me uneasy knowing there was still so much they didn't understand about us. My fire was coming back, and while Sophie kept her distance when she could, it was only a matter of time until someone started to take it personally.

"Now, do you see that patch of trees up there on the hill?" Jade pointed to the dense horizon. "That's where we're going. Keep a sharp eye out for lynx and wolverines, they like to hang out around here because of the hares, and we don't want any trouble."

"Okay," the kids said in unison, as if wolverines and lynx were akin to raccoons and other everyday backyard critters.

"Lead the way." Jade flung her hand out like she was releasing the greyhounds, and happily, Beau and Thea made their way up the hill, hunting with the grown-ups forgotten, for now. They struggled through the deep snow, but I reveled in the eminent exhaustion our morning excursion would bring. Koda barked and hopped through the snow with Thea, happy to be out of his kennel and part of the commotion.

I took in the wild landscape, sparkling whites and midnight greens against a cloudless blue sky. The world was pristine in the sunlight, reminding me how small we were once again. I made a valiant effort not to move my arm much as we hiked up the hill, each step sending a twinge of pain through my side.

Sophie could know things about people and I could turn to flame, but aside from the men in Slana with evil hearts, I wondered what else people could do. Was there someone out there who could heal themselves? That would come in handy. My burning energy had saved my life twice, but what other abilities did people have? They couldn't all be bad. Which powers were people using for good?

"Do you think there are colonies of people banding together?" I looked at Jade who seemed to see the good and hopeful in all things. "For all we know, the lower forty-eight are up and running and we're still up North, clueless. One day, I half expect a helicopter will fly overhead and I'll feel that grand sense of relief that it's all over."

"Do you think?"

I shook my head regretfully. "No, I don't. It's already been four months. I feel a sense of hopelessness in my bones, knowing that if it was going to happen, it would have already."

"You never know," Jade said as she scanned the wooded hillside for dangers. "The world might surprise you. And yes, I think there are other survivors banding together. It's the human way, caring for and helping one another. Don't let a few bad eggs make you lose hope."

Jade and I continued the rest of the trek in silence, listening to Beau and Thea chatter about the squirrels and hares that had left footprints in the snow.

"Why can't we see any?" Thea tossed a stick for Koda to retrieve, though it didn't make it more than a few feet. Her nose and cheeks were rosy, and her braids bounced against her puffy jacket with each perky step. She jumped on a pair of tiny footprints.

"Hey genius, it might be because you're scaring them away with all your talking and jumping," Beau told her. "Plus, we look like aliens to them."

"And we're big," she added.

Beau looked down at her. "You're not big."

"Yeah-huh!" she retorted, puffing her chest out and glaring at him.

Jade sighed. "Is it strange that I enjoy hearing them bicker?"

"Not at all," I said with a chuckle. "It helps things feel normal.

"No bickering now," Jade called, though her voice was light with amusement. "It's just up here." She began to walk more quickly. "The winds are stronger on the hill," she explained, pointing to the split branches and broken twigs covering the ground. "They break easily under the weight of the snow since they're frozen deep down to the core." There was an awe in Jade's voice I admired, a sense of wonder that captivated me when she spoke. I wanted to soak up every bit of knowledge she had, and be just like her one day—centered and confident. I wanted to be content.

"Now," Jade said. "These—" She picked up a thick, white stick. "These are birch branches good for burning. These are the ones we want. All shapes and sizes, as long as we can pull them down the hill. Got it?"

"What about these?" Thea asked, lifting a wispy, needle covered twig.

"That's a spruce. We can use the big branches for building. It's hardwood and strong, good for hanging poles in the smokehouse and in the skinning shed, but not for burning. We'll come back for those when we have more help, okay?"

Everything Jade knew from living in the wild was like liquid gold. We needed every ounce if we would make it in a world without noise to stave predators away, without factories to make our clothes or the materials for our homes. We would have to relearn the ways of the past to make it in the future.

"Let's make sure we remember what Jade's telling us," I told them. "And ask a lot of questions if we have them. We can teach Sophie, Alex, and Jackson when they get back, and Sophie can put them in her book."

"Okay," Beau said, scouring the thick snow beneath the shelter of the trees.

Koda barked at ptarmigan, white and hidden in the snow, and

sniffed fox trails that looped through the woods, disappearing deeper inside.

We gathered branch after branch, Beau and Thea making it a timed game to see who could collect more wood the fastest, and we were done before too much time had passed.

"Okay, I think we need to be done," I told them. I wasn't sure we could make it down the hill without some of them sliding off as it was. "The load is looking pretty heavy."

"Here," Thea said, adding more tinder to the top of the pile.

Jade brushed her gloves off on her pants and peered up at the sky as the clouds moved in front of the sun. "Elle's right, we should head back and see if we can get a nice warm fire going in the cabin and something to eat."

I wiped my brow with my forearm. I was wearing a long-sleeve shirt, but had only worn a tank top underneath to help keep my body temperature down. It wasn't working. "Plus, we've still got wood to pile up before the sun goes down," I added. "Let's head back." *So I can strip down.*

Jade nodded and picked up her discarded .22. "Oh, look, Thea. This is the perfect sized walking stick for you." Jade picked up a scraggly birch branch and broke off the pointed, wispy end.

"It's as tall as me," Thea mused, standing up beside it. With a final measure of approval, Thea followed Jade down the hill, stick jabbing through the snow with each step.

"Ready—" I glanced over my shoulder, waiting for Beau to grab the sled rope, but I lost my voice before I could say his name. He stood a few yards behind me, the black wolf from last night pensive in the sea of trees, staring at him once again.

"Beau," I breathed, slowly reaching for my pistol, but it wasn't on my belt.

I looked behind me, afraid to call out for Jade already halfway down the hill, completely unaware. I wanted to scream for her, but I couldn't bring myself to do it. Amidst the desperation that tightened every muscle and the terror of uncertainty, something kept my feet from moving and my mouth from opening.

The wolf stood as it had the night before, its head down and its yellow eyes fixated on Beau. A voice screamed at me to pick up branches and scream and shout at the wolf to go away, but fire-Elle, the part of me who knew impossible things were happening all around us, knew Beau was safe. They were ten times stronger than Beau and just as tall, yet they hadn't hurt any of us yet. Curiosity overwhelmed my instinct to be afraid.

The wolf sniffed the ground, its eyes fixed on Beau. Their silent stare down dragged on until a few thrashing heartbeats later, the wolf blinked and looked away, and as if it was satisfied, it took a step closer.

Fear won out and I took a slight step closer. "Beau," I said flatly, reaching out my hand.

Neither he nor the wolf seemed to notice I was there, let alone register that I'd spoken.

"Beau, give me your hand," I told him. "Now."

Finally, Beau looked up at me, but he just stared at my hand.

"Beau," I warned and wiggled my fingers. "Come on, take my hand please."

Obediently, he stepped closer and linked his hand with mine. "She won't hurt me." His voice quivered a little, but I wasn't sure if he was sad for having to leave or a little scared.

"Maybe not, but that's plenty close enough for one day."

The wolf brought its head up, watching me so close I wondered if I'd made the wrong choice.

A gunshot pierced the air, and the wolf fled back into the woods. I couldn't move at first, my heart pounding like a hammer, staking me into the ground where I stood. My hands began to shake as I realized how horribly that could have ended.

I glanced back at Jade, the .22 at her side. "Let's go home," she said, her chest heaving. I saw the fear in her eyes, and the bewilderment. "Koda!" she shouted, running a hand through her hair as she turned to head back down the hill again.

Koda ran out of the trees, trotting up behind her with his tongue hanging out of his mouth and his tail wagging. "What are you good for anyway," she groused, and leaned down to pat his side.

I took Beau's hand in mine again, gripping it as hard as I could to keep the tremors from worsening.

"She won't hurt you either," Beau said quietly, and I looked down at him.

"How—how could you possibly know that?"

He shrugged and picked up the rope to the sled. "I just do."

47

JACKSON
APRIL 14

B rittle, winter-ravaged brush crunched under our feet as we made our way toward a rocky knoll. There was no trail to follow, just Del's photographic memory from years of hunting the land. We'd tracked the caribou and needed a bird's-eye view for a proper shot. Although we'd had many target practices over the past several months, none of us had done any hunting.

"Where are the caribou going?" Sophie asked a few steps ahead of me.

"Del said they're heading for their calving spots," Alex said, shoving a piece of jerky in his mouth.

"Does that stuff line your pockets or something?" I joked. The kid never seemed to leave camp without it.

His eyebrows waggled and he offered me one. "Maybe. This is some of the stuff Took made. You want some?"

"You mean the stuff he won't stop bragging about? Sure, why not."

Alex grabbed another chunk out of his pocket, picked off a piece of lint and handed it to me.

"Thanks." I tore off a bite and pulled my rifle strap further up my shoulder. I eyed the moose jerky as I gnawed on it. It was smoky but not too over the top that it tasted like a campfire. I shrugged, pleasantly surprised. "Not too bad."

"Shouldn't there be more of them then?" Sophie asked and peered out at the small herd in the distance. "I thought the point of having so many members of a herd was to protect themselves and their young; the more bodies and movement, the more confusing it is for their predators."

"Woodland caribou are more solitary, Soph." My attention was half focused on Del as he brought the binoculars to his eyes. "And they're more predictable, which makes them easier targets for poachers and trophy hunters."

"You don't like hunters then?" she asked.

"I don't like people who break the law for a rack they can hang on the wall and then leave the rest to waste."

"Well, we won't be doing any of that," Del said from a couple yards ahead, and he waved us onward. "If we're lucky, you'll have an entire caribou to take with you to Whitehorse." He pointed to a patch of woods on the other side of the clearing. "There's likely another small herd over there, if history is anything to go by. I've seen them there a few times." Del glanced back the way we came. "Since we have the two snowmobiles, we can take back double the load. We may not get another chance before they're gone." Del wasn't one to be overly emotional—sad, excited, or otherwise—at least not that I'd seen in the few days of knowing him, but he was glad we were there, you could tell with each lively step and hear the smile in his voice. Part of him missed civilization, and while I wouldn't claim we were high society, we were new faces and animated conversation, and I was glad we could give that to him.

He peered up at the sun then appraised the herd, lying around about a half a mile out. "These guys will be on the move after the first shot. Then we'll be on the hunt again and we're wasting daylight." He nodded toward a rocky bluff ahead with a few evergreens scattered around it. "It's as good a place as any," he said. "Careful though, the boulders are slippery." He stepped over one and pointed to a dozen tiny dots across the field. "Bulls only. It's hard to tell, so look for big, wide racks."

"You said big racks," Alex snickered, and Sophie rolled her eyes.

"Wow, real mature," she chided.

The three of us followed Del up the knoll, our dusky jackets resembling rocks from a distance, and the caribou couldn't smell us downwind. It was our first hunting trip and even if we shot nothing, I'd still feel proud. Of all of us though, Sophie seemed the most excited, and I was glad to see her spark was back and that she was interested in being a part of the team again.

"Are you ready for this?" Alex looked at Sophie as we reached the top.

Del offered her his hand as she made the final climb, and she shook her head. "I'm fine, thanks." She smiled and stared out at the herd. "But I *am* ready for hunting. It's been a while since I practiced my aim, but I'm as ready as I'll get."

"Well then, you're up," Del said, crouching behind the boulder as he peered through the scope on his rifle.

"There's no pressure, Soph." Alex handed her his rifle. "In fact, if you don't get anything it will make me look better when I go next." He grinned. "So, please, feel free to miss."

I crouched down, out of the way to watch and wait. "Do you remember what I told you, Soph—"

"Safety on until I'm settled, and keep my finger off the trigger until I'm ready to shoot."

She glanced at me. "It's hitting the target I'm more concerned about."

"It's all a learning experience," Del said. "From bullet to bowl, today's the day you learn how to kill, dress, and store your meat," he said eagerly and rubbed his hands together excitedly. I imagined he and Jet enjoyed hunting together, and I wondered what it would be like after we left. Took and Del, at it again, only we wouldn't be around to distract them from the void Jet left in their lives.

"Now, get into position," he told Sophie. "They're moving around a lot, so you might have to wait for a good shot."

She propped the rifle on the top of a boulder and peered through the scope.

Alex grinned and plopped down on the ground beside me. "She's totally going to get one and show me up, just to spite me."

"You and me both," I guessed.

Del lifted his binoculars and studied the herd again. "I see a few bulls to the right. Can you see them?"

She grunted and quirked her mouth in concentration. "Yeah, I think so."

"The shot's yours when you're ready, Sophie. Anywhere behind the shoulder blade." Del watched the herd as she finished settling in. She fidgeted with the rifle, trying to find a comfort zone, then she took a deep breath and licked her lips.

I waited with bated breath until she pressed the trigger. The shot cracked through the stillness and the herd startled.

"I'll be damned, girl. You got 'em!" Del shouted, and the caribou Sophie shot wavered and fell into the snowfield. "We're on the move, gang!" Del shouted joyously. Grabbing his gun, he headed down the knoll to the snowmobiles.

"Great shot, Soph," Alex said, and he reached down to help her to her feet.

She took his hand with a triumphant grin, but as she stood, she yanked her hand back again, causing Alex to stumble into a boulder and shout with pain as he slipped and landed on a rock.

"What the hell, Sophie?" he growled, wincing as he climbed back up to his feet. I reached for him to offer some leverage. Alex grabbed hold of my forearm and heaved out a breath.

Sophie clamped her hand over her mouth, eyes wide and head shaking. Alex snatched his gun from her.

"I'm sorry," she gasped. "I didn't mean to do that." Her voice trembled as she glanced from me to Alex. "I just—you can't touch me. Okay? *No one* can touch me."

He looked at his palm, as if he was registering it. "You feel it too, don't you?" he realized.

"Feel what?" I asked, glancing between them.

"The . . . *thing* I was telling you about." Alex's eyes met Sophie's again, a silent conversation passing between them and he shook his head. "What do you know, Sophie? What's going on— why do I feel a wave of uncertainty every time I touch you."

"I don't know," she whimpered. "I don't know what you're feeling. I only know what I feel."

"Which is what?" I asked. Their chests heaved so violently, I thought both of them might be on the brink of tears. "What the hell is going on?"

"It was fine for a while," she said, mostly to herself. "But—" She looked Alex right in the eyes. "Something's wrong with me. Ever since Whitely."

"Whitely?" I blurted. That was nearly five months ago.

"Then tell me. What's wrong with you?" Alex begged. "You're freaking me out, Sophie."

"Good, because it's fucking scary," she blurted.

"The charge?" I asked, looking at Alex. "Is this about the charge you feel around her?" I was beyond lost, but it was the only thing I could think to grab hold of.

Sophie shook her head and took a step back, like the world was closing in on her and she was going to make a run for it. "I know it, all of it—everything you don't want to feel." Sophie looked at me this time. "I know it and I can feel it, too." The look on her face was one of disgust as she let her hands fall at her sides and paced back and forth.

"Say that again?" I asked. "What don't I want you to know?" I had no secrets—nothing to hide. Nothing that would make her fear me.

"Your wife," she bleated. "Molly . . ."

"Hannah?" *Molly?* I'd never told Elle or anyone else my daughter's name, at least not that I could remember.

"I know how bloody your hands were as you buried her—I can feel what it cost you, the part of you that died that day. I know how much you loved her, how much you still love her and that it's hard for you to be around us—"

"Stop!" I told her. "Just—just stop."

I ran my fingers through my hair as dizziness set in, and I turned away from her. Sophie knowing anything about my life before was like my flesh had been peeled away, every dark part of me gaping and exposed.

"How?" I breathed, forcing myself to face her. "How do you know any of that?"

Sophie's head shook. Her chin trembled. Her eyes clouded with tears. "I—I don't know. I don't know how any of it is possible. We're just—different." She looked at Alex. "And somehow you feel it too."

Alex stepped back like he was petrified of the very thought. "No. I don't see that shit. I feel something, but I don't know any of that—I don't want to."

Sophie reached for his hand, desperate to show him.

Alex's mouth opened in protest, but the words never fell from his lips. The creases in his brow deepened, his lips pinched together, and his eyes shimmered with unshed tears before he had the wherewithal to tear his hand away from her.

I gawked at Alex, weighing his reaction, then at Sophie with disbelief. Sophie's words were impossible—what was happening *was impossible.*

"It's only when someone touches me," she explained. "Except for you, Alex. I feel a connection with you, but I've always shied away from it because I don't want to know more. I don't want to know everything."

Dark shadows filled Alex's eyes. "Why didn't you say something? At least I would've known I didn't repulse you."

She blinked at him, her gaze softening. "Why haven't *you* said anything?"

"This is what you were trying to tell me in the truck?" I considered Alex's words, and tried to understand how I'd missed so much.

Alex shook his head and threw his hands up. "I have felt weird touching Sophie and Elle, but I didn't know what it—" He looked at Sophie. "Wait, is that why Elle wears gloves? Because she feels it too?"

"No, she had them before—it's because of the fire."

"The what?" Alex and I blurted.

Sophie glanced between us, licking her lips as she took a step back. "We're different," she said. "But you"—she looked directly at me—"you should ask her about it."

It was like all the knots in my stomach from the past four months twisted together, tighter and tighter until I couldn't stand it any longer.

"Elle's had plenty of time to tell me," I grounded out. My hands clenched at my side and I looked into Sophie's secretive blue eyes. "Tell me. Now."

Sophie lifted her chin, almost defiantly, and swallowed thickly. "She didn't mean to do it," she prefaced.

"Do what? Why does she wear the damn gloves, Sophie?"

"The men in Slana," she started. "We shot two of them, but the other burned alive."

"You're saying her hands are fire?" Alex confirmed, barely able to believe it himself, but then recognition widened his eyes and lit his face. "So, that's what I feel when I touch her."

"That's impossible," I rasped. It couldn't physically be possible. I'd seen her hands, hadn't I? They were normal, just like everyone else's.

The gloves are because of the fire . . .

My mind was screaming at me, telling me this wasn't real. These *abilities* weren't even possible, and if Elle had known about them—if she could kill a man with her hands—she would've told me.

While Alex considered the implications of his touch, all I could think about was why Elle had kept what she could do from me. "Did she think I wouldn't believe her?" I thought aloud. She'd told me the men in Slana had been dangerous, that survivors were changed, but like this? It wasn't just the men who could do unnatural things. *She* was different. All three of them were.

"How long?" I met Sophie's gaze, subdued and crestfallen in a way I'd never seen before. "How long have you been keeping what you see a secret?"

"It's only gotten worse the last couple months."

"And Elle? How long has she been hiding this?"

Sophie's brow furrowed.

"How long?"

"A while."

Alex looked at his hands like he might see flames burst from them.

"How long is *a while*?" I repeated.

"I felt it the night I met her, at your apartment, Sophie." He paused and shook his head. "She touched me, and a weird feeling —I thought I was just crazy."

"That's what we've been worried about. It's why we haven't said anything."

Alex's eyes narrowed at a memory. "The guy in her house . . . I can't imagine killing someone with my bare hands . . ."

My heartbeat shuddered and I peered down at Sophie's delicate hands.

Like one of Alex's electric charges zapped through me, the pieces fell into place. *The guy in her house?*

Elle wasn't just hiding what she could do, she was hiding what she had done.

48

ELLE

APRIL 14

I sat at the table with Jade, mending the wear and tear in our clothes I'd neglected for months. I turned one of Jackson's wool socks inside out, deciding on a red thread since I didn't have black to match. I tied a knot in the end of the string, only for it to pull its way all the way through the wool, and I groaned.

"You need a larger knot at the bottom," Jade said, peering over the rim of her glasses. She didn't normally wear them, but they suited her.

"It feels like a cruel joke," I said, staring at the pile of clothes.

"What's that?" She pulled the needle through a tattered quilt she was re-hemming.

"We'd planned to stock up on clothes before we left, but leaving in such a hurry, we hadn't gotten to it. It's the end of the world and we could go on the biggest shopping spree of our lives, and yet here I am, sewing our holey socks and underwear because we only brought enough to get by."

I stared at my thermal tops. Case in point. What I really needed were t-shirts. I wiped the moisture from my brow and glanced at the low burning fire in the stove the kids huddled beside, whispering. "Where did you two sneak off to after chores, anyway?"

"Nowhere," they said in unison.

I lifted a skeptical eyebrow. "Is that so?" They'd been conspiratorial since we'd returned. "Maybe you should wash that sap off your hands then," I told them. "You wouldn't want to leave any evidence."

Beau looked at his hands, then at his sister's. "Thea," he groaned, and helped her to her feet. They walked over to the washtub, their whispers fading when they noticed my eyes on them. "I hope you haven't been getting into trouble. Took might not take you fishing tomorrow."

"We didn't do anything," Beau griped, and while part of me wanted to tell him to watch his tone, I couldn't bring myself to do it. After what happened with the wolf, he'd been distracted, and I couldn't blame him. I couldn't stop thinking about it either.

"It must be nice to have so many people care about you and want to keep you safe," Jade told Beau with a soft chuckle. She winked at me and rose to her feet.

"Not really," he grumbled.

Jade lifted her mug. "Care for some tea?" she offered. "Tundra tea with a little honey. I make it from a shrub that grows heavy around here in the spring. I don't make it very strong unless I'm using it for medicinal reasons, but I've grown to like the taste more over the years."

"Yes, please. I'd love some."

While Jade puttered around in the kitchen, I silently rejoiced completing the sock-mending pile.

Jade brought two mugs back to the table and sat one down in front of me. I lifted the mug to my nose and inhaled. I could smell the honey mingling with something unrecognizable but a bit bitter.

"So," Jade said, more quietly than before. Her eyes shifted to Beau. "Will you tell Jackson about what happened today?"

"Yes. When he gets back. I have a lot to tell him."

"You're worried?"

I inhaled like it might make the tension in my chest and shoulders dissipate. "I've sort of been stockpiling conversations we need to have. Let's just say he won't be happy with me." I lifted the mug to my mouth and took a sip. It was scorching hot, but I only remotely felt it. "I'm talking to him tonight though." I couldn't put it off any longer—*Jackson* couldn't put it off any longer. He'd been avoiding me too.

Like Jackson could hear his name on the breeze, the snowmobiles hummed toward the house. The kids jumped to their feet and were out the door before I could tell them to grab their jackets.

I set my mug on the table and met Jade's pewter gaze.

She smiled reassuringly, and squeezed my hand. "Whatever it is, you'll be fine. You both only want what's best for the children and each other, so you'll work things out."

I nearly snorted a laugh. "I'm glad someone has so much faith in me."

Jade and I rose to our feet and headed for the door. I'd spent the past few weeks preparing myself for this conversation, and while I was half petrified, another part of me had no energy left to worry about the outcome.

When I stepped outside, Alex and Sophie climbed off one mobile, more somber than I'd expected, and Del climbed off the other. They had two sleds of caribou meat, but there was no Jackson.

When Sophie saw me standing on the porch, she glanced furtively away with reddened cheeks.

"What is it?" I asked stepping off the porch. "Did something happen?"

It wasn't until Alex met my gaze, his eyes darting directly to my hands, that dread began coiling inside me.

"Jackson knows," Sophie said so quiet it was almost lost to the sound of the sled being drug across the snow. It was a warning, but I felt relief as the burden of my secret dissolved to nothing. But in realizing Jackson wasn't with them, apprehension settled quickly in its place.

"He needs space," Alex said over his shoulder.

Needing space I understood, but the questions were whether he was coming back and if he did, would he stay?

49

JACKSON
APRIL 14

The night I met Elle in Anchorage, I debated whether I should save her life. It went against every fiber in me not to, but I'd seen too much and had expected the worst, even as the three men surrounded her. It was a split-second of indecision, but I knew I would never forgive myself if I walked away, knowing there was a chance an innocent might die, even if she proved to be as crazy as the rest in the end. Noticing the kids she was trying to protect, only helped me pull the trigger. And as she stood over her assaulters' lifeless bodies, shaking but determined not to look away, she compelled me to offer them a safe place to stay.

I saw myself in her that night, on the brink of breaking as she sat on that couch, but instead of giving up, she used her fear to bolster her strength. At least that was what I thought I'd seen. After the shock of learning the truth of who she was and what she could do wore off, I questioned everything I thought I knew.

I stared into the dark forest as I walked through the snow, drawing closer to the cabin with each step.

Elle had been lying from the first night I met her. I didn't blame her for not telling me who she was back then, but I blamed her for hiding it the moment she joined me and for hiding it every day since. As much as I understood her fear, she hadn't even tried to tell me the truth. I felt like an idiot, commending her on her quirks and strength, unaware the entire time of the truth. I'd berated myself this whole time for putting her and the kids at risk, while Elle wasn't only capable and strong, she could be deadly if she wanted to be.

I rolled my shoulders, willing the tension to disperse as I peered up at the main cabin's chimney, billowing with smoke. Sophie had kept what she could do from all of us, too. I didn't like the fact she was walking around with my memories—memories no teenager should have to witness—and yet her silence didn't hurt as much as Elle's did.

Across the yard, I saw the light under the skinning shed door and headed toward it, passing the house and determined to keep my hands and mind busy for as long as possible.

"Jackson?" Elle's voice was barely a whisper, and I tried to ignore the way my chest ached as I walked past.

"I'm not talking about this now," I told her, forcing myself to keep walking. I was weak around her, and I hadn't realized how much until tonight.

"I know you're angry with me, but there's something I need to tell you—"

"There's more?" I spun around. "Really?"

She stepped off the porch into the moonlight, her eyes like liquid malachite and shimmering. I felt senseless satisfaction, knowing she was hurting too. Even if I knew Elle wasn't malicious, she'd made a conscious, daily decision not to tell me the truth about what she had done and what she could do, and betrayal stung like a bitch.

"Jackson, I know I should've told you. I was scared—"

"Scared? You could've fried me with one touch and you're scared of *me*—?"

"I would never hurt you—"

"You already have!" I shouted.

She flinched and her dark hair fell in her face as she took a sudden step back.

"I already knew my dad was crazy, Elle. He loved his damn dogs more than me and shot them for God's sake. You knew how crazy I felt as I put the pieces together about what happened to him —that I knew something was wrong—and you didn't tell me."

"I didn't know if you'd believe me—"

"Oh, that's horseshit," I spat. "We've been partners in everything." I hated that my voice wavered, that any of this mattered so much. I was supposed to be indifferent, just going through the motions until it was time to part ways, and yet each of her omissions felt like a burning hole in my gut. "At least I thought we were—and take those gloves off, they aren't protecting anybody." I shook my head.

Her shoulders heaved, but so did mine. My face burned, like my chest, and I couldn't catch my breath. I hated myself for being angry with her, but I couldn't help it either.

The door to the cabin cracked open, and Beau stepped outside. "Are you guys okay?" He leaned against the porch post, the corners of his mouth pulled down with worry.

Elle wiped the tears from her cheek.

"Yeah, kid." My heart squeezed as I realized whatever world I'd been living in all this time was only a false sense of belonging. "We're fine."

Unwilling to risk more of a scene, I turned on my heels and headed for the skinning shed.

I opened the door and shut myself inside, trying to catch my breath.

When I looked up, Took, Del, Alex, and Sophie were looking at me, their faces brightly lit by the lantern light.

Sophie looked away immediately, cheeks reddened. Del wasn't an idiot. He didn't know what I was upset about, exactly, but he knew enough to look at me with a sympathy I didn't want.

"What's left to do?" I pulled my gun strap over my shoulder

and leaned it against the wall.

Del held up his knife. "We're learning about the best angle for proper precision and the right type of blade."

I shrugged my jacket off, tossed it over a pallet of canning jars, and stepped closer. "Don't stop on my account."

Took handed me the knife. "I'll let you take over," he said. "I need to check on something."

Alex pointed to the hindquarter strung up on a crossbeam, waiting to be taken to the smoker. "That one's ours," he said. "I'll hang it up."

"I'll help," Sophie added, and they disappeared before I could say anything. At least the two of them had made amends, or so it seemed.

"What are we cutting?" I asked, peering down at the hunk of meat on the stone top.

"We're cutting half the steaks into stew bits. It's easier to thaw and more versatile that way."

I followed his lead, grateful for a task to focus on.

Del looked at me. "Should I even ask?"

"Nope."

"Have it your own way," he muttered. We cut meat slab after meat slab until the steak strips were tied and the stew bits were sealed in jars to go into the underground freezer. "We'll get a new block of ice tomorrow while we're ice fishing, before the lake completely melts. That will keep everything cold throughout the summer."

Tomorrow—summer . . . it all seemed too distant in the future. I needed to get through tonight first.

"Sounds good—"

"Jackson!"

I glanced up at the door as it flung open, creaking on its rusty hinges. Elle stood breathless in the doorway. She winced as she handed me the satellite phone.

"It's Ross—he's trying to reach you."

50

JACKSON
APRIL 14

I grabbed the phone, my hands trembling as I brought it to my ear, only this time I wasn't shaking with dread, worried I wouldn't get a response.

"Ross?" I had to force the word out and I held my breath.

Muffled movement was all I heard at first. "Jackson? It's damn good to hear your voice."

My heart swelled at his familiar timbre. "You son of a bitch," I rasped. Tears stung my eyes. I hadn't experienced joy in so long I'd almost forgotten how light and liberating it was. "Where the hell have you been? I've tried calling you for months."

"Where haven't I been?" he said dryly. "I had to deviate a little."

"Yeah, no shit. I almost gave up hope." I looked at Del, forgetting he was standing there. Then, I looked at Elle. She averted her gaze, chewing her bottom lip.

Getting too warm in the shed's confinement, I stepped out into the brisk night.

"I know, brother. It's been awhile."

I hated to ask, but it seemed insensitive not to. "Kelsey?"

"Who? Oh, no. She didn't make it."

Who? God only knew what he'd been through since Anchorage, but *who?*

"Where are you, Ross?"

"I'm in Fairbanks," he said. I waited for him to say more. "What about you, where have you been?"

"All over the fucking place," I told him. "I've been traveling with some people though. I haven't been alone."

"Oh, good. Me too. I met a guy here in Fairbanks." While I knew what we'd been through would change us, it was hard to tell if Ross was being intentionally vague, if he was crazy, or maybe just broken in so many pieces he'd never be the Ross I remembered. Either way, I was beginning to worry. "Is everything okay?"

He chuckled. "Not at all, are you?"

"I'm serious. Where the fuck have you been?" I felt like a broken record, but as the sleepless nights and discoveries of the day set in, all I felt was relief. Ross was alive. "I thought you were dead."

"I know, Jackson. Shit—I'm sorry, brother. It's a long story. Nothing I can get into now. But I promise, I *will* tell you, everything."

Ross was true to his word, always, and my gut told me that while I felt sick to my stomach for a dozen reasons, I knew I could trust him. So I did.

"Are we still meeting somewhere?"

"Whitehorse," I told him. "I'm in St. Elias territory, though. I'll head to the Midnight Sun Lodge as soon as I can. I can probably be there in a week."

"Great. That gives me time to fuel up and get the truck ready."

"You still in the work truck?"

He laughed. "That thing has saved my life a few times," he said. "You weren't exaggerating when you said people were fucking bonkers."

I could only imagine what he'd come across in Fairbanks. "I'm just glad you're breathing," I told him. It was all I'd wanted after radio silence for so long.

"Back at you, brother. I'll call you when we're ready to leave. Deal?"

"Same."

It was silent as Ross breathed into the phone, and I wondered what else there was to say. It felt like there should've been a thousand things, but knowing he was alive was enough, for now.

"Hey, Jackson," Ross said, tentative.

"Yeah?"

"Stay safe, my man."

"You too, Ross." After another hesitant pause, he ended the call.

I stared at the phone in my hand. It had been practically glued to me since Anchorage but his calls never came. There had been a hollowness I carried, a void of every life I cared about being taken, but knowing Ross was alive was like an overflowing bowl of sustenance I needed at the perfect moment. Ross sounded different, but I was different too.

Bottom line, I would get to see him after all these months of thinking he was dead.

Tears burned my eyes. Exhaustion solidified. For the first time in months, all I wanted to do was sleep.

51

ELLE

APRIL 15

Jackson didn't want to talk to me, but his anger toward me and what I had done aside, he needed to. Everyone knew he'd finally found Ross, and it was only a matter of time before he would leave. Jackson had found his friend, there was no reason for him to wait around with us any longer. But we needed to know when he was leaving. He still didn't know about Beau and the wolf either, but maybe he wouldn't care either way.

He'd been gone all night, and while I didn't blame him for needing his space, it was morning, and I needed him to think about the kids.

Heart in my throat, I walked over to the side of the Tacoma, where he sorted through the supplies brought in from the road. I'd already organized them and taken inventory, but I wouldn't stop him from his maniacal searching.

He glanced up as I approached, squinting in the sunlight. "Have you seen the fishing line?" he asked, lifting the lid to the hunting bin. That he acknowledged me at all was a good sign.

"It's in the craft box."

He glowered. "The *craft* box?"

I nodded to the bin beneath the camping supplies behind him.

"It's more of a junk drawer, but you'll find a spool in there."

He lifted one bin off the other and began rifling through rubber bands and zip ties, the miniature sewing kit and safety pins.

"I know you don't want to talk," I said, straightening my shoulders. "And that's fine, but the kids—"

"The kids what?" He found the spool and clicked the lid back onto the box and put it into the truck bed.

"They know you talked to Ross last night and they're worried."

He flipped opened a toolbox. "Why would the kids be worried?" He seemed almost indifferent to my standing there as he fingered through the nuts and bolts.

I crossed my arms over my chest, feeling my side twinge, but it was bearable. "Are you going to leave?"

"That was always the plan." He pulled out a drawer, didn't see what he needed, then shut it. Opened another drawer and shut it just as quickly.

"What are you looking for? Maybe I can help you."

"The sharpening stone."

"It's with the box cutter and scissors in the Do Not Touch bin."

He continued to move the bins around.

"Jackson, would you—" I reached for his arm, determined to make him stop for a single second to look at me.

He paused, eyes fixed on my hand gripping his bicep, so I let it fall away. It wasn't fear in his eyes, even if he'd said I was dangerous, it was something much more distant. "You can be mad at me, but that's not what this is about—"

He straightened and turned to face me fully. For the first time since I'd known him it felt like he was looming over me, almost threatening. Somehow, his reserve was much more fearsome than his shouting at me last night, and I felt uncomfortable under his scrutiny.

I shoved my hands in my back pockets. "They care about you," I said, my voice barely a whisper. "They think you will leave them."

Pain creased the corner of his eyes before he glanced away. "I'm not leaving yet," he said, staring at the cabin.

"Will you talk to them? Sophie feels responsible, and she knows you're angry."

"I'm not angry," he said, though I knew it was a lie.

"Will you tell her that? She thinks I'm only saying it to make her feel better."

"Yeah, I'll talk to her," he said. "And I'll talk to Thea and Beau while we're at the lake."

My eyes widened. "You're still going?"

Jackson's gaze hardened. "Why wouldn't we?"

I opened my mouth but couldn't find the words. I was uncertain what to think anymore. "I don't know. I guess I thought you might decide . . ."

"To what, blow them off, like suddenly I don't care about them?" His jaw clenched. "Glad to know you think so highly of me."

"I—" I didn't like this indifferent side of him, like the old Jackson was back and he was distancing himself from me again. "I didn't mean that. My not telling you wasn't because I don't trust you."

"Wasn't it, Elle?"

He spoke the words so easily, I questioned for a split-second if they were true. "No, it wasn't. I wanted to tell you," I told him shakily.

"But you wanted my help more and thought I'd leave." There was no anger in his voice, barely any emotion at all, just simple facts.

"At first, maybe. But it got more complicated than that." He grabbed his toolbox like he was finished talking to me.

"I don't blame you for being angry—"

"I told you, Elle. I'm not angry."

"Well, maybe you should be!" I shouted then clamped my mouth shut.

"What the hell do you want from me, Elle?" He took a step closer, his hazel eyes fierce in the sunlight. "Do you want me to shout at you? Do you want me to tell you that it's all bullshit because you had months to tell me and you *chose* not to. And you know what . . ." He stared down at my gloved hands. I would've rather had him lash into me, like he just needed to get it out of his system and then things could go back to the way they were, rather than have him stare at my gloved hands in silence, like they disgusted him.

"I didn't ask for this," I told him, almost a plea for him to understand. He might not want to talk about it anymore, but I did. "I woke up one day to a man in my house who was trying to kill me. I thought I was going to die and then a horrifying, miraculous thing happened." The tears welled in my eyes, and I tried to blink them away. "You can judge me for not telling you what I did to your father, and you can be angry for my not telling you what I can do. But you can't be angry at me *because* of what I can do—"

"Elle—"

"Just listen, please," I begged. "I didn't tell you what I did when we met because it seemed impossible and you would think I was crazy like the rest. *I* worried I was crazy. And you're right, I was scared with four kids and I needed your help to keep them safe. But I *kept* it a secret because I didn't want to hurt you and I don't want to lose you." I wiped the tears from my cheeks and took a step back. "Something crazy is happening, Jackson. Something I don't understand, and it's not just me. Beau and Sophie . . ." I shoved my hands back into my pockets. "They're scared. I just hope you can find the time to say goodbye before you disappear."

Having said enough, I turned back for the cabin. If Jackson was the man I thought he was, he'd make things right with them before he left. If he wasn't, then the five of us were back where we started: scared and determined, and we'd figure it out on our own.

52

SOPHIE
APRIL 15

They say an old soul is a person who has the knowledge and wisdom of someone much older than they are. The only person who ever told me I was an old soul was an elderly woman in my building who mistook me for Holly Lynch, a girl who hadn't lived on my floor for over ten years, or so I was later told. But watching Elle and Jackson argue with each other made me feel like an old soul.

It was weird and not because it felt like they were a mix between pseudo-parents and older siblings to me. It was because it felt like I knew both of them better than they knew themselves sometimes. I didn't know what they were feeling and thinking all the time or anything like that—my power didn't work that way—but I'd learned plenty about them since all this craziness started, stuff I don't think even they were aware of.

Being only eighteen, I wasn't supposed to know those types of things. A person was supposed to accumulate knowledge over the years and gain wisdom in their old age through experience. Instead, it was like reading sections of a biography in a single touch, absorbed into a photographic memory complete with live action, color, and all the feels. Good or bad, each glimpse became

LINDSEY POGUE

part of the library, all because I let someone pat my shoulder or because one of them would grab my hand when I wasn't expecting it and there was a spark of a connection. When it happened and what I saw were out of my control.

Stretching my legs out on the porch step, I stared at the skinning shack across the yard where Alex and I played butcher-the-caribou last night. I'd hunted—I'd *shot* an animal. I hadn't seen that one coming. I was the pale girl with weak hips and twisted ankles who had to wear leg braces most of her childhood so that her mother's image of perfection wasn't shattered and it would keep the bullies at bay. The day I'd gotten sick I was worried about teen pregnancy, now I was learning how to live off the land like *Swiss Family Robinson*—six survivors living in a wild world wrought with dangers.

Day one of surviving together had been awkward.

Week one had been eye-opening, to say the least.

Week two I'd finally bought into the dynamic of staying together—love them or hate them—and everything else was history.

The difference was everyone only saw Sophie Collins, the strange delicate girl who needed extra care and acted crazy sometimes, yet when I thought of Elle, Jackson, and Alex, it felt like I'd known them a lifetime. There wasn't a TMI switch I could shut off when I was on overload, and those were the days I wanted to disappear in a dark cave and hide. Forever.

The door to our cabin opened, and Alex stepped out onto the porch. He'd been avoiding me, which I knew would happen.

"I thought you'd be out doing . . . whatever you do when you're not hanging with the kids," he said.

"Yeah, well, there's no reason to hide anymore." The cat was out of the bag. I lifted up the science book that Jackson had gotten for me. "Besides, I've been doing some light reading," I told him.

Alex crouched down beside me, a waft of wood smoke filling my nose.

"You could've told me, Soph," he said softly. "I wouldn't have thought you were crazy." While his voice was gentle for reassurance, he still sat three feet away from me.

"You wouldn't?" I knew enough about him and his character to know there were a hundred things he'd never want me to know. Like the first time he was with a girl and how incredibly awkward it had been; what life was like with his real family before his dad died and the guilt he carried because of it ever since.

"I would rather have known why you were keeping your distance than assumed the worst."

I looked at him, right into his beautiful green eyes. "Are you sure about that? You're not so much an open book as you like people to think you are. I know you hate me knowing things about you."

He didn't bother denying it.

"Besides," I told him. "I already feel crazy enough. I didn't want you, of all people, acting weird around me . . . or for you to look at me differently." Alex had been an unexpected gift since the day I'd met him, even before our entire apartment building was infected with the virus. I hadn't known him twelve hours, and he'd saved my life in more ways than one.

"I might not like that you know, but it doesn't change anything." His voice was like a lure that hooked me and pulled me out of whatever fog I sometimes found myself in. And it also sounded like he meant it, but as my superpower strengthened, so would his discomfort.

"Maybe not," I said, but Alex had never had a sense of place, and I knew the minute I'd first felt his memories of his family, that he'd push me away if I got too close to his truth. "Did you have a girlfriend, before I mean?" I stared down at my broken nails, jagged and dirty. I'd come a long way from the mayor's groomed and picture-perfect daughter. *If my mother could see me now . . .*

Alex smiled. "No. Why, are you interested?" His eyebrows danced at the insinuation.

"No, of course not," I said too quickly. "That would be weird, right?" I tried to laugh it off.

"Yeah, I guess," he said, but he didn't laugh with me. "Especially since you've been pushing me away the past few months. Besides, all-knowing wizard that you are, wouldn't you already know if I'd had a girlfriend?"

I shrugged. "No, not unless I made a habit of touching you. I've kept my distance from everyone for a reason, remember?"

"Why do you ask, seriously?"

"Oh, because," I drawled. "I wanted to know what she was like."

In December I had a subpar boyfriend and was on the brink of an emotional breakdown, and that was before the virus. After was even worse. Alex had been my rock, and he'd seen me at my absolute worst, weak and desperate and grieving for my dead parents. Even though I knew he felt *something* for me, I didn't want Alex to want me because I was a girl he liked to save. I wanted him to like me because I was strong and useful and came with a TNT Flammable label, not Fragile - Handle With Care.

"What sort of stuff *do* you know?" he asked, and I felt my face flush as I scooted around to face him, one leg crossed over my lap. He wasn't asking about Elle and Jackson.

Everyone had dark pasts.

What I know changes nothing—not how I feel about you, Elle, or Jackson.

I wanted to give him a dozen reassurances but I didn't. It wouldn't do any good if I did.

So, what did I tell him if not the full truth? I knew he had burn marks on his arms from his mother. I knew the hairline scar on his right temple was from being bullied when he was little because he was poor. I knew what his stepdad did to him the day he died.

"Random stuff," I said instead, and it was true—I saw whatever people were feeling in the moment, and the memories that linked to it in one way or another. "Personal stuff," I added. The emotions were the worst part. The happy ones tended to fade, just like optimism on a shitty day. The bad ones clung like weights, and I assumed because they were so much stronger with all the anxiety and doubt everyone felt all the time now.

"But like what, exactly? My favorite color? The first time I smoked weed in middle school? Or like, the crazy shit?" He knew it was more than colors and rap sheets, but if I didn't tell him something, the curiosity would eat away at him.

"I know you always marked 'Other' on intake forms instead of 'Hispanic' because you don't know who your real dad was." I told him. "And I know that you've always wondered if you had any siblings. And I know why you bought me that pregnancy test the day we first met."

The amusement dulled in his eyes and he pursed his lips.

"I won't tell anyone," I promised.

Even if Alex didn't like my knowing things, he knew he could trust me. His face softened. "I know, Soph."

We stared at each other for a few long seconds; the cool morning breeze was refreshing against my warming skin.

"What about you?" I asked, glad I wasn't the only screwed up one. "What have you seen?"

"Yesterday was the first time," he said. "You were worried your hair was out of place—"

I pretended to throw the textbook at him. "Shut up. That's not what I worry about."

He grinned.

"Sometimes you do," he said with a smirk. "Admit it."

"Well, I don't want to look like a bush woman." His smile was infectious, and I laughed. "Stop staring at me."

"I can't help it. Now it's all I can think about—Sophie the Alaskan bush woman."

I rolled my eyes. "I'm glad to see you're having so much fun with this."

"I'm only playing. That's not what I saw." His voice sobered and his eyes glazed over like he was standing on that rocky knoll again, eyes wide and terrified. "I saw Elle and that man in Slana. Not the whole thing but bursts of images and I could feel her power, though I wasn't sure if it was actually hers or your perception of her."

"Could've been both, I guess." It was hard to discern my emotions from others sometimes because my reactions to theirs were often similar.

Alex let out a breath and leaned back against the porch post, then he laughed and dragged his fingers over his head. "This is so crazy. We're talking about this shit like it's normal."

"Yeah, trust me, it feels anything but normal."

He shrugged. "It's that or freak the fuck out." And that was probably one of the most real things Alex had said to me, even if he thought he'd meant all the rest.

I looked at him, studying the verdant depths of his eyes.

"What?"

"Has anyone ever told you you're an old soul?"

"Oh boy. Now we're getting too deep," he teased, jumping to his feet. "Come on, let's go get some breakfast. My treat."

"Oh, a granola bar. Lucky me."

53

JACKSON
APRIL 15

"I've never fished before," Thea said, peering out the window of the truck. I glanced at her in the mirror, then at Beau. While Thea talked enough for the three of us, Beau seemed even more out of sorts than usual.

"Well, hopefully you'll have fun," I told her. "I enjoyed fishing when I was your age." I hadn't ice fished in years, but soon the ice would melt completely and they might miss their chance to learn.

Beau was quiet in the back. He stared out the window, his mind somewhere else. "How about you, Beau? Are you excited to try fishing for the first time?"

"I went once, with my dad," he mumbled.

"Good, maybe you can teach me. I'm a little rusty."

He leaned back in his seat, his head bouncing as we drove through the woods. The plow came in handy; creating roads that would be easier for us to follow on our way back. "What's eating at you, kid?"

He met my gaze in the mirror. "Are you and Elle still fighting?"

I cleared my throat. "We're not fighting, we just disagree on some things."

"It sounded like you were fighting," he said. "Is it because of me?"

"No, bud. We aren't fighting because of you or anyone else." Elle hadn't told me what was going on with Beau, but then things had escalated quickly and there hadn't really been an opportunity for that. "Why would we be fighting about you, Beau?"

"She doesn't like the wolves."

"What do you mean?"

He sighed. "She thinks they're dangerous and doesn't want me around them."

"They're really nice," Thea chirped. "I like the black one the best."

Beau smacked Thea on the arm and glared at her.

"Hey, no hitting," I chided.

Beau crossed his arms over his chest. "You have such a big mouth," he muttered, glaring at her.

"Nuh-uh."

Beau rolled his eyes. "Whatever."

As Thea's words sank in, I tapped on the brakes, bringing the truck to a stop. Then, I turned around in my seat. "You've been playing with the wolves?" I wasn't sure why I was surprised. Beau had been pushing his luck with them for weeks.

"They won't hurt me," he grumbled, just like I had done when I was a pissed off and defiant at his age.

"Beau, they're wild animals." I pointed to Thea. "What about your sister? They aren't pets. You guys could get hurt."

"You don't understand," he growled. "How come Elle can use her power but I can't use mine?"

"Your *power*?" I didn't even know how to answer his questions.

"Yeah, Elle killed that guy with her bare hands and she's not in trouble."

"Elle did what she had to do to save you," I reminded him. "She didn't want to hurt those men."

"Well, I know the wolves won't hurt me either. It's like the same thing."

The image of a wolf mauling Beau made my stomach flip-flop and the hair on the back of my arms stand on end. "How do you know they won't hurt you, Beau?"

"I just do," he said, voice sharp with impatience. "Why won't you guys trust me?"

"I'm sorry kid, wolves aren't particularly cuddly animals. They're not pets."

"Well, mine are."

Mine? I rubbed my forehead and continued down the trail left by the snowmobile. Things were getting weirder by the hour and I didn't know how to navigate questions about how baby caribou were born let alone superpowers. "Does Elle know you've been playing with them?"

He met my gaze again and regrettably shook his head.

"I'll tell you what," I started, grasping at straws. "Tonight we'll talk about it, okay? All of us, together. We'll figure out what's going on, and we'll get some ground rules in place. But until then, no more playing with the wolves, okay?"

I brought the truck to a stop near the water's edge where Took and Del had their snowmobile parked. Then, I turned around to face him. "Beau, do we have a deal?"

Reluctantly, he nodded.

"If you promise, I'll take you hunting before I leave."

His brow furrowed.

"What, suddenly you don't want to go hunting anymore?"

"I do," he said. "But . . . when are you leaving?"

My throat constricted, and I hated that it was becoming so difficult to talk about. "Soon," I admitted. "But not for a few days at least. I'll take you hunting before I go, okay?"

Beau nodded, but his heart wasn't in it, and I felt the excitement of the day officially dampened. "Do you guys even want to fish anymore?"

"I do!" Thea chirped and she flung open the door.

I looked at Beau, praying we could salvage what was left of the late morning. Fishing was supposed to be a fun trip, but I hadn't expected I'd have to address superpowers, wolves, and lady-fuck-ing-phoenix, too. "You don't have to," I told him.

Beau stared at me for a few heartbeats. "I still want to fish," he said. He climbed out of the back seat and shut the door.

I watched as he and Thea ran over to Took and Del unloading their things from the sled. Nothing was easy anymore. Everything that was supposed to be good was complicated; everything that was meant to be easy was problematic. The plan had been the same since day one and suddenly I had a fraying knot in the center of my stomach telling me it was wrong to leave. My best friend was alive and I should be more ecstatic. Elle killed my dad, which shouldn't have felt okay, but I was glad she did. He would've killed her instead, and I would've never known her or the kids; they'd never have been a part of my life.

I wanted to be angry at Elle for lying because it was easier than admitting I cared about her in a way that made me feel like a disloyal piece of shit to my dead wife's memory.

Beau stepped in front of the truck and tapped the hood. "Come look!"

I climbed out of the truck, grabbed the tackle box from the passenger seat and the poles from the back, determined to enjoy the day like we'd come out to do. The rest could wait for a few hours. It had to. I needed a break.

"It's so pretty!" Thea squealed, clapping her hands.

Took stood at the bank, pointing at a patch of sunlight. Ice crystals floated in the air around it like suspended, blinking diamonds.

"They're called dust diamonds," Took said with a crooked smile. "We only get 'em a couple times a year, when the weather clears up. It's one of Jade's favorite things."

"I've never actually seen them before," I admitted. "My mom

used to tell me stories about it though. She said the ice danced to the silent song of sunlight."

"It *does* look like they're dancing," Thea said, voice radiating with awe. "Is this what heaven looks like in the daytime?" We hadn't talked about death much, even though it had surrounded us all winter.

I didn't know what heaven looked like, or if it existed, but I agreed, it would be a beautiful place if it did. "I hope so. What do you think it looks like at nighttime?"

"The lights, silly. Like Jade said."

I smiled. "How could I forget?"

Inhaling the sharp scent of ice and evergreen, I soaked in the snow-capped mountains that surrounded us, and the crystalline sky that shimmered.

"We picked a good day to come," Beau said.

"We sure did," I said, content.

Del used the ice spud to measure the thickness a few yards out on the lake. The sun had been shining longer and higher in the sky, but the world was taking its time to melt. But like every natural part of Alaska it was hard to predict, and we had no idea what was already shifting under the frozen surface of the water.

"Some ice is thicker than others, you guys. Stay in the areas where Del is putting the holes, okay?"

They nodded, and I pointed to a prickly, fallen tree angled half frozen in the water, a perfect haven for bottom feeders and shadow dwellers. "What about there, Del?"

"Yeah, we'll get nibbles in the debris for sure," he called. "It's just over five inches. It's safe, but be careful." He began to pick a fishing hole in the ice with the chisel.

"All right you two, you heard him." I handed the kids their poles. "Stay in these areas. The last thing I need is one of you falling in."

"Oh, man." Thea giggled. "That would be so cold."

"Yeah, and Elle would kill me," I told her. "So be careful."

"Where are the fishing jigs we carved last night?" Took grumbled, searching through their toolbox.

Beau opened our tackle box. "Right here." Careful, so as not to hook himself, he handed Thea hers and studied his own.

"Alaskans have been carving their own jigs for thousands of years," I told them. "You couldn't have a better teacher than Took, I'm sure."

Thea looked up at me, blinking as she mouthed *thousands* with awe.

"Let me see your handiwork." I crouched down between them. To a fish, their jigs would look like a piece of driftwood, but they weren't bad for a nine- and six-year-old's first time. "I didn't have fancy poles like you growing up, but that's another skill for another time."

I grabbed a container of frozen guts to use as bait while Took helped them attach their jigs to the fishing line.

"Some guts for you," I said, handing a frozen piece to Beau. "And, some guts for you . . ." Thea's face crinkled with disgust, but she didn't hesitate to take it.

"It's not so bad when it's frozen," Beau told her.

"Okay now, shove them on your hook and we'll let it dangle in the hole just a little, so that other fish will think it's still alive."

Thea pursed her lips as she struggled to bait her hook. It got stuck to her mitten, but she was determined to do it on her own.

"Ready!" Del said. "Come pick your holes."

Thea chose her hole first, and Took helped her drop her line. Del helped Beau with his, and I grabbed a stick as thick as my finger from the bank and tied fishing line around it, making a rod of my own.

"What kinda fish are we getting?" Beau asked. He stood there with his fishing pole in hand, waiting.

"Oh, well," Del said. "I don't know what we'll get. Could be grayling or whitefish. And if we're lucky, maybe even trout."

"That's my favorite," I told them.

"Don't all fish taste the same?" Beau asked. "They're all fish."

Took chuckled to himself and straightened, stretching out his crooked, old back.

"No," Del said. "They don't all taste the same. You'll see."

"I had a fish once," Thea said. "Fuzzbucket ate it though."

"What's a Fuzzbucket?" Took asked. "A bigger fish?"

"It's a cat, silly." Thea laughed.

"Oh. Okay." He eyed her skeptically.

I crouched down over my own hole and braced my stick over it, making sure the line went as far down as possible to float with the water, which I would check on later.

Once the rods rested in carved out holes and the lines were set, Took, Del, and I made camp on the bank. We unfolded chairs and built a fire to blazing, simple and quiet, just as I'd hoped it would be.

"Now what do we do?" Thea plodded over, her braids hanging messily on each side of her face.

I tugged her beanie down further over her pink ears. "We keep warm and wait for the fish to come."

"But . . ." She pursed her lips in disapproval. "But that's boring."

Chuckling, the guys and I looked at each other. "That's fishing, Thea. It's a game of patience."

"Well, then this was a mistake," Beau muttered. "Thea sucks at patience."

"I do not," she retorted.

"Do too."

"Shut up."

"Okay you guys," I said. "No bickering while we're fishing. It's one of two rules."

"What's the other?" Beau asked.

"Safety," I told them.

"Well, it's his fault," she retorted, walking back out to her hole. "I'm going to wait for my fish."

"Don't touch mine," Beau told her and followed after her.

"I have hot chocolate when you want some," I said. "And snacks."

"Okay," they called, but I was officially an afterthought to them.

"Don't they know a watched pot never boils?" Took asked, shaking his head.

"They'll get it, eventually, just like Jet did." Del nodded with certainty. "You'll see."

"At first I thought it was beginner's luck," Took added. "Suddenly he was catching all the fish." He batted the notion away. "I stopped fishing with him."

"Ouch." I chuckled.

"Jet had patience, Took. You're like Thea when it comes to fishing. I'm surprised you enjoy it."

"I don't. Just because I know how doesn't mean I like it."

Del threw his hands up with a chuckle. "Then why do you do it all the time?"

"Because you like it. I'm not sending you out here alone."

Del and Took bickered back and forth, half as bad as Thea and Beau, and I admired their relationship as much as I envied it. The more I watched them and heard their stories, the more I looked forward to having happy, memorable stories of my own one day.

"So, Elle said you might leave soon." Del poked the fire with a long stick. "You still going to Whitehorse?"

I stared into the embers, uncertain how to answer. "That was the plan."

"Was?" Took raised his eyebrows, looking more perturbed than curious.

"Was. Is. I'm not sure which."

Del leaned forward, resting his elbows on his knees. "Pardon my prying, but seems like if you're uncertain, it might not be the right answer."

"Yeah, well, things are—"

"Complicated," Del and Took finished in unison.

"Elle keeps saying the same thing," Took grumbled. "Life is complicated. You still gotta make decisions. Do you want them to be good ones or bad ones? I'll tell you what the bad ones are—"

"Please excuse my father-in-law, he thinks highly of his own opinion."

"Well, I'm not sorry," Took said tersely. "In the grand scheme of things, it's really not that complicated. Do you want to be alone or be with people you care about? Trust me, time flies and all that."

"I get what you're saying, Took, but—" I glanced out at the ice and rose to my feet. "Where are the kids?"

"Probably just exploring," Took said. "That's what I'd be doing."

I walked out onto the ice, relieved to see their poles were there and they hadn't fallen in. I glanced around the frozen lake. They weren't out in the middle of the ice, which had been my fear. I headed toward the curve in the bank, and was about to call for them, when I saw Thea sitting at the water's edge through a thicket. I prepared my scolding speech to give them for going off on their own when I saw something move in front of her. I took a few steps closer.

My gaze latched onto a twig that spun around and around on the ice in front of her, moving at the same pace her finger twirled. I blinked, barely able to believe my own eyes, and couldn't open my mouth to say a single anything.

Beau walked further out onto the ice with a much larger branch and stopped a few yards out. "Try to roll this one back to you," he told her, gaze narrowed on the branch intently. "It's the biggest one so far."

Though I felt the need to caution them, I couldn't look away either. Thea could move things with her mind. Elle was right, it was all impossible. All of it was, and until yesterday, I would've thought Thea was crazy had I not seen it for myself.

I held my breath as Thea squeezed her eyes shut, then blinked them open in concentration. The log at Beau's feet moved, only trembling at first. But as Thea continued to stare at it, it hedged and began to roll slowly toward her.

"You did it!" Beau shouted, but his excitement was short lived. When he noticed me watching him, he leapt into a run to get off the ice, and his foot went straight through. He screamed as he fell into the water.

"Beau!" I shouted and took off running. "Fuck—"

Thea screamed from the top of her lungs as she ran to where the water sloshed over the ice. "Get back!" I told her, and fell to my knees when I reached the hole. I couldn't see him through the murky water. There was no flailing, and the horror he might not know how to swim eviscerated any shock immobilizing me.

I jumped into the water after him. It was so intensely cold, it felt like I was surrounded by fire and a net of razor blades. I didn't see Beau at first and panic was a blaring cry as I tried to focus in the icy water. My eyes burned. My fingers and legs were numb. But as the ice was chipped away from the surface, I could see more clearly. The white of Beau's jacket against the darkness floated like it was suspended in the air, and Beau wasn't moving.

I pulled my body through the water without thought, clutching Beau's hand in mine as I forced my limbs to send me to the surface. Arms reached into the water next, helping me pull him to the top. Del and Took lifted Beau out first, then their hands frantically grabbed at me as I used every ounce of willpower I had left to kick and pull myself out of the water.

The hard ice felt like a miracle, almost warm against my freezing skin, and I peered around for Beau. "Is he breathing?" I cried as Took helped me onto my knees. "Is he breathing!" I shouted and scrambled over to the bank where Del crouched over Beau's body.

"Del," I pleaded. "Is he breathing?"

Thea cried behind me, screaming her brother's name, and all I could think was I'd been too stupid and slow to react. I should've gotten him off the ice. I should've jumped in faster.

"He's only . . . in shock," I prayed, my voice frozen in my throat. Every ounce of training I'd had was like a rock sunk to the bottom of my gut; my head was empty and the energy that was left drained from my body as hot tears streamed down my face.

Finally, Beau doubled over, gasping for air as he choked up water.

"Oh, thank God," I breathed. "Thank God." I held his forehead against mine and pulled him against me, trying to warm him. "Are you okay? You scared the shit out of me."

"I—I think so," he chattered. Took held Thea in his arms, trying to console her as she cried.

"He's okay, Thea," I told her, but it was hard to believe myself.

"Here," Del said, removing his coat. "We've got to get you guys warmed up."

I helped Beau to his feet, ignoring the ache in my body as I stood and lifted him in my arms to carry him toward our camp. "Sit next to the fire," I told him, setting him down in one of the chairs. "We'll get you something warm to wear, okay bud?"

Beau nodded, shivering but alive and okay.

"Del, get his clothes off, would you? I might have something in the truck we can use."

"What about you?" Del said. "You need dry clothes too."

"Yeah, him first though," I called over my shoulder.

Del murmured about wet socks and boots as I opened the truck for an extra jacket or flannel. Finding a towel and dirty thermal shirt, I grabbed them and shut the door.

"This is all I could find—" I stopped at the front of the truck, my body ice cold while fear burned red and hot straight through me. A black wolf crept out of the woods, furtively glancing around at us as it timidly made its way toward Beau.

Slowly, Del stepped toward the gun propped against a spruce a few feet away. He looked at me, and as crazy as it was, I shook my head.

The wolf stopped at Beau's feet and licked his shaking hand with a whine.

On trembling legs, Beau climbed out of the chair and plopped down on the ground beside the fire. The wolf waited for him to settle in—half-naked by the flames—and it laid against Beau's little body to keep him warm.

"It chose him," Took whispered, pulling me out of my trance.

"What?" I shivered, but as my body numbed, I wasn't sure if it was from cold or sheer awe.

Del lifted the discarded jacket off the ground. "It looks like the kid's got it covered. You're the one we have to worry about now."

54

ELLE
APRIL 15

"Now, we let the fat boil and the rendered tallow that comes to the top will become our wax once it hardens," Jade explained. "We can get a dozen candles out of this batch, and all the membrane and meat that's left, we'll freeze for Koda's food during the winter."

"It's as easy as that?" I stared at the empty mason jars on the table, and the thin wooden wicks piled beside them.

"It's messy, but yes. It's fairly straightforward—"

Koda barked outside as the truck and snowmobiles rumbled closer.

"They're back early," Jade mused. Wiping our hands off on our aprons, we headed for the front door.

The instant I saw Beau was in the truck bed, wearing clothes that were too big and hair stuck in a frozen mess, I knew something was wrong.

I stepped off the porch as Jackson climbed out of the passenger side of the Tacoma, his clothes stuck to him and covered with frost.

"What—"

"I'm fine," he said, pointing behind him. "We need to get Beau inside." There was a frustration in his voice I wasn't sure was aimed at me, but I didn't argue.

I hurried around the bed of the truck and nearly fell back. "Oh my," I breathed, my hand clamping over my mouth. A black wolf lay beside Beau, its yellow eyes lifting as we gathered around, though it didn't lift its head or bare its teeth like I expected it to do.

Beau quivered a little, draped in an oversized coat that shook around his shoulders, but his skin was pink and full of color.

Jade gasped beside me, none of us moving.

"Jackson," I whispered, uncertain what to do.

"It's been keeping Beau warm since we pulled him out of the water," Del explained as he shut the driver side door of the truck.

"Time to go inside, bud," Jackson said, coming around to the tailgate. He nodded to Beau as if they'd had an agreement.

Beau nudged the wolf, and though it seemed inconvenienced having to move, it stood up and jumped out of the back of the truck. Beau scooted to the edge of the tailgate, held out his hand, and the wolf stepped closer for Beau to pet the top of its head. The wolf's eyes closed and its ears flattened, and for a few breaths I watched as Beau and the wolf had a silent communication.

Then the wolf's eyes darted around at us, it trotted past Koda's kennel, and disappeared into the woods.

I gathered Beau against me, ignoring the twinge in my side as I squeezed. "Are you okay?" He was warm, despite his hair frozen on end. I desperately wanted to lift him into my arms, but refrained. "What happened?" I pulled back, waiting for him to say something, but he only glanced at Jackson before sliding onto the ground.

Jade reached out to offer Beau her hand. "Let's get you all bundled up inside and warm," she said.

Sophie and Alex ran over, Alex's eyes trained on the forest. "What the hell was that?"

Sophie took Thea's hand in hers. "Sounds like you had an interesting morning."

"Yeah," Thea murmured. "It was *really* scary." Alex followed them inside, the air buzzing with questions and curiosities, but my mind was still reeling as I watched them disappear into the house.

Although I could fill in some of the missing pieces, I wasn't sure how or why Jackson and Beau had fallen into the water, and the remnants of what happened—Thea's face still red from crying, and Beau and Jackson soaked to the bone—I couldn't help the uneasiness that settled in a little deeper.

The door had barely closed when Del popped back out in a new jacket and settled his cap back on his head. "We still have gear at the lake and a snowmobile. We'll be back."

As Del closed the Tacoma door, I sidled up to the window, glancing between him and Took, though both of them tried to avoid my gaze. "What happened?" My voice was surprisingly calm, and I peered past them at Jackson heading to the smaller cabin. "Is Jackson all right?"

"Physically, they're both fine." Del's choice of words didn't put me much at ease.

Took nodded in Jackson's direction, offering me a silent nudge, then the truck rumbled to life, and Del rolled up the window. And as quickly as they had driven into camp, they followed their tracks back out again and disappeared through the trees.

I considered going inside to check on Beau, but there were enough people fussing over him, so I headed toward the cabin. My heartbeat thudded like a bass drum and I braced myself for whatever might transpire between Jackson and me when I stepped inside. He probably didn't want to see me, but I cared too much to let him be.

I creaked the door open. Jackson stood half-clothed in wet pants beside the wood stove. He shivered as he stared at the wall, ice frozen to his mustache and hardened to his pants. I didn't bombard him with questions I knew he wasn't ready to answer, so I grabbed a folded quilt from the bed and shook it out. Standing on tiptoes, I tried to drape it over his bare shoulders, struggling as my side twinged.

Jackson reached out for the blanket, pulling it around him haphazardly. He didn't look at me though, just stared at the fire-place. Lost. In shock. Maybe even angry still.

"Take your pants off," I whispered, and went over to his bag for a pair of sweats and wool socks. "You need to get out of those clothes." I placed them on the bed next to a thermal shirt for him to change into and opened the woodstove to build a fire. My hands moved quickly. Splinters and scratches weren't something I had to worry about, though my gloves were plenty scarred and discolored from so much use. Shoving tinder beneath the crossed wood, I lit it with a match and breathed life to the bourgeoning flames.

Eventually, Jackson dressed behind me, unhurried and word-less. One boot scuffed the floor, then another, as he took them off. The floorboards creaked under his weight, and then heavy, soggy clothes thudded to the floor.

I rubbed my gloved hands together against the growing warmth, acutely aware of the irony as I tried to keep my mind from wandering. The fire may have sizzled in my veins, but the flush of my skin seemed to deepen as I realized this was the first time Jackson and I had been alone in so long I couldn't remember. It felt different than before—charged from the turbulence of the days passed and uncharted.

Once he finished changing, and the flames were roaring, I closed the stove door and looked back at him. Though Jackson stood tall and his presence often filled the room, he seemed differ-ent. An emotion I hadn't seen before eclipsed his hazel eyes. Instead of haunted by the past, he looked dazed and uncertain.

I stood and stepped toward him. "Are you okay?" Hesitantly, I rested my hand on his arm, offering whatever reassurance I could.

Jackson's eyebrows drew together, almost painfully, and his gaze drifted to my hand. I was about to remove it when he took my wrist, stared at my glove, then began to pull it off.

"No—" I tried to tug away, but he whispered my name and I stilled. With bated breath, I stared into his eyes. He was completely still. Determined.

Slowly, he inched the glove from my fingers. The air was cool against my skin as the glove dropped to the floor, and my eyes fluttered closed at the relief I felt. I took them off sometimes, but only when I dared to chance the outcome and was alone.

Jackson placed my hand against his chest and my eyes fluttered open. His chest was solid and cold, and I could feel the rhythmic thud of his heart against my palm.

Bah-bum. Bah-bum. Bah-bum.

His eyes closed, and he spread his freezing palm over mine. I could feel the cold waning from his fingers as the heat from my hand seeped into him. Jackson calmed me in a way I never understood, and in a frisson of desire and curiosity, I pressed my fingertips more firmly against his chest, letting a flood of heat fill us both. I wasn't afraid, but content.

"What's happening to us?" he whispered, lifting my hand from his chest. He stared down at it, lost in wonder. Any uneasiness from before was gone.

"I don't know." My voice was quiet but seemed to echo in the room. "I've been trying to figure that out myself."

Jackson blinked at me, his lashes wet but no longer icy, and water dripped from his beard onto my boot. "I didn't know if he would be okay," he finally said, his voice thin.

"Beau? He'll be fine," I told him. "He had a wolf blanket to keep him warm." I lifted my shoulder with a slight smile, like it was just an ordinary day.

Jackson's brow puckered again and he let go of my hand. "Thea moved a log with her mind," he said.

My eyes widened. That was a new one I hadn't heard yet. And I couldn't help but smile. "Really?"

He nodded slowly, and his frown deepened. "When they caught me watching, Beau ran for the bank and the ice broke under him."

"And let me guess, you jumped in after him," I said knowingly. That's what Jackson did, he saved people, even if he didn't realize it. All of us were proof of that. "I guess all of our secrets are out now. What's yours?"

He shook his head. "I have no idea. I don't think I have one."

Thoughtful quietness surrounded us, broken only by the crackling wood and a sigh as Jackson sat down in the chair. "What now?" he asked. He picked my glove up from the floor and handed it to me.

"Well, I'll get a towel for your defrosted hair for starters," I teased. I grabbed a towel from the clean stack by the door. "And we need to talk, all of us." I handed him a worn, brown towel fraying on the ends. "I'll give you some space."

I turned to leave and Jackson reached for my hand again. "Elle?"

"Yes?"

His eyes sought mine, and he squeezed my hand, rubbing his thumb over my wrist. "Thank you."

My chest warmed, and I exhaled a shaky breath of relief. It was a look of forgiveness and gratitude, and I couldn't have asked for anything more.

55

SOPHIE
APRIL 15

"Where are my pants?" Thea groaned, glancing around the room with her hands on her hips.

"Here." I pulled them out from under my sweatshirt on the floor. "Clean socks are in your bag."

Privacy was something you sort of forfeited when you lived with so many people, especially since being safe meant sticking together. That's why the girls dressed first, then we switched with the boys. It was our current routine, though revisions tended to happen quickly as our location changed.

As an only child, I'd always had privacy. Well, not where my mom was concerned. She hovered, making sure I did my homework and showered—like I needed reminding—and did my leg stretches that hadn't been necessary for eight years. She didn't want all of our hard work and the physical therapy she'd paid for to get my weak legs in tip-top shape to go to waste. Part of me wondered if that's why it was so hard to lose her.

My mom had been a nagging reminder of everything I needed to do, hadn't done, and would one day become. Without her, I wasn't sure who I was. I'd spent my teen years pushing back, trying to prove I wasn't a baby girl anymore and would never be her perfect Sophie. Not having her around made me feel like I was just sort of . . . lost.

When I first started seeing and feeling other people's memories, I thought it was just my mind breaking down and my weakness showing through, and *that* was the hardest part to imagine. I'd always felt like the weak link and now, when I needed to be strong to survive, it wasn't just my bones I had to worry about anymore, it was my mind, too. If I'd had Elle's power I wouldn't have to worry about shrinking away at someone's touch or going out of my way to avoid them.

"Ready!" Thea chirped.

"Switch!" I called, and Elle creaked the door open to find the three guys sitting on the step, patiently waiting.

"Done!" Thea sang.

Alex looked at his imaginary watch as he stood up. "You almost beat your record."

"Ah, see Thea," I nudged her. "We *are* getting faster." Being around Thea and Beau was easier, and I wasn't sure why exactly, only that their memories didn't seep into me, wringing me out from the inside. I had a feeling it had to do with their resilient ability to keep moving forward and not overthink and hold onto things.

Alex sidestepped me as us girls filed out the door. He grinned, of course, because that's what Alex did. He acted like life was what it was and you had to roll with the punches. Inside, though, he was all about survival. Each day was about proving his worth and that meant being the person he thought we all wanted him to be, and hiding from his past. Being with all of us had given him a purpose for the first time in his life, but now I could learn things he didn't want me to. So he kept his distance, and things were different between us. Already seeing so much about him, I anticipated that would be his reaction when he learned what I could do, and it's part of why I kept my silence for as long as I could.

A logical person would understand why he was wary, and of

course I did, but the distance still stung. I wasn't just a random person he wanted to keep secrets from, I was supposed to be his friend—more than that in some ways—after all we'd been through. We'd had a connection since the day we met, and suddenly none of it mattered. I had become something else to him; no longer just Sophie, but *dangerous* Sophie.

"You better hurry," Thea sang through the door. "If we beat you, you're making us breakfast tomorrow."

"I'm already making you breakfast tomorrow," Alex called back.

"Besides," Beau griped. "That wasn't part of the bet."

I leaned against the porch post and stared up at the sky. The night was cold, the air crisp. A few clouds dappled the inky blue, moving quickly across the moon.

Jade, Took, and Del asked very few questions, though all of them had seen enough to know we were different than they were. They didn't know about my touch, but I'd been careful to keep my distance as much as possible. It felt wrong to touch them, to see their private lives—especially since what happened with Jet. I couldn't control the things that I saw, at least not yet, and I didn't want to trespass more than I already had. I thought maybe it was the memories closest to the surface that I felt most, but without practicing I couldn't be sure. And if I was honest, I didn't want to have to hold any more fear or pain. My mind was already chock-full, and it was difficult to ignore. So I kept my hands to myself as much as I could.

"The coast is clear," Alex said, opening the door. "And we made excellent time."

"I don't know," Thea drawled, and she pointed at Beau who was still pulling his shirt down. "He's not even ready!"

"Yeah-huh," Beau said.

"Nuh-uh—"

"How about we call it a tie tonight, guys?" Elle prompted. "We're all tired and we can start again tomorrow."

Jackson closed the door to the wood stove, still in his sweats from earlier. He'd been shaken up after what happened at the lake, but it was nice to see he was finally coming around—a little worse for wear. Beau was the one who fell in, and he was unfazed, maybe even relieved to show everyone he was right about the wolves. Of course Beau could talk to wolves, Thea could move things with her mind, and Elle could kill a man with a single touch. While I carried the burden of it all—me, the weak one—as if it was my own. I fleetingly wondered if my mom would be proud.

"Everyone grab a seat," Jackson said.

Thea and I crawled up onto the bed where Beau already sat, fluffing his pillow. Alex took his cot under the window.

"Before everyone goes to sleep," Elle started, standing at the foot of the bed. "We need to talk about all the new things that are happening." She met Jackson's gaze as he laid the pallet of sleeping bags out on the floor.

"We never talked about what I did to that man in Slana," she said.

Beau stiffened beside me, which was strange, but then he'd watched Elle fry a man, which wasn't something I liked to relive either.

"You did it to protect us," Beau said. "You had to."

"Yes, I did it to protect us, but we all know that killing isn't okay, right?"

"I know I wasn't there," Alex said, elbows resting on his knees. "But what are you worried about? That we're scared of you or that we think it's okay to kill people?"

"Both, I guess. We've seen a lot of death, and we've been very afraid."

"Of the bad people," Beau said.

"Yes, there are bad people, and the things we can do now can hurt people, so we have to be careful because there are good people too, like the Ranskins. We can't walk around pretending we know what we're doing and how to control it, especially around Jade, Took, and Del because they might get hurt. Do you agree?"

I nodded with the kids. Even if my ability couldn't physically hurt them, the emotional scars people carried were their own to bear, and I had no business intruding.

Elle looked at Beau. "Are there any other animals or capabilities you've discovered we should know about?"

He shook his head. "Just the wolves . . ."

But Beau didn't seem certain, something we all seemed to pick up on. Elle tilted her head. "There's nothing else, Beau. What about you, Thea? We won't be angry. We want to help each other."

Beau looked at his sister, his chest rising and falling more quickly.

Thea stared at him and I could practically feel their worry buzzing in the air between them.

"I heard you can do something pretty dang cool, Thea. You can tell us," I said and ran my fingers through Thea's brown hair.

In an instant, Beau was standing over Thea's bed, his pajamas wrinkled but his coat was on. "Get up. Come on—we have to go!"

She climbed out, head fuzzy and skin still hot with fever, but Thea did what her big brother commanded.

"Mom says the bad guys are coming," he told her and took her hand in his.

I blinked. The memory shifting in a flash.

Frigid, howling wind whipped through a dark hallway. The way only lit by Beau's flashlight as he hurried ahead. Debris littered the ground—crumbled concrete and copper piping. His hand was in his mother's. It was Katie, my teacher, alive. Her blonde hair was disheveled, her pajamas soiled.

"Mama, what's wrong with you? Where are we going?" Beau hurried obediently beside her, trying to match her pace.

"Shut up and hurry," she told him. "We have to hurry . . ."

Graffiti covered the cement wall, and I could almost feel the coldness of the wind against my skin. Katie glanced back. Her brown eyes were bloodshot and sores dotted the corners of her mouth. "They're coming," she warned, panic in her voice. "The bad men are coming."

Thea moved as fast as her little legs would carry her, petrified of the bad men coming, but it wasn't fast enough. "Hurry!" Katie shouted, reaching back with spindly fingers, nails bit to the quick. Thea whimpered, her head a throbbing mess of hazy confusion and fear. Katie grabbed hold of Thea's arm, tugging her forward. "I said they're coming," she muttered. "The bad men are coming!"

Thea stiffened against her mother's touch, and Katie tugged her harder and more ferociously.

"You're hurting her," Beau cried, tears in his eyes. "Mama, you're hurting Thea!"

"Stop being a little brat!" Katie shouted, dragging Thea up the flight of stairs, as Thea kicked and pulled to get away.

Beau shouted and pulled at her to let go of his sister, but Katie shoved him into the wall, oblivious as he fell to the ground.

"Stop it!" Katie screeched at Thea. "Stop it! We're almost there—"

"No!" The more Thea struggled against her, trying to pry her mother's fingers from her wrist, the more terrified and obstinate Thea became. The haziness began to vanish from her mind.

Thea's panic was like a shock wave coursing through me. It wasn't Mrs. Gunderson snarling at them. It wasn't even their mom. She was a woman so sick I prayed the inevitable end would come already.

They were in a room.

Thea stood shaking in a doorway as her mother demanded them to jump. "It's the only way," she said. "It will be like flying." She peered out the broken window.

"Come, Beau." Katie tried to grab him but he stepped away.

"No!" he shouted at her. No longer sobbing with fear, but determined to protect his sister. "Come on, Thea," he said, choking in a breath.

Thea shook with cold as he reached for her, the chill seeping through the floor and into her boots, chasing away the final remnants of the fever.

"Get back here!" Katie shouted, and she grabbed onto Beau's hood and tugged him so hard he fell back and hit his head.

"Stop it!" Thea shouted, eyes blurred with tears. The shock, the fever—all of it wearing off as she realized it wasn't her mother standing in front of her. Thea ran to Beau to help him up, but Katie reached for him first. Grabbing hold of Beau's jacket, she tugged him toward the window.

"If you won't jump—I'll push you out!" And as Beau's pleas and Thea's screams comingled, I could feel the shift in the room.

The air in Thea's lungs caught and her thoughts hardened with resolve. Desperate to make her mother listen and disappear, Thea began to scream. She screamed so loudly her mother's body lifted off the floor and was flying out the window before Thea even understood what was happening.

Eyes blurred with tears, I blinked myself back to the cabin. It was warm, Beau and Thea were safe, and Elle was still talking as if only seconds had passed. "Jackson said you moved a branch with your mind." Elle's voice was easy and open, even excited. "Is there anything else you can do?"

I wiped the moisture from my eyes and forced myself to breathe, rooting myself back to the moment. That I'd felt anything from Thea at all was new, but that she and Beau had been carrying their mother's final hours around like a buried secret was inde-scribable.

"Um, well—" Thea looked at Beau for approval. He shrugged, and Thea licked her lips, glancing furtively around the room. "I can do things like this," she said, making a piece of firewood tremble in the basket.

Elle and Alex's eyes widened.

"Sometimes I can move things, but only when I'm really

scared or thinking really, really hard." She fidgeted with her fingers in her lap, eyes darting around at everyone.

"You mean, you could've been doing my chores this whole time?" Alex teased.

Thea looked at Beau again, waiting for him to say something, but he just stared down at his hands, disappearing inside himself before my eyes.

"You don't have to be afraid," I told Thea, barely able to get the words out. "We all love you, both of you. And we know you're good. You'd never do anything bad you didn't have to do." A tear escaped my lashes and I wiped it hastily away.

Elle studied me, brow furrowed.

"You can tell them," I urged them both.

Beau looked at me, understanding widening his eyes.

I nodded for him to take the leap. "I'm right here." I forced a reassuring smile and rubbed his shoulder, pushing the flicker of emotion I felt away with all my might. I needed to be here with them in this moment.

Thea licked her lips and took a deep breath. "One time," Thea said with a ragged breath. "I saved Beau from the bad lady." Her eyes shimmered. "I thought it was a bad dream," she added. But as she sat there, really thinking about it, I saw the realization dawn in her brown eyes. Even though she understood the fever and had understood what happened to her mom, the weight of what she'd done finally began to settle over her. Then, her chin trembled and she began to cry.

Hating my power and every horrible thing that came with it, I wrapped my arms around Thea and pulled her closer, trying to ignore anything she'd unwittingly let me see. "It's okay," I whispered, squeezing my eyes shut. I wanted her to feel my love, so she could feel something good and true.

"It was an accident," Beau bleated, beside us. "She didn't mean to do it." When I opened my eyes, his face was red with tears and he balled the blanket up in his hand.

"Hey, kid," Jackson said, crossing the room. "Whatever it is, it's okay." He took Beau's hands in his, so tiny in comparison, and rubbed Beau's shoulder as he sniffled back tears. "We aren't mad at you or Thea."

As I wiped the tears from my eyes, Alex looked at me, his own eyes glistening in the firelight. The day he found Beau and Thea, Alex had told me about their mom's body, and about their strange silence and secrecy. I knew Katie had lost her mind, I just didn't realize . . . I hadn't thought . . .

Elle looked at me, distraught and lost, but I couldn't bring myself to say the words aloud. I was losing count of how many times it felt like my heart had broken, but it cracked and everything strong inside of me poured out.

Half sitting on the bed, Jackson wrapped his arms around Beau and let him cry into his chest.

"She was sick," Beau explained through choked sobs.

Understanding widened Elle's eyes and she covered her mouth with her hand. Everyone had thought she'd killed herself in front of her children, but the truth was far worse, and whatever was happening to us, this was only the beginning.

56

JACKSON

APRIL 16

It was past midnight when the kids finally zonked out. Elle and I sat on the floor against the wall in companionable silence. I leaned back, my arms draped over my knees, completely spent of every possible emotion as a result of the past few hours. Grief and exhaustion. Anger. Fear and uncertainty. Love and understanding. More than anything, I was broken hearted for Thea and Beau.

"I hadn't seen that coming," I whispered, my voice hoarse.

"Me either."

Snot and tears stained both of our shirts and I had to chuckle to myself. Four months ago, I hadn't expected to be taking care of kids, let alone to feel so endeared to them. Now, I wouldn't have it any other way.

I looked at Elle. Her cheeks were rosy from the heat of the room, and her hair was in a disheveled ponytail that hung messily around her ears. She crossed her legs out in front of her and sighed. She was barefoot and wearing a t-shirt and sweats. I could imagine her at home this way, hair mussed, eyes gleaming in the flickering light. She'd spent the past months working her fingers to the bone—chopping firewood, insulating bedrooms, and lugging around 30-liter jugs of drinking water. But like this, still and thoughtful beside me, there was a softness about her I'd rarely seen before. It made me want to touch her skin, but I looked away instead.

"They need to practice what they can do," I said. "All of them. They need to know how to use their capabilities and how to control them."

"We all do." She looked at me. "Even you. I mean, there has to be something, Jackson. You can't be the only one without a power."

"My power is that I worry," I told her. "I have the ulcer to prove it."

She nudged me and heaved out a breath.

For the first time in months, I felt like I could let my mind rest for a little while, like there wasn't something looming overhead, and I closed my eyes and let the feeling sink in.

"I worry too," Elle whispered. "Sophie told me something once, right before the accident. She said, there are good guys and bad guys."

"Always," I breathed, letting my eyes flutter closed. "We know some survivors are homicidal, out there sniffing the air for their next victim."

My eyes popped open, remembering what she'd told me about the man in Slana.

"But," she continued, "if we're the good guys, how are we going to protect each other from the bad ones?"

"Other than practicing what you all can do? The five of you would be a force to reckon with. Especially if Alex can draw powers from all of you—the bad guys wouldn't stand a chance—"

"Jackson, I'm serious."

"So am I."

Elle dropped her head in her hands and groaned. "Sometimes I'm so scared."

All of us were scared all the time, but it was the first time I'd heard Elle say it out loud.

She looked at me, lips pursed as she inhaled a deep breath. "What if there are bad guys in Hartley."

"You could decide not to go," I told her, tired of fighting every part of me that wanted to make all of this work. "We could come up with a different plan, together."

I half expected her to smile with relief, but instead, she frowned. "What about, you know . . ." She hesitated. "Your dad and—"

I leaned my head back against the wall. "You were right, this is bigger than us. I don't want to dwell in the past anymore. I want to do something that feels right for a change and whatever all of this is, it feels like this is it. Maybe this is the family I was meant to have." The words were toxic and I cleared my throat. I hadn't meant to say that, and it felt wrong. But even as my eyes blurred, it also felt true. "I think Hannah would want me to do this."

Elle's eyes lingered on me for a few seconds, then she looked at the kids, still sleeping in their beds. She remained quiet, which I appreciated. I was confused enough without her questions.

The kids' chests rose and fell slowly, sounds of their soft breaths filling the small room. "I wish I could sleep like that," Elle said, smiling contentedly at the kids. "They're down for the count."

"Are you still having trouble sleeping?" I asked. There had been so much moving and commotion since we arrived, I wasn't sure.

"Yes, a little. But it's not like it was before."

"What do you mean?"

She shrugged. "I used to see things and have lucid dreams where my stepfather stood at my bed—I hated thinking about him . . . remembering." She blinked and shook her head. "It's not like that anymore. My mind just won't shut off. Lack of sleep is definitely catching up with me though," she said with a yawn.

It was difficult to picture a frightened Elle, lying in her bed, and yet I wanted to comfort her all the same. I just wasn't sure how, or that she even needed me to.

"It's times like this I wish I still had a camera," she mused, staring at Alex. His face was smooshed against his pillow, his mouth agape. "Incriminating evidence is fun."

Climbing to my feet, I hauled myself over to my scavenging bag that hung on the wall of hooks and coats. In all the craziness, I'd forgotten about the camera. As quietly as I could, I pulled it out of my bag with one hand and grabbed the box of film, and then I shoved the dark chocolate Milky Way into my sweats pocket.

"I have no idea if this is any good," I said, turning around. I held out my hands as I took a few steps closer. "But, I thought you might be able to use it."

With another yawn, Elle looked at me. Her green eyes grew big and round. "What the hell . . ." A wide, toothy grin like I'd never seen consumed her face. "No way." She climbed to her feet, practically stumbling in excitement. "And it's analog?" She practically giggled as she took it greedily.

I grinned as she turned into a giddy school girl before my eyes. "I figured digital was pointless, but we'll have to figure out how to develop the film."

Elle turned the camera over in her hands, analyzing every number and every button. "This is a great camera."

"Yeah, ten years ago."

"No, still," she insisted. "And the film will be easy to figure out." She sighed, her smile still pinned from ear to ear. "I just—I can't believe you got me a camera, that you even thought of it."

"I might not've been sober all the time, but I was listening." I pulled the Milky Way from my pocket.

"No way," she chirped and covered her mouth immediately, glancing back at the kids. "It's been months since I've had one of these."

I'd never heard Elle laugh with pure joy—an excited-to-the-core laugh—and it made me happy.

She stepped closer, and leaned forward. My heartbeat skipped and my chest warmed as she pressed her lips to my cheek. Resting her warm palm on the side of my face, she whispered, "Thank you."

I closed my eyes, soaking her in.

57

JACKSON
APRIL 16

S itting in the chair beside the stove, I pulled my boots on by firelight. Like clockwork, I woke up with the sun. Spring made for longer days, which I was accustomed to when I was working. Spring also meant warmth and a break from the snow, so I welcomed it.

I peered down at Elle, curled up on the pallet, a canteen and her pistol beside her pillow as she slept. Unlike the rest of the clan wrapped in blankets, she wore a t-shirt and shorts, her blankets wrapped only around her feet.

As if she could feel my gaze on her, she stirred in her sleep, turning onto her back and folding her arms over her face. I smiled. Her gloves were still off. Maybe she finally trusted herself the way I trusted her, even if I knew what she could do was dangerous.

Schlepping into my jacket, I grabbed my rifle leaning against the doorframe. I reached for the door to head out for my predawn perimeter check when a groggy voice reached my ears. "Jackson?"

I turned around.

Beau sat up in bed, hair tousled as he rubbed his eyes. "Can I go with you?"

Relieved he wasn't shying away after all that had happened last night, I nodded and pressed my finger to my lips.

Quietly and carefully, Beau climbed out of bed, glancing at his sister and at Sophie wrapped up in blankets beside him. Neither of the girls stirred.

Content to spend the morning with Beau after such a tumultuous twenty-four hours, I stepped outside to wait for him. The morning air was perfect. A refreshing jolt after a night of gut-wrenching revelations.

I knew Beau and Thea weren't going to be okay, not deep down, after something like that. But at the same time, I didn't know how to help them.

The door cracked open behind me, and Beau stepped outside, the floorboards creaking on the porch as he zipped up his jacket, his beanie in hand.

"You couldn't sleep?" I whispered as I closed the door quietly behind him.

"Not really," he said, but it wasn't with sadness. Scanning the gray morning, he stepped off the porch into the snow, and tugged his beanie over his head.

"Ah, I see." I lifted an eyebrow, staring down at him. "Too excited about your new friends?"

Beau shrugged, like he didn't care, but I knew better than that. "You can be happy about your power, Beau." I realized that it might feel wrong to find joy in one's own ability if everyone else was scared of what they could do. "You just have to be smart—and careful," I added.

He blinked up at me, eyes cloudy with sleep, then he nodded.

I glanced at the main cabin. A small swirl of smoke was coming from the chimney, but no lights flickered inside. Like the rest of the Ranskins, Koda was still sleeping in his doghouse. "It looks like it's just you and me out here this morning."

Beau grabbed hold of my arm and shook his head. "Wait." He pointed to the north end of the property. At first I saw nothing but morning shadows, then a gray wolf stepped out, stretching with a yip, like it had just woken up. Next, a white and tan wolf came into view.

I had to fight back the urge to be afraid, instinctually at least. They were large and powerful, with jaws of steel and a ferocity to match when it suited them, especially when they were together. But they were awesome too, majestic and otherworldly in so many ways.

I swallowed thickly. "Do they sleep out here every night?"

"They hunt at night," he said matter-of-factly.

I knew wolves were nocturnal, but that wasn't exactly what I'd meant. "Where is their home?"

Shrugging, he started walking toward them. "They live here."

I didn't know if they were the same wolves from Slana, but I had a sneaking suspicion they were. "Have they *always* been here?"

The gray one, whose tail wagged more vigorously the closer we drew, darted into the trees. "No," Beau said over his shoulder as he started walking faster. I could barely hear him through the sound of my boots crunching in the snow.

The white and tan wolf darted in to the trees next, and Beau ran in after them.

"Beau," I said carefully. "I think you should come back toward the house." I was all for him practicing his communication with the wolves, but I wasn't sure about disappearing into the woods with them. I gripped my gun tighter. "Beau—"

"Come on!" he called. "You can say hi to all of them."

The ever-present disquiet I had that always kept me on edge, dimmed a little, and I knew Beau was right. I *could* say hi to a wild wolf because he said I could, and they were his friends. Instinctively, I knew it was safe, even if I questioned my sanity deciding to do so.

Beau's white jacket flashed against the trees as the sunlight filtered through their leafless boughs.

My stride quickened, my heart racing as my body warmed. "Where the hell are you taking me?" I muttered, but Beau was too far ahead to answer.

There were so many questions, like why wolves, and why had his power taken so long to fully manifest? How the hell did the virus make any of this possible?

Wings fluttered in the trees above, and my heartbeat raced until finally, Beau slowed.

"How do you communicate with them?" I asked, inhaling the dark woods around us.

"I know what they're thinking," Beau explained, staring down at the wolf tracks. "I see it in pictures, and I can feel if they are scared or happy."

The gray and tan wolves trotted further ahead.

I stepped over a log, waiting for the hair on the back of my neck to rise. I couldn't believe the words on the tip of my tongue, but I said them all the same. "So, what *are* the wolves thinking? Feel free to leave out the gruesome details." It was only a joke, but part of me wondered what exactly Beau saw when he talked to them.

I heard a few yips in the distance, and my gaze flicked forward.

"They just want to play," he explained. "They think I'm one of them."

"And you know they don't want to hurt you. You can sense that?" I wanted him to be absolutely certain.

Beau laughed at me. "Yeah. I'm certain. I mean, they get scared sometimes, but then they don't come around. I told them you wouldn't hurt them though."

"Well that's good," I mumbled.

"There are eight. Taiga and Luna and their six kids."

"Eight," I breathed. "That's a big number." Under different circumstances, we could've been marching to a feeding frenzy for all I knew.

"Taiga—like the snow forest, where they live—is the dad.

Luna is the mom. Her favorite part of the night is when there's a full moon."

They already had names, of course they did. "Have you been sneaking out to play with them since Slana, Beau?"

He stopped ahead of me, clearly guilty, as he hesitated to answer. "Only a couple times. I didn't want to get in trouble and they were still scared of me a little, I think."

"I see," I said with a huff. My nose was cold from the brisk morning and my skin was dampening with sweat. Beau, on the other hand, seemed completely unfazed by our morning excursion.

Beau bit the side of his mouth, waiting for me to say something, but I nodded him forward. "Lead the way," I told him. There was no undoing the past.

A small smile grew in place of his uncertainty. "We're already here." He led me to a cluster of boulders on the side of the mountain, covered with snow. Four wolves lounged together on the rocks. Two others ran up to Beau.

I stopped where I stood a few yards away, watching Beau interact with a pack of wolves with bated breath. All of them came out to greet him. Tails wagged. They sniffed and nuzzled him. They yipped happily as he ruffled their fur and patted their heads. The biggest smile I'd ever seen engulfed Beau's face.

"This is Rocky," he said, glancing over at me. He petted the chocolate-colored wolf's head, and it licked his glove in return. "He likes to lie on the rocks in the sun. He's the youngest."

"Rocky, huh?" I crouched down, watching from the sidelines as he laughed with true happiness I'd never heard in him before.

"Come on. You can pet him," Beau said, leading Rocky over. Beau grabbed my hand for Rocky to sniff it. "He likes attention the most."

I waited for the ominous warning inside me to blare back to life like it did so frequently, but still nothing came. I had no apprehension whatsoever, just like when I was around Elle, knowing what a simple touch from her could do.

Unable to resist, I pulled off my glove and reached out to the wolf. His mane was soft but thick, and Rocky's eyes met mine, softly blinking as he succumbed to all the attention.

"He likes your beard," Beau said. "It makes you less strange than the others."

I chuckled, uncertain how to take that other than hairy beasts liked hairy beasts, I supposed.

The other wolves sauntered over, less quick to welcome me than Rocky but equally curious. The knot in my stomach never returned as eight wild wolves sniffed me and licked my clothes like I was nothing more than another friend.

As Beau and I played with them, I realized maybe there was something different about me, and there had been all along.

58

ELLE

APRIL 16

Aurora borealis broke through the clouds as I made my way to the firepit. The others were still getting dressed for a night under the stars, but I was content in my jeans and long sleeves. Fleetingly, I wondered if that's how it would be for the rest of my life, always warm or overheating, and what summers would be like. Miserable? Either way, Jackson was right. The more we practiced, the more control we would have and the more we'd know. Even if I feared I'd hurt someone, it didn't mean I couldn't practice on my own.

Instead of trying to deny my ability, like I had for nearly five months, I was sort of excited to embrace it. Knowing I wasn't the only one now made it less intimidating somehow.

When I came to the firepit, I glanced around to see if anyone else was headed over yet. The Ranskins didn't know openly that we were different, but between my argument with Jackson for all to hear, and what had happened with Beau, they had to have some inkling that we weren't a typical family.

Satisfied that only Koda rustled over by the main house, I knelt down by the logs of the unlit fire. My rib was on the mend, but it still hurt like a bitch. Part of me wondered if it would hurt even more if I didn't have the insane amount of energy I had coursing through me all the time.

Since Slana, the burn had been slowly building up again, and it was time to see if I couldn't let some of that pent up energy out in a new way. With another quick glance around the property, I reached out to touch one of the logs, disappointed when nothing happened. I wasn't entirely surprised though. Jackson had let me touch him with my bare hands and nothing had happened. While I now understood his keen sense of impending danger, I'd thought he was a real daredevil before. Why would an inanimate log provoke anything different?

Feeling even sillier, I leaned closer and tried to blow the fire to a start. Nothing happened.

Shutting my eyes, I reluctantly thought about what had happened in Slana. I remembered the fear that had me running up the stairs toward the sound of the kids screaming. I felt the clawing desire to kill and protect, and imagining the intruder looming over them with menace in his eyes had my blood burning hotter.

Fear, I realized. It was the rising fear and desperation that stoked the fire inside. I just had to harness it.

I tried to light the fire again, latching onto the fear and the dread that resurfaced, and the burn shifted inside of me, blooming in my chest and heating the tips of my fingers. The fire still didn't start, however, something *was* happening in the blood that ran through my muscles and limbs.

"Do you need a fire starter?"

I jumped and turned around at the sound of Jade's voice coming up behind me. She was wrapped in a wool shawl, her eyes sparkling from the dancing lights above.

"Oh, uh, yeah," I said dumbly, and I sat back into an empty chair.

"Trying to start it yourself?" She lifted an amused brow and settled into the seat a couple of chairs down. She blew on her hot mug and glanced at me over the brim.

"I—I," I stammered. "Yes, actually." It was a relief to say. I took a deep breath and held up my palms. "I know that sounds crazy, and I'm sure—"

"Crazier than a wild wolf crawling into a little boy's lap to keep him warm? Crazier than Sophie telling me she loved the Moon drawing I gave my son three years ago because she forgot she'd only seen it in a memory?"

I swallowed thickly.

"I thought *I* was crazy when that bag of oats fell over while Thea and I were on the other side of the room. Her proud smile was impossible to ignore," Jade explained.

My cheeks burned red, and it wasn't from my unnatural kind of heat.

Jade looked at my hands. "And, you aren't wearing your gloves," she pointed out with a smile.

I tilted my head, uncertain I could believe she was so content with it all. "All of these unfathomable things are happening and you aren't freaking out, even in the slightest?"

"It's unexpected; it's not every day a little girl can stir your gravy for you from the other side of the room while you finish folding the laundry." She winked. "It started a bit messy, but we were practicing this afternoon."

"We weren't sure how you would take it," I admitted. "I wanted to tell you sooner, I think we all did, but . . ."

"When I was eleven," Jade started. "I woke with a horrible premonition that my mother would die. I remember having tears in my eyes the instant I opened them; it felt so real. I ran from my room and told my father I saw her drowning in the river—that she would fall through the ice and be swept away by the current, but he didn't believe me. I was a child who woke up from a nightmare in his eyes, no matter how desperate I was to stop her from leaving. But it wouldn't have made a difference anyway because she'd already left with my uncle and grandfather. It was their annual fishing trip northwest, at a river that has claimed many lives."

Jade's eyes were soft and somewhere far away. "She never came back from the trip."

My lips parted, caught somewhere between surprise and sadness. "She drowned?"

Jade dipped her chin slowly and took another sip of her tea. "I believe in things unseen," she said. "And there are many things still unknown about our spirit and purpose in this life." She paused, a thought lifting the corner of her mouth before she continued. "I think we all have something inside of us we don't fully understand. It's always there, and sometimes it remains undiscovered. I don't know if it's the sickness you've all been through or something more infinite than that, but perhaps with everything you've been through, you've found yours—all of you have—and that's something I think should be celebrated. Your purpose has always been there, only now, it's known."

I'd never considered there was an innate part of me that had been dormant and would still be that way if I hadn't visited the fiery depths of the sickness before I came out the other side.

"The human mind is so complex and still so unknown." I repeated the words Dr. Rothman had told me many times.

"So is the intricacy of all life in this place, no matter what you believe. I'm certain most would agree we know little in the great scheme of things." Jade peered up at the lights in the sky. "Sometimes a little something incredible is all we need to give us the boost we need to figure things out."

Jet was up there in the rainbow of lights, so was Jade's mom. "I'm sorry about what happened to her," I said. "Your mother, I mean." I couldn't imagine losing my mother because she never a part of my life. But I could imagine losing one of the kids, and how devastated I would be. I figured multiplying that by a hundred wouldn't come close to the love between a mother and daughter.

"Thank you, but it was many years ago. I went to live with my grandmother who was very old fashioned," she said, pointing to the lined tattoos on her chin. "As you can tell." I barely noticed them anymore; they were just a part of who she was.

"What do they mean, exactly?"

"Maturity," she said. "Womanhood—achievements in my life, this one is Jet." She pointed to the middle line. "This last one is Del."

"How fascinating," I thought aloud. Jade was such an interesting human, I wanted to cling to her like lichen on a rock and absorb all her knowledge and insights about life and people.

Smiling, she nodded to the abandoned fire. "Perhaps you need something to give you a little spark."

"Oh, right." I stared at the logs, untouched and lonely. "Maybe . . . But I haven't needed one before." I took a match out of the camping box beside the fire and stared at the striking tip. I wasn't sure I wanted to attempt this with her sitting there, but I had little choice.

Closing my eyes, I thought about the intruder's face again, saw the gauntness of it, and the fever in his yellow-tinted eyes. I touched the tip of the match, barely pressing my fingertips against it, but intent on burning the image of his face away.

At first, it felt like the typical tip of a match, until my fingers warmed and I felt heat against my face. I opened my eyes, watching the flame flicker on the end, burning slowly down the stick. I grinned, brimming with a sense of accomplishment, even if it was only just the start.

The closer the flame moved toward my fingers, the more curious I became.

The door to the small cabin opened across the yard and I heard Beau and Thea bickering before they stepped outside.

I tossed the match into the fire, and quickly lit another one with a single touch. With a victorious smile, I reached out and watched the tinder catch flame.

"Thank you," I whispered, gaze flicking to Jade, like we had a secret.

She smiled back and brought her mug to her lips.

I held my bare hands to the fire, enjoying the growing warmth without my gloves to hinder the sensation. "I thought using my fear and anger would make it work like before," I mused. "I guess I was wrong."

"Memories of fear and anger aren't the same as the heat of the moment," she said, and I restrained from laughing at her choice of words.

"I guess that makes sense." At least for everyone but Sophie. Unfortunately she couldn't escape it.

"Yeah-huh," Beau said, trudging over from the cabin.

"Nuh-uh," Thea retorted, hustling to catch up. Her puffy jacket made her little arms bounce as she ran.

"Whatever. They already have names. You can't change them, Thea. And you can't name a boy Flower if he doesn't want that to be his name." A white and gray wolf with a black spot on the top of his head trotted over behind them.

Thea took an empty seat by the fire and scratched the wolf's neck as he plopped down between her and Beau. "Pretty Flower," she cooed.

"You're so annoying," Beau grumbled.

"What is this one's name, Beau?" I asked. I had already met Luna, the one who had kept him warm, but the rest were still new to me.

"Little Foot," Beau said, pointing to his back leg. "He was born with a smaller foot in the back. But he still runs faster than the rest."

I reached beside Beau to Little Foot at his side and offered him my hand. "I probably smell like smoke," I realized. The wolf sniffed me, his cold nose brushing against my skin, and he lowered his head for me to pet him.

Took and Del came out of the main cabin next, thermoses in their hands. "Did everyone bring their cups?" Took asked and unscrewed the lid of his.

"Yes," Beau said, and Sophie straggled over behind them. I was glad to see she seemed to be doing better after last night. She'd been distraught for Beau and Thea, and rightly so, but she smiled now, even if it seemed faint with exhaustion.

Took walked the circle of chairs, pouring each of us a full mug of hot cocoa. He was a man of tradition, like Jade, but he'd taken to nightly hot chocolate with the kids, nature walks with Thea, and carving with Beau.

"He'll be sad to see them go," Sophie muttered, like she could read my thoughts. Her eyes met mine as she sat down beside me, then shifted to Alex. Her expression was less easy with him again. I knew he was pulling away from her a bit since he'd learned about her power, I just hoped time was all he needed to accept it, for both of their sakes.

Alex flashed everyone a smile as he sat down on the other side of me, between me and Jade. He snuggled down into his jacket and stared into the fire.

"Penny for your thoughts," I said.

Alex's mouth lifted in the corner and he yawned. "I'm tired. Jackson and I were working on the trailer all afternoon. I think the axle's finally fixed, but my shoulder is shot."

The wolf whined and his ears tilted back as Jackson strode up behind us. Hands in his pockets, he glanced around at all of us and took a seat in the empty chair across the fire.

"Where did you disappear to after dinner?" Jade asked. "Making the rounds?"

Jackson chuckled. "Out of habit, yes, but I guess I don't need to anymore with these guys hanging around." Little Foot trotted over as if he and Jackson were old friends, and Jackson patted him on the neck. "And," he said. "I've been thinking."

"Oh boy," Alex said playfully. "Here we go." He leaned forward to warm his hands against the flames.

"Is it about you leaving?" Sophie asked, I could hear the reluctance in her voice and it made the anticipation all the greater.

"About all of us leaving, together, actually. If you want."

"You're coming to Hartley?" Alex straightened. "I mean, that's awesome, but I thought you weren't feeling the whole community vibe."

"That depends," he said. "What do you all want to do?"

"I don't want to go to Hartley anymore," Beau said.

"You don't?" I shot a look to Jackson. "Why not, Beau?"

"What about the wolves?" he said. "I can't leave them, and they can't live there."

I hadn't considered the wolves in any of our plans. "Are you sure they'll want to come with you?"

"Yes, they do, and Hartley won't let me keep them, and they might try to hurt them—"

"It's okay, kid, we'll figure it out," Jackson said. "It's up to everyone else, too." He peered around at the others. "What about the rest of you?" His eyes landed on Sophie.

"What do you and Elle want?" she asked, flicking her gaze at me. If I knew Sophie, she knew the answer before we did.

"I want to do what makes the most sense," I told her. "I want us to be safe, and I want us all to agree if we can. We can't stay here forever. We need to find someplace to call home."

"Not to speak out of turn," Took said, and we all looked at him. "But you can stay here. We have land. We can build on it."

"Took—" Del chided.

"What? It's true. We have the space."

"Of course you're welcome to stay," Jade said, gesturing to all of us. "We would love to have you. But there is no obligation, I know you want to start new lives and there's still a lot you don't understand. Maybe you can find answers out there, somewhere."

It was a beautiful thought, staying with them and continuing to learn what they knew about the land. It would be much simpler than starting over and risking new places and people.

"What about your lodge, Jackson?" Alex looked at him. "What about Whitehorse?"

I half-expected Jackson to shy away from the idea given it meant so much to him and his wife, but he lifted his shoulder, as if it was a possibility. "We could do that," he said. "Or at least check it out. I'll be meeting up with Ross there, regardless," he said. "I have to see him."

"I think," Sophie began, holding her mug tightly in her hand. "I think we should at least visit Whitehorse, even if it's just a short trip to see what it's like. If we don't," she looked more pointedly at Jackson, "we'll always wonder about it. And you have Ross to think about now, too."

I thought of Jackson changing his plans for us, on top of foregoing Whitehorse, and having to worry about choosing between us and Ross, now that we knew he was alive.

"If you're already going to see Ross," Alex said. "We can go with you and figure it out then."

Jackson nodded, thoughtful as he picked at a loose string in his folding chair. "We can always come back."

"And, if we stay in Whitehorse," Sophie added, looking at Jade. "We won't be as far from you as we would be in Hartley. So we can still visit."

Jade's lips parted in a relieved smile. "That would be wonderful."

"We could still go hunting with you guys each spring," Alex added. "It could be like an annual thing."

"And either way," I said, winking at Beau. "You can keep your wolves."

Jackson glanced around the circle, meeting each pair of waiting eyes that blinked back at him. "It's decided then. We plan for a trip to Whitehorse to check things out." He looked at me with a nod. "I'll call Ross."

59

ELLE
APRIL 18

I t was twilight by the time we reached the Yukon. In the middle of nowhere, we didn't have to worry about cars abandoned on the highway or roadblocks to get around. All we had to worry about was snow and fuel, and we'd been lucky with both.

We'd been on the road for nearly ten hours and had stopped only three times between fuel refills and bathroom breaks. With six people in two vehicles, the Pathfinder Jackson found yesterday, following behind the Tacoma as it plowed the harrier roads, we'd taken every safety precaution, from tow straps to toilet paper to extra snacks for the kids, just in case. We were cramped but it was worth it.

Whitehorse was a sprawling city but it was the surrounding mountains we were heading toward. I was content leaving the city and the horrors that likely came with it behind and eagerly continued south. I knew Whitehorse was a place of deep-rooted, native culture, and I wondered how many other remote villages and homesteads in the area had missed the outbreak, or even knew about it.

"Elle?" Alex's voice came through the CB radio.

Sophie clicked it on. "This is Sophie."

"We're going to follow the Yukon River through the city," Jackson said on the other end. "Keep to the highway. The fewer people that hear or see us coming, the better."

"Got it."

"We're looking for signs for Midnight Sun Lodge, it should be about ten or fifteen minutes down the highway."

"Okay, we'll keep our eyes out."

"And Elle," Jackson hedged, his voice grave. "Don't stop for anyone, okay?"

I glanced at Sophie, hating this part of traveling near cities. "I won't."

The radio went silent, and I glanced in the rearview mirror, glad to see the kids were asleep. I didn't want to have to worry about what might happen or what they might see along the way.

"At least we're almost there," Sophie said encouragingly. "I could use a nice leg stretch."

"Tell me about it. My fingers are stuck like this." I smiled and held up my hands, fingers bent like claws.

Sophie sighed and stared at the passing mountains beyond the window. "What do you know about Jackson's friend?" she asked, lifting her foot up onto the dash. "I mean, other than they worked together?"

"I know nothing about Ross," I admitted. "Other than he's all Jackson has left from his life before, and he's important to him."

"Do you think we can trust him? I mean, he was gone all those months. He's got to have a power too, right? How do you even broach the topic to begin with?" She muttered the last part.

"I don't know, but I trust Jackson," I told her. "And his ability to sense things." Jackson had a natural gut instinct about things, it was something I could always rely on.

Sophie looked at me. "That doesn't mean we have to go in blind," she said. Although she was genuinely offering to use her power to learn his intentions, it would come at a cost. It always did.

"You don't have to do that every time, Sophie."

She shrugged. "I think I do now, Elle." It was a sad realization and I hated that it fell on her shoulders. "There has to be a way to control it better."

"In time." Now Sophie was the one reassuring me.

I smiled, grateful to have her with me in all of this. "Team Good Guys, right?"

"For sure," she said with a grin. "We need to come up with a name though. Something epic."

We sat in silence for the rest of the drive, taking in the dark roads that were lit only by our headlights. The sky was clear, and the world had a moonglow about it, even if we couldn't stop to appreciate the stars.

When the sign for Midnight Sun came into view I glanced at Sophie. "Wake the kids up, would you?" I scanned the signs ahead.

Sophie twisted in her seat, half leaning in the back as she shook Beau awake. "We're almost there."

I glanced in the rearview mirror, just as Thea stirred. "We're here," Beau told her, and she gripped her stuffed duck closer and threatened to fall back to sleep.

"Wake up," Beau groused again, and her eyes blinked open languidly.

"I'm tired," she whined.

"You guys remember what we talked about, right?" Beau met my gaze in the mirror. It was imperative they remembered.

"No talking about powers," he said.

"Or the wolves," Thea added sleepily.

"And," Sophie prompted, "we stick together until we're comfortable around our new friends, right?"

"Yes," they agreed in unison.

"If you see anything strange," I warned. "Tell one of us, okay?"

I followed Jackson down a muddy road and saw the lights on in the lodge before I could make out the building.

"They have power?" Sophie asked.

"Or generators, maybe."

"That's . . . awesome." She could barely contain her surprise.

Or wasteful, but I kept that thought to myself. I didn't want to give the kids a bad taste in their mouths before we met up with everyone. I was just scared, and I needed to remind myself that not everyone was evil outside the six of us. Jade, Took, and Del had proven that.

When we got further down the drive, a Chevrolet truck with a plow on the front was parked behind the building.

Jackson pulled off to the side, and I followed next to him. Though I was excited for Jackson, I was nervous about what the next twenty-four hours might bring.

You are formidable. It was a necessary reminder. I wasn't helpless; I hadn't been for a long time, even if I was still getting used to the idea.

I waited for the cue from Jackson, and when I got a thumbs up, I shut off the engine. "All right." I pushed the driver side door open. "We're here, but remember the rules."

The kids climbed out of the back seat.

"Put your jackets on," Sophie told them, stretching her legs. With the sun long set and the heat of the car escaping, it felt like the arctic again.

Carefully, I stretched out my neck, stiff from gripping both hands onto the steering wheel.

I peered up at the lodge. It was huge compared to anywhere we'd stayed during the past five months, a log chalet with a wrap-around porch surrounding it. Three chic cabins with angled roofs were snuggly situated a few yards behind it. Land surrounded us; mountains and forests spreading as far as the eye could see; all of it glowing in the moonlight.

Jackson and Alex stretched and groaned as they met us in the center of the driveway.

"It doesn't feel wrong, but it doesn't feel right either," Jackson said without ceremony. His gaze shifted between the lodge and us.

I wondered how much of his reluctance had to do with his wife verses the people that waited inside.

"I guess we'll see," Sophie told him.

"That was the *longest* car ride ever," Thea groaned. "Huh, Beau?"

But Beau was too busy peering around the property to answer. We were nestled in the forest; the wolves would have plenty of areas to hide.

I leaned down and whispered in his ear. "Are they here?"

He shook his head. "Not yet, but soon . . . I think."

"Good." His connection to them increased daily, and I knew he wouldn't settle in until they were. *I'd* feel better once they arrived, too.

"Well, should we go look inside the house?" Alex asked. The front door flung open as he took Thea's hand.

"Hot damn!" A man's voice boomed in the crisp night air, and he stepped off the porch with his arms wide and welcoming. "It's been too long."

"Brother," Jackson breathed, relief easing his shoulders a little. The two men embraced, and I took the infamous Ross in as they patted each other on the back. Ross wasn't as tall as Jackson, but he had broad shoulders and filled out his clothes just as well. He had shorter hair and a bit of scruff on his face, but more than anything he was open and animated where Jackson was reserved.

"I thought your ass would never get here," Ross said with a final squeeze.

"You and me both." Jackson gestured to the five of us. "Meet the gang. Gang, this is my best friend, Ross."

Ross's smile widened, and he leaned forward, offering his hand to Thea first. "Well, little lady, my name's Kyle Ross, you can call me, well, Kyle or Ross, I guess."

"I'm Thea," she said shyly. "And this is my brother, Beau." She pointed to Beau who eyed him carefully.

"Hey little dude. Nice to meet you."

"I'm not that little," Beau replied curtly, and Ross chuckled.

"No, I guess you're not are you." He straightened and looked at Alex, offering him his hand.

"I'm Alex," he said with a quick shake.

"Nice grip," Ross said, peering down at their clasped hands. "Young *and* strong. I like it." He clapped Alex on the shoulder and looked at Sophie, next in line.

"Sophie," she said reaching out her hand. Her lips were pursed and her expression pensive though she forced a smile as he took her hand. "Nice to meet you."

"It's good to see another ginger in the group," he said, jokingly. "And one even better lookin' than me." He winked at her with a chuckle. "And you've got a firm grip, don't you?"

Jackson and I watched Sophie closely, the strain in the corner of her eyes giving her turmoil away. Her smile tightened and she dropped his hand and took a step back.

Sophie nodded reassuringly, and wiped the moisture from her eyes.

"And you must be Elle." Ross stood in front of me. His eyes widened ever so slightly, but I wasn't sure if it was out of surprise, or if his ability allowed him to know what I could do.

"Yes. Nice to meet you." I offered him my good hand, and his grip was soft but strong. I could smell alcohol on him, and I wondered if his smiles were covering what the alcohol couldn't.

"Jackson made it sound like he was palling around with a bunch of kids," he added, in awe. "You guys look like warriors."

"Sometimes," I joked, glancing at Jackson. He eyed his friend with a waning smile.

"Well . . ." Ross put his hands on his hips and scanned all six of us. "Aren't you a big happy family. You always wanted one of those, aye, Jackson?" He patted him on the back, and Jackson's easiness faltered.

"You have travel companions as well?" I prompted, eager to

change the subject. It was apparent Ross didn't realize how hard the past months had been for Jackson.

"Yep, that would be old Bert, he's passed out on the couch. He's a lush, just to forewarn you."

"Can you show us around the place?" I asked, trying to move the conversation along. It was clear Jackson and Ross, no matter how close they had been were uneasy in each other's company now, and the awkwardness made me restless. "That way we can figure out sleeping arrangements and where to put our things."

"You bet." Ross turned toward the place. "Jackson, you probably know this place better than I do, but I'll show you around."

"So," I said as we all trailed after him and Jackson into the lodge. "What *is* the situation here? You have electricity?" All the lights were on, though I didn't hear a generator anywhere inside.

"Yeah, for now. Isn't that great? You picked a primo spot, Jackson." Ross gestured to the large industrial kitchen as we stepped inside. It was updated and modern with rustic-chic everything; exactly what I would expect to see in an upscale lodge for tourists.

"Don't mind the mess," he said, bypassing the dirtied kitchen. "Some of us are still celebrating the fact we finally got here." He walked further into the house. Everything had clean lines and welcoming, warm tones with light wood and landscape photography lining the walls. It made me long to watch the sunset once the winter clouds were gone for good.

"We got a community space here," Ross said, waving away the drunk old man. All I could see was gray hair and maybe a mustache. "Anyway," Ross continued, "In there is another space." He pointed to a formal living room and a game room or den. There were large vertical windows everywhere draped with moss-colored linen.

The air was cool but not freezing, which might've been my body temperature.

"There are three bathrooms and five bedrooms upstairs, and then there are a few cabins adjacent to this one."

We made our way up the stairs. The loft area was an office, with a large shaggy rug to cover the cold hardwood, and a minimally decorated but wide hallway shot off either end, one toward the master bedroom with two other rooms and a bath, and the other hall led to a final two, narrow rooms and the last bath.

There were bathrooms everywhere and I longed for a steaming hot shower, despite my internal temperature.

"Do the bathrooms work?" Sophie asked.

"They sure do. This place has all the fancy bells and whistles to protect the pipes and the well, at least for now." He shrugged. "I haven't showered yet but I used the hot water in the kitchen." Ross pointed to a closed bedroom door. "I'm in one room down here, but the rest are open."

"It's bigger than I expected," I mused, staring up at the vaulted ceilings and down over the landing, into the living room. "Plus the detached buildings."

"Yep, it was a good call meeting here, Jackson," Ross said, but Jackson lingered in the doorway behind us, staring into a darkened room.

Ross made his way downstairs again, but I exchanged a look with Sophie.

It was their room, I assumed. The one he'd shared with his wife. I'd forgotten how difficult it must be for him to be there without her, and yet, I imagined it might give him a sense of closure, too.

Leaving Jackson to his thoughts, Sophie and I followed the kids back downstairs. Jackson had been doing so well, I selfishly hoped being here and seeing Ross wouldn't change the way things had been among all of us.

"Where's all of your luggage?" Alex asked, poking his head back into the kitchen. "Supplies and clothes and stuff?"

"Ah, we've only unpacked what we've needed." Ross grabbed a beer bottle from the twelve pack on the counter. A tequila bottle sat beside it. He popped the cap off the bottle, and slurped down a few glugs before he came up for breath, smiling. "Can I get you all anything? We have beer and there's canned food in the pantry if you're hungry."

"Why don't we check out the other cabins so we can get settled," Jackson said, coming back down the stairs. He nodded to the back door. "The kids are exhausted."

Ross's easiness wilted briefly—looked almost sad—but he nodded and held up his beer. "Sounds good."

Alex led the way, Beau at his side. Sophie and Thea followed behind him.

"There weren't any bodies when you got here?" I asked him, suddenly worried what we might stumble upon. "Nothing weird we should know about?"

"Nothing weird." Ross shook his head. "There were two women, they're in the garage. I figured we could deal with that tomorrow." He tossed Jackson a ring of keys hanging from a long line of hooks. "You'll need these. The cabins are locked."

Jackson nodded in thanks and followed me out the door, pulling it shut behind us. "I want us all in the same room tonight," Jackson said.

I eyed him, willing him to tell me what was going on in his head. "Should I be worried?"

He hesitated to answer. "I don't know," he said. "It's a weird vibe but nothing hair-raising. Ask Sophie. I know Ross is in bad shape, drunk, which isn't like him." I could hear the concern in Jackson's voice. "Four months ago he would've been pulling the bottle out of my hand and telling me to keep my shit together."

"We've all changed since December," I reminded him. "We don't know what happened to him in Fairbanks or anywhere else he's been."

Both of us glanced at Sophie grabbing her bags out of the car. She was the only one who did.

I peered at Ross sitting inside at the table, hand on head as he rubbed it methodically and stared at his beer. "He's right there," I whispered. "Why don't you go ask him?"

Running his hand over his face, Jackson sighed. "I just imagined this feeling different," he admitted. "Seeing him again."

"Maybe things will feel better in the morning, after you've both had a decent night's sleep." For Jackson's sake, I hoped I was right.

60

JACKSON
APRIL 18

W hile Elle and the kids unpacked their things, Ross and I sat at the counter in a strangely awkward silence as the past and present settled between us. Or, maybe it was a mixture of relief and fatigue. He took a swig of his beer, and I eyed the large, half-folded map with starred locations of northern Alaska next to him. None of the areas were part of his original plan, so I was curi- ous. But then, my plans had skewed off course too.

"What were you looking for?" I asked, glancing at the map.

Ross cleared his throat. "Answers," he said and took another swig.

He offered me one, but I held up my hand. "I'm good."

At first, Ross shrugged like it was my loss, then his eyes flashed with comprehension. "You stayed dry." I wasn't sure if it was awe or surprise in his voice, but there was a difference between the two—awe meant he commended me, surprise meant he didn't think I was capable. He would've been right.

"No," I said. "I didn't. But I need to be now. It's been a really long winter." I stared at a piece of scratch paper sitting on the countertop. The King Corporation. It sounded familiar, but I brushed it aside, more curious about the note written on it. Addresses throughout Fairbanks and the Tanana River.

"What are those places?" Each of them but the last were hastily scribbled out.

Ross's gray-blue eyes glazed over as he stared at it. "All the places I went to check to find her."

"Did you?"

He nodded. "I found her, it just took a while. Her mom was dead but she wasn't there."

"Where the hell was she?"

"She was parked at a bus station. It took me a few weeks to figure that out." He took a swig of his beer. "I don't want to talk about depressing shit tonight, Jackson." He waved toward the cabins outside. "Where'd you get all those kids, anyway? You and Elle . . ."

I waited for him to finish his sentence, but he looked at me, expectant. "Me and Elle what, popped out four kids in the past four months?" I chuckled. "No."

He punched me in the shoulder and took another drink. "Smart ass."

"I met them in Anchorage the day after you left. We were heading in the same direction and—"

"And now it's more than that," he finished for me.

I shook my head and rubbed my eyes. Yes, it was more than that, and as simple as that too.

"Are you sure you and your lady don't want to shack up in the house?"

"Don't say it like that," I told him.

"Okay, fine. Would you and Elle like to have a room in the house?" he said like a robot. "The kids will be fine out there, if that's what you're worried about."

"It's not like that with her," I told him, and it was true. Whatever Elle and I were it wasn't what he imagined.

"No shit?" he asked, eyes like frisbees. "What's wrong with you, are you broken or something?"

"No," I said, trying not to laugh. "Don't be an asshole."

"Jackson, it's okay. My sister is dead. You're alive and—"

I shot to my feet, infuriated even if his words were true. "Don't say it like that," I warned him.

Ross rose to his feet just as quickly. "Why, because it hurts? Fuck yeah, man. All of this fucking sucks, but it is what it is. Hannah ain't coming back—*Kelsey* is not coming back." He heaved out a breath. "The sooner you come to terms with that the better."

"Oh, like you have?" I bit out, glaring at the bottle in his shaking hand. "When was the last time you were sober because you look like shit, brother. I've tried coping that way, and it doesn't work, trust me." I shook my head. "Don't be a dick."

Every hard line on Ross's face softened, and he sat back down, glugging what was left in his bottle. Ross wasn't ever much of a drinker. A few beers at a BBQ maybe, but he never went for the hard stuff. He was also a compulsive neat freak, a soldier through and through, though by the looks of him you'd never know it.

"I thought you said there are showers here?" I leveled my eyes on him. "Take one. As your friend and housemate, it's not a request." We weren't getting anywhere tonight, not like this. I slid the stool in with my boot. "I'm going to bed." I stared at the old guy passed out on the couch in the game room. "He good for anything or did you bring dead weight?"

Ross glowered. "He's not dead weight. Despite what he looks like, he's a brilliant old fart; he was an engineer in another life."

"Good. Now, go to bed, would you? We have a lot to talk about tomorrow." I turned for the door.

"Sweet dreams, princess," he grumbled.

"You too, buttercup." I flipped him off for the hell of it. "See you in the AM."

The instant I shut the door behind me, I felt better. I couldn't say if it was that niggling feeling that dissipated or just my concern for Ross.

The cold air shook me awake as I walked toward the cabins. Peering into the darkness, I tried to remember the last time I looked at a watch. Daylight was all that mattered anymore; time felt obsolete. With a final glance toward the house, I quietly opened the door into the narrow cottage.

Candlelight flickered over the walls, casting familiar shadows. They'd pushed a queen bed against the wall to leave more room on the floor for two twin mattresses and a folding cot where Alex lay, already passed out. Beau was lying in his bed, eyes heavy as he blinked at me, and Thea and Sophie were on the other. And, like music to my ears, the water was running in the bathroom.

Sophie looked up at me from combing Thea's hair. "The boys brought in the mattresses from the next cabin so no one would have to sleep on the floor."

"I noticed." I stepped inside. It was like Christmas had come early. Comfy beds and plumbing. "You and Elle get the bed," she said with a quirked brow.

"I'm fine on the mattress. You kids can have the bed—"

"Elle said the bed was fine."

"Yeah, well, Elle's having a euphoric shower right now, she wouldn't care about much of anything else I'd imagine."

Sophie laughed. "True."

I took off my coat and draped it on the edge of the bed. "Are you okay?" I'd been worried about her since her meet and greet with Ross.

She nodded without bothering to look at me. "Parts of his memory are blurry. He feels really lost."

I didn't need her to fill in the rest. She didn't need to think about it anymore than she already had before bed.

"No lights, huh?" I asked, taking in the darkened room.

Sophie shrugged. "It feels weird sitting in the bright lights," she mused. It made sense after all this time, and I wasn't complaining.

Beau's eyelids flitted open.

"Did your friends arrive?" I asked him.

His chin dipped slightly.

"Do you think they'll mind keeping an eye on things tonight?"

"They will," he murmured, his lips barely moving.

"Thanks, bud." I pulled his sleeping bag up over his shoulder.

A week ago I might've slept with my gun, knowing eight wolves were outside the house. Tonight, I didn't feel like I needed it at all. I stopped at the vertical windows, peering out into the crystal-clear night. It wasn't that I didn't trust Ross, but I wasn't sure I knew him anymore. He'd gone AWOL for months and the unknown of where he'd gone and what he'd done worried me.

The bathroom door opened and Elle stepped out. Her silhouette flickered in the window's reflection. "You're back," she said quietly so not to wake the boys.

I made the mistake of peering over my shoulder to answer and my tongue lodged in my throat.

Of course I'd noticed Elle was attractive, you had to be a corpse not to, but until now she'd just been Elle. Well, mostly. The maternal and responsible one. She'd been the person who kept our lives running like a well-oiled machine most of the time. But standing there with her hair long and dark over her shoulders, and the wet tips soaking into her strappy pink tank top, she was more than that. Her shirt clung to every curve of her chest, and I cleared my throat.

"Is everything okay?" She wrapped her hair in a towel and glanced at me. "Did you get a chance to talk to Ross?"

I shook my head. "Yeah, he's—uh—he's fine. I told him to get some sleep." I plopped into a cushioned chair beside a corner desk and pulled off my boots.

"Good." She smiled with relief and I forced myself to look away.

"Your bag's there," Sophie said with a grin. I didn't have to look at her, I could hear it in her voice.

"Thanks," I muttered and threw a dirty sock at her.

I pulled my shirt over my head as Elle rifled through her bag. I needed sleep. A lot of it. "I was hoping there might be warm water left for me," I said, glancing at her.

"Of course. Let me get my things out of the shower." Elle disappeared into the candlelit bathroom and I grabbed my bag.

"You're acting like a goober," Sophie said. I could feel the burn in my cheeks.

"I thought you were going to bed," I deadpanned, which only earned me a pleased smile. As prompted, Sophie and Thea crawled under their respective sleeping bags, both of them yawning.

"It's all yours," Elle whispered and stood at the edge of the queen bed, folding up her "dirty" clothes to put into our dirty bag.

I walked past her, into the steamy bathroom. It was warm and muggy, like a sauna. While the heat felt like a small miracle, I wasn't sure how Elle of all people could stand it.

"Here's a clean towel," she said. The bathroom was probably 5' x 8' but felt more like 4' x 4' as she leaned in and set it on the counter.

I pulled out my razor and Elle paused, appraising me in the mirror. "Grooming, huh?"

"I figured I could at least make my goatee look less like a beard."

Elle chuckled softly and turned to leave. "Enjoy your shower."

"I plan to," I told her as the door clicked shut behind her. I stared at my reflection, somewhat horrified. I wasn't sure of the last time I'd actually looked in anything other than a rearview mirror. My hair was shaggy and nearly to my shoulders, which is why it was always pulled back. My mustache was long enough to tickle my lip and any remnants of a goatee were long gone. Yes, grooming and a hot shower were in order before my head hit the pillow.

Sleep couldn't come fast enough, and yet I took my time in the bathroom, soaking under the hot water as I scrubbed the dirt from every muscle. I'd almost forgotten what it felt like to be really, truly clean. I let the water roll over me until it cooled, then climbed out to dress.

The air was brisk, but the tile was warm beneath my feet from the steamy room and I towel dried my hair then brushed my teeth. Dressed and cleaned, I blew out the three-wick candle, halfway burned, and opened the bathroom door.

A candle on the headboard was all that lit the room. Elle was curled up under the covers, facing the wall with only a sheet covering her. I smiled; she didn't have to pretend to be cold anymore.

I padded around the bed, setting my dirty clothes and toiletries on top of my bag to deal with tomorrow. And with great anticipation, I pulled up the comforter and crawled in beneath it.

All I could feel was Elle's warmth. It emanated off of her like she was made of the sun, and as much as I tried to ignore it, my instinct was to pull her close.

It had been a while since I laid on a mattress or slept in an actual bed with a woman. My wife. The months she'd been gone felt more like eons, and yet like it was only yesterday, too. I wondered if it would ever get easier imagining my life without her. Or if I ever wanted it to. To my surprise another question popped into my mind too: what if I miss my second and last chance to truly live?

"Goodnight," Elle whispered.

I stared at her back, at the damp hair that splayed against her pillow. "Night, Elle."

I blew out the candle and rolled to my other side, then tried and failed to fall asleep.

61

SOPHIE
APRIL 19

A dele. Journey. I was even guilty of listening to a little Bieber and One Direction from time to time, especially when my boyfriend Jesse and I were fighting. I missed my stereo and social media, watching other people's ridiculous problems so I didn't have to think about my own. Now the world was small even if it was bigger than before, more vast and unpredictable. Or maybe it had always been that way, only now I lived in it and could actually feel it.

There was a peace in the woods here, different from Jade's house. The lodge felt like a fresh canvas of white views and jagged peaks—a promise of something new and sort of exciting. Even if more housemates came with it.

I peered up at the wraparound deck where Ross and Bert had been chatting over their morning coffee. I needed to get my power under control, and figure out what exactly I'd found in Ross's head. He wasn't a bad guy, just very broken and even more lost. His mind was different, and I wasn't sure if it was part of his PTSD or because of something else. Even though I wanted to know, mostly I didn't.

I stopped at the crest of the hill and stared out at the pines and willows that jetted up toward the sky like fingertips trying to reach the sun. If I held my breath, I could almost hear the Yukon River flowing beyond them. If it hadn't been for my dream, I would've been able to enjoy it.

I heard the crunch of Alex's steady footsteps. "Is everything okay?"

I wanted to ask him the same question. He was the one who had been none too subtly avoiding me again. "Yeah, I'm fine."

"Come on," he said. "Tell me."

"I just woke up on the wrong side of the bed."

"Bad mattress?"

I shook my head. "Bad dream."

"Intriguing."

I glared at him. "There were intruders and my legs were broken," I told him. It was a recurring dream I had growing up, worrying my legs wouldn't work properly. My mom drilling into me when I didn't keep up with my leg exercises, even when the doctor said I was fine, didn't help either. There had never been psychopathic villains in my dreams before though.

"I couldn't stand or reach my gun in time and they shot me." Not having a power that would help me save my life if I needed it was even more depressing.

"Geez, Soph. That's—rough."

"What's your greatest fear, Alex?"

His eyebrow twitched and he tilted his head, like I'd asked him to commit a crime or something. "Why?" he asked warily. "I mean, don't you already know?"

I shook my head, not because I didn't already have an idea, but because I wanted him to tell me something about himself. "I don't know everything about you, Alex. I already told you that."

He widened his stance and crossed his arms over his chest. "I don't know," he said, tapping his chin. Theatrics. Dramatics. Jokes.

It was always something with him. "I try not to think about what scares me." That part was true. He shoved everything into a vault, pretending it wasn't there—until the vault was overflowing.

"Mine is being weak," I admitted.

"Why, because of those stupid leg braces I saw in photos at your house in Whitely? A lot of kids have those—"

"It's not only that." It was a lot of things. "My power, too."

He threw his arms up. "Why does that make you feel weak?"

"Well, for starters, I hesitated shooting that guy in Slana. Oh, and my power is pretty useless. It's not like feeling someone's emotions sucks the life out of them. And that would be shitty if it did; I don't want to have to suffer in order to use my ability. Oh, wait. I already do," I uttered.

"Don't be like that, Soph. You'll get a handle on it, and once we're settled we can start target practice again to make you feel more comfortable shooting. And I bet Ross knows some good moves, being in the Army. Or Jackson, he was going to teach you self-defense at some point. Right?"

I nodded. "True."

"Okay, look—" he stepped in front of me. His eyes searched mine as he formulated a plan. "I promise to help you once we get settled okay? We can learn shit together."

"You already know how to fight," I told him. His openness immediately faltered and I hated my mouth in that moment. More memories I had that he wanted kept in the vault.

"No, I don't know how to fight." He exhaled and shook his head. He hated that part of him, the street kid who did what he had to. The kid who saw and did dark things to stay alive. He didn't understand how strong he was, but of course I couldn't tell him how much I saw and how I felt about it.

"Well, you can't fight and I can't fight, so I guess we're even," I said more bubbly to break the stillness. "You're right, we'll train together. The next guy who breaks in won't be so lucky."

"Good," he said, but for the first time, I wasn't sure what Alex was thinking when he looked at me. It looked like uncertainty and affection, but which kind of affection—sisterly or something more —I wasn't certain of either. "We'll work every day until you feel safe, with or without Jackson and Elle or anyone else's help, for that matter."

Somehow, even when I knew Alex was uncertain how to act around me, he could still be so genuine. Everything he ever told me—*seriously* told me—felt like a promise. His words always nestled their way into the cold spots in my bones and warmed me from the inside out.

He stared at my biceps through my jacket. "But we do have our work cut out for us," he teased.

"Hey, Alex," Jackson called from the deck. We both glanced back at him.

"Shit, I was supposed to get you and Elle." Alex looked at me. "Jackson wants us to circle up so we can iron things out."

Jackson stared down at us, frowning. It had been permanently etched in his brow since he'd woke up. "Where's Elle?"

"I'll get her," I offered. "She's at the river taking photos."

He glanced toward the water. "Thanks. We'll meet up in the living room."

I waved in answer, then headed down the trail toward the water. I'd come a long way from a fourteen-story building, and I tried to imagine what life would look like a few years from now. Would I be a badass? I sure as hell hoped so. Would Alex still be around or will he have completely pushed me away by then? God, I hoped not.

I sighed and followed the muddy trail down to the water. Willows and scratchy, defrosting branches lined the path and I tried to imagine how beautiful everything would be in full bloom during the spring.

"Elle? Jackson wants to meet." I heard a rustle in the bushes and followed the bend in the path a bit farther as I rounded a boulder.

I gasped when I saw a mass of black and froze. My heart thudded, and I was about to scream, then everything went black.

62

JACKSON
APRIL 19

I paced the window, waiting for Elle and Sophie to come up the trail. I'd had a bad feeling since I woke up and now wasn't the time to worry about taking pictures.

"Where the hell are they?" I glared at Alex. "It's been almost an hour."

Alex set the maps in his lap on the coffee table and walked over to the window. "You know as much as me. Sophie said she would get Elle . . ." He scanned the tree line, like I hadn't done it a hundred times already.

I'd finally gotten drunken Bert off the couch long enough to get some coffee in him. Ross was up and showered, hell, the kids were easier to wrangle than the rest of the lot.

Apprehension mounting, I headed out the sliding door onto the deck. "Elle! Sophie!" I hurried down the steps and stopped on the crest of the hill. "Let's wrap it up!"

But a sickening feeling settled inside of me when they didn't answer. "Elle?" Resting my hand on my Glock, I marched through the yard, past the fire pit, and down the path. "Elle!" I shouted, but it was fear lacing my voice, not anger.

The sickening feeling coiled, alive in my chest as I ran the length of the trail. My heart raced as I thought of everything that could've happened. Bears. A lunatic. That they'd fallen in the Yukon and gotten swept away.

I stopped at the end of the path at the muddy bank of the water. I looked upstream and then down. The water drifted, but not strong enough yet to carry them away. "Sophie!"

My boot slipped in the mud, and I caught myself on the trunk of a pine tree. I blinked, staring down at bootprints on the bank, different sizes overlapping each other, and I held my breath and stared.

No. Whatever this was, it wasn't happening.

Muscles wound so tight it hurt to breathe, I crouched down with my gun clutched in one hand as I felt the mud with the other. Some prints had grip outsoles, which could be any tactical shoe, but they were too big to be Sophie and Elle's. And they were fresh, wet and glistening in the sunlight.

"Fuck!" I kicked brush and twigs out of the way, scouring the water's edge for more shoe prints, but there were none that I could find. There was nothing but a slight breeze and rippling water. I analyzed the branches, looking for some that were broken and would give me some sign. There was nothing.

"Fuck!" I trampled through the trees, running my fingers through my hair. I needed to get a grip. I needed to calm down and think.

"What is it?" Alex ran to a stop at the mouth of the trail.

"Elle's gone," I breathed, grabbing my head. "Elle and Sophie are gone." I hit my fist against a hapless tree trunk. "Someone was here." We hadn't been in Whitehorse twelve hours and my worst fears had already come true.

Ross and Bert ran up behind Alex, and I spun around. The shoe prints were military grade, just like the shoes he was wearing. Grabbing Ross by his collar, I lifted him to his feet. "Where are they?" I roared.

"Fuck, Jackson, I don't know!" His eyes were wide with

surprise, his chest heaving but not as much as mine was, with fear and pure rage.

"You've been acting weird since we got here. I know you know something. Tell me or I swear—"

"Jackson!" Alex shouted. "Calm down. We don't know it was him. He's been with us this whole time."

Ross glanced at Alex then back at me. "Listen to the kid, Jackson. You're out of your damn mind if you think I was behind this."

I let go of him, and Ross stumbled to the ground, trying to catch his balance. "Jesus, Jackson. How did I go from your bro to being your number one suspect?"

"You're the only one who knows we're here," I growled.

He laughed, humorless and fuming. "Are you shitting me, man? You drove a fucking caravan through an empty city last night, *everyone* knows you're here."

I took a step toward him. "There are survivors then?" People who would hurt Elle and Sophie the first chance they got.

"I don't know, Jackson. I didn't exactly walk into town with an old drunk and knock on doors looking for psychopaths who were interested in post-apocalyptic Girl Scout cookies."

I frowned.

"Look, Jackson. I know this looks bad and is the last thing you want to hear right now, but we know what sort of people are out there. Anyone could've taken them."

My mind began to swirl, and I was in the hospital all over again, surrounded with the cold sweat of fear and desperation.

Alex grabbed my arm, his eyes wild with the same desperation I felt. "We have to find them."

I nodded. Yes. We did. And Elle wasn't like Hannah. She wasn't helpless. Elle was strong, and she was fierce, and she would protect Sophie and herself, we just had to find them.

I ran past Alex and Ross, toward the house.

"Where are you going?" Ross called, and I heard the clomp of footsteps running up behind me.

I needed Beau. "I'm getting more help."

63

ELLE
APRIL 19

My mind flicked on, like a switch turning on the light in a dark room, and I opened my eyes. I blinked as my vision adjusted to the darkness, sprinkled with filtered light from outside the room. I was confined and the cement floor beneath me was cold as ice. I hadn't been cold in so long, it seeped its way into my body, riddling my bones. The sharp scent of metal and stale air filled my nostrils.

A man sat on a chair outside the door, bathed in a halo of light that shone from the skylight above him. His face was cast in shadows, and my thoughts flashed to an unwanted, familiar form standing beside my bed. A breath caught in my throat, and I tried to move back—to crawl as far away as I could—but my hands were tied behind me. I moved barely an inch before I slammed into a cold wall instead.

Dr. John wasn't standing there though. It was a trick of the mind, because he was dead.

Wasn't he?

"Who are you?" I ground out. My voice was a hollow sound that echoed in the sterile room surrounding me. An open door was all that separated me from him.

"Mornin' sunshine," he said with easy amusement.

My eyes opened wider and I pursed my lips. It was a unique voice, a *familiar* voice I tried to place. Not Dr. John's, but it belonged to someone I knew. I searched the foggy depths of my mind for a memory.

Then, the man from the river flashed to mind. I'd been crouched down, taking a picture of morning dew in a spider web, when I turned around and a man in a hood stood behind me, and just as suddenly everything had gone black.

My blood boiled, but not with the anger and rage and the fear I knew I could use to my advantage—but, I couldn't feel the fire at all, and panic wound its way through my veins in its place.

"What do you want?" I bit out, trying desperately to grasp hold of my vehemence rather than my fear. There was no telling what power he had, or what he was capable of. "Whatever it is—"

"I just want to talk."

"And you had to kidnap me to do that? You couldn't simply ask?" I spat, not buying a single word.

"Truly. No need to get angsty." There was an intrigued lilt to his words that worried me.

"Talk about what?" I seethed. "Because this isn't a great way to make friends."

He tossed his head back and chuckled. "Good point." The man stood up, still covered in shadow as he walked closer to my cell. His footsteps echoed against the concrete. "You're right though, I'm being rude. I'm very sorry about all this."

"Sorry for what, abducting me?"

He laughed again. "I guess that is what it looks like, doesn't it?" He paced back and forth, like a warden might do, but his steps were less rigid, even if his fatigues were standard issue. He clasped his hands behind his back and rocked on his feet a little. There was no doubt in my mind that he was crazy. "These days," he said, contemplative, "it's not exactly smart to assume good intentions, am I right? I'm not one of the bad guys, though. I promise."

I tried to wiggle my wrists free of my bindings, what felt like cuffs and rope combined. "Funny. That's what all the bad guys say."

He shrugged. "I have a couple questions and then I'll let you go. It's that simple. Or, I might decide to lock you in here forever. I haven't decided yet."

"You mean, you'll let me go *if* you like my answers," I clarified.

He wagged his finger at me as he stepped into the light. "You're smart, and you've got some fire in you." He was a middle-aged man with crazy blonde hair and a beak-like nose. He had beady eyes and a permanent smile parting his lips, exposing the gap between his straight white teeth. "I like it." He nodded appreciatively. "It means you're not easily swayed."

I couldn't listen to his psychobabble much longer. The room felt like it was closing in on me, like this might be the last place I'd ever see, and if that was the case, I wouldn't go down without a fight. "Jackson!" I screamed. "Help, Jackson! I'm in here!" I waited for the fire in my blood to surge and swirl, but it never came. "Jackson!"

"It's okay, scream. Go ahead. Get it out." He began to pace, like he expected it, and tears burned the backs of my eyes. "Scream until your heart's content. No one can hear you."

"Beau! I'm in here!" I tugged against my binding, squeezing my eyes shut. "Beau!" Maybe no *person* could hear me, but if the wolves could hear me, maybe Beau would too. I was probably underground in a bunker. I hit my fists on the floor, my chains clanking, and I shouted from the top of my lungs.

The man turned on his heel to leave. "When you're ready, let me know and we can talk. I'll pop in to see your friend in the cell down the hall while you get the shouting and the screaming out of your system."

He could only take one step before I screamed, "Wait!" My

heart lurched to a screeching halt. I could barely form the words. "What—who? Please don't hurt them—"

"Uh, I didn't get a name before we snatched her," he mused, tapping his scruffy chin with his crooked index finger. "She's younger, about five-foot-six or so with reddish-blonde hair."

"Sophie," I breathed. "Please, don't hurt her, she's just a kid."

"I won't hurt her unless I have to," he said so nonchalantly, I wanted to rip his head off.

"Fine, ask me then, whatever you want. Ask me and I'll tell you." I wanted him to forget Sophie was in the other room. I needed his attention on me while I figured out a plan. If I could lure him closer maybe the fire would return.

"So," he said, pulling his chair from the shadows so he could sit closer to the doorway. "I want to know why he sent you." His army fatigues were old and tattered.

While I understood the words, I didn't understand the question. I blinked. "What?"

The psychopath chuckled again, laughing at everything that didn't go exactly his way. I contemplated whether he'd been crazy before or if it was because of the outbreak. Either way, this kind of crazy was unpredictable, which meant there was a chance of getting out alive, and a chance this cell might become my cement tomb.

"Look," I said, and spoke slowly and as carefully as I could. "No one sent me. I was passing through Whitehorse with Sophie, and we'd stayed at an abandoned house by the river. That's all."

"Are you related?" he asked, catching me off guard. "You two don't really look related."

"Uh, no. We're not related. We're just . . . family," I said, blinking back tears. "Did any of your relatives survive?" I hedged, wondering if this was a tangent I could take advantage of.

"Not that I'm aware of," he said easily. "But then," he said more thoughtfully, crossing his arms over his chest. "I never really had any family, not for many years, at least. I've been what most people would call a 'strange bird' all my life. Very introverted, a little crazy, but all the best people are, am I right?" He pointed at me as if he expected me to laugh with him too.

I tried to smile, to act like he didn't petrify me, but I couldn't manage it. "Sophie's just a teenager. Please, let her go."

He stared down at his hands as he made a show of thinking about it. "But she's not just an ordinary teenager, is she?" He peered up then, looked right into my eyes, past the shadows covering half my face, past whatever threat he saw in me. It wasn't really a question. He already knew way too much.

My chest heaved and my chin trembled.

"Don't worry, I'm not like those kooks you've seen out there. I'm not after kids. I'm on the lookout for military folk, yellow-bands and black-bands. I hear they're out in force these days, and I, quite frankly, want to kill every last one of them. So," he said, his easiness solidifying to something more terrifying. "Are you here on his behalf, and do I need to kill you?"

"Whose behalf?" I whispered, knowing I would never get out of here if he thought I was part of some delusion. "I don't know what bands you're talking about—I don't know who *he* is."

The angles in his face sharpened. Whatever amusement he'd had was gone.

He stood up, and began pacing. Then, he turned and walked closer to my open door again. "I've been telling people for years the government would do this. They would unleash a super killer that would take out the world, but in all fairness, I was wrong about one thing. The Virus didn't take out the world, just 90 percent of human life."

My breath caught in my throat. "You're the voice from the radio."

"Oh, good!" A grin engulfed his face, exposing the gap in his teeth again. "You've heard the show. The name's Woody. I don't have much of an audience these days." He shrugged. "But what are you gonna do?" He lifted a shoulder, not expecting an answer and leaned against the door frame. "I might've been wrong about the specifics, but I think I still earned that point. In my opinion, at least."

"This *was* the government?"

"I've known something was coming for years," Woody said, talking over me. "Yet somehow people are surprised." He chuckled to himself and shook his head. "I tried to tell them. Doesn't it suck always being right?"

The more Woody paced, the more desperate I was to find the fire inside that had been gaining strength for months. Where was it when I needed it; why wouldn't it come?

"I should probably tell you that your mutated capabilities won't affect me," he said. "Or anyone in here, for that matter."

"What—" I tried not to dwell on how *many* people he was referring to. "How did you . . ."

"I might be crazy, but I'm not stupid," he explained. "I wasn't gonna bring you down here just so you could kill me, silly." Woody grinned, amused by my confusion. "But, all jokes aside, I will kill you if you don't tell me what you're doing here. I'm a fair man, but my patience tends to run out when I get bored. Probing to get the truth is fun," he mused, "but a bit messy. I don't like to get my hands dirty if I don't have to." He tapped his chin with his index finger again. "It's a quirk of mine, I guess. I've always had it."

"I told you!" I shouted, done listening to him talk in circles. I hit my fists on the ground, regretting it instantly. "I don't know what you're talking about! I don't know about different colored bands or know anything about the government—I don't know anything!" I waited for the pain to shoot through my side and chest from my cracked rib, but everything in my body felt funny. Everything felt wrong. The heat was gone. The fire and the hum inside me—all of it was numb.

I let my head roll back and swallowed a whimper. "What else do you want me to say?" I croaked. "I. Don't. Know. Anything. I don't know how the virus spread or what it even is. I don't even know what's wrong with me. I thought I was dead and then I woke up, and now I'm not the same. Just let me see Sophie. *Please*!" Silent tears streamed down my cheeks, a cold sweat making me feel sick to my stomach, like the fever was coming on all over again.

"What do you think, Stanley? Is she telling the truth?"

"Oh my God," I groaned. He was talking to himself now too. I lifted my head and saw another shadow drawing closer up the hall, footsteps barely echoing. I blinked. Waited. Held my breath. I imagined an executioner in blood-stained robes coming to take me to a chamber much worse than the one I was in. My eyes blurred as tears breached my lashes, and my throat burned.

I only saw the tips of his pointed shoes before an unassuming man peeked his head into the doorway to look at me. Stanley wasn't a monster. He was thin and tall, with combed back hair and black-rimmed glasses. He wore a dark suit and yellow bow tie. I wasn't sure if his presence made me feel worse or better.

He whispered something to Woody, but I couldn't make it out.

"You'll have to speak louder, Stanley. That's my bad ear."

"She's telling the truth," he murmured, glancing in at me. He looked almost sympathetic.

Stanley's words were like a warm blanket of hope. I wanted to reach out and hug him for saying such a glorious thing. Even if he was likely crazy, he was also my only hope.

"Does she know the General?" Woody eyed me warily.

Stanley shook his head. "I, um . . . I don't think so."

Woody sighed and crossed his hands over his chest. "Do you know the General, Elle?"

I gasped. How did he know my name?

"Tell the truth now, you're doing so well."

I glanced between the two men, praying this wasn't a trick. I shook my head. "No," I whispered. "I don't know the General."

Woody's eyes narrowed on me and I could see the contours of

his jaw flexing in the dim light. The seconds felt like minutes until as he contemplated, then suddenly, his brow lifted and he smiled, big and wide, and crazier than before. "Well, why didn't you say so from the start?"

A door shut down the hall, and I realized Stanley was gone again.

"In that case," Woody said, walking into the doorway, his hands on his hips. "Sorry for the inconvenience, Elle. You should've told me you were one of us."

"Wait—what?" I stared at him, gaping. His behavior was worse than whiplash.

"It's all just a precaution." He waved my confusion away. "You can't trust the government, you can't trust the General . . . they have spies everywhere."

He was waiting for me to stand. "Come on now, let's get you out of these silly bindings. I'll take you to your friend."

My adrenaline rushed through me, making me almost dizzy. Whatever I'd woken up to, whatever fear I had for my life, was still hovering, and I wasn't sure I could trust him.

He took a step closer and I took a step back. "You broadcast your show from a dungeon? And you're not military," I processed aloud, trying to put the pieces together.

He chuckled. "Not anymore. And it's not a dungeon, they don't make those anymore."

I laughed this time, hysteria bubbling up inside me. I still wasn't convinced that he wasn't going to have another change of heart.

Woody motioned for me to turn around, and he pulled a key out from his pocket.

It couldn't have been that simple. He was crazy; he wouldn't just let me go. "What's the catch?" I took a step further back. "You kidnap me, threaten me, and now you're just . . . letting me go?"

"No catch, but just remember," he said, reaching for my cuffs again. "Your powers won't work here, not until you leave."

"What about Stanley," I said. "His powers worked."

Woody lifted a bushy, blonde eyebrow and held the key just shy of my lock. "Stanley is my friend, I allow his Ability to work."

I was too overwhelmed to process all that could mean, but my mind raced with the possibility of my overtaking him; I had finger-nails, I had sheer desperation and willpower.

Woody's smile faltered a little as he put the key in the lock. "Don't try anything stupid, either." He dipped his chin. "Promise?"

I nodded, if a little hesitant. "Promise."

"Good. Let's get you to your girl." The bindings clanked to the concrete, my hands feeling weightless without the heavy metal holding them down. I rubbed at the raw skin and took two steps back from Woody.

He gestured out the cell door, but I didn't move. "I'm not going to bite."

"No, you were only going to probe me," I told him, skeptical. I pressed my palms to the cold cement wall behind me. "*Were* you really going to probe me?" I was unable to resist asking. I hoped he was just exceedingly convincing.

Woody hooted, which wasn't entirely unexpected. He enjoyed all of this far too much. "Does it matter? I don't need to now, do I?"

Definitely not. I shook my head and rubbed my arms, shiver-ing. The adrenaline made it impossible to stop shaking, that or the cold I wasn't used to feeling. More than anything, I prayed Sophie was really here, wherever we were, and that Woody was taking me to her. I had no reason to trust him, but I also had little choice.

"Now," he said, gesturing toward the cell door again. "There are a few things you should probably know. Shall we?"

64

SOPHIE

APRIL 19

I stared down at the sterile white table, wondering where all the bodies in the prison had gone. The place didn't smell, in fact, it was strangely clean, like there'd been upkeep over all the months since the world stopped. And the electricity still worked here, just like at the lodge.

I picked at the syrup-saturated fruit cup Phil had given me, then stared up at him. He stood guard beside me, tactical gear on, though it didn't look military, and he had a gun in his belt. He was young, like Alex and me, with chubby white cheeks and fluffy brown hair. He had a lot of freckles on his nose, like I did, and he definitely didn't look like a killer, but I knew better than anyone that looks were *always* deceiving.

"How old are you?" I asked him, staring into his brown eyes. "And what the hell are you doing at a place like this? Is Woody your crazy uncle or something?"

Phil's eye shifted to mine, but he didn't answer.

I'd been sitting in the room for so long with silent Phil to keep me company, all the heart-racing fear I'd had diminished more and more by the minute. They hadn't hurt me and they'd given me water and food. I was antsy and annoyed more than anything, waiting for Elle, praying she was okay. Somehow I knew she was.

This place was strange. Everything felt huge and vacuous without people sitting at the white tables or standing in line at the food counter. I glanced up at the cameras mounted on the ceiling. I wasn't sure if they were from before, or if someone was watching me.

Maybe I wasn't overly worried because I knew if Woody tried anything with Elle, she'd fry his ass. But I wasn't sure it was that either. Phil didn't seem like a killer, not like the ones I'd seen so far anyway. Woody, on the other hand, was clearly crazy, though whether or not he was the dangerous kind, I hadn't decided yet. He promised I'd be fine if Elle gave him the info he needed about the General, but since we knew nothing, I wasn't sure how he'd react.

My stomach turned as I considered just how much they could hurt us if they really wanted to, because even if Alex and Jackson found us, it wasn't easy getting into a prison. In fact, they might die trying.

I speared at a syrup-soaked grape. I'd felt strangely lighter since I'd woken up, too. I actually liked it, even if I didn't know why. *Maybe that's why I wasn't worried.* "What is it you can do?" I asked Phil, wondering if he'd engage if I just kept asking question after question. He might get tired of my voice and decide to give in.

His eyes shifted to me again, but only for a second before he refocused on the bathroom sign located on the other side of the cafeteria. "It doesn't hurt to talk, right? I mean, you guys can't get *that* many visitors around here." I stabbed a diced peach, deciding I'd eat that at least. "The place isn't exactly inviting," I muttered. "And," I said, pointing to the hallway with my plastic fork. "Who was that slinky guy walking down the hall earlier? The one with the bow tie."

Phil remained silent.

"I mean, why was he so dressed up? Who does he have to dress nice for? Woody?" I choked out a laugh.

I had half a mind to reach out and touch Phil just to see what I could find out.

"I could get the answers from you myself, you know?" It was true. Even if what I could do wasn't exactly petrifying, it was enough to get his thoughts wandering a bit.

Phil shifted his weight, finally looking at me. "You mean your Ability?"

My eyebrows rose, nearly touching my hairline. "My what?"

"The powers . . . They're called Abilities."

"Um, okay . . ." I rolled my eyes. "Why can't I call it what I want?"

"I'm just saying that's what they're called."

The fact that he was willing to argue with me was promising, so I egged him on. "Says who?"

"Stanley," he answered tersely. "He knows everything about the Virus."

"*Everything?*"

Phil nodded. "He was with the General until the Re-gen Rebellion."

I didn't know what the hell a Re-gen was but a *rebellion* sounded terrifying. "I didn't realize there were enough of us left for there to be a rebellion," I mused. "Wait, who's *The General* first of all?" It sounded like a crazy tale having to do with Woody's conspiracy radio broadcasts, but a part of me knew that if Elle could turn herself into a lady phoenix and I could find out who Phil's best friend in third grade was with a single touch, crazy, impossible, and unbelievable were all relative now.

"The General created the Virus." Forgetting his plans to ignore me, Phil sat down across from me at the table, making the whole thing shift and squeak and my fruit cup slosh around. "Woody said Stanley was one of the General's most trusted Truth Guards, so he knew how to get out of the Colony when the timing was right."

Frowning, I leaned closer. "And of *all* the places Stanley could've gone, he went to Woody?"

Phil nodded with too much excitement, and I began to think he really was insane. "Rumor has it," he continued, "Woody was on the General's watch list of potential threats a decade ago, but the General thought he was too crazy to worry about, so he didn't bother silencing him."

"As in, murder him?" I gulped, but I wasn't sure why I was surprised.

"He did kill nearly everyone in the world—on purpose," Phil deadpanned.

Okay, so maybe Phil wasn't crazy, just naive? "What's a Truth Guard then? You said Stanley was a Truth Guard."

"A truth teller—the General's paranoid, so he surrounds himself with people whose Abilities he can use to manipulate and control everyone. Some of his men were mind-controlled."

"And the others?" My eyes were wide, and my mind swirled with far too many questions I feared to ask, yet felt I had to. It was a fascinating and horrifying tale that seemed fictional, but Phil's words were shaking with truth. He was either brainwashed or he'd seen enough and heard enough to believe a power-hungry fanatic was trying to control the world, or what was left of it anyway.

"The others follow him willingly," he spat and pursed his lips. "They help him because they believe in what he's doing."

"Or they're too scared not to," I thought aloud. If a lunatic with an arsenal of powers behind him wanted my help and my only defense was a shotgun since my power couldn't help me, I might do the same. "Where's the General now?" I breathed, frightened to hear the answer.

"He has a colony in Colorado. I've heard the radio broadcast; they've been urging survivors to go there since December."

"But, if the General caused the virus—"

"Then it can't be good."

I shook my head. "No, it can't." It was hard to imagine how all of what Phil was saying could've been going on while we'd been trying to survive the winter. I narrowed my eyes and glared at him, staring into his watchful, brown eyes. It was probably all a ploy. "Why are you telling me all of this?"

"I'm—well . . ."

I tilted my head and crossed my arms. "You're trying to distract me or put nonsense in my head—how do I know *you're* not the General?"

Phil's entire face changed and he stood up. "My entire family is dead," he snapped. "You think I wanted to watch my sister and mom die?" He pointed out the door then let out a breath. "At least you have her." His cheeks burned red, and he shook his head. "I shouldn't even be talking to you." Phil took his stance at the end of the table again and resumed his glare at the bathroom sign.

"I'm sorry," I whispered. I'd clearly hit a nerve. "But you *did* kidnap us. So . . ."

His eyes shifted to me again, lingered, then the double doors to the cafeteria creaked opened as Elle and crazy-haired Woody walked in.

Brimming with relief, I ran to Elle, apparently more worried Woody wouldn't keep his word than I'd thought.

"Soph," Elle breathed, cringing as I wrapped my arms around her. Her body was so cold through her long sleeves and pants. But she was okay, and Woody *had* kept his word. "Are you all right? Did they hurt you?" She glanced from me to Phil and then to Woody.

"No, they didn't hurt me." I took a step back and assessed her crooked ponytail and her red wrists. Gently, I grabbed her hand, feeling no spark at all when I touched her.

"The fire's gone," she whispered, registering the confusion on my face.

I nodded, staring at my hands in hers. I felt and saw nothing. "Me too."

"Yeah, about those Abilities," Woody said, sitting down at the

LINDSEY POGUE

cafeteria table. He took my fork and skewered the last two pieces of fruit into his mouth. "There's a way to block them, but we won't go into that right now." He leaned his elbow on the tabletop and folded his hands in front of him. "When you leave, they'll come back. Don't worry your pretty heads."

I didn't bother mentioning it was actually a relief not to have mine. It was an incredible lightness I'd never appreciated before and hadn't been able to in months.

"Fine. Now let us go. We answered your questions," Elle told him. "We did what you needed. Our people are probably—"

"Look," Woody said in all seriousness, "I'm happy to let you both go on your merry little way, but I have a proposition for you first."

65

JACKSON
APRIL 19

Three hours. One hundred and eighty-nine minutes was what it took to get gear, jump in the truck, and follow the wolves until they found Elle and Sophie's scent four miles upriver.

We'd ditched the trucks on the side of the road, hoofing it behind the wolves as they scattered and sniffed, searching for whatever trace they could find that would take us to them. The closer to the city we drew, the more panicked I became.

"A boat!" Alex shouted from ahead, and I ran through the trees, toward him. "They can't be far then, right?"

"God, I hope not," I said, pivoting to search the mud for more tracks.

"Guys, they found something!" Beau shouted.

I nodded for Alex to follow Beau and the wolves as I holstered my gun in my waist strap and conducted a quick search of the boat. Other than an emergency kit strapped to the side, there was nothing that would help us.

I glanced up, barely able to see Alex's green jacket through the trees as he followed the wolves further and further away. I exchanged a quick look with Ross, who was still angry with me for accusing him of having a part in it, and then jogged after Alex and

Beau. I weaved through the willow trees with Ross at my side, grateful to have him there, despite my accusation.

"I told you I'm sorry. It was a feeling. I've had it since I got here. I thought—"

"You thought your best friend could do something like that," he bit out. "Yeah, I got it."

"Over here!" Beau shouted brusquely as he ran behind the wolves toward the road. There were tracks in the mud as we jogged through the trees. We didn't know where they led or where we would end up. We were losing daylight, so creating a solid plan would have to come later, once we knew what we were up against.

"Are you sure Thea's okay with Bert?" It might've been my tenth time asking, I was losing count.

Ross scanned the woods behind us for unwanted followers. "She'll be fine. Now do you want to worry about Bert and Thea or find Elle and Sophie?" he ground out.

As we broke through the trees at the highway, a rumble in the distance echoed through the still air. "Hold up!" I shouted, heart fumbling to a halt. "Hurry! Back into the forest!" Everyone darted behind cover, but something urged me to stay at the edge of the road.

"Jackson!" Ross called. "Get your ass in here."

I couldn't move. Deep down I needed to stay put as a beat-to-shit, lifted Chevy Blazer with blackened windows slowed to almost stopping a few dozen yards away.

I lifted my gun, hearing everyone behind me shift their own in their hands, followed by the sound of bullets sliding into their chambers. At least whoever was inside wouldn't be unscathed if they tried anything.

The passenger door swung open and two feet hit the ground, and a familiar strawberry blonde jumped out.

"Sophie!" Beau shouted. Her face lit up as she saw us, and she jogged over. I wasn't sure I believed what I was seeing, an unscathed Sophie.

Then Elle climbed out the back seat. She looked unscathed and it made no sense.

Apprehensive, I debated lowering my gun until Beau ran over to her, a pack of wolves trotting behind him.

Elle pulled Beau into her arms, squeezing her eyes shut as she kissed the top of his head.

It was definitely her, but how? It was too easy. "Elle?" I breathed. My feet moved of their own accord. Part of my brain told me it was a trap, she wasn't really there, or she was bait, while the other part had me pulling her into my arms before I knew what I was doing. "What the hell—"

"I'm okay," she whispered, warm and real against me. I gripped her tighter. I'd been terrified of what might happen to her, but until that moment I hadn't realized I thought I might never see her again, at least not alive. If I would've lost her, like I'd lost Hannah, I would never come back from it. Especially if she never knew how I felt.

I balled my hands in her hair and lifted her face to mine.

"I'm okay," she repeated, cheeks red and eyes shimmering. "He didn't—"

I pressed my lips to hers with bruising force, needing to show her—needing her to see what she was to me. An almost imperceptible sigh hummed through her and I kissed her deeper.

Gasping for breath, I rested my forehead to hers, eyes shut as I breathed her in, willing her warmth to consume me. She was more than my partner in all of this. I knew that now.

When I opened my eyes, she was staring at me. She cupped my hand in hers and kissed the inside of my palm as she looked up at me.

"Well, what do you know? I didn't see that one coming." The man standing by the brown Blazer chortled.

My eyes shot to him. He had unruly blonde hair and an unnervingly wide smile. Then, I glanced at the driver who aimed a rifle at me through the window.

"Don't worry, we come in peace." The man held up his hands in supplication then pointed to the wolves. "Who's the animal whisperer? The kid?" He shook his head and smiled with amusement. "This just keeps getting better and better." He stared at Beau and the wolves fanned protectively around him, their teeth bared and hackles raised.

I took a step forward and lifted my gun to aim directly for the man's head. Victory never felt so righteous as the amusement dulled from his face.

"Jackson!" Elle pleaded, reaching for my arm. "Stop—look at me," she demanded.

"What?" I whipped around to glare at her. "He *took* you both!" My hands were shaking with rage. I searched for Sophie, relieved to find she was standing beside Alex, and Ross still aimed his rifle at the crazy-haired son of bitch.

"I know, but it was a mistake," Elle said. "This is Woody, and . . . you need to hear what he has to say."

66

ELLE

APRIL 19

W e sat around the large table in the dining room at the lodge. Jackson eyed me cautiously, still blindsided by the past ten hours; so was I. Sophie, less so, as she sat by Alex, Bert, and Ross, staring down the far end of the table at Phil and Woody. I kept asking myself what we'd gotten ourselves into coming to Whitehorse, wondering if it was better to know what they were telling us or to be blissfully ignorant. It wasn't like we didn't have enough to worry about already. But as I continued to absorb the information as Woody retold it to the rest of them, I knew it was better to be prepared than completely unaware, like we had been in Slana. Three crazed survivors with powers was nothing compared to what else was out there.

"So," Ross said, taking a swig of his beer. "Let me get this straight." He stared at Woody and Phil as they finished their bowls of soup, like they hadn't kidnapped us and just brought our oblivious sense of security crashing down on us. "You're telling me that we're all alive because this *genetically engineered* virus was meant to kill off the weak and we're the strong?" Ross leaned onto the kitchen table. Hands clamped into fists in front of him, like he was trying to keep his shit together.

"Genetically speaking," Sophie said with disbelief. "Isn't that ironic," she muttered. I knew her childhood was punctuated with doctor appointments and physical therapy, just like my entire adulthood had been one therapist after another telling me I wasn't crazy or weak, though deep down I questioned it frequently. Yet here we were, part of the few among the living.

Woody took a bite from his bread roll and pointed to Ross. "Yes, we are the strong—that's exactly what I'm saying. In fact, we're stronger than ever. That's the General's manifesto for crying out loud—build a clean, stable, crime-free civilization where the next evolution of mankind can thrive in peace."

"*After* he kills everyone else in the entire world," I clarified.

Woody's hands flew up. "Hey, I might be crazy, but I'm not insane, and trust me, there's a damn difference. This megalomaniac is the very definition of insanity." He shook his head. "I've been telling people for years," he muttered. For the first time, I wondered how different the world might be now if more people had listened, instead of having followed the pied piper so blindly.

"So, why are you here?" Jackson asked. "What do you want from us in exchange for giving us this information?"

Woody nodded with a smile. "No bullshit, I like you." He took a gulp of his beer and glanced around the table at all of us. Half of us were in shock, the others in disbelief, but all of us were smart enough to know nothing was predictable or safe anymore. "The General has outposts everywhere," he said. "They've been around for years—the Virus was a longtime coming. He didn't cook it up overnight. And a man like him is never done. My sources tell me he's still on a mission to take over and rebuild what's left to his satisfaction, and we sane survivors need to stick together. He has an entire army of people with Abilities just like yours." Woody looked at Beau and Thea, then at Sophie and Alex, but his eyes settled on me.

Jackson squeezed my hand under the table. His palm was hot, even against *my* skin.

"I'm not trying to scare ya, I'm just being real, and we need to be prepared."

Inhaling deep to chase away the exhaustion and overwhelming uncertainty, I considered what might be next for us, and let out a deep breath. "What is it you want us to do, Woody?" I met his gaze, unblinking. "We're not soldiers, we can't fight him."

"And let's hope you'll never have to," he said, shaking his head. His crazy hair jostled. "All I'm saying is keep your eyes open and your ear to the ground. Tell me if you see something. There are rumors his yellow-bands have been in these parts, and I just ask that you share what you know with me, just like I'll share what I know with you."

Jackson tilted his head, studying Woody, though I wasn't certain he was much closer to figuring anything out. It was weird. All of it was catastrophically, horribly, impossible and yet it was real. Just like the end of civilization, just like the end of anything normal. All of it was gone.

"Do you have a personal vendetta against this guy or something?" Jackson finally asked. "You should be shitting your pants if this man is as horrible as you say he is, not plotting with a band of five misfit soldiers in your prison—"

"With strong Abilities," he added. "We're not helpless, and we gotta keep each other safe."

"And you knew we were here—"

"The caravan was hard to miss," Phil grumbled, and Ross shot Jackson a satisfied look.

"*And*," Jackson continued, "you kidnapped Elle and Sophie specifically, why? Because they are women?"

He laughed, full and throaty, and leaned back in his chair. "Not at all! In fact, Elle's the strongest of all of you," he said, pointing to me. "Trust me on that."

I glanced at Jackson. Was I?

"Like I said, I heard a rumor a yellow-band was here last week, one that fits Elle's description," he said. "And I most definitely wasn't going to take any chances. I needed to get you away from everyone, figure you out . . . I'm a little nutty sometimes, but not stupid. I couldn't exactly interrogate you at the water's edge now, could I? If you were here on the General's behalf I needed to get you alone, and Sophie here was just the bargaining chip I needed."

With a straight face and no-nonsense, Woody looked Jackson in the eye and said, "I'm not looking for a fight with you guys or with General Herodson, because I'm not suicidal, but I wasn't born crazy, and that son of a bitch ain't ever getting his hands on me again, I can guarantee you that. It never hurts to be prepared, paranoid—whatever you want to call it. I was as ready as I could be for all of this, wasn't I?"

"What about you?" Ross asked Phil. "Woody's got his reasons, but what's your story? Why are you following the crazy man blindly?"

Phil tilted his head, glaring at Ross defensively, but his face softened when he looked at Sophie and he heaved out a breath. "I was in Whitehorse on vacation with my family when everything happened. Woody found me. Fed me. Took me in."

"Where do you call home?" I asked softly. He was just a teenager. I hated to think of Alex or Sophie alone in this world.

"Florida."

My eyes widened, imagining how lost and scared he must've felt. At least the rest of us were used to Alaska and were familiar with how harsh she could be. He, on the other hand . . .

I eyed his empty bowl. "Phil, would you like more soup? I can heat some up for you."

Phil shook his head. "No, thank you."

"That was damn good, though," Woody said, slurping what was left in his bowl. He looked between Sophie and me.

Both of us deferred to Alex, still glaring at Woody with his arms crossed in the chair across the table.

Woody lifted his torn roll in gratitude. "It's delicious."

"Thanks. I started it this morning, so it would be ready for lunch," he drawled. "We never got that far." *Thanks to you* went unsaid.

With a chuckle, Woody tapped his index finger on the dark wood tabletop. "Should I stop in around the same time next week for more? I love a good home-cooked meal. None of us bachelors cook all that much. What they say about Twinkies is true, you know? And MREs, I've learned to like them."

The rest of us sat quietly as Woody sighed, full and content and he rubbed his belly like he hadn't just dropped a life-threatening bomb on everyone.

"So, what are we supposed to do now?" I needed big-picture problems answered before I could handle any more small talk. "You're holed away in a prison to await a war that might never come. We just want to be left alone and live our lives."

"Then you should do that," he said. "I encourage it even. You stay off the grid and out of town, out here in the backcountry where no one knows where you are, and you stay here."

"But?" Jackson said, we could all feel a warning coming.

"But that doesn't mean trouble won't find you, and you gotta be ready for that. That's all I'm saying."

"We build a fortress then," Bert spoke for the first time. The hard-set lines around his mouth were etched with more than a dusting of age. His expression was grim, just like his tone, and his eyes crinkled with decisiveness. He had been quiet since we'd returned. Thoughtful or shocked, I wasn't sure which.

Ross nodded. "Something easy to protect. Spring and summer —it's the best time to get it done."

"What, like a castle with a drawbridge or something?" Sophie asked.

The thought of anything more than a simple home in the middle of the woods seemed impossible as my mind grew too full and heavy with things out of our control.

Jackson untangled his fingers from mine and excused himself

from the table. Without bothering to grab a jacket, he opened the sliding door and stepped out onto the deck.

Part of me thought I should leave him alone with his thoughts, but that's not how I wanted to be with him anymore. After everything we'd been through, we were more than partners in this; we were in this together until the end. All of us were. Jackson was no longer alone, and he hadn't been for a long time.

I scooted out of my chair and followed after him. Quietly, I slid the glass door closed, shutting the commotion inside behind me.

The air was cold and refreshing now that the heat ran in my veins again, a slow, increasing burn since Woody, Sophie, Phil, and I had left the prison.

"We can't put Jade and Del at risk," Jackson said, his voice a rumble in the still night. "We can't go back, at least not to stay."

"I know," I whispered and stood beside him, shoulder to shoulder. "Woody said Phil can sense abilities, so chances are the General will have someone who can too. Even if he's not out looking for survivors, we can't risk it." I rested my head on his bicep, winding my arms around his.

"All of us were science experiments," he said, disgusted. His chest lifted with a heavy sigh.

"Hopefully they'll just leave us alone up here and forget about us." It was wishful thinking. We'd learned long ago that nothing was simple or came easily anymore. It didn't mean we couldn't hope though.

Jackson took my hand in his. The light from the house poured over him and he turned to face me. "Why don't we carve a place out here somewhere that's hidden and just ours. No one will care—nothing's changed. Not really. There's a psychopath in Colorado. Well, we're more likely to die from one out here than ever meet the General."

I nodded, because Jackson was right if the last four months were anything to go by.

"We live a life we want for as long as we can. We keep to

ourselves. No one will find us." His hazel eyes searched mine, frantic. It was an urgency I'd only seen the instant I stepped out of the Blazer. "I thought you and Sophie were dead," he breathed. "And Woody isn't even the craziest son of a bitch out here."

I squeezed his fingers in mine. "I know."

"Ross and Bert can set up their fortress if they want and we can help each other, sure, but I don't want to be a hamster in a cage like the one we found in that pet store. I want us to live full lives, as much as we can. And if any of those Colorado fuckers come close, Alex can grab your hand and the two of you can fry the shit out of them."

I laughed, not because it was funny but because it might actually be possible, and we were willing to do whatever it took to live a life away from all the craziness; it was what we'd all come to want, and for now, we could still have it.

"Okay," I said, knowing there was nothing better we could hope for.

Jackson's cold hand cupped my face, his thumb brushing a rogue tear from my cheek. He waited for me to change my mind or protest, but I wouldn't.

"Let's do it," I breathed. I rose to my tiptoes, and wrapped my arms around his neck. It was quite probable we wouldn't be able to avoid the General or people like him in the uncertain world we now lived in, but like the rest of the survivors, we had a whole new life to build and new discoveries to make about ourselves and those around us. I was more than okay with selfishly wanting my life with Jackson to begin, to see where our story would take us.

His eyes glistened, searching my face, and fire danced beneath the surface of my skin. Without another moment's hesitation, I pressed my lips to his, letting it consume us both.

THE END

ALSO BY LINDSEY POGUE

THE ENDING WORLD

Savage North Chronicles

The Darkest Winter

The Longest Night

Midnight Sun

Fading Shadows

Untamed

Unbroken

Day Zero: Beginnings

The Ending Series

After The Ending

Into The Fire

Out Of The Ashes

Before The Dawn

Beginnings: Origin Stories

The Ending Series: World Before

The Ending Legacy

World After

OTHER SERIES INCLUDE:

Forgotten Lands

Borne of Sand and Scorn Prequel

Dust and Shadow

Earth and Ember

Tide and Tempest

<u>Saratoga Falls Love Stories</u>

Whatever It Takes

Nothing But Trouble

Told You So

For more information visit: www.lindseypogue.com

A SPECIAL NOTE TO READERS

To all of you who have been reading my books since The Ending Series, thank you. To all of you who are new to my stories and quirky shenanigans, welcome! I know authors say this all the time, but I keep writing because you keep reading my books. And you *actually* seem to like them.

I can't speak for every author, but I can tell you this: writing is a constant psychological minefield, fraught with self-doubt, distractions, impatience, and the list goes on. But being an author is also one of the most extraordinary things I've ever done. I'm constantly challenged and forced outside my comfort zone; I've come to grips with "failure" even if I don't particularly like it; and if at the end of a smack-my-head-against-the-wall sort of day I can still hang out with you, it makes every ounce of turmoil worth it.

It's been years since Lindsey Fairleigh and I first published *After The Ending* (2013), and even longer since we began writing it —our hairbrained blog idea that turned into so much more than that. And while The Ending Series has continued to gain momentum, it's you, dear readers, who have enabled me to write adventures in other lands far, far away from here. It's because of you that I hope to write many more.

This is a long-winded, over-the-top way of saying, thank you for making my dreams come true. I might have started writing for myself, but I continue to write for you. Oh, the places we will go…

ABOUT LINDSEY

WWW.LINDSEYPOGUE.COM

Lindsey Pogue has always been a sucker for a good love story. She completed her first new adult manuscript in high school and has been writing tales of love and friendship, history and adventure ever since. When she's not chatting with readers, plotting her next storyline, or dreaming up new, brooding characters, Lindsey's generally wrapped in blankets watching her favorite action flicks with her own leading man. They live in Northern California with their rescue cat, Beast.

You can follow Lindsey's shenanigans and writing adventures just about everywhere.

Author Lindsey Pogue:

CPSIA information can be obtained
at www.ICGtesting.com
Printed in the USA
BVHW091631230621
610215BV00007B/1373

9 781638 488750